The Best of BETTY NEELS

With This Wish

MILLS & BOON

WITH THIS WISH © 2022 by Harlequin Books S.A.

SATURDAY'S CHILD
© 1972 by Betty Neels
Australian Copyright 1972
New Zealand Copyright 1972

First Published 1972
First Australian Paperback Edition 2022
ISBN 978 1 867 25726 4

HILLTOP TRYST
© 1989 by Betty Neels
Australian Copyright 1989
New Zealand Copyright 1989

First Published 1989
First Australian Paperback Edition 2022
ISBN 978 1 867 25726 4

GRASP A NETTLE
© 1977 by Betty Neels
Australian Copyright 1977
New Zealand Copyright 1977

First Published 1977
First Australian Paperback Edition 2022
ISBN 978 1 867 25726 4

Except for use in any review, the reproduction or utilisation of this work in whole or in part in any form by any electronic, mechanical or other means, now known or hereafter invented, including xerography, photocopying and recording, or in any information storage or retrieval system, is forbidden without the permission of the publisher.

This book is sold subject to the condition that it shall not, by way of trade or otherwise, be lent, resold, hired out or otherwise circulated without the prior consent of the publisher in any form of binding or cover other than that in which it is published and without a similar condition including this condition being imposed on the subsequent purchaser.

All rights reserved including the right of reproduction in whole or in part in any form. This edition is published in arrangement with Harlequin Books S.A. Cover art used by arrangement with Harlequin Books S.A. All rights reserved.

This is a work of fiction. Names, characters, places, and incidents are either the product of the author's imagination or are used fictitiously, and any resemblance to actual persons, living or dead, business establishments, events, or locales is entirely coincidental.

Published by
Mills & Boon
An imprint of Harlequin Enterprises (Australia) Pty Limited
(ABN 47 001 180 918), a subsidiary of HarperCollins
Publishers Australia Pty Limited (ABN 36 009 913 517)
Level 13, 201 Elizabeth Street
SYDNEY NSW 2000
AUSTRALIA

MIX
Paper from responsible sources
FSC® C001695

® and ™ (apart from those relating to FSC®) are trademarks of Harlequin Enterprises (Australia) Pty Limited or its corporate affiliates. Trademarks indicated with ® are registered in Australia, New Zealand and in other countries. Contact admin_legal@Harlequin.ca for details.

Printed and bound in Australia by McPherson's Printing Group

CONTENTS

SATURDAY'S CHILD 5

HILLTOP TRYST 227

GRASP A NETTLE 385

Romance readers around the world were sad to note the passing of **Betty Neels** in June 2001. Her career spanned thirty years, and she continued to write into her ninetieth year. To her millions of fans, Betty epitomized the romance writer, and yet she began writing almost by accident. She had retired from nursing, but her inquiring mind still sought stimulation. Her new career was born when she heard a lady in her local library bemoaning the lack of good romance novels. Betty's first book, *Sister Peters in Amsterdam,* was published in 1969, and she eventually completed 134 books. Her novels offer a reassuring warmth that was very much a part of her own personality. She was a wonderful writer, and she will be greatly missed. Her spirit and genuine talent will live on in all her stories.

Saturday's Child

CHAPTER ONE

THE ROOM WAS chilly and severe, as was the woman sitting behind the desk in one of its corners. The desk lamp, which only partly held at bay the fog of the darkened January sky outside, also served to illuminate her features, and the girl who had taken the chair on the opposite side of the desk in answer to the woman's brisk nod occupied herself in giving her interviewer a softer hair-style, appropriate make-up and a more becoming dress. These alterations, mused Miss Abigail Trent, as she admitted to that name, would take away at least ten years from the age of her unconscious interviewer, who looked up and repeated, 'Your age, Miss Trent?'

'Twenty-four.'

'Your education?'

Abigail murmured the name of a well-known girls' boarding school. When her father had been alive there had been money enough...

'You are State Registered?'

Abigail nodded and when asked to give the name of her training school mentioned a famous teaching hospital in London.

'Have you family ties?'

She thought of the two cousins in Canada; they sent her Christmas cards each year, but they could hardly be described as ties, nor, for that matter, could Uncle Sedgeley, her mother's brother, married to a peer's sister and landed gentry, and totally disapproving of her father, her mother's marriage to him and to Abigail herself. She said quietly in her pleasant voice: 'No,' and when she was asked what branch of nursing she had most recently been in, said: 'Surgery—the operating theatre too.'

'You're willing to travel?'

It sounded like the beginnings of an advertisement in the Personal Column of *The Times*. She said, 'Certainly,' and smiled at the woman, who didn't smile back but looked at her watch as though time was rationed for her interviews and she had used it all up on Abigail. She got up briskly and went across to the filing cabinet against one wall and started pulling out its drawers. Presently she came back with a small folder and sat down again. 'I think we could offer you a post immediately if you are prepared to take a medical case. A patient in Amsterdam—an American woman staying with friends there, in their flat. She has been in hospital with severe gastric symptoms and is now back with them—still in bed, of course, pending the doctor's decision. She didn't care for the hospital, for she speaks no Dutch and found the regulations a little trying. She is, I gather, rather...' She wisely left the sentence unfinished and went on: 'You will be paid twenty pounds a week and receive your board and lodging, and she is prepared to pay your fare at the end of a fortnight. The flat is, I believe, in one of the best parts of the city. You will have two and a half hours free every afternoon, and such other times as you can arrange for yourself. Should you take the post, you will pay this agency twelve and a half per cent of your salary until such time as you leave.'

She finished speaking and sat, tapping her ballpoint on the blotting pad in front of her. After perhaps half a minute she enquired, 'Well, Miss Trent, do you care to take the case?'

It wasn't quite what Abigail wanted, although she hardly

knew what she did want—only to get away from London—from England, for a while, so that she could adjust herself to a future which no longer held her mother. And she needed the money. She got to her feet. 'Yes, I'll take it,' she said. 'When do you want me to go?'

'Please sit down again.' The woman looked more severe than ever. 'I'll give you the patient's name and address and advise you on the easiest way of getting to the case. I suggest that you fly over early tomorrow, so that you will arrive in Amsterdam by lunch time—that should give you time to unpack, see your patient and begin your duties without delay.'

Abigail blinked the fine silky lashes of eyes which were her sole claim to beauty in an otherwise ordinary face. They were brown and large and the brows above them were silky too. But her nose was too short, her mouth too wide and her hair too mousy to give her even a modicum of good looks. She wasn't sure at this moment if the change would be for the better; probably not, but she could always go back to hospital again. She held out a hand in its slightly shabby glove and took the papers which the woman was holding out to her.

Two minutes later she was outside in the street, standing rather uncertainly on the pavement while the passers-by pushed and jostled her first one way, then the other; not meaning to treat her roughly, but intent on getting to wherever they were going as quickly as possible. Presently she crossed the road, drawn by the cheerful lights of a Golden Egg restaurant, and went inside. It was almost twelve o'clock on this damp and foggy day in the first week of January; lunch in a pleasant warmth seemed a good idea. She chose egg and chips and coffee and while she was waiting for them got out her little notebook and started doing sums. Twenty pounds a week would be a godsend; she hadn't earned any money at all for three months now. When her mother had fallen ill, she had given up her job at the hospital and stayed at home to nurse her, because the doctor had told her that her mother had only a few months to live anyway, and Abigail couldn't bear the thought of her living out those last few weeks in some strange hospital bed. She had gone home for almost three months, and her mother had had every small comfort and luxury she wished for or needed, and Abigail had spent what money she had saved, which wasn't much, to pay for them. Her mother's pension had paid the rent of their small flat and the household expenses, but when she had died there had been nothing left at all. The furniture went with the flat, her mother's jewellery, never very valuable, had been sold over the last five years, and Bollinger, who had served her father faithfully until his death and had refused to leave them after it, was owed almost a year of his low wages. The funeral had taken almost all the money she had, and now today, barely a week later, she had gone out to get a job, and it had had to be private nursing—that way she would get her board and lodging free and would get paid sooner.

The egg and chips arrived and she ate them, still doing sums in her head. She would just about be able to get to Amsterdam and have a pound or two in her purse until she was paid. Two weeks wasn't long to wait, and anyway it didn't look as though she was going to get much free time in which to spend her money. Even when the twelve and a half per cent had been deducted, she would still be able to send Bollinger some money. He would retire now, she supposed, but he would only have his old age pension, and that wouldn't go far in London. She began to worry about where he would live; after that night they would have to leave the flat and she wasn't going to leave him to struggle on his own after the years of service he had given them, and he had been so kind and helpful to her and her mother. The food on her plate became dimmed by the tears in her eyes, but she fought them back and doggedly went on eating the chips on her plate and drinking the coffee she didn't want any more.

She took a bus back to the flat, the small top flat just off the Cromwell Road where they had lived since her father died and Abigail had started her hospital training. As she put her key in the front door at the top of the long flights of stairs, she could hear Bollinger in the kitchen; he came to its door as she went inside and said comfortably:

'There you are, Miss Abby, the kettle's on and I treated us to some crumpets. Nothing like a nice hot crumpet.' He went back to the gas stove. 'How did it go?'

'I've got a job, Bolly—twenty pounds a week, in Amsterdam, nursing an American woman. I'm to go tomorrow, and isn't it lucky I've still got my passport from that trip we had to Ostend? So everything's going to be OK.' She cast her coat and hat over the back of one of the wooden chairs at the table and went to get the teapot from the dresser. 'Now, about you—did you manage to find anything?'

'I did—the woman at the paper shop, remember her? She's got a daughter with a house just round the corner from here. I can have a room and me meals with her and her husband. Four pounds and fifty pence a week—leaves me plenty, so don't you worry your pretty head about me.'

She looked at him with deep affection, loving him for the cheerful lie. He was almost seventy, she knew, and he had worked very hard around the flat since they had moved into it, shopping and cooking and repairing fuses and waiting on her mother hand and foot. It was impossible to repay him, but at least she would see that he got the money which they owed him and then a small weekly pension after that so that he could find a proper home and not some small back room where he would be lonely. Years ago he had been her father's gardener and odd job man, and when her father had died he had somehow stayed on with them, smoothing her mother's path, offering practical advice when it was discovered that there was no money at all, and Abigail had never quite discovered how it was that he had persuaded her mother to keep him on at such a ridiculous wage.

She made the tea and they sat down together with the plate of crumpets between them. 'I'm glad you've got somewhere to go for the present,' began Abigail. She opened her handbag. 'They gave me five pounds in advance on my salary,' she went on mendaciously. 'I've got more than enough and this'll help you to get started, then each week, once I get my pay, I shall send you some money,' and when he began to protest, 'No, Bolly dear, you're my friend and you were Mother's and Father's friend too—I can well afford to pay you back the wages we owe you and then pay you a little each week. It won't take me long, you see, for I get my room and my food for free, don't I? And in a little while I'll get a hospital job again and perhaps we can find a small place and you can come and run it for me while I work.'

She smiled at him, trying not to see that he was getting quite elderly now and wouldn't be fit to do much for many more years—something she would worry about when the time came, she told herself vigorously. She poured more tea and said cheerfully: 'How funny Uncle Sedgeley was yesterday. I wonder what he and Aunt Miriam would have done if I'd accepted their invitation to go to Gore Park and stay with them? They hated Father, didn't they, because he was a Methodist parson and hadn't any worldly ideas and they hadn't been near...' She paused, unable to bear talking of her mother. 'Aunt Miriam told me how fortunate I was that I had a vocation, for all the world as though I'd taken a vow not to marry.'

'Of course you'll marry, Miss Abby,' said Bollinger, quite shocked.

'That's nice of you to say so, Bolly, but I'm afraid she may be right, you know. I'm twenty-four and I've never had a proposal—nothing even approaching one. I'm a sort of universal sister, you know, because I'm plain.'

'You're talking nonsense, Miss Abby. You just haven't met the right man, that's all. He'll come, don't you fret.'

'Yes? Well, when he does I shan't marry him unless he lets you come along too,' she said firmly. 'Now let's go and see this room of yours and then I'll treat us to the pictures.'

A remark which would have shocked Uncle Sedgeley if he

could have heard it; to go to the cinema barely a week after her mother's funeral—unthinkable! She could just hear him saying it, but it didn't matter what he thought; her mother would have been the first one to suggest it. Life went on and you didn't forget someone just because you sat in the stalls and watched some film or other without seeing any of it, and at least it would be warm there and infinitely better than sitting in the little flat talking, inevitably, of old times with Bolly, something she couldn't bear to do.

She said goodbye to him the next morning and started her journey. She had booked her flight when she had left the agency, obedient to the severe woman's instructions, and had packed her case with the sort of clothes she considered she might need, adding the blue uniform dresses and caps and aprons she had been forced to buy, and now on the plane at last, she got out her little notebook again and did some anxious arithmetic. With luck she wouldn't have to spend more than the equivalent of a few shillings; stamps for her letters to Bollinger, small odds and ends for herself. She hoped that her patient might need her for more than two weeks—three, or even four weeks at twenty pounds a week would mount up nicely, and they were going to pay her fare too. She closed the little book, opened the newspaper the air hostess had handed her and read it with grave attention, fearful of allowing her thoughts to wander, and was surprised when far below she saw the flat coast of Holland, glimpsed through the layers of cloud.

Schiphol, she discovered, was large, efficient and pleasantly welcoming. With hundreds like her, she was passed along the human conveyor belt which eventually spilled her into the open air once more, only to be whisked up once more into the waiting bus which would take her to Amsterdam. It covered the ten miles to the capital with a speed which hardly gave her time to look around her and she got out at the bus terminus, still not quite believing that she was in Holland. It seemed such a very short time ago since she had said goodbye to Bollinger, as indeed it was.

Mindful of her instructions, she took a taxi to the address in the Apollolaan. It was, she quickly discovered, away from the centre of the city, for they quickly left the bustling, older part behind, to drive through modern streets lined with blocks of flats and shops. When they stopped half way down the Apollolaan, she got out, paid the driver from her small stock of money and crossed the pavement to enter the important-looking doorway of the building he had pointed out to her. It was of a substantial size, and from the cars parked before it, inhabited by the well-to-do, and inside the thickly carpeted foyer and neatly uniformed porter bore out her first impression. He greeted her civilly, and when she mentioned her name, ushered her into the lift, took her case from her and escorted her to the fourth floor. Here he abandoned her, her case parked beside her, outside the door of number twenty-one—occupied, according to the neat little plate at the side of the door, by Mr and Mrs E. Goldberg. Abigail drew a heartening breath and rang the beautifully polished bell.

The door was opened by a maid who, in answer to Abigail's announcement of her name, invited her to enter, waved her to a chair, and disappeared. Abigail looked at the chair, a slender trifle which she felt sure would never bear the weight of her nicely rounded person, and stood looking around her. The hall was carpeted even more lushly than the foyer; the walls were hung with what she considered to be a truly hideous wallpaper, embossed and gilded, and as well as the little chair she had prudently ignored, there was a small settee, buttoned fatly into red velvet, and another chair with a straight back and a cane seat which looked decidedly uncomfortable. A wall table of gold and marble occupied the space between two doors, burdened with a French clock and matching vases. Abigail, who had a nice taste, shuddered delicately and wished that her mother could have been with her and share her feelings. For a moment her opulent surroundings faded to give place to the little flat in the Cromwell Road, but she resolutely closed her mind to her memories; self-pity helped no one, she told herself firmly, and turned to see who was coming through the door on the other side of the hall.

It had to be Mrs Goldberg, for she looked exactly like her name. She was middle-aged, with determinedly blonde hair, blue eyes which were still pretty and a baby doll face, nicely made up, which, while still attractive, had lost its youthful contours. She smiled now, holding out her hand, and when she spoke her voice was warm even though its accent was decidedly American.

'Well, so you're the nurse, my dear. I can't tell you how glad we are to have you.' She added dramatically, 'I am exhausted, absolutely exhausted! Night and day have I been caring for our dear Clara—she is so sensitive, you know, we couldn't leave her in hospital, although I'm sure they were kindness itself to her, but she's used to the little comforts of life.' The blue eyes looked at her a shade anxiously. 'We hope that the worst is over; Doctor Vincent will be in after lunch and this evening he'll bring a specialist—the very best to be got, I assure you— to see dear Clara, and he'll decide whether to operate or not.' She paused to take breath and Abigail asked quickly: 'You'd like me to take over immediately, I expect? If I could go to my room and change...'

Mrs Goldberg smiled widely, showing a hint of gold tooth. 'My dear, will you? I simply must rest. We lunch at half past twelve—so early, but when in Rome, I always say—If you could get into your uniform and make poor Clara a little more comfortable?'

'Of course.' Abigail smiled understandingly, hoping at the same time that Mrs Goldberg might suggest a cup of coffee or tea. Half past twelve was an hour away and she was, while not exactly tired, in need of a few minutes to collect herself, but Mrs Goldberg made no such offer, but followed her from the hall and into a short passage and so to her room. It was nice, with a view over the Apollolaan and comfortable anonymous furniture so often found in guest rooms, and it had the added attraction of a bathroom next door. As soon as she was alone Abigail unpacked her uniform, washed her face and hands, put her mousy hair up into its tidy bun, perched her frilly cap on top of it, buckled her belt around her trim waist and with a nicely made-up face, went back into the hall.

Mrs Goldberg must have been waiting for her; she appeared suddenly, like a cheerful outsize fairy, from one of the doors and said approvingly:

'My, how quick you've been, and what a quaint outfit—that cap, it's not a bit like our nurses wear back home.'

Abigail explained quickly that her hospital took pride in allowing its trained nurses to wear that particular headgear—it had been worn for a very long time and no one, least of all the nurses, wanted it changed.

'Mighty becoming,' commented Mrs Goldberg, 'it sure will tickle poor Clara pink.'

Abigail, following her companion through another door, wondered if her patient felt well enough to be tickled by anything. At first sight it seemed not. Mrs Clara Morgan lay uncomfortably hunched against far too many pillows. Some of these she had tossed to the floor, the remainder were crowding into her back, which probably accounted for her petulant expression. She acknowledged Mrs Goldberg's introduction languidly and said tiredly, 'I'm glad you've come, Nurse, I'm very poorly and I need a great deal of skilled care and attention.'

Abigail murmured suitably and enquired if the doctor had left any message for her.

'No,' said Mrs Goldberg, 'because he'll be here in a couple of hours. Clara will tell you all about herself, won't you, Girlie?'

Abigail judged it a good idea to get her oar in before her patient did, for she looked ill and tired and that was probably why she looked peevish. Her voice was persuasive. 'Would you like me to give you a bed-bath and a fresh nightie and make you more comfortable? You'll feel better for it.'

Her patient agreed, and while she submitted to Abigail's kindly hands, discoursed at length upon her condition, its seriousness, the possibility of an operation, the need for her to return to the States as soon as she could, and the kindness of her friends the Goldbergs. That there was a thick thread of self-pity winding through her narrative was natural enough; it hadn't taken Abigail long to gather that her patient was rich, spoilt and self-indulgent. She had, it transpired, been widowed twice, and, a still attractive woman in her early forties, was prepared to marry again should she find someone she liked sufficiently. Abigail listened without envy, because it wasn't in her nature to be envious, and a certain amount of pity, because it seemed to her that Mrs Morgan was lonely too, despite her silver-backed hairbrushes and silk nighties and enormous bottles of perfume. But talking cheered her up, and by the time Abigail had smoothed the last wrinkle from the sheets, she declared that she felt a new woman.

'I do believe we're going to get on just fine,' she declared. 'I must admit that the idea of an English nurse didn't appeal to me, but I'll admit to being mistaken, though your uniform is pretty antiquated, isn't it?'

Abigail admitted that perhaps it was. 'They're trying to change the uniforms in England, but you see, some of the hospitals are very old and they like to keep their own, however old-fashioned. Especially the caps—it's like a regimental badge, everyone knows which hospital you were trained at just by looking at your cap.'

'Well, I must say whoever thought of yours had a nice eye for something sexy.'

Abigail was folding towels neatly. No one had ever called her cap sexy before! She remained silent, nonplussed, and then said:

'I think a nice milky drink, don't you? I'll go along and see about it.'

Milk and water, in equal proportions with afters of Mist. Mag. Tri., were her patient's portion for lunch. Abigail measured carefully, arranged the two glasses on a little tray with a pretty cloth and bore them away to the sickroom, where she put the tray on the bed table, together with a selection of novels, the daily paper and a handful of glossy magazines, and then, quite famished, found her way to the dining room.

Mr Goldberg had come home to lunch. A small fat man with large glasses and a fringe of greying hair, possessed of a charming smile. Abigail liked him at once and wasn't surprised to hear that he was something important to do with a permanent trade mission—anyone with a smile like that deserved to have a top job! They sat her between them at a large rectangular table and plied her with food. It was cold and grey outside, but here in the warm, over-furnished room, there was no need to think about the weather. She drank her soup, accepted a glass of wine and embarked on beef olives while she listened to her host and hostess and made polite replies to their questions whenever they asked them, which was frequently. She would have liked to have lingered over coffee with them, but she was on a job, after all. She excused herself and went back to her patient to find her asleep.

It seemed a good opportunity to unpack her few clothes and scribble a quick note to Bolly; most likely she would have the chance to post it before bedtime; if not, surely the hall porter would do it for her. She wrote the address with a little lump in her throat, because Bolly would probably be sitting by himself in that dreadful little back room with no other view than the house behind.

Dr Vincent came shortly afterwards. He was a tall man in his thirties, with regular features and an excellent command of the English language. He was obviously relieved to see Abigail and after he had examined Mrs Morgan and talked to her for a little while, he retired to the sitting room with Abigail so that he might discuss their patient. They sat opposite each other, on the edge of over-stuffed and very large easy chairs, because to sit back in them would have meant a complete loss of dignity on both their parts and the doctor was nothing if not dignified. He took her carefully through the ins and outs of Mrs Morgan's illness. 'This evening a specialist will come, Nurse—I shall of course accompany him. He is a consultant surgeon at several of our big hospitals and very well known. I feel that his opinion will be invaluable. It would be a pity for our patient to undergo an operation unless it is absolutely necessary. If we can get her well enough, she would much prefer that she should return to the United States with all speed. You are prepared to stay here until she returns, I hope?'

Abigail said that yes, she was. 'What have they in mind?' she wanted to know. 'A gastrostomy? Surely if it's a bad ulcer they'll have to do an end-to-end anastomosis.'

Dr Vincent eyed her warily. 'I think, Nurse, that we must leave such things for Professor van Wijkelen to decide.'

With a name like that, Abigail thought flippantly, a man ought to be able to decide anything. He would have a beard and begin all his remarks with -er. She would probably dislike him. Dr Vincent was speaking again, so she listened carefully to his instructions and forgot about the professor.

He came that evening, an hour or so after her patient had had another glass of milk and water with its attendant powder, and Abigail herself had had a short break for her own tea. Mr and Mrs Goldberg were out, and it had been brought to her on a tray in the sitting room. It had been pleasant to sit down for a little while on her own, while she had it, and then have the time to tidy herself, powder her ordinary nose and put on more lipstick. The results weren't very encouraging, she considered, looking in the bedroom mirror. She had gone back to her patient's room and taken her temperature and pulse, and sat her up more comfortably against her pillows, and was on a chair in her stockinged feet, reaching for a vase of flowers which someone had placed out of reach, and which, for some reason,

Mrs Morgan had taken exception to, when there was a knock on the door and Doctor Vincent came in. The man who came in with him eclipsed him completely. He was a giant of a man, with a large frame which radiated energy despite the extreme leisureliness of his movements. He was handsome too, with pale hair, thickly silvered at the temples, a high-bridged nose and a well-shaped, determined mouth. His expression was one of cold ill-humour, and when he glanced up at her, still poised ridiculously on the chair, Abigail saw that his eyes were blue. It struck her with something of a shock that they were regarding her with dislike.

She got down off the chair, the flowers clutched in one hand, hastily put them down on one of the little tables which cluttered the room, crammed her feet into her shoes and reached the bedside at the same time as the two men. Doctor Vincent introduced the professor, adding a corollary of his talents, and Mrs Morgan, suddenly interested, shook hands. 'And our nurse,' went on Doctor Vincent, 'arrived from England today and is already, I see, attending to the patient's comfort. Miss Trent, this is Professor van Wijkelen, of whom I spoke.'

She held out her hand and he shook it perfunctorily and said nothing, only looked at her again with the same cold dislike, before sitting on the side of Mrs Morgan's bed and saying, 'Now, Mrs Morgan, will you tell me all your troubles, and perhaps Doctor Vincent and I can help you to get well again.'

His voice was charming, deep and quiet and compelling, and Mrs Morgan was nothing loath. Her recital, with various deflections concerning her own personal courage in the face of grave illness, her fears for the loss of her good looks and the fact that she had been twice widowed, took a long time. The professor sat quietly, not interrupting her at all, his eyes upon her face while she talked. He seemed completely absorbed and so, to his credit, did Doctor Vincent, who, Abigail guessed, must have heard the tale at least once already. She herself stood quietly by the bed, a well-trained mouse of a girl, her eyes, too, on her patient, although she would very much have preferred to fix them upon the professor.

Mrs Morgan finished at length and the professor said, 'Quite, Mrs Morgan,' and went on to ask her several questions. Finally, when he was satisfied with the answers, he turned to Abigail and asked her to prepare Mrs Morgan for his examination. He asked courteously in a voice of ice; Abigail wondered what had happened to sour him and take all the warmth from his voice as she bent to the task of getting Mrs Morgan modestly uncovered while the two men retired to the window and muttered together in their own language.

'He's ducky,' whispered Mrs Morgan, and then sharply, 'Don't disarrange my hair, honey!'

She lay back, looking, to speak the truth, gorgeous. Abigail, obedient to her patient's wish, had been careful of the hair; she had also arranged her patient's wispy trifle of a bedjacket to its greatest advantage. Now she stood back and said briskly, 'Ready when you are, sir,' and watched while the professor conducted his examination. He prodded and poked gently with his large, square hands while he gazed in an abstracted fashion at the wall before him. At length, when he had finished and Abigail had rearranged Mrs Morgan, he said: 'I think that there will be no need for an operation, but to be quite sure there are several tests which it will be necessary to do, and I am afraid that they must be done in hospital.' He paused to allow Mrs Morgan to pull a pretty little face and exclaim:

'Oh, no, Professor—I was so utterly miserable when I was there just a week ago, that's why I engaged Nurse Trent here.'

'In that case, may I suggest that you take her with you to hospital? She can attend you during the day and I am sure that we shall be able to find an English-speaking nurse for night duty. I should suppose that three or four days should be sufficient, then you can return here to await the result of the tests. If they are satisfactory, a week or so should suffice to see you on your feet again and well enough to return home.'

'If you say so, Professor,' Mrs Morgan's voice was just sufficiently plaintive, 'though I'm sure I don't know how I shall get on in that hospital of yours. Still, as you say, if I take Nurse with me, I daresay I'll be able to bear a few days.'

She smiled at him after this somewhat frank speech, but he didn't smile in return, merely inclined his head gravely and offered his hand.

'You'll come and see me again, Professor?' Mrs Morgan was still smiling. 'I sure feel better already, you've a most reassuring way with you.'

If the professor was flattered by this remark he gave no sign. 'Thank you, Mrs Morgan. I think that there is no necessity to see you again until you enter hospital. I will arrange that as soon as possible and you will of course see me there.'

'I look forward to that—and be sure that I have a private room. I'm so sensitive, I can't bear the sights and sounds of hospital, Professor.'

He walked to the door and then turned to face her with Doctor Vincent beside him. 'I feel sure that Doctor Vincent will arrange everything to your liking, Mrs Morgan, and you will have your nurse to shield you from the—er—sights and sounds you so much dread.' His smile was fleeting and reluctant, a concession to good manners, and it didn't last long enough to include Abigail. He nodded curtly to her as he went away.

Surprisingly, he came the following day, late in the afternoon when Abigail had returned from her few hours off and was sitting with her patient, reading the *New York Herald Tribune* to her. She read very nicely in her quiet voice, sitting upright in a truly hideous reproduction Morris chair. She had enjoyed her afternoon off, and wished that her patient lived in one of the old houses beside the canals, because she would have dearly loved to see inside one of them. The flat in the Apollolaan was comfortable to the point of luxury, but all the same, she wouldn't have liked to live in it for ever, but the brick houses with their gabled roofs reflected in the still waters of the *grachten*—they were a different matter; it would be wonderful to live in their serene fastness.

The morning had been successful too; Mrs Morgan seemed to like her, for she had chatted animatedly while Abigail performed the daily nursing chores, talking at great length about Professor van Wijkelen. 'A darling man, Nurse,' she mused. 'I must find out more about him—such good looks and such elegance.' She smiled playfully at Abigail. 'Now mind, dear, and tell me anything you should hear about him. You're bound to find out something in the hospital, aren't you?'

Abigail had said that probably she would, provided she could find someone who could speak English. She had gone to lunch with Mr and Mrs Goldberg after that, and they had asked her a great many questions about her patient and seemed, she thought, a little relieved that dear Clara was to leave them for a day or two. Without someone in constant attendance, she must have put quite a strain on their good-natured hospitality.

Mrs Goldberg had asked her kindly if she had everything she needed and to be sure and say if she hadn't and then told her to hurry out while she had the chance. And Abigail had, wrapped in her well-cut but not new tweed coat against the damp cold winds of Amsterdam. She hadn't been able to do much in two hours, but at least she knew where she would go when next she was free; the complexity of *grachten,* tree-lined, their steely waters overlooked by the tall, quaintly shaped houses on either side of them, needed time to explore. There was no point in looking at the shops, not until she had some money to spend, but there was enough to see without spending more than the price of a tram fare.

The knock on the bedroom door had taken them both by surprise. Mr and Mrs Goldberg were both out, neither Abigail nor her patient had heard the maid go to the front door. She came in now and said in her basic English, 'A person for the *Zuster*.'

Abigail put down the paper, which she was a little tired of anyway, saying: 'Oh, that will be instructions from the hospital as to when we're to go, I expect. I'll go and see about it, shall I?' and followed the maid out of the room. The visitor was in the sitting room. Abigail opened the door and went in and came to a standstill when she saw the professor standing before the window, staring out.

'Oh, it's you!' she declared, quite forgetful of her manners because of her surprise, and was affronted when he answered irritably:

'And pray why should it not be I, Nurse? Doctor Vincent has been called out unexpectedly and finds himself unable to call, and I had to come this way.'

'Oh, you don't have to explain,' Abigail said kindly, and went on in a matter-of-fact voice, 'You'll want to see Mrs Morgan.'

'No, Nurse, I do not. I wish merely to inform you that there will be a bed in the private wing tomorrow afternoon. Be good enough to bring your patient to the hospital at three o'clock. An ambulance will fetch you—you will need to bring with you sufficient for three days, four perhaps. Be good enough to see that Mrs Morgan fasts from midday tomorrow so that no time is wasted.'

He spoke shortly and she wondered if and why he was annoyed, perhaps because he had had to undertake Doctor Vincent's errand, although surely he had a sufficiency of helpers to see to such mundane things as beds... He looked very arrogant and ill-humoured standing there, staring at her. She said briskly, 'Very well, sir—and now if you'll excuse me, I'll go back to my patient.'

He looked faintly surprised, although he didn't bother to reply. Only as she started for the door did he ask, 'What is your name?'

She barely paused. 'Trent, sir.'

He said impatiently, 'I am aware of that—we met yesterday, if you care to remember. What else besides Trent?'

It was on the tip of her tongue to tell him to mind his own business, but she wasn't given to unkindness and perhaps he had some very good reason for looking so irritable all the time. 'Abigail,' she offered, and watched for his smile; most people smiled when they discovered her name; it was old-fashioned and quaint. But he didn't smile.

'Why?'

'I was born on a Saturday,' she began, a little worried because he wasn't English and might not understand. 'And Abigail…' She paused. 'It's rather a silly reason and I don't suppose you would know…'

He looked more annoyed than ever, his thick almost colourless brows drawn together in a straight line above a nose which to her appeared disdainful.

'You should suppose nothing. I am sufficiently acquainted with your English verses—Saturday's child has to work for her living, eh? and Abigail was a term used some hundreds of years ago to denote a serving woman, was it not?'

'How clever of you,' said Abigail warmly, and was rewarded with another frown.

'And were your parents so sure that you would be forced to work for your living that they gave you this name?'

She said tight-lipped, because the conversation was becoming painful:

'It was a joke between them. You will excuse me now, sir?'

She left him standing there and went back to her patient, who, on being told who the visitor was, showed her displeasure at not receiving a visit, although she brightened again when Abigail pointed out that she would see a good deal of him in hospital once she was settled in there. They spent the rest of the day quite happily, with Abigail opening and shutting cupboards and drawers in order to display various garments to her patient, who, however ill she felt, intended to look as glamorous as possible during her stay in hospital. It was much later, when Abigail had packed a few things for herself that, cosily dressing-gowned, she sat down before her dressing-table to brush her hair for the night. She brushed it steadily for some time, deep in thought, and she wasn't thinking about herself, or her patient or Bollinger, but of Professor van Wijkelen. He was the handsomest man she had ever seen, also the most bad-tempered, but there had to be a reason for the look of dislike which he had given her when they had met—as though he had come prepared to dislike her, thought Abigail. She finished plaiting the rich thickness of her mousy hair and stared at her face in the mirror. Plain she might be, but in an inoffensive manner—her teeth didn't stick out, she didn't squint, her nose was completely unassuming; there was, in fact, nothing to cause offence. Yet he had stared at her as though she had mortally offended him. She put the brush away and padded over to the bed, thinking that she would very much like to get to know him better, not because he was so good-looking; he looked interesting as well, and for some reason she was unable to explain she found herself making excuses for his abrupt manner, even his dislike of her. She got into bed wondering sleepily what he was doing at that moment—the idea that he was a happily married man dispelled sleep for a few minutes until she decided that he didn't look married. She slept on that surprisingly happy thought.

CHAPTER TWO

THE HOSPITAL WAS hidden away behind the thickly clustered old houses and narrow lanes of the city. It was itself old, although once inside, Abigail saw that like so many of the older hospitals in England, it had a modernised interior despite the long bleak corridors and small dark passages and bare enclosed yards which so many of its windows looked out upon. Mrs Morgan's room was on the third floor, in the private wing, and although small, it was well furnished and the view from its window of the city around was a splendid one. Abigail got her patient safely into bed, tucked in the small lace-covered pillows Mrs Morgan had decided she couldn't manage without, changed her quilted dressing-gown for a highly becoming bedjacket, rearranged her hair, found her the novel she was reading, unpacked her case and after leaving the bell within reach of her, went to find the Ward Sister.

Zuster van Rijn was elderly, round, cosy and grey-haired, with a lovely smile and a command of the English language which Abigail found quite remarkable. They sat together in the little office, drinking the coffee which one of the nurses had brought them, while Zuster van Rijn read her patient's notes and charts and finally observed:

'She does not seem too bad. Professor van Wijkelen never operates unless it is necessary—he is far too good for that, but she must have the tests which have been ordered—she can have the X-ray this afternoon and the blood test—tomorrow the test meal—just something milky this evening for her diet. You're to stay with her, the professor tells me.'

'Yes, Mrs Morgan is a little nervous.'

Zuster van Rijn smiled faintly. 'Yes,' her voice was dry. 'There's a room ready for you in the Nurses' Home—would you like to go there now? There is nothing to do for Mrs Morgan for half an hour and one of the nurses can answer the bell. I will tell Zuster de Wit to go over with you.'

Abigail went back to her patient, to explain and collect her bag, and then followed the nurse down one flight of stairs, over a covered bridge, spanning what looked like a narrow lane of warehouses, and so into the Nurses' Home. Zuster de Wit hurried her along a long passage and then a short one to stop half way down it.

'Here,' she said, and smiled as she flung open a door in a row of doors. The room was comfortable although a little dark, for its window overlooked another part of the hospital, but the curtains were gay and it was warm and cheerful. Abigail smiled in return and said, 'How nice. Thank you,' and Zuster de Wit smiled again, said *'Dag'* and hurried away. Obviously she had been told to waste no time. Abigail, listening to her rapidly disappearing feet, hoped that she would be able to find her own way back to the ward again as she began to unpack her things. She had bought only a modicum of clothes—mostly uniform and her thick winter coat and a skirt and sweater, boots and the knitted beret and scarf she had made for herself during the weeks she had nursed her mother. It took only a few minutes to put these away and another minute or so to powder her nose and tuck her hair more tidily under her cap. It was almost four o'clock, as she shut the door she wondered about tea—perhaps they didn't have it; there were several things she would have to find out before the day was over. She went back over the bridge and found her way to her patient's room, to find her asleep.

Working in an Amsterdam hospital was almost exactly the same as working in her own London hospital; she had discovered this fact by the end of the day. Once she had become used to addressing even the most junior nurses as *'Zuster'* and discovered that she was expected to say *'Als t'U blift'* to anyone she gave something to, and *'Dank U wel'* each time she was given something, be it instructions—mostly in sign language—or a thermometer or a holder for the potted plant someone had sent her patient, she felt a little less worried about the problem of language. She had had to go without her tea, of course—they had had it at three o'clock, but she went down to supper with the other nurses at half past six; a substantial meal of pea soup, pork with a variety of vegetables, followed by what Abigail took to be custard and as much coffee as she could drink.

She went back to the office to give her report and then returned to sit with Mrs Morgan who was feeling a little apprehensive about the test meal. At half past eight, just before the night nurse was due on duty, a house doctor came to see the new patient and a few minutes later Doctor Vincent. He listened patiently to her small complainings, soothed her nicely, recommended her to do as Abigail told her, and went away again, and presently when the night nurse came and Abigail had given her a report too, she went herself, over the bridge to the Nurses' Home and to her room.

She hadn't been in it for more than a minute when there was a knock on the door and the same nurses she had seen at supper took her off to their sitting room to watch TV which, although she was tired, Abigail found rather fun because Paul Temple was on and it was amusing to watch it for a second time and listen to the dubbed voices talking what to her was nonsense. For so the Dutch language seemed to her; she had been unable to make head or tail of it—a few words and phrases, it was true, she had been quick enough to pick up, but for the most part she had had to fall back on basic English and signs, all taken in very good part by the other nurses. It had been a great relief to find that the night nurse spoke English quite well; enough to understand the report and discuss Mrs Morgan's condition with Abigail, and what was more important, Mrs Morgan seemed disposed to like her.

After Paul Temple she was carried off once more, this time to one of the nurses' rooms to drink coffee before finally going to her own room. She slept soundly and got up the next morning feeling happier than she had done for some time; it was on her way down to breakfast that she realised that the uplift to her spirits was largely due to the fact that she would most probably see the professor during the course of the day.

Her hope was to be gratified; he passed her on the corridor as she made her way to her patient's room after breakfast. She saw him coming towards her down its length and watched with faint amusement as the scurrying nurses got out of his way. When he drew level with her she wished him a cheerful good morning and in reply received a cold look of dislike and faint surprise, as though he were not in the habit of being wished a good day. Her disappointment was so sharp that she took refuge in ill temper too and muttered out loud as she sped along, 'Oh, well, be like that!'

She found her patient in good spirits; she had slept well, the night nurse had understood her and she had understood the night nurse, and the Ryle's tube had been passed and the test meal almost finished. The night nurse, giving the report to Abigail in the privacy of the nurses' station further down the corridor, confided in her correct, sparse English that she herself had enjoyed a quiet night and had got a great deal of knitting done. She produced the garment in question—a pullover of vast proportions and of an overpowering canary yellow. They had their heads together over the intricacies of its pattern when the professor said from behind them:

'If I might have the attention of you two ladies—provided you can spare the time?' he added nastily.

The Dutch girl whipped round in much the same fashion as a thief caught in the act of robbing a safe, but Abigail, made of sterner stuff and unconscious of wrongdoing, merely folded the pullover tidily and said: 'Certainly, sir,' which simple remark seemed to annoy him very much, for he glared at her quite savagely.

'You are both on duty, I take it?' he asked.

'No, me,' said Abigail ungrammatically in her pleasant voice. 'We've just discussed the report and Night Nurse is going off duty.'

'When I need to be reminded of the nurses' routine in hospital, I shall say so, Nurse Trent.'

She gave him a kindly, thoughtful look, her previous temper quite forgotten. Probably he was one of those unfortunate people who were always ill-tempered in the early morning. She found that she was prepared, more anxious to make excuses for him.

'I didn't intend to annoy you, sir,' she pointed out to him reasonably, and was rewarded with a sour look and a compression of his well-shaped mouth.

'The test meal,' he snapped, 'when is it complete?'

She looked at her watch. 'The last specimen is due to be withdrawn in fifteen minutes' time, sir.'

'If the patient doesn't tire of waiting for your return and pull the Ryle's tube out for herself.'

'Oh, no,' said Abigail seriously, 'she'd never do that—you see, I explained how important it was for her to do exactly as you wish. She has a great opinion of you.'

Just for a moment she thought that he was going to laugh, but she must have been mistaken, for all he said was, 'I want Mrs Morgan in theatre at noon precisely for gastroscopy. The anaesthetist will be along to write her up. See that she is ready, Nurse Trent.'

He turned to the night nurse, who had been silent all this while, and spoke to her with cold courtesy in his own language. She smiled at him uncertainly, looked at Abigail and flew off down the corridor, leaving behind her the strong impression that she was delighted to be free of their company. Abigail picked up the report book and prepared to go too, but was stopped by the professor's voice, very silky.

'A moment, Nurse Trent. I am interested to know what it was you said in the corridor just now.'

She wished she could have looked wide-eyed and innocent, or been so pretty that he really wouldn't want an answer to his question. She would have to tell him, and probably, as he seemed to dislike her so much already, he would say that he wanted another nurse to work for him and she would have to go back to England. Did one get paid in such circumstances? she wondered, and was startled when he asked, 'What are you thinking about? I assure you it is of no use you inventing some excuse.'

'I'm not inventing anything. What I said was,' she took a deep breath, '"Oh, well, be like that."'

'That is what I thought you said. May I ask if you are in the habit of addressing the consultants in your own hospital in such a fashion?'

She considered carefully before she answered him. 'No, I can't remember ever doing so before, but then, you see, they always said good morning.'

She studied his face as she spoke; perhaps she had gone a little too far, but she didn't like being treated in such a high-handed fashion. He looked very angry indeed—she waited for the outburst she felt sure would come and was surprised when all he said, through a tight mouth, was:

'Young woman, you disturb me excessively,' and stalked away, leaving Abigail with her eyes opened very wide, and her mouth open too.

She didn't see him again until she entered the theatre and she thought it unlikely that he would notice her, disguised as she was in theatre gown of voluminous size and nothing visible of her face, only her nice eyes above the mask.

The morning's work had gone exactly to plan. It was precisely noon. Theatre Sister and two nurses were there and of course the anaesthetist—there was to be no general anaesthetic, but Mrs Morgan had had a pre-med and would need a local anaesthetic. He was a nice sort of man, Abigail thought; his English was fluent if a little difficult to understand and he had smiled kindly at her. Mrs Morgan, her hand held in Abigail's comforting grasp, was dozing in her drug-induced sleep; she had joked a little about it before they went to theatre because she would miss seeing Professor van Wijkelen, and Abigail had consoled her with the prospect of further visits from him, for there were still one or two more tests to carry out, though once the professor had done the gastroscopy and had made up his mind whether he needed to operate or not, there wasn't much more to be done.

Abigail arranged the blanket over her patient, turning it down below her shoulders so that it wouldn't get in the surgeon's way once he started. Mrs Morgan made a little whimpering sound and opened her eyes, and Abigail said instantly in a soothing voice, 'It's all right, Mrs Morgan, the professor is just coming.'

He was in fact there, standing behind her, talking quietly to Sister. He finished what he was saying and went closer to his patient, ignoring Abigail completely—something she had expected.

He spoke quietly to his patient. 'You feel sleepy, don't you, Mrs Morgan? We are going to spray your throat now and it will feel numb, but you will feel nothing else—a little uncomfortable perhaps, but that is all. It will take only a short time. Your head will be lifted over a pillow now and I am going to ask you to open your mouth when I say so.'

The small examination went well and Mrs Morgan, whom Abigail had expected to be rather difficult, didn't seem to mind at all when the professor inserted the gastroscope and peered down it, his great height doubled, his brows drawn together in concentration. At length he said, 'That will do. Kindly take her back to the ward, Nurse.'

Which Abigail did, to spend a rather trying few hours because Mrs Morgan was under the impression that the local anaesthetic would wear off in ten minutes or so, and when it didn't she was first annoyed and then frightened. Abigail, explaining over and over again that the numbness would disappear quickly and that no, Mrs Morgan couldn't have a drink just yet, longed for an hour or so off duty. It was already three o'clock; she had been relieved at dinner time, but no one had said a word about her off-duty. Probably the Ward Sister thought that she wouldn't mind as long as someone relieved her for a cup of tea.

The door opened and she looked up hopefully, unaware that her face plainly showed her disappointment at the sight of the professor standing there, for he certainly hadn't come to release her from her duties. She got to her feet, wondering why he stared so, and fetched the chart for him to study. He hadn't spoken at all and since he seemed to like it that way, she hadn't either. She had half expected to hear more about their morning's meeting, but now she rather thought that he wasn't going to do anything more about it. She took the chart back again and stood quietly while he spoke briefly to Mrs Morgan. Presently he turned away from the bed. 'Nurse, I shall want another blood count done and the barium meal will be done tomorrow at two o'clock. Attend to the usual preparations, please. I can find nothing very wrong, but I shall need confirmation of that before I make my final decision.'

She said, 'Yes, Professor,' and admired him discreetly. Forty or more, she concluded, and unhappy—though I don't suppose he knows it.

His voice, cutting a swathe through her half-formed thoughts, asked:

'You are comfortable here, Nurse? Everyone is kind to you? You have your free time?'

'Yes, thank you,' she answered so quickly that he said at once, 'Today?'

'Well, not yet, but I'm perfectly all right. Mrs Morgan is my patient, isn't she, and the ward is very busy. I'm quite happy.'

He said surprisingly, 'Are you? I should have supposed otherwise, although I daresay you do your best to disguise the fact.'

She was appalled, and when had he looked at her long enough to even notice? 'I—I...' she began, and was instantly stopped by his bland, 'No need to excuse yourself, Nurse Trent—we all have our worries and sorrows, do we not—and never as important as we think they are.'

Abigail went brightly pink. She blushed seldom, but when she did, she coloured richly from her neck to the roots of her hair. He watched her now with a detached interest, nodded briefly, and went away.

She was relieved shortly after that and after a cup of tea in the dining room she tore into her clothes and went out into the city. The night nurse had explained how she could get to the shops in a few minutes; now she followed the little lanes between the old houses, pausing frequently to make sure that she could find her way back again, and came all at once into a brightly lighted street, crowded with people and lined with shops. She spent half an hour peering into their windows, working out the prices and deciding what she would buy when she had some money. That wouldn't be just yet; as soon as she had her first pay she would have to send it to poor old Bollinger. She wasn't happy about his room—it had looked cold and bare and although the landlady seemed kind enough she hadn't looked too clean, and supposing he were to become ill, who would look after him? She stood in the middle of Kalverstraat, suddenly not sure if she should have left him.

Mrs Morgan stayed in hospital for another three days, becoming progressively more cheerful because it seemed unlikely that she would need an operation after all. Besides, the professor visited her each day and she made no secret of her liking for him. He spent ten minutes or so listening gravely while she explained some new symptom she feared she might have, and then courteously contradicted her, impervious to her undoubted charm and quite deaf to her suggestions that he might, in the not too distant future, pay her a visit at her Long Island home. He seldom spoke to Abigail and when he looked at her it was with a coldness which she admitted to herself upset her a great deal more than it should have done.

They went home on the sixth day, this time in Mr Goldberg's Buick motor car; the professor had paid a visit the evening before and had stayed a little longer than usual, reassuring Mrs Morgan as to her future health, and had bidden her goodbye with his usual cold politeness, nodding briefly to Abigail as he went away. On her way off duty, half an hour later, she had seen him in the main ward, doing a round with his registrars and housemen, Sister and attendant satellites of students, nurses, physiotherapist and social worker. He looked very important but completely unconscious of the fact, an aspect of his character which she found strangely endearing.

The days following passed pleasantly enough. Mrs Morgan was out of bed now, although she preferred to keep to her room, walking a little and talking incessantly about her flight to the States, which she anticipated with all the impatience of someone who always had what they wanted when they wanted it. Abigail was impatient too—although she damped it down—for pay-day. She had had several letters from Bolly and from the sparse information they contained as to how he fared, she guessed that life was being difficult for him. She had already decided that she would send almost all her money to him, for she was almost certain that Mrs Morgan would ask her to stay another week, perhaps longer, and she didn't want him to wait any longer for it. The moment she got back to London she would go to the agency again and ask for another job. She reviewed her plans almost daily, and behind all this careful scheming was the thought that she would never see the professor again once she had left Holland. A ridiculous thing to worry about, she told herself scornfully, for she very much doubted if he would notice if she were there or not. She dismissed him firmly from her thoughts and went out each day, exploring Amsterdam.

It was on the morning that she was due to be paid that Mrs Morgan asked her if she would stay another week. 'I know I don't really need you, honey,' she said, 'but you are such a comfort to have around, and Dolly and Eddy don't need to worry about me at all. I've booked a flight for next week—a week today—if you would stay and see me safely away?'

She opened the crocodile handbag with the gold fittings which looked almost too heavy for her to carry and took out an envelope. 'Here's your salary, honey—I got Eddy to see to it for me. You'd rather have the cash, I'm sure. I bet you've got your eye on something pretty to buy with it.'

Abigail agreed pleasantly. She had grown quite fond of her patient while she had been looking after her and she saw no point in disturbing her complacent belief that the rest of the world lived in the same comfortable circumstances as herself. She put the envelope in her pocket and picked up the guide book of Holland which she had been reading to Mrs Morgan. Later, when she was free that afternoon, she would go to the post office and send the money to Bollinger, and perhaps now that she knew when she would be finished with the case, she should write to the agency and ask if they had anything else she could go straight to. The problem remained at the back of her mind while she read aloud about the delights of Avifauna and the best way of getting there, she was interrupted half way through by her companion telling her with enthusiasm that she intended to return. 'Because,' said Mrs Morgan, 'this is a sweet little country and I must say some of the people I've met are well worth cultivating.' She giggled happily and Abigail, who knew that she was talking about Professor van Wijkelen, smiled politely and wondered what success she would have in that quarter.

With her patient tucked up for her afternoon nap, Abigail was free to go to her room and open the envelope. There was two weeks' salary inside and her fare—but only her single fare. She had expected to be given the return fare and had neglected to ask anyone about it. Perhaps she was only entitled to half her travelling expenses; on the other hand, Mrs Morgan might give it to her with her next week's pay. She put the fare away in her bag, popped the rest into the envelope she had ready and got into her outdoor clothes.

It was cold outside and bleak with the bleakness of January. The clouds had a yellow tinge to them and the wind was piercingly cold. She hurried to the post office some streets away, where there were clerks who spoke English and would understand her when she asked for a registered envelope.

The post office was warm inside. The walk had given her eyes a sparkle and put some colour into her cheeks. She had perched her knitted beret on top of her head and wound its matching scarf carelessly round her throat. She took her gloves off and blew on her cold fingers and went up to the counter.

It took a little while to understand the clerk and then she was so disappointed that she could hardly believe him. She had taken it for granted that she could send either the cash or a money order to Bolly and it seemed she had been hopelessly at fault—she could do no such thing. Go to a bank, suggested the clerk helpfully, where there would be forms to be filled in and a certain amount of delay. But she wanted Bolly to have the money now—within the next day or two. If she waited until she went back herself that was a whole week away—besides, she had promised Bolly. She sighed and the clerk sighed in sympathy and she said, 'Well, thank you very much for explaining. I should have found out earlier, shouldn't I?'

'Can I help?' The professor—she would have known his icy voice anywhere. She whirled round to face him.

'Oh, how funny to meet you here, sir. I don't think so, thank you. It's just something that was my own silly fault anyway.'

'Why should it be funny, Nurse Trent? I also write letters, you know.'

'Yes, I'm sure you do, only—only I should have thought that you would have had someone to post them.'

'Indeed? I am not particularly interested in your suppositions, but I find this one extraordinary. How can I help you?'

Persistent man, he wasn't going to take no for an answer. She explained in a matter-of-fact voice and apologised again for being stupid.

'Why should you be stupid?' he asked irritably. 'You were not to know before you asked. How much money did you want to send?'

'Forty pounds. No—I've got to take some off...' she began to reckon twelve and a half per cent of forty pounds in her head and the amount came different each time she did it. Finally she asked, because he showed signs of impatience, 'How much is twelve and a half per cent of forty pounds?'

'Five pounds. Why?'

'Well, that's what I have to pay the agency for as long as I work for them.'

'Iniquitous! It so happens that I am going over to London this evening. I will take the money, since you seem so anxious to send it.'

She stared at him, astonished. 'But you don't even...you're very kind, but I couldn't trouble you. I shall be going back myself in a week's time.'

The professor tweaked her out of the queue forming behind her.

'Ah, yes—I should be obliged if you would remain in Amsterdam for a further few weeks. I have a patient upon whom I shall be operating in ten days' time, and he will need a special nurse in hospital and probably to accompany him home when he is sufficiently recovered. Your usual fee will be paid you.'

Abigail's voice sounded a little too loud in her own ears. 'But you don't…' She stopped—what had his personal opinion of her got to do with it anyway? He wanted a nurse and she was available. She answered him with her usual calm good sense, 'Yes, Professor, I should be quite willing to stay on for as long as you require me.'

He nodded carelessly, as though he had known all along that she was going to say yes.

'Very well, we will consider the matter settled,' and when she looked at him it was to find him smiling. Perhaps it was because she had never seen him smile that her heart lurched against her ribs and her breath caught in her throat. It transformed his handsome face into one of such charm that if he had at that moment suggested that she should remain in Holland for the rest of her life, she would probably have agreed without further thought. But her idea wasn't put to the test; the smile vanished, leaving him looking more impatient than ever.

'Give me the address of the person who is to receive the money,' he suggested, 'and I will see that it reaches him—or her.'

'Him,' said Abigail, and would have liked to tell him about Bolly, but quite obviously her companion was anxious to be gone. She handed him the envelope with the letter inside and the forty pounds hastily pushed in with it. She had forgotten about the agency fee, but he hadn't.

'Twelve and a half per cent?' he wanted to know.

He really was in a hurry. 'I'll—I'll take it out of my pay next week. You're sure…?'

He interrupted without apology, 'Stop fussing, Miss Trent.' He stuffed the envelope into a pocket with a nonchalance, Abigail thought vexedly, of a man who found forty pounds chicken feed, wished her a curt goodbye and walked away. She began to walk back to the flat, her head bent against the sneering wind, telling herself that the reason she felt so happy was because

Bolly would have the money by the following evening, or at the very least, the morning after.

The professor came to see Mrs Morgan three days later. He paid his visit while Abigail was out for her afternoon walk and left no message for her at all. It wasn't until the evening previous to Mrs Morgan's departure that he came again. Abigail was packing her patient's clothes, surrounded by tissue paper, orderly piles of undies, innumerable hats and an assortment of suitcases. Evidently Mrs Morgan never worried about excess baggage. That lady was reclining on the couch, directing operations; she looked very well and remarkably attractive, which was more than Abigail felt, for her head ached and her usually neat hair was a little untidy, nor had she had the time to do anything to her face for some time, and over and above these annoyances she was worried about Bolly; she had had a cheerful letter from him, thanking her for the money, but she sensed that he was hiding something from her. She was thinking about it now and frowning—she was still frowning when there was a knock on the door and Doctor Vincent and the professor walked in. They both wished her a good evening and she flushed a little under the professor's brief, unfriendly glance, very conscious that she wasn't looking her modest best. They stayed perhaps ten minutes, made their farewells and started for the door. But this time Professor van Wijkelen made a detour and came to a halt by her and her pile of luggage.

'I understand that you will be taking Mrs Morgan to Schiphol tomorrow morning. You will be fetched from there and taken straight to the hospital. Perhaps you can arrange to have your luggage with you.' His eyes strayed over the ordered chaos around them. 'I trust you have a good deal less than this.'

'One case,' Abigail told him briefly, and he nodded. 'I will leave a message for you at the hospital tomorrow,' he stated. 'Good evening, Nurse.'

He had gone before she could thank him for posting her letter.

Mrs Morgan was actually bidding Abigail goodbye at Schiphol when she interrupted herself to exclaim, 'There, I knew there was something, honey! I've clean forgot to give you your money.' She made to open her unwieldy bag, but it was too late; a smiling official indicated the passenger conveyor belt which would take her one stage nearer the plane. 'I'll post it to you,' she called, waved and smiled and nodded, and was borne swiftly away; so easy for her to say it, thought Abigail a little forlornly, but where would she send the money to? Mrs Morgan knew that she was going to another job, but she hadn't asked for any details and Abigail hadn't volunteered any. Perhaps she would send the money to the agency. If so, would the severe woman who had interviewed her send it on, or would she keep it and expect Abigail to call for it? And what about the rest of her fare—she hadn't had it yet.

She stood pondering, pushed to and fro by the hurrying people around her. She had been silly; she should have asked for her salary and her fare sooner. But she hadn't liked to, even though the money was rightly hers. And now she had landed herself with only a few pounds. Supposing the professor had changed his mind about employing her for his next patient? She had been rash enough to buy herself a pair of shoes the day before, and now she was left with less than her fare to England. She moved at last, back to the reception area to fetch her case. She had been foolish twice over; the professor had said that she would be fetched from the airport, but how was she to know who was looking for her? Supposing they couldn't find her and she was left—supposing they forgot all about her, supposing... Her gloomy thoughts were cut short by the professor's voice. She hadn't seen him, but here he was beside her, taking her case from her as relief as well as delight flooded through her, although her quiet 'Good morning, Professor,' was uttered in her usual voice. She received an ill-tempered grunt in reply and a brief, 'Come along, Nurse,' as he made for the door.

She trotted beside him because otherwise she could never have kept up with him, and to lose him now would be unthinkable. There were a great many cars outside and she wondered which of them was his.

He stopped in front of a black Rolls-Royce Silver Shadow, sleekly and unobtrusively perfect among the other cars, opened its doors, told her to get in with the cold courtesy she had come to believe was the only alternative to his ill-humour, and went to put her case in the boot. He didn't speak when he got in beside her, and was still silent as he edged the car away from the crowded bustle of the airport and on to the main road. They were tearing along the motorway to the capital when she ventured helpfully:

'I expect you came yourself so that you could save time telling me about the patient.'

She looked at him as she spoke and he turned to meet her gaze briefly. She wished that he would smile again, but he didn't, although when he did speak she had the impression that somewhere, deep down inside him, he was laughing. Imagination, she told herself roundly; why should he laugh?

'A doctor,' he stated flatly. 'Professor de Wit, seventy years old. He's to have a gastroenterostomy—CA, of course, but everything's in his favour, he's got a sound heart and chest and a great desire to live. He is to have a room in the private wing and you will be working under Zuster van Rijn with whom you will arrange your off-duty, please.'

Having thus given her the bare bones of the case he fell silent once more, and Abigail, not knowing if he was occupied with the intricacies of the day's operating list, forbore from disturbing him. It was only when he drew up in front of the hospital entrance and called to the porter to come and collect her case that she said:

'Thank you for posting my letter. I heard from—that is, it arrived safely. I'm very grateful to you.'

He looked at her with quick annoyance. 'There's no need to say any more about it,' he stated with such finality that she felt snubbed, so that she too was annoyed. 'I shan't,' she told him crisply. 'Obviously gratitude and thanks are wasted upon you, sir.'

She walked briskly into the hospital, not waiting to see what the porter was going to do about her case. She was half way across the width of the entrance hall when she was amazed to hear the professor laughing. It was a deep bellow and sounded perfectly genuine.

It was surprising to her how quickly she slipped back into the routine of hospital. She had been given the same room again and this time it was so much easier because she knew some of the nurses and they greeted her as an old friend. Zuster van Rijn seemed glad to see her again too; they were short-staffed on the surgical side, she told Abigail, and specialling could be awkward unless there were enough nurses.

'Will you work as you did before,' she asked, 'and take an afternoon off? I know it's not quite fair that you shouldn't work shift hours as the other girls do, but that way I can spare a nurse to take over while you're off duty. There will be the same night nurse as you have already worked with, and you shall have your days off, of course, but how or when I do not know at the moment. You are content?'

'Quite content,' Abigail told her. Days off didn't matter, not for the first week at any rate, for she hadn't any money to spend. The problem of how to get the money over to Bolly was looming heavily again too; she had done nothing about it because she had expected to return to England, now she would have to start all over again. She dismissed her problems and followed Sister, prepared to meet her patient.

She liked him on sight. He was lying in bed and although his face was pinched and white with his illness, he was still a remarkably good-looking old man. Excepting for a thick fringe of white hair, he was bald, but the fringe encircled his face as well in rich profusion and his blue eyes were youthful and sharp. She shook his hand—gently—because she could see that he was an ill man, and despite his alert expression and merry eyes, probably in pain as well.

Zuster van Rijn left them together after a few minutes and Professor de Wit said, 'Pull up a chair, my dear, and let us get to know each other. I believe Dominic wishes me to spend a week in bed before he operates, physiotherapy and blood transfusions and all the other fringe benefits of his calling which he so generously offers.'

Abigail laughed with him. So the professor's name was Dominic—she stored the little piece of information away, though what good it would do her she had yet to discover. She listened to the old man's placid talk in his slow, almost perfect English and by means of gentle questions of her own found out that he slept badly, ate almost nothing, had lost his wife twenty years previously, had a doting housekeeper to look after him, and a dog and a cat to keep him company, as well as a half-tamed hedgehog, a family of rabbits and a pet raven. They were discussing a mutual dislike of caged birds when Professor van Wijkelen came in.

The two men, she saw at once, were old friends. It was also apparent that the older man trusted the younger completely. He lay listening quietly while the professor told him exactly what he was going to do and why.

'It sounds most promising, Dominic. I gather I am to be a new man by the time you have finished with me.'

'Shall we say soundly repaired, and fit for another ten or fifteen years—and that's a conservative estimate.'

'And what does Nurse say?' It was her patient who spoke.

Her smile lighted her ordinary face with its gentleness and sincerity.

'I never think of failure—Professor van Wijkelen will operate and it will be a complete success, just as he says.' She looked across at him as she spoke and found him staring at her, and there was no mistaking the faint sneer on his face, but because she liked him, she saw the hurt there too. Someone at some time had turned him into a cold, embittered man; she wondered who it was and hated them. Once, just once, he had smiled at her and she wanted him to smile like that again, but that, at that moment, seemed unlikely.

She settled down to a steady pattern of work, the same work as she would have been doing in a London hospital, even though the language was different, but all the doctors and a good many of the nurses spoke English and she herself, with the aid of her dictionary and a good deal of good-natured help from everyone else, managed to make herself understood. The days passed quickly. Under her patient's kindly direction she went each afternoon to some fresh part of the city, sometimes to a museum, sometimes to gaze at the outside of some old house whose fascinating history he had described to her delighted ears while she was fulfilling the various duties which made up her day. He was looking a little better, mainly due to the blood transfusions, to which he submitted with an ill grace because they interfered with his movements in bed. He was a great reader and an even greater writer and a formidable conversationalist. Abigail became fond of him, as indeed did anyone who came in daily contact with him. The day before his operation he paid her, handing her an envelope with a word of thanks and a little joke about him being strong enough to do it the following week, which touched her soft heart because although she had complete faith in Professor van Wijkelen, things quite outside his control could go wrong. She tucked the envelope away under her apron bib and as she did so wondered for the hundredth time why Bolly's last letter had been so strange; asking her not to send him any more money for at least another week. A good thing in a way, because she had not yet discovered the best way of sending it to him, all the same, she felt a vague disquiet.

Professor van Wijkelen came each day, treating her with his usual polite chill, at direct variance to the obvious regard he had for his patient. She stood quietly by while they talked together and longed for the warmth of his voice to be directed just once at herself. A wish which was most unlikely to be fulfilled, she told herself wryly, handing him charts and forms and reports and at the end giving him her own report very concisely in her clear precise voice. He liked to take her report outside the patient's room and did her the courtesy of giving her his full attention. And now, on this day before he was to operate, he listened even more carefully than usual. When she had finished he said, as he always said: 'Thank you, Miss Trent,' and proceeded to give her detailed instructions as to what he wished her to do on the following day.

The operation was a success, although only the next few days would show if the success was to be a lasting one. Abigail had taken her patient to the theatre and remained there to assist the anaesthetist. For a good deal of the time she was free to watch the professor at work. He was a good surgeon completely engrossed in his work and talking very little. When at length he was finished, he thanked the theatre sister and stalked away without a word. He was in his old friend's room within minutes of his return to it, though. Abigail was still getting the old man correctly positioned and adjusting the various tubes and drip when he came silently through the open door.

'I don't want him left, Nurse. I have spoken to Sister—if you wish to go off duty, she will send someone to take over. Is that clear?'

'Perfectly, thank you,' said Abigail, and because she was checking the closed drainage, didn't say any more. She had no intention of going off duty; she had promised Professor de Wit that she would stay with him and she could see no reason why she shouldn't do just that. She was, when all was said and done, his special nurse. Professor van Wijkelen said abruptly:

'He'll do—with careful nursing,' and turned on his heel and left her.

She didn't leave her patient again, only for the briefest of meal breaks and the professor came in twice more as well as his registrar, a portly little man whom Abigail rather liked. He spoke a fluent, ungrammatical English and she got on famously with him and she was grateful to him too, because he came often to check on the patient's condition and cheer her with odd titbits of gossip so that the day passed quickly. It was half an hour before she was due off that Zuster van Rijn came rustling down the corridor to tell her that the night nurse had been struck down with a sore throat and a temperature and wouldn't be able to come on duty, and there was no one to take her place. 'I can put a nurse on until midnight, though, and then she need not come on until the noonday shift. Could you possibly…?'

'Yes, of course,' said Abigail. 'I'll go off at eight, have supper and a sleep and come back here at twelve.'

Zuster van Rijn looked relieved. 'That is good—tomorrow morning I will get someone to take over while you go to bed for a few hours.'

So it was that when Professor van Wijkelen came at one o'clock in the morning, it was Abigail who rose quietly from her chair near the bed. His glance flickered over her as he went to look at his patient; it was only when he was satisfied as to his condition that he asked curtly:

'Why are you on duty? Where is the night nurse?'

'It's quite all right, sir,' said Abigail soothingly. 'Nurse Tromp is off sick and there wasn't time to get a full-time night nurse. I've been off duty, I came back at midnight.'

'Until when?'

'Until I can be relieved. Zuster van Rijn will arrange something.'

'Have you had your days off?'

'I'd rather not have them until the professor is better.' She spoke uncertainly because he was looking annoyed again. 'I imagine that my days off can be fitted in at any time, as I'm not a member of the hospital staff.'

'You have no need to state the obvious, Nurse. You must do as you please and I daresay Zuster van Rijn will be glad if you remain on duty for a few days until Professor de Wit is on the mend.'

He spoke carelessly as though he didn't mind if she had her days off or not, and indeed, she thought wearily, why should he?

He went away then and she spent a busy night, because there was a lot of nursing to do and the professor had regained consciousness and wished to be far too active. But presently, after an injection, he dropped off into a refreshing sleep and Abigail was free to bring her charts up to date, snatch a cup of coffee and then sit quietly between the regular intervals of checking one thing and another. It was, she mused, a splendid opportunity to think quietly about the future, but perhaps she was too tired, for when she tried to do so, she seemed unable to clear her mind. She gave up presently, and spent the rest of the night idly thumbing through her dictionary, hunting for words which, even when she found them, she was unable to pronounce.

The professor came again at seven o'clock. Abigail, with the help of another nurse, had made her patient's bed and sat him up against his pillows; she had washed him too and combed his fringe of hair and his whiskers and dressed him in his own pyjamas. He looked very old and very ill, but she had no doubt at all that he was going to pull through, for he had a good deal of spirit. She was drawing up an injection to give him when Professor van Wijkelen arrived; he looked as though he had slept the clock round, and now, freshly shaved and immaculately dressed, he sauntered in for all the world as though he were in the habit of paying his visits at such an early hour. His good morning to her was brief; so brief that it seemed pointless, but she answered him nicely, smiling from a tired face that had no colour at all, unhappily aware that there was nothing about her appearance to make him look at her a second time.

He didn't say much to his patient but motioned her to give the injection, walked over to the window and sat down at the table there and began to study the papers she had laid ready for him. He had given her fresh instructions and was on the point of leaving when he remarked:

'You look as though you could do with a good sleep, Nurse.'

'Of course she needs a good sleep,' Professor de Wit's voice was testy even though it was weak. 'Just because you choose to work yourself to death doesn't mean that everyone else should do the same.'

'I have no intention of working anyone to death. Nurse is doing a job like anyone else and she has a tongue in her head. If she cannot carry out her duties, she has only to say so.'

He didn't look at her but flung 'I shall look in later,' over his shoulder as he went.

'Such a pity that...' began her patient, and fell asleep instantly just as Abigail was hopeful of hearing why something was a great pity—something to do with Professor van Wijkelen, she felt sure.

The next few days were busy ones. Her patient continued to improve, but there was a great deal of nursing care needed and Abigail was a conscientious nurse. She took her daily walk because she knew that she needed the exercise in the fresh air, despite its rawness and the bitter wind which never ceased to blow, but her days off she saved up; she would take them when the case was finished. There had, as yet, been no talk of sending Professor de Wit home although it had been made clear to her that she was to accompany him. They would be in hospital another week at least—two probably; if it hadn't been for the niggling worry about Bollinger, she would have been happier than she had been for a long time. She had made some friends in the hospital by now and she was battling on with her Dutch, helped a great deal by her patient, who now that he was feeling better spent a fair proportion of his waking hours correcting her accent and grammar.

It was the day after the drip came down for the last time and the old man had walked a few steps on her arm that Professor van Wijkelen had come to see him and on his way out again had said in his usual austere way:

'Nurse, if you are free tomorrow afternoon, I wish you to come with me—there is someone who wants to meet you.'

'Who?' asked Abigail, who liked to know where she was.

'Shall we say you must wait and see?' he enquired silkily, and then suddenly, as though he sensed that she was about to refuse, he smiled with such charm that she would have agreed to anything he wished. 'Please,' said the professor.

She nodded, knowing that when he looked at her like that she wanted nothing more than to please him. She was thoughtful after he had gone and Professor de Wit said nothing, although she had expected him to. When she saw that he didn't intend to discuss it with her, she launched into an argument on the subjunctive in the Dutch language, concentrating fiercely upon her companion's learned comments, because Professor van Wijkelen was taking up much too much of her attention these days.

CHAPTER THREE

THE PROFESSOR WAS waiting for her when she reached the hospital forecourt the following afternoon. He greeted her with unsmiling courtesy as he opened the car door for her to get in, and because he so obviously didn't want to talk, she remained silent as he took the car through the gates and into the narrow streets beyond.

'You don't want to know where I am taking you?' he enquired blandly.

'Yes, of course I do, but I daresay you wouldn't choose to tell me, so I shan't ask.' Abigail spoke matter-of-factly and without rancour.

'We are going to my house.'

That startled her. 'What ever for?'

'There is somebody you should meet—it seemed the best place.'

'Oh, I see.' She didn't see at all and she was longing to ask him who it was and didn't because he would be expecting it.

'Very wise of you,' he commented silkily, answering her unspoken thought. 'I've no intention of telling you. How do you find Professor de Wit?'

She obligingly followed his lead. 'Determined to get well as soon as possible.'

'Yes—I have every hope that he will. The operation wasn't quite straightforward.' He launched into details and then said to surprise her:

'He likes you, Nurse Trent. I hope that you will be prepared to go home with him for a few days?'

'Certainly,' said Abigail. There was nothing she would like better, for a variety of reasons, which for the moment at least, she didn't intend to look into too deeply. She looked about her. They were travelling along the Herengracht, beautiful and picturesque with its old houses on either side of the tree-lined canal. Some way down its length the professor turned the car into a short arm of the canal—a little cul-de-sac, spanned by a narrow footbridge half way down its length. Houses lined the cobbled streets on either side of the water and across its far end, and trees, even in their winter bareness, crowded thickly along its banks.

The Rolls slid sedately along its length and came to a halt outside one of the houses at the end, facing the canal. It was a very old house, with double steps leading to a great door and another, smaller door tucked away under those same steps. The windows were high and narrow and climbed up the front of the house. The higher they climbed the smaller they became, until they terminated in one very large one, heavily shuttered under the steep gable of the house. There was a tremendous hook above it, because that was the only way to get anything in or out of the houses' top floors.

It was peaceful in the small backwater, away from the traffic, with only the wind sighing around the steeple roofs. Abigail got out and looked around her while the professor opened his house door, and then at his bidding went inside.

It was all she had expected and hoped for, with its black and white tiled floor, its plasterwork ceiling and plain white walls, upon which were hung a host of paintings, and its carved staircase rising from one side.

The furnishings were in keeping—a heavy oak table along one wall, flanked by two carved oaken chairs which Abigail thought looked remarkably uncomfortable, while the other wall held an oak chest upon which reposed a great blue and white bowl, filled with spring flowers.

Abigail rotated slowly, trying to see everything at once. 'How absolutely beautiful—it's quite perfect,' she said, and was instantly sorry she had spoken, because when she looked at her companion he was looking down his long nose at her as though she had been guilty of some offending vulgarity. She went a faint, angry pink, which turned even brighter when he remarked austerely:

'I feel sure, from the ferocious expression upon your face, that you are on the point of bidding me not to be like that, or some such similar phrase, Miss Trent. May I beg you not to do so—I am easily irritated.'

'So I've noticed,' Abigail told him tartly. 'The smallest thing... And now, Professor, if I might meet this person.' Her eyes swept round the empty hall; the house was very quiet, she allowed her thoughtful gaze to rest upon the man beside her and was on the point of speaking when he interrupted her:

'No, Miss Trent, I can assure you that there is nothing of sinister intent in my request to you to accompany me here.' He smiled thinly. 'You surely could not have seriously supposed that?'

It was annoying to have her thoughts read so accurately. Abigail said crossly, because that was exactly what she had been thinking, 'No, of course not. I'm not such a fool—you have to be joking.'

He said nothing to this but opened a door and said: 'Perhaps you would like to wait in here?'

She went past him into a small panelled room, warm and snug in the light of the fire burning in the steel grate. It was furnished in the utmost comfort with a number of easy chairs, leather-covered; a charmingly inlaid pier table against one wall, one small round table, inlaid with coloured mosaic work, conveniently close to the hearth, a revolving bookcase filled with books and a small Regency work-table. The professor pressed a switch and a number of table lamps bathed their surroundings in a delicate pink, highlighting the walls, which she could see were covered with red embossed paper, almost hidden along two sides of the room by the pictures hung upon it, and completely hidden on its third side by shelves of books. The room called for comment, but this time she held her tongue, walking to the centre of the room and standing quietly, waiting for him to speak first.

He didn't speak at all, but went out of the room, shutting the door behind him, and Abigail for one split second fought an urge to rush to the door and try the handle. Instead, she turned her back on it and went to examine the paintings on the walls. Mostly portraits of bygone van Wijkelens, she decided, who had undoubtedly passed on their good looks with an almost monotonous regularity. She was peering at a despotic-looking old gentleman in a tie-wig, when the door opened behind her and she turned round to see who it was.

Bollinger stood there. She cried on a happy, startled breath: 'Bolly—oh, Bolly!' and burst into tears. He crossed the room and patted her on the shoulder and said: 'There, there, Miss Abby—I gave you a shock, eh? Thought you'd be pleased and all.'

'Oh, Bolly, I am! I'm so happy to see you, that's why I'm crying—aren't I a fool? But how did you get here?' A sudden thought struck her. 'In the professor's house?' She whisked the spotless handkerchief he always carried out of his pocket and blew her nose and wiped her eyes. 'Does he know?'

'Course he knows, love. It's him as thought to do it. You see, he comes along one night and gives me your letter and the money, and I asks him to have a cuppa, seeing as it's a cold night, and we gets talking and I tells him a bit about us, and he says to me, "Well, Bollinger, seeing as how Miss Trent's going to be in Amsterdam for a week or two yet, why don't you get yourself a little job and be near her?"'

"'Well,' I says, 'that's easier said than done,' and he says: 'I'm looking for a gardener and odd job man for a week or two while my man has his bunions done—how about it?' So here I am, Miss Abby, came yesterday. He paid me fare and I'm to get my wages, so I'm in clover, as they say—no need for you to give me any more money.'

'It's fantastic,' declared Abigail. 'I simply can't believe it—do you like him, Bolly?'

'Yes, that I do, Miss Abby—a bit of a toff, you might say, but a gent all right.'

Abigail blew her nose again to prevent herself from bursting into another bout of tears. 'Oh, Bolly, it's like being home again. And of course I shall go on paying you your money—have you any idea how much it is we owe you? Don't you see, Bolly, I must pay you back now that I know about it and can afford to do so?'

'Well, if it makes you happy, Miss Abby. How long do you think you'll be here?'

'I'm not sure. Another two weeks, perhaps three. What have you done about your room?'

'I give it up, it wasn't all that hot. This professor, he says he knows someone in London lets rooms, very nice—a bit more than I got, but if I save me wages...'

'And I pay you each week while you're here, and by the time I get back to London and you're running a bit low, I'll be in another job and be able to send you something each week.' She hugged him. 'Oh, Bolly, it's all so wonderful, I can't believe it. Are you happy here? Where do you live?'

'Here, of course, Miss Abby. I got a room at the top of the house—very snug and warm it is too.'

'You don't have to work too hard?'

'Lord love you, no, Miss Abby—nice little bit of garden behind, and I does the odd job—and I'm to go to his other house in the country once a week and see to the garden there.'

Abigail stood silent, digesting this new aspect of Professor van Wijkelen. 'Well…' she began, and was interrupted by the door opening to admit a small round dumpling of a woman with a pleasant face. She shook Abigail by the hand and said in very tolerable English, 'The housekeeper, Mevrouw Boot,' and Abigail, mindful of her Dutch manners, replied: 'Miss Abigail Trent.'

Mevrouw Boot eyed her with kindly curiosity as she spoke. 'The professor begs that Miss will return to hospital when she must. There is a car at the door in five minutes. He excuses himself.'

She smiled again and went quietly out of the room, and Abigail looked at Bollinger and said with unconscious sadness, 'He doesn't like me, you know,' and had this statement instantly repudiated by Bolly who exclaimed in a shocked voice:

'That I can't believe, begging your pardon, Miss Abby—a nice young lady like you…'

'Well, it doesn't matter in the least,' said Abigail with such firmness that she almost believed what she was saying—but not quite, because it mattered out of all proportion to everything else. 'I'd better go, I suppose it's a taxi and I oughtn't to keep it waiting. Come to the door with me, Bolly.'

They crossed the hall, lingering a little. 'The professor says you're to come whenever ye're inclined,' Bolly explained, 'but not the days I go to the country.'

She nodded and stopped. 'All right, Bolly, I'll remember. I'm very grateful to him. Do you suppose I should write him a letter?'

He looked astonished. 'You see him, don't you, can't you do it then?'

She shook her head. 'I told you he doesn't like me,' and as if to underline her words one of the doors opened and Mevrouw

Boot came into the hall and before she closed the door behind her, Abigail and Bollinger had an excellent view of the professor sitting at a desk facing it—the powerful reading lamp on it lighted his face clearly; he was staring at Abigail with no expression, giving her the peculiar feeling that she wasn't there, and then lowered his handsome head to the papers before him. The door closed and when the housekeeper had gone, Abigail said softly:

'You see, Bolly? He doesn't even want to see me, let alone speak.'

She smiled a little wanly, wished him a warm goodbye and went outside. The Rolls was before the steps, an elderly man at the wheel. He got out of the car when he saw her and opened the door, smiling nicely as he did so although he didn't speak, and she returned the smile, for he had a kind face, rugged and lined—like a Dutch Bolly, she thought as she settled herself beside him for the journey back to the hospital. During the short ride she tried her best to reconcile the professor's dislike of her with his kindness to Bollinger. There had, after all, been no need to offer the old man a job, even a temporary one. She hoped that Bolly hadn't told him too much, although she discounted as ridiculous the idea that he might have acted out of sympathy to herself as well as Bollinger. It was all a little mysterious and she gave up the puzzle and began to ask her companion some questions about Amsterdam, hoping that he could understand. It was an agreeable surprise to find that he could, and moreover, reply to them in English.

At the hospital, she thanked him for the ride, wondering who he was and not liking to ask for fear the professor would hear of it and consider her nosey. She went back to her patient with her curiosity unsatisfied, to find him feeling so much better after a refreshing nap that he wanted to know what she had been doing with her afternoon. She told him, skating over the more unexplainable bits, and rather to her surprise he made very little comment, and that was about herself and Bollinger. About the professor he had nothing to say at all.

The days slid quietly by, each one bringing more strength to Professor de Wit. He was to go home in a week's time, said Professor van Wijkelen when he called one morning soon after Abigail had been to his house, and as he had said it, both he and his patient looked at her.

'You'll come with me, Abby?' asked her patient, who considered himself on sufficiently good terms with her by now to address her so. The professor's cool, 'I hope you will find it convenient to go with Professor de Wit for another week, Nurse Trent,' sounded all the more stilted. She said that yes, of course she would, hiding her delight at the idea of seeing the professor, even if he hated her, for another few days, and the lesser delight of knowing that she would be able to repay Bolly quite a lot of money. She went away to fetch the latest X-rays the professor decided to study, walking on air.

She told Bollinger about it the next day when they met, as they often did, for a cup of coffee and half an hour's chat. Bollinger, she was glad to see, looked well, and he was happy with his gardening and the odd jobs he was doing around the house. He had been to the country too, but Abigail didn't press him with questions about this; somehow she felt that the less she knew about the professor's private life, the better it would be.

She hadn't been back to the house on the *gracht*—not since the time when he had looked right through her, as though she were someone he didn't want to see there. Each time Bollinger suggested it, she had some excuse, but when she went home with Professor de Wit, she would have to do better, for she discovered that the older man had a small house within walking distance of the professor's home, and Bolly would expect her to go and see him quite often and she could think of no good reason why she shouldn't. The professor had even told Bollinger to use the small sitting room where they had met, and offer Abigail tea if she wished, which, considering the lack of friendliness he showed towards her, puzzled her very much.

She took care during the next few days to keep herself busy, both in her work and her leisure; under her patient's tuition, she was beginning to make a little headway with her Dutch, and because it pleased him excessively and kept him interested in something while he struggled through the unrewarding days of convalescence, she spent a good deal of time outside her working hours with him, not admitting to herself that it served her purpose very well and gave her a real excuse for not going to the house on the *gracht*.

The professor came daily, sometimes twice, but beyond wishing her a good day and asking her in a strictly professional manner how his patient did, he made no effort to talk to her. About Bollinger he had said nothing at all, and the short, painfully careful note she had sent him had been ignored.

But she was not able to follow this rather cowardly scheme for any length of time; Professor de Wit took her to task for not going out enough, and dispatched her to Kalverstraat on her next free afternoon to fetch him some books he had ordered. She knew her way about by now and hurried down the narrow lanes, wrapped warmly against the snarling wind and the first powdering of snow from a heavy sky. There were several ways in which she might reach the bookshop; she chose the longest of them, because although it didn't pass Professor van Wijkelen's house, it went close to it, which, she told herself sternly, was the silliest reason for taking it.

There were several alleys connecting one *gracht* with the next. She went down one of them now, her head bent against the quickening snow, her feet sounding loudly on the uneven cobbles and echoing against the silent warehouses, leaning, crooked with age, against each other on either side of her. She was nearly at the end when a movement in the gutter drew her attention—a slight movement, made without sound. She slowed her pace to investigate, crossing the road gingerly; it might be a rat, and she was afraid of rats. But it wasn't a rat, it was a kitten, a very small one, its dirty black and white fur clinging wetly to its bony body, a few drops of blood on its filthy white shirt-front. She stooped and picked it up with care, fearful of hurting it, and exclaimed with pity at its pathetic lightness. It was an ugly small creature, with a large nose; even when clean and well fed, she doubted if it would be worth a second glance. It gave her a penetrating glance from blue eyes and mewed, and all thought of fetching her patient's books went out of her head. She wrapped the waif in the ends of her long scarf, cradled it against her and hurried on. The professor's house was only around the next corner. She would go there and get Bolly to take care of it after she had examined it to see where it had been hurt.

At the house she hesitated. To ring the front door bell and ask to go in so that she might attend to a stray kitten seemed to her to be taking advantage of the professor's message that she might stay for tea with Bolly—and probably it had been mere civility on his part, with no thought of her accepting. She didn't think he was at home—there was no car to be seen and the house stood silent in the snow. She knocked on the little door beneath the steps and waited.

Bollinger opened the door, his face lighting up at the sight of her. 'There, Miss Abby,' he exclaimed, 'I knew you'd be along—on such a nasty day too. Come in and we'll have a cuppa.' He opened the door wider, saying: 'But I don't know if you should come in this door. The one above's for you.'

'Well, no—I shouldn't think so,' Abby stated. 'I haven't been invited you know—besides, I've got something—look.'

They carried the kitten to the kitchen at the back of the house, a surprisingly bright room overlooking a small walled garden, now shrouded in snow. There was no one there; Bolly explained that Mevrouw Boot had gone out to see some relative or other and the daily woman who came in to do the rough work had gone home. 'Let's put the little beggar in front of the stove,' he suggested, 'get him warm, then we can have a look.'

Which they accordingly did, to be rewarded after a few minutes by a faint movement from the small creature, who put out a pink tongue and weakly tried to lick its fur. 'There,' said Bolly, who knew every old wives' tale and believed them all, 'she'll get better—she's licked herself.'

Looking at the bedraggled kitten, Abigail refrained from saying that she considered that a too optimistic statement. Nevertheless, they must try to do something. Because there had been nothing else, she had wrapped it in her scarf; now she produced a handkerchief and started to clean its dirty fur. She did it very gently because she was afraid of hurting it, but she managed to get off enough of the muddy wet to discover where it was hurt. There was a cut on its puny chest, not a large one, but probably deep.

'If I had a pair of scissors...' she began.

Someone had come into the kitchen and joined them. 'If I might take a look?' the professor enquired almost apologetically.

It was Bolly, who had gone to the stove to warm some milk, who answered him. 'Ah—good thing you've come, sir—this here beast don't look too good, Miss Abby found him in one of them alleys round the back.' His tone implied that the alleys in question failed to win his approval. 'She brought him here.'

'And quite right too.' The professor was on his knees beside the scrap stretched on Abigail's scarf, his capable hands busy. 'I didn't hear the house door bell,' he commented mildly, and looked at Abigail.

'No—well, I didn't come in through the big door.' At his raised eyebrows she hurried on, 'I—I had to take the kitten somewhere and I was close by and I thought that Bollinger might help—so I rang the bell of the little door under the steps.'

He had picked the kitten up and was inspecting the cut. 'It is, of course, no concern of mine, Miss Trent,' his voice was smooth, 'but I can assure you that you have no need to—er—creep in the tradesmen's entrance of my house.'

'I didn't creep...' began Abigail indignantly. 'I didn't know you were here.'

'And if you had known?'

She went pink, longing to tell him that ringing the door bell of his house was something she would never willingly do, knowing herself unwelcome in it. She said nothing, but took the saucer of milk from Bolly. She asked:

'Can it have this? Is it likely to need an anaesthetic?'

His mouth twitched, but he said gravely enough, 'I think there will be no need of that. Give him a little of the milk and I'll put a stitch in. He'll be all right in a day or so—he's nearly starved to death.'

He got to his feet and went away, to return presently with a needle and gut, scissors and a spray of local anaesthetic. 'Bring him over here,' he commanded Abigail, 'and hold him still on the table. Bollinger, turn on the light, if you please.'

He was very quick and the kitten lay still, licking the last drops of milk from its small chops. When he had finished, the professor unbent himself and gathered up his odds and ends.

'And now what is to become of the creature?' he wanted to know blandly. 'You intend to take him back with you, Miss Trent?'

Abigail removed her finger from the kitten's clutches and stared down at it. It was unthinkable that it should be turned into the streets; she would have to take it with her, and heaven knows what they would say about it in hospital—perhaps she could keep it in her room and take it back to England when she went... Her thoughts were interrupted by the professor's voice. 'No doubt you think that he should remain here?'

She looked at him then. He had never been particularly pleasant to her, but she refused to believe that he was an unkind man. 'I don't think you would turn anyone or anything away if they needed help,' she stated flatly, and added, 'That's if you don't mind.'

The stare from his blue eyes was shrewd; when he didn't answer she went on quietly, 'It's quite all right if you don't want to be bothered. I'll manage. Thank you very much for being so kind.' She smiled at him and the plainness of her face was changed to a kind of beauty. She picked up her scarf and began to arrange it around the kitten, then buttoned up her coat. Her fingers faltered at the top button when the professor spoke.

'I beg your pardon for teasing you. Of course the animal shall stay here.' His manner changed to a fierce mockery. 'In any case, how could I refuse after your pretty speech?'

'I meant it,' said Abigail, trying to keep the hurt out of her voice. 'Thank you, Professor. It won't be any trouble to you, I know Bollinger will keep it out of your way, won't you, Bolly?' she besought the old man, who said at once, 'Of course I will, Miss Abby, don't you fret your pretty head, I'll do me best—you won't know him when you come.'

'Your thoughtfulness does you credit, Miss Trent, but I assure you that the kitten will be welcome. I have a dog who will be delighted to have company when I am not here, and as the kitten is a female, I foresee no difficulties.' He started for the door. 'Bollinger, perhaps you would be so good as to make a pot of your excellent English tea and bring it to my study. Miss Trent, be so good as to accompany me.'

Abigail was astonished to a state of speechlessness. 'Me?' she wanted to know, and then, remembering, 'But I can't—I've got to go to the Kalverstraat and get Professor de Wit's books.'

Her host's eyes flickered to his watch. 'No matter, I have to go there myself this afternoon—I'll bring them with me when I call in later.'

He held the door open for her, so certain that she would do as he wished that she saw no other course open to her. She went past him and up a few steps, old and worn uneven by countless feet over the years. There was a door beyond them which he pushed open and they were, as she had guessed, in the back of the hall, which they crossed to enter a room she took to be his study. The walls were lined with books, a large circular table standing in the centre of the room held more books as well as papers, unopened letters as well as opened ones, several copies of *World Medicine* and *The Lancet* and a great many journals in the French and German tongues. She turned, round-eyed, from this businesslike disorder, to view the desk in one corner, very tidy, although there was a sheaf of papers pushed to one side as though he had risen from his chair in haste. That same chair was tall and straight and definitely not for lounging, but there were two leather armchairs on each side of the brightly burning fire, and a table lamp beside one of them cast an inviting glow. It was a well-lived-in room; she could imagine the professor sitting here working and reading; the thought conjured up a picture of a lonely, bookish life, which she felt sure was quite erroneous; with his good looks and unmarried state, not to mention the fact that he was undoubtedly wealthy, he would be much in demand among his friends and acquaintances. She frowned because it was foolish of her to speculate upon his private life, but the frown turned to a delighted smile as a Great Dane came from behind the desk and offered a paw. Abigail shook it and hugged him as well. 'Beautiful,' she addressed him, 'and so...' she remembered just in time how vexed the professor had looked when she had admired the hall. She said instead, 'What's his name?'

'Colossus.' And she, forgetting to be wary of him, chortled: 'Oh, how apt—Julius Caesar, isn't it? Something about petty men walking under his huge legs,' she added admiringly. 'How very clever of you.'

She smiled at him and encountered a look of such fierce derision that she got to her feet and said instantly, 'I don't th' I'll stay for tea, if you don't mind.'

The look had gone. 'I must beg your pardon for th'

time this afternoon,' he smiled unexpectedly and she felt her heart tumble. 'Please stay, Abigail.'

She would never understand him; it was like going along a winding road wondering what would be around the next corner. She sat down in one of the chairs and asked in a voice which forgave him, 'What will you call the kitten?' She pulled Colossus's ear and heard the dog sigh with pleasure, and at that moment Bollinger came in with the tea-tray and the professor said:

'We want a name for the kitten, Bollinger. Any ideas?'

Bollinger put the tray down by Abigail, smiled at her and then frowned in thought. 'Well,' he said at length, 'she's an orphan, isn't she? So she'll be Annie.'

He looked at them hopefully. 'Little Orphan Annie,' he explained, and beamed at the professor when he declared: 'A splendid name for her, Bollinger. Annie it shall be. When she's a little more herself, Colossus shall go down to the kitchen and make friends.'

'She's having a nap,' continued Bollinger, 'I haven't moved her, so snug she lies. I'll feed her presently.'

'Every two hours—milk, Bollinger, and not too much of it.'

'OK, boss,' said Bollinger comfortably. 'I'll say bye-bye for now, Miss Abby.' He sounded wistful and she was quick to hear it.

'I'll meet you for coffee—tomorrow, Bolly, and you can tell me about Annie.'

The professor's voice was blandly polite. 'May I suggest that you come here? I shall be away for a couple of days and I think it would be as well if you kept an eye on Annie until I return.'

'Now that's an idea,' said Bollinger enthusiastically. 'No reason why you shouldn't, is there, Miss Abby?'

Abigail said that no, there wasn't, in a rather prim voice which concealed sudden delight. She wanted to come to this old house again; she could think of nothing nicer than living in it for ever and ever. She lifted the teapot and almost dropped it again, struck by the knowledge that the house meant nothing at all without the professor in it—bad temper, frowns, sneers and all. Somewhere behind that forbidding manner must be the man she had fallen in love with—once or twice he had allowed himself to be glimpsed and she dearly wished that he would allow it again. She had no illusions about herself; the professor was as likely to fall in love with her as the moon would turn to cheese, although miracles did happen... She handed him his tea and poured some for herself, asking in a matter-of-fact voice whether Colossus found city life a little trying.

'No—not really. He has a good walk each morning and another some time in the evening and he goes with me to Friesland, where I have another home. He can exercise there to his heart's content.'

'Friesland,' wondered Abigail, 'isn't that a long way?'

'No, a hundred and thirty odd kilometres. An hour and a half's driving—less.'

'Is that where Bollinger went?'

'Yes—there is quite a large garden there. He enjoyed himself enormously.'

He handed Abigail a dish of little cakes and she took one and bit into it. It tasted as delicious as it looked. 'Yes, he loves gardening, but I expect you know that. He has green fingers.'

'Green...? What does that mean?'

'He can grow things and they grow for him because he understands them.'

The professor sipped his tea. 'How interesting. I shall look forward to a beautiful garden this spring.'

Abigail put down her cup and saucer—delicate, paper thin and transparent with a white and purple pattern; she would make a note of them and ask Professor de Wit about them later on—the teapot too; silver and very plain with a rounded lid. 'I think I'd better go,' she said politely, while she longed to stay, but her companion, while making pleasant enough conversation, had shown no great delight in her company, nor did he press her to stay. He got up as she did and went with her into the hall. There were red tulips, dozens of them on the chest today, she noticed. They were half way to the front door when the professor stopped.

'One moment, Miss Trent—your scarf. You made a bed for the kitten, did you not?'

'Yes, but it doesn't matter. I'm not cold and it's a short walk.'

He ignored this and turned on his heel and went to a pillow cupboard at the back of the hall and came back with a silk square. 'This will do.' He unbuttoned her coat, tied the scarf round her neck and buttoned the coat up again, and when she murmured her thanks made no reply, but went ahead of her to the door and flung it open on to the snow outside. The Rolls was by the steps.

'Jan will take you back. Goodbye, Miss Trent.' As she went down the steps she thought indignantly that he sounded relieved that she was going, and possibly he was, but he might have had the decency to pretend—and he had lent her his scarf, but then he would have lent a scarf to anyone in an emergency. She refused to tease herself any more and began a determined conversation with Jan, which lasted until they reached the hospital entrance.

She had spent two happy afternoons at the house on the *gracht,* playing with a slowly recovering Annie and listening to Bollinger's cheerful talk. She had been able to give him some more money too, which he had refused to take until she had pointed out that the quicker she paid her debt to him the quicker she could make a fresh start.

'There's nothing you can do about it, Bolly,' she told him, 'so don't argue. Besides, I'm to be a week at Professor de Wit's house and I've got my fare back to England and some money besides.' She didn't mention that she had heard nothing from Mrs Morgan—she could always go to the agency and ask what to do about it. The prospect of going back to England depressed her, but she was too level-headed to allow it to dominate her thoughts. She had told Bolly that when she knew for certain when she was leaving, she would let him know and he could either come with her or follow when it was convenient. As far as she could make out, he and the professor had a very easy-going agreement between them, and Bolly had said that the man whose work he was doing wouldn't be well for a few weeks yet; he might stay until he was and that would give her time to find another job, this time where she could live out and get a small home together for them both.

The transfer of her patient went without a hitch. Professor de Wit's house was much smaller than his friend's but just as old. It had no garden though, just a few square feet of paving stones and a high wall, but the rooms were delightful. His bedroom was on the first floor and hers next to it, because, as he pointed out to her, after his stay in hospital he was a little nervous of being quite by himself. His housekeeper, Juffrouw Valk, seemed to Abigail to be a sensible and kind woman and perfectly able to look after the professor once she had been told about his diet and what he might and might not do. She spoke no English, which, Professor de Wit pointed out with some glee, was splendid for Abigail's Dutch. And so it was; by the end of the afternoon Abigail had managed to communicate quite a lot to Juffrouw Valk, who smiled and nodded and encouraged her and went to a great deal of trouble to have things just so.

Abigail and her patient ate their dinner together in the small dining room at the back of the house after she had spent some time in the kitchen showing the older woman what Professor de Wit might eat and how much, and immediately the simple meal was finished, she helped him climb the stairs and got him to bed, for he was tired and happy and exhausted. She had settled him nicely in his bed and was getting his spectacles and newspaper for him when Professor van Wijkelen arrived. He stood in the doorway of the bedroom, looking larger than ever, and, Abigail was quick to perceive, very out of humour. Or perhaps it was only herself who caused that expression on his face, for it cleared as he went over to sit by his patient's bed, and after a minute, seeing that she wasn't needed, she slipped away, downstairs to the kitchen, to help Juffrouw Valk with the washing up and improve her Dutch at the same time. She was forced to go back upstairs very soon, though, because the professor called to her briskly from the head of the narrow little staircase. She followed him into his patient's bedroom and stood, very neat in her uniform, waiting to hear what he had to say.

'We have been discussing you, Miss Trent. Professor de Wit agrees with me that another week of your excellent nursing and he will be able to dispense with your services—with regret, I must add.'

He sounded not in the least regretful himself. Abigail fastened her eyes on the glowing silk of his tie and remembered, for no reason at all, that once, quite by accident, he had called her Abigail.

'This suits me very well, however,' went on the professor, 'for I have another patient in need of your care for a week or so. A Scotswoman who lives in one of the houses in the Begijnhof—you have probably been there?'

Abigail nodded. It was peaceful and beautiful and the little houses couldn't have changed much since they had been built centuries before. 'A week should suffice,' went on the professor smoothly, 'a short delay for you, I know, Nurse, but you would be doing her a great kindness—she is a charming person.'

He smiled at her, and even as she heard her own voice saying that yes, she was quite prepared to take another case for him, she was chiding herself for being a fool. Now that he had got what he wanted he would doubtless be as morose and irritable as before; it was an ever-recurring pattern which she weakly never attempted to alter. She only had to say no. She peeped at him—he wasn't smiling now and she saw that he looked very tired, so that his hair looked more grey than it really was and the lines of his face were etched more deeply. He looked up and his eyes held hers for a brief moment and the smile on her lips froze before their coldness. She looked away quickly and he turned back to Professor de Wit, and presently got up to go. It hardly seemed the right moment to give him back his scarf, but she went and fetched it all the same and handed it to him with a word of thanks, remembering how gentle his hands had been when he had tied it round her neck. He took it carelessly now and stuffed it in a pocket. Abigail went downstairs with him and let him out into the coldness of the winter evening. He didn't reply to her sober good night.

'I shall miss you, Abby,' declared her patient when she went back upstairs, 'but Dominic is quite right, I shan't really need you. I've surprised even him, I believe. But I'm glad you will still be in Amsterdam. You must come and see me when you can.'

'I should like that, though I shall only be here for another week after I leave you, shan't I? I must write to the agency in London and see if they have another job for me.' She smiled at him. 'Otherwise I might have to wait a few days for a case and I should prefer to go straight to a patient.'

'What—no days off, Abby?'

'Yes—that is, no, I can't...don't let's talk about me, it's so dull.'

'Dull? My dear Abby, you are the last person I should describe as dull. Tell me, how is that ridiculous kitten you wished on Dominic?'

They spent the rest of the evening talking about nothing in particular and when she had finally tucked the old man up for the night she went to her own room and got ready for bed too. It was marvellous, she told her reflection in the little shieldback mirror on the dressing-table, that she had another patient to go to, and marvellous, said her heart, that she would see the professor for a further week. 'And a lot of good that may do you,' she admonished her mirrored face, 'for he only speaks to you when he's got something unpleasant to say or when he wants something.' Her face reflected sadness; she made a derisive face at it and got into bed and lay awake, thinking about Dominic van Wijkelen. He had looked so very tired that evening, and although the house on the *gracht* was a beautiful home and his housekeeper everything she should be, it surely wasn't quite the same as going home to a wife and children. Even if he were tired to death, he would open the great front door and find them waiting for him. It would be lonely in that house…a tear slid beneath her lids and she blinked it away. 'At least he's got Annie,' she reminded herself, and went to sleep on that ridiculous thought.

The week went pleasantly by. Professor de Wit, now that he was home again, began to take up the thread of his life once more; he was still weak, but he managed the stairs on his own now and spent an hour or more each day working on the book he was writing—a lengthy treatise on biochemistry, which Abigail strove to understand, when, carried away by some theory or other, he would talk at great length about the fascinations of cell life. And his friends came; learned gentlemen who spoke kindly to her and drank a great deal of coffee while her patient sipped his milk.

Juffrouw Valk had proved a treasure; not only had she obtained extra help in the house, she had proved a quick and willing learner when it came to Abigail explaining her patient's diet and what he might and might not do. She wrote it all down in laborious Dutch too so that Juffrouw Valk couldn't forget, and that lady, far from laughing at Abigail's efforts, praised her kindly and tactfully pointed out the mistakes. Abigail could see that she would be leaving Professor de Wit in excellent hands.

Professor van Wijkelen came daily, sometimes briefly, sometimes to stay long enough to play chess with his old friend, and each time he came he brought news of Annie and Bollinger—both, it seemed, in the best of health and firm friends. On one of his visits he suggested that she should go to see them and when she replied quietly that she had been that very afternoon he answered dryly, 'Ah, yes—while I was away from home on operating day, as you very well know.'

The afternoon before she was due to leave Professor de Wit's house, she walked round to see Bollinger once more and enquire after Annie. Despite the professor's words, she had formed the habit of ringing the bell of the little door under the steps, with the vague, half-formed idea that if the professor were home she could, if she wished, beat a hasty retreat. But he was out that afternoon, she had a cup of tea with Bollinger, admired Annie, who had turned from the miserable little waif she had been into a plump, enchanting kitten, and petted Colossus, who chose to have tea with them, taking up a good deal of room before the fire. He stretched out now with Annie balanced on his paws while she tidied away her whiskers after the saucer of milk Bollinger had given her.

'So you're off again, Miss Abby,' he commented, and Abigail detected the satisfaction in his voice. 'The boss says it's a Scotch lady this time—very nice too, specially as his gardener ain't going so fast as he might with his bunions.' He sighed happily. '"No hurry," he tells me, "you're far too useful a man to go before you need."' He added proudly, 'I help Jan with the cars—cleaning 'em, you know.'

Abigail hadn't seen him so happy for a long time, not since her father had been alive and Bolly had seen to the garden and driven and serviced their old-fashioned, solid car, and between whiles made himself useful in the house. She wondered how he would like London again; even if she was very lucky and got a job where she could live out, it would have to be a furnished flat, and a small one at that. She said now, her nice voice urgent:

'Bolly, when I go back to London, don't come with me, not if there's still a job for you here. Stay on a little while, until I can get a home for us.'

'And who's going to look after you?' he demanded fiercely.

'I'll be fine, Bolly. I'll get a job where I can live in for a couple of weeks, that'll give me a chance to look round.'

It sounded easier than it would actually be, but it lulled the old man into a sense of security; he needed very little persuasion to do as she asked and she knew that secretly he was happy to be staying.

When she got up to go she said, 'I don't know exactly when I'll be here again, Bolly. I'll have to see how the new patient is, but I'll come as soon as I can.'

'Right, Miss Abby. The boss'll tell me how you go on, he always does.'

Abigail, on her way out, stopped. 'Does he? Does he really? I shouldn't have thought...' She walked on again, having uttered these rather obscure remarks, said her goodbyes and went back to her patient.

The professor came early that evening. They had barely finished their simple dinner when he was announced by Juffrouw Valk, who in the same breath offered coffee and perhaps, if the professor was a hungry man, a little something to eat. He declined the little something but accepted the coffee, which Abigail poured for him, listening with a sympathetic ear to his patient's gentle complaints about not being allowed to drink that beverage. Abigail offered him his milk with such a motherly air, explaining how good it was for him, that he chuckled and said:

'Abby, I find I do a great many things I don't care about, as a consequence of your persuasive ways. I can see that in due course you will wheedle your husband and children most shamefully into doing exactly what you want.'

Abigail laughed at his little joke and hoped that it didn't sound hollow. She saw no prospect of marriage, and even if she did, she only wanted to marry the professor, sitting beside her now, drinking his coffee and taking no notice of her at all. She got to her feet.

'I expect you would like to talk, and there are several things I have to do.'

'Stay where you are,' the professor's voice was a little sharp and when she looked at him in surprise he added: 'Please.'

So she sat down again, looking at him with a calm face, wondering what it was he had to say.

'I shall fetch you tomorrow,' he spoke in a no-nonsense voice. 'Kindly be ready by three o'clock. My patient is nervous of returning home alone, and it seems to me that getting to know each other over a cup of tea might be best for you both. I should imagine that you will be with her for a week or ten days and I have told Bollinger this—he knows that he is free to leave when he wishes. I don't know what arrangements you have made, but he seemed to think that he would stay here while you—er—find a home.'

'Yes,' said Abigail briefly. It was, she told herself, no concern of his.

'Which is no concern of mine, is it?' concluded the professor with uncanny perception. He turned back to Professor de Wit. 'I'll be in to see you each day, but you are making good headway now and you have Juffrouw Valk, who, Nurse tells me, has proved an apt pupil in the compiling of your diet and so on.'

Abigail perceived that he had finished with her. She was still not sure what her patient was suffering from and if he didn't choose to tell her, then she wasn't going to ask. She got to her feet again, and this time no one suggested that she should stay.

She was quite ready by three o'clock, with her case in the narrow hall and her outdoor clothes on. She had said goodbye to Juffrouw Valk, promised Professor de Wit that she would visit him before she went back to England, extracted a promise from him to be good and do exactly what he should and thanked him with charm for the gloves he had given her. They were lovely ones, warm brown leather, fur-lined. She hadn't had such a pair for a very long time. She put them on and declared that as long as winter lasted she would wear them every day, and because he looked so lonely sitting there she put her arms round his thin shoulders and kissed him, just as the professor came into the room.

'Ah, Dominic, envious?'

His visitor smiled bleakly and turned such a look of ice upon Abigail that she blinked under it. He said briefly to his patient,

'Hullo,' and advised him that he would call in later, and then asked, in a voice to freeze her marrow, 'You're ready, Nurse?'

She told him yes, she was, in a voice as cold as his own, though it warmed as she bade her patient goodbye and followed the professor out to his car.

She sat silently beside him because it was obvious that he was in a towering rage about something or other. He had woven the car through the traffic on the Herengracht before he spoke.

'Your patient,' he began, 'Mrs Macklin—she has been ill for some time. A peptic ulcer—I operated some six weeks ago, but she has been slow to recover. She is now much better, but naturally after so long a stay in hospital, she's nervous of going home alone. She has no relations and isn't the type to bother her friends. She has very little money, by the way—you will be good enough to say nothing to her about your fee. If she should ask tell her that it will be settled later. I will see that you are paid.'

Abigail took a quick look at him. He was staring ahead, his profile fierce and unfriendly, as though daring her to make any comment, so she said in a matter-of-fact voice, 'Just as you wish, sir. How old is Mrs Macklin?'

'Sixty-five. She is the widow of a Scottish Presbyterian parson.'

He didn't speak again, even when he pulled up in the Begijnsteeg, got her case from the boot of the car and crossed the quiet Begijnhof to the end house on the semi-circle of quaint dwellings surrounding the church. The steps leading to its door were narrow and worn, and the front door creaked with age as he turned its handle and walked in, saying, 'Hullo there,' in a cheerful voice, the sort of voice he never used towards Abigail. She stifled a sigh and followed him into one of the smallest houses she had ever been in.

CHAPTER FOUR

THE HALL CONTAINED two doors and a small circular staircase at its end, its wooden steps worn crooked with age, its floor was brick with a hand-made rug upon it, the walls were white plaster, upon which was displayed a fine plate of Delft Blue and nothing else. The professor opened the door nearest him and ushered Abigail inside, into a room which was small, low-ceilinged and rather dark, although the early February afternoon largely accounted for this.

It was an attractive room, though cluttered, with small tables laden with photographs in silver frames, a writing bureau against one wall and a display cabinet on the other. There were footstools and several small comfortable chairs; there was one large easy chair by the small old-fashioned pot stove set in its traditional tiles; the woman sitting in it spoke to them as they entered.

'Dominic, my dear, how punctual. I won't get up—you won't mind? And is this my nurse?'

'It is. Miss Abigail Trent—Mrs Macklin. I'll take the bags up, shall I?'

He went out of the room again and it seemed much larger

without his bulk half filling it. Abigail said how do you do and stood quietly while she was inspected, carrying out her own inspection at the same time. Mrs Macklin was tall, though how tall it was hard to say until she stood up, she was also very thin, with a long, sharp-nosed face and bright dark eyes. Her iron grey hair was screwed into an old-fashioned no-nonsense bun, skewered with equally old-fashioned hairpins. After a moment they smiled at each other and Mrs Macklin said, 'You're exactly as Dominic described you. Shall we have a cup of tea together? Could you put the kettle on? The kitchen is behind this room and you'll find the tray already laid. A neighbour kindly did it for me—she was here waiting when Dominic brought me home a couple of hours ago.'

Abigail took off her gloves and unwound her scarf and went to find the kitchen, small and a little old-fashioned, with a gay gingham frill round the mantelshelf above the small electric cooker and a row of pot plants on the windowsill. She filled the kettle and put it on, listening to the creak of the stairs as the professor descended them with measured tread. He had very large feet, thought Abigail lovingly, but then he was a very large man. She could hear the murmur of their voices in the room next door as she made the tea in the brown earthenware pot, put it on the tray and carried it through to the sitting room.

The professor took the tray from her at the door and Mrs Macklin smiled at her and said, 'My dear, there's a fruit cake in the tin on the middle shelf of the cupboard,' so Abigail went back and found the cake, a plate to put it on, a knife and three little porcelain tea plates, all different in design and, she guessed, very old.

They had tea to the accompaniment of cheerful small talk, and Abigail, under the impression that she now knew the professor quite well, discovered another side of him entirely. It was as though Mrs Macklin had charmed away his ill temper and coldness, and although he spoke seldom to her, and then only briefly, she was aware of this. She didn't talk much herself, but sat listening to her new patient and the professor mulling over the city's news.

The professor got up to go presently, saying as he did so: 'Be good enough to come with me to the door, Nurse Trent, I have one or two instructions for you.' He wasn't looking at her and his voice was as cold as ever it had been, but at the door, just as he was going, he halted and said in quite a different voice: '*Hemel*, I forgot the cat—I intended to fetch him...'

'You have enough to do,' called Mrs Macklin from the sitting room, 'you know you haven't a minute to spare this evening.'

'I'll get him,' Abigail offered. 'I know my way around Amsterdam very well now and I'm sure there'll be plenty of time this evening.' She had a sudden unsatisfactory picture of the professor, spending his evening wining and dining some gorgeous girl who could make him smile instead of scowl as he was at that moment.

'I can't allow you to go trudging all over Amsterdam after a cat.' His voice was polite and quite impersonal.

'You exaggerate,' Abigail pointed out reasonably. 'I never trudge anywhere—you make me sound like Little Orphan Annie...' She stopped, because although she wasn't Annie she was an orphan. She fixed her gaze on the fine cloth of his car coat and clenched her teeth to stop the tears coming into her eyes. She gulped back the lump in her throat and said:

'I shall enjoy it.'

'And will you enjoy the shopping and housework and the cooking?' he enquired.

'Yes. There isn't much nursing for me to do, is there? And it's such a tiny house.'

'I will get some kind of household help for Mrs Macklin by the end of the week. In the meantime I should like you to restrain her from doing everything. She has always been a very active woman and likes to have her own way.'

'Most people do,' remarked Abigail, and looked at him, to surprise an expression on his face which set her pulse racing—it was such a peculiar look, half wonder, half amusement, wholly tender. She met his eyes squarely and waited for him to speak.

'I didn't know that there were girls like you left in the world,' he said slowly, and put up a hand and lifted her chin gently with his forefinger and scanned her face as though he hadn't really looked at it before. 'You've almost restored my faith in women, Abigail.'

He dropped his hand, turned on his heel and was out of the door, wishing her good afternoon in a perfectly ordinary voice before she could draw a difficult breath.

She had no time to ponder his remark because she went to fetch Jude the cat soon afterwards, and when she got back and had settled him with his mistress, Mrs Macklin began at once to talk.

'Sit down, my dear. You must be wondering about me and why I should need a nurse, for I'm sure Dominic neglected to tell you anything at all, except the number of pills I'm supposed to take each day. I was his mother's dearest friend, you know, and when she died I promised that I would keep an eye on him, because I've known him ever since he was a baby, but now I'm older and the boot is on the other foot. It's he who keeps an eye on me now, although I will say that he still listens to me with a fair amount of patience and even takes my advice from time to time. When this silly ulcer business started, nothing would do but that I must go into hospital, and when he saw that medical treatment wasn't going to cure me, he operated himself and insisted on me staying there much too long, I consider. He seems to think that I need a nurse for a short time, though I told him that I was as fit as a fiddle, and now he tells me that he's arranging for someone to come each day and help in the house when you go.' She snorted delicately. 'I never heard such nonsense, though I must admit, my dear, that I'm going to enjoy your company—to tell you the truth, I was just a little nervous, and since he tells me that it will cost me nothing... I didn't know that the *Ziekenfonds* paid for private nurses, but they've improved these things so much in the last few years, haven't they, and I've never had occasion to make use of them before.'

Abigail made a sympathetic murmured reply. So that was what the professor had told her patient, and that was why she was to say nothing about fees. He was paying them out of his own pocket. She reflected with brief tenderness upon him, then remarked calmly:

'I'm sure the professor knows best; it really does seem a bit strange when one comes back from hospital. We could use this week finding out just how much you can do without getting tired, don't you think? Then if you have someone in to do the housework, you'll be able to cope with the cooking and perhaps the shopping—isn't that a good idea? Now, shall I get some supper for us—and what about Jude, he'll want a meal, I expect—supposing you sit there and enjoy his company for a while and I'll explore the kitchen.'

Mrs Macklin agreed to these suggestions readily enough and Abigail retired to the kitchen; her patient was more tired than she wished to say, and a week of cosseting would do her good. Abigail nodded her neat head in confirmation of her own opinion and began opening cupboard doors and peering at their contents.

She saw her patient into bed quite early that evening, with Jude on his own shawl at her feet and a bell within reach, and then crossed the landing to her own room. It was extremely small and rather sparsely furnished, but the bed and the chest in the window and the chair beside it were very old and glowing with the loving polishing of many decades of housewives. She undressed slowly, despite the chill, thinking about the professor and wondering what exactly he had meant that afternoon. Why had he lost his faith in women in the first place—or had he been joking? That was unlikely—he wasn't a man to make that kind of a joke. She went downstairs, dressing-gowned and slippered, and had a shower in the cubicle squeezed in beside the kitchen, then crept upstairs again and into bed, her thoughts still centred on him. Perhaps he was in love with someone who didn't love him, although this seemed to her to be quite inconceivable—she was still worrying about it when she went to sleep.

She got up early the next morning to find a light powdering of snow once more and a snarling wind whining round the little square. She made tea and took Mrs Macklin a cup, suitably weak, then let Jude out for his morning prowl. Mrs Macklin, sitting up in bed to eat her breakfast, said cheerfully that she had slept like a top and she hoped that Abigail had too. 'And my dear,' she went on. 'I really cannot call you Nurse or Miss Trent—I shall call you Abigail, such a pretty name and seldom heard these days. Was there a reason for it?'

Abigail explained, and her companion said admiringly: 'What a good idea—how imaginative some people are.' She bit into a slice of paper-thin bread and butter with relish. 'I was sorry to hear about your mother, child.'

Abigail almost dropped an empty porridge plate she was removing to the kitchen. 'My mother?' she faltered. 'How could you possibly know?'

Mrs Macklin gave her an innocent look. 'Dominic told me, of course—should he not have done so?'

Abigail shook her head. 'No, it's not that—it's just that I didn't think he knew...!'

'Dominic knows everything,' remarked her patient complacently, 'as you will discover for yourself, no doubt.'

She spent the morning tidying the house and shopping and cooking their simple meal, which they had barely finished when the professor arrived. The visit seemed more social than professional; he greeted Abigail with his usual distant manner and then sat for ten minutes with Mrs Macklin, talking about nothing in particular. As he got up to go he remarked to Abigail, 'I see you brought Jude safely back. You had no difficulty in finding the place?'

Abigail said that no, she hadn't, thank you, and forbore from mentioning that she had had to pay a week's board for the animal before they would let her have him. The professor had paid all the previous bills; he had forgotten this, the final one; a mere thirty gulden for him perhaps, but a large slice of the money she had left in her purse. She hoped that he would remember it when he paid her, for she had given Bollinger most of the money she had earned from looking after Professor de Wit. She still had her fare to England, but not a great deal besides.

He nodded carelessly in reply. 'I imagine Mrs Macklin is going to rest for a couple of hours. Get your hat and coat and I will take you along to see Bollinger—and Annie.'

Abigail opened her mouth to refuse this high-handed disposal of her free time, but was thwarted by her patient.

'What a splendid idea!' declared that lady. 'I shall lie down here on the sofa and take a nap until you return. Run along and put on your things, Abigail, Dominic can make me comfortable.'

Abigail, running a professional eye over Mrs Macklin when she came downstairs again, had to admit that he had done his work very well—the old lady looked not only comfortable, but pleased with herself. She wished her goodbye and followed the professor out of the house and walked with him across the cobbled square and into the car. He didn't speak for the entire journey, and she, who had hoped that perhaps his remark of the previous day might have meant a breaking of the ice between them, was disappointed. They got out, still silent, at his front door and went inside, where he cast his coat in an untidy heap into one of the chairs, his gloves after it, and strode across the hall to the room where she had had tea with Bollinger. And all he said was: 'Bollinger will be in directly,' as he went away.

It was nice to see Bolly again—and Annie, tucked cosily under his arm. They sat by the fire and drank their coffee which Mevrouw Boot had brought to them and Abigail listened to Bolly's account of his day in Friesland and saw how happy he was. It seemed a pity that he couldn't stay for always. She voiced the thought. 'Bolly, if the professor asked you, would you stay here? It's just what you like, isn't it, and it suits you, doesn't it?

I should be perfectly all right in England—you know what private nursing is, first one place, then the other. I shall be away from home a great deal.'

He looked shocked. 'Miss Abby, what's ever come over you?' he wanted to know. 'I must own it's nice here, but the other bloke'll be back before long anyway and I doubt if the professor would want me. Besides, we want a home, don't we?'

'Yes, of course, Bolly,' she agreed hastily, 'it was only an idea. How's Annie?'

'See for yourself, Miss Abby. Flourishing, and such friends with Colossus; sleeps with him too, and sits in the dining room while the boss has his meals. He's that fond of her.'

'I'm so glad.' She stroked the kitten on her lap. 'I didn't think he would be—I mean, I knew he'd be kind to her and give her a home...'

'Lord love you, miss, the boss ain't a bit like he seems—very soft-hearted, he is. Does a lot, quiet like, so I hear.'

'I'm sure he does, Bolly—and now I must go because I don't want to be too long away from Mrs Macklin. I'll come again very soon. I still think it would be the best thing for me to go back alone and you follow me when I've found something.'

He nodded reluctantly. 'OK, Miss Abby, anything you say, and you're to go out the front door, the boss says. Real narked, he was, that you should use the servants' entrance.'

Abigail's nice eyes rounded with surprise. 'Was he? I should think that would be the last thing to worry him.' A thought struck her. 'Bolly, did you tell him much about us—I mean Mother and...'

'Only a trifle, here and there, so to speak.'

With which remark she had to be content. She wished him a warm goodbye and went, obedient to the professor's wish, through the house door. At the bottom of the steps stood the Rolls with Jan at the wheel. He got out when he saw her and said: '*Dag,* miss. I take you back, the Professor's orders.'

She wondered how long he had been waiting there and why

the professor hadn't told her. Probably he hadn't given it a thought after he had given Jan the order. She got in and immediately embarked on a conversation with Jan in her laborious Dutch, without mentioning his master; she knew without being told that Jan would hear no word of criticism against him.

She was out shopping when the professor called the next day. Mrs Macklin told her in a satisfied voice when she returned that he was sufficiently pleased with her progress to allow her to do a little cooking. 'So I shall cook supper, my dear, though I doubt if I shall feel much like washing up the dishes afterwards. And tomorrow if it is fine, I should like to come with you, just to the grocers in the Begijnsteeg. Dear me, how pleasant it is to get back to normal life, and with you here, not nearly as frightening as I had imagined.' She added hastily as if to explain her change of attitude, 'One gets lazy in hospital and too secure.' She smiled at Abigail. 'How pretty you look in that woolly thing, dear, and such pink cheeks. Oh, I nearly forgot to tell you, Dominic has got someone to do the housework, a Mevrouw Rots, she'll be coming in a week's time. What happens to you then, Abigail?'

'I go back to England, Mrs Macklin.'

'You have a home to go to—relatives?'

'No—cousins in Canada and an uncle and aunt who don't want to know about me. But don't worry, all I have to do is to go to the agency and they'll find me another job—at once, the same day, perhaps.'

'How appallingly efficient,' said Mrs Macklin dryly, 'and how very dull for you. All work and no play...'

'Oh, I daresay I'll take a day off.'

'Big deal,' commented her patient unexpectedly, and Abigail laughed with real amusement. 'That's better. You should laugh more often, Abigail.'

Abigail had nothing to say to this and her companion went on in the most casual manner, 'Dominic doesn't laugh enough either. Did you get all the shopping?'

The day passed at a gentle pace, for although Abigail found enough to do in the little house there was no hurry over the doing of it; during the morning Mrs Macklin told her its history and added, 'I was lucky to get it, because they're really almshouses, I suppose. It's so central and the rent is low—besides, it's close to my friends. Are you going to see Bollinger today?'

'I thought I might go and see how Professor de Wit is—he was my last patient, you know.'

'Yes, Abigail, a good idea. He's an old acquaintance of mine too. Dominic has promised to take me to visit him one day soon—he has been very ill, I understand, but you know more about that than I do. Dear me, how dull life would be for us elderlies if we were without Dominic to keep a watchful eye upon us. He has never allowed me to be lonely—he was fond of my husband.'

Abigail made some reply; Mrs Macklin must know the professor very well; perhaps during this week she might tell her a little of his life. It would be nice to know; she mused over the interesting fact that he appeared to be Doctor Jekyll and Mr Hyde, for according to her patient there never was a better man. Undoubtedly there was a great deal more than met the eye. She said now: 'Bollinger thinks the world of him and I can quite understand why, for he made it possible for him to leave the most dreary room imaginable—he was so lonely, too, and here in Amsterdam he's happy.'

'Yes?' Mrs Macklin sounded interested. 'Dominic mentioned in the vaguest way that he had been lucky enough to find someone to take Jaap's place until he got back to work, but he didn't tell any of the circumstances.' She gave Abigail a shrewd glance. 'Sit down, dear, and tell me about yourself and Bollinger, and your parents too, that is if you can bear with an old woman's curiosity.'

It was a delight and a relief to be able to talk to someone about Bolly and her mother and their life in London and how she missed the hospital; she told about the agency too and made

Mrs Macklin laugh with her description of the stern woman in charge of it. At length when she had finished, Mrs Macklin leaned back in her chair and sighed. 'You poor child, life hasn't been very kind to you in these last few years.' She studied Abigail's face. 'But you're not sorry for yourself, are you?'

'No—well, almost never. Sometimes when I see a lovely dress or some fab jewellery, or a girl with everything, you know—lovely face and hair and up-to-the-minute clothes and the men looking at her—then I wallow in self-pity.' She laughed as she said it and her companion laughed with her.

'Bunkum,' said Mrs Macklin firmly. 'Go and put on your hat and coat and visit Professor de Wit and give him my best wishes.'

Abigail spent a pleasant hour with the old man; he was as thin as ever and still pale, but he had lost none of his zest for life; he wanted to know exactly what she was doing and if she was happy, and listened to what she had to say about Mrs Macklin. 'She's a dear,' said Abigail. 'You know with some people you can be friends at once, just as with others it's quite impossible.' Of course she was thinking of the professor and her elderly companion gave her such a penetrating look that she went a guilty red, although he had said nothing, and changed the conversation. 'I'm going back to England next week,' she volunteered.

He looked surprised. 'You'll like that?'

'I—I suppose so. I like Amsterdam, though at first I thought it would be a bit difficult and lonely, but it's not—there are Bolly and Annie and you and Mrs Macklin, as well as the nurses in the hospital.'

She omitted the professor and her listener appeared not to notice, for he said jokingly, 'Quite an impressive list! We shall all miss you. And now, my dear, run along to the kitchen and see if our good friend Mevrouw Valk has made that abominable weak tea I am forced to drink.'

Abigail, who liked her tea strong, sipped the tasteless beverage with him and listened intelligently to his theories on cell life, while at the very back of her mind she wondered what the professor was doing. He was, in fact, in the act of pulling the door bell and appeared a moment later before them, dwarfing everything in the room behind him. He greeted his old friend warmly and Abigail with the cold courtesy she had come to expect. She offered him tea and took care not to catch his eye because she happened to know that he detested weak tea, and this was pale and insipid and, what was more, tepid. She sat for another ten minutes for the sake of good manners, then rose to go with the excuse that she should return to Mrs Macklin before that lady, refreshed from her afternoon nap, decided to do something beyond her strength.

The professor got up too, observing that he would show her out, and when she assured him that she was very well able to see herself to the door, he remarked, 'Don't be bird-witted, I have something to say to you.'

She bade Professor de Wit goodbye with the hope that she would see him again before she left Amsterdam, and went out of the room closely followed by the professor. In the dark, panelled hall which was barely big enough for the two of them, he said to surprise her into speechlessness:

'It is the hospital dance in five days' time. I should like you to come—it is to commemorate its foundation.'

Abigail's heart tripped, steadied and turned right over. She spoke quickly before that treacherous organ should make her change her mind.

'Thank you, Professor, but I don't think I'll accept your kind...'

'Why not?'

She stared up at him, looming over her in the dimness and much too near for her peace of mind, trying to think of a really good excuse. 'Well...' she began, not having the least idea what she would say.

'Don't tell me that you have nothing to wear,' he remarked with faint amusement, and she, who had been on the point of saying just that, exclaimed roundly, 'Certainly not, I have several...' She paused, unwilling to utter such a trivial lie to him. 'I don't know anyone,' she offered with sudden inspiration.

'Me?' he queried.

'Oh, don't be ridiculous!' Abigail's voice was a little gruff and she had the uneasy feeling that she was being rude; all the same she went on: 'You're hardly likely to spend the entire evening...' She broke off.

'No, probably not,' he agreed with infuriating readiness, 'but my junior registrar professes a desire to get to know you, and Professor de Wit will be there...'

'You're never allowing him to dance?' Her voice squeaked in protest.

'I should have thought a woman of your good sense would have known better than to have asked such a silly question.'

It was annoying to be addressed as a woman of good sense; if that was how he thought of her then she would go to this dance and she would find a dress to fit his detestable opinion. Something grey or mousey with a high neck and one of those awful shapeless draped fronts.

He asked sharply, so that she jumped guiltily, 'What are you plotting? You will buy a dress— pink, I think, deep pink and of a style to suit you. I believe that I shall come with you to buy it.'

'Indeed you will not,' declared Abigail, her fevered imagination picturing him selecting delectable gowns without once looking at their price tickets.

'And who will carry all the parcels?' he enquired silkily. 'There will be shoes as well.'

'No, thank you, Professor, I would far rather go alone—it would be distracting.'

'Do I distract you, Miss Trent?'

She fumed silently at his awkward questions. 'No—y don't know—you see, I shall want to have a good look first.'

'Yes? I should have thought that you could have fou

you wanted within minutes at Dick Holthaus or Max Heymans.' Two dress shops which she, after only a short stay in Amsterdam, had discovered matched high prices with high fashions—they were the sort of shops she would have loved to have gone to. She frowned, wondering how it was that the professor knew about them, and then remembered to look casual as she said carelessly:

'Oh, I daresay they have, but I still want to look everywhere first.'

He opened the door for her. 'As you wish, but pink, remember, and pretty.'

She walked back to the Begijnhof with a head full of ideas pushing each other round and round; she would never be able to buy a dress with the money she had. True, she had been paid the day before, but the professor had obviously forgotten about Jude's fees and she wasn't going to ask him for them. And she, like a fool, had given Bolly half straight away. She could borrow on her fare, for she would be due another week's salary when she left Mrs Macklin and there was still the money from Mrs Morgan, surely waiting for her at the agency. She did some rapid sums in her head, and when she got back to Mrs Macklin, asked that lady if she knew of a dressmaker.

'Of course, my dear,' said that lady without hesitation. 'There's Juffrouw Blik, three doors down—a *dominee*'s daughter and crippled in one foot, poor woman, but charming. Don't be put off at the sight of her, Abigail, she's not a very fashionable sort of woman, but she's very good with clothes, especially with something pretty.'

She gave Abigail a questioning look and was instantly told all about the invitation. 'I'd rather like to have the dress made,' said Abigail, 'then I can get exactly the material and shade I want.' Quite unconsciously she spoilt this by adding, 'Is she expensive?'

Mrs Macklin bent her head over her knitting. 'No, dear, about twenty-five gulden, I should think, and for these days it's ridiculously cheap. Why not go to the Bijenkorf tomorrow and see if you find what you want? I know they have a silk sale on, but there'll be other materials, not in the sale.'

They spent the evening discussing the sale, the dance, the dress, the most suitable shoes to go with it and Abigail's hair.

'Leave it as it is,' urged Mrs Macklin. 'It suits you, it's pretty.'

'Pretty? It's mousy and straight.'

'Mice are pretty little creatures,' her patient pointed out, 'and they have straight hair.' She began to talk about the numerous dances she had been to in her youth and not once during the evening did they mention the professor, although Abigail thought about him a great deal.

She found just the material she wanted in the Bijenkorf—rose pink chiffon and a matching silk to line it, both at sale price too, although even then their purchase made a great hole in her purse. But she was feeling reckless by now; drunk with the prospect of spending an evening in the same company as the professor, she purchased some silver slippers and a handbag and walked back happily clutching her purchases, and after getting the lunch for her patient and herself and settling her for a nap, went to see Juffrouw Blik.

Juffrouw Blik's house was really a flat, for she lived on the ground floor; the floor above was rented to a retired schoolteacher. Her sitting room was the same size as Mrs Macklin's but seemed even smaller, if that were possible, because of the number of half-finished garments hanging around its walls and over the chairs, and the old-fashioned treadle sewing machine taking up all the space under the window.

Abigail, eyeing Juffrouw Blik's dumpy, unfashionable person, felt a little dubious about handing over her precious material to the dowdy little woman, then took heart when she remembered that Mrs Macklin had recommended her very highly. In her difficult, halting Dutch she explained what she wanted, showed the pattern she had bought, made a date for a fitting and, with an eye to the urgency of the matter, allowed herself to be measured.

The dress was a success. Abigail, trying it on the day before the dance, had to admit that the professor's demand for rose pink had been completely justified, for the soft colour of the gossamer fine material gave her face a glow and Juffrouw Blik had cut it with panache so that it fitted where it should and the wide, wide skirt swirled around her as she turned and twisted before the mirror. And to complete the outfit, her patient had produced a Russian sable coat, its Edwardian cut exactly right for the dress, and when Abigail protested that she couldn't possibly borrow so valuable a fur she had declared, 'Nonsense, child—I wear it once, perhaps twice a year—it needs an airing. You will be the belle of the ball.'

At which remark Abigail had looked very doubtful, but since she had been invited to go, the least she could do was to look her best. She had seen very little of him during the past few days—true, he had spoken to her during his visits to his patient, but only upon matters which concerned that lady's welfare. Not once had he mentioned the dance, nor for that matter had he given her any sign that he had invited her to attend, which had such a damping effect on her spirits that by the day of the dance she felt no excitement at all, only a secret fear that he had forgotten all about it, and she would dress and then sit and wait in Mrs Macklin's little sitting room, watching the clock ticking through the hours, and he would never come.

It was the morning of the dance, after he had paid his visit to Mrs Macklin, professed himself pleased with her condition, reiterated that the daily help would come in three days' time and reminding her that she was no longer a young woman, that he turned to Abigail, standing like a silent, well-trained shadow beside him.

'You will be called for at nine o'clock,' his voice was pleasant and completely disinterested. 'The dance will not end until the small hours; if you become tired or wish to return here you have only to say so.'

As though she were an old lady or a cripple like poor Juffrouw Blik! thought Abigail, bursting with indignation. Perhaps he was hoping that once having done his duty in inviting her, she would choose to leave early, leaving him unencumbered to dance with the countless lovelies who would most certainly be there. She said coolly, 'I shall be ready, Professor,' and went with him to the door and showed him out with a convincing and utterly false calm.

She was ready by a quarter to nine that evening; she had cleared away the supper, made everything ready for her patient's night and then gone upstairs to the little room of which she had become so fond, to dress. The result was gratifying; she was no beauty, nor would she ever be, but there was no doubt at all that pretty clothes did a lot for a girl. She had taken Mrs Macklin's advice too, and put her hair up in its usual simple style and used the very last of the Blue Grass perfume she had been hoarding for just such an occasion as this one. Wrapped in her borrowed sables, she stood in front of the mirror and promised her reflection that she would enjoy herself and what was more, stay until the very last dance, despite the professor's offer to send her home early. Anyone would think that I was ninety! she told her face in the mirror. You go and enjoy yourself, my girl.

When the doorbell rang at exactly nine o'clock she flounced downstairs rather defiantly. That would be Jan, she supposed, or a taxi. She flung open the sitting room door, exclaiming: 'Will I do?' and stopped short at the sight of the professor, very grand in his white tie and tails, warming himself before the stove. He inclined his head by way of greeting and said nothing at all, which she found so disconcerting that her defiant mood ebbed away and she looked appealingly at Mrs Macklin, who said satisfyingly:

'Abigail, you'll have a lovely evening, no doubt of look delightful.'

A sentiment hardly echoed by the professor, judging by the expression of his face, for he was glaring down his long nose at her and just for a moment she was tempted to turn round and go upstairs again and tear off her finery and not go at all, but common sense prevailed—there was no reason why she shouldn't have a good time once she got there. She glared at him, disappointment raging under the pink chiffon, to lose all other feelings but one of delight as he told her:

'You take my breath away.' He sounded his usual austere self, but at least he was paying her a compliment. 'I hardly recognised you,' which rather spoilt the compliment, but he actually smiled and she smiled warmly back, her eyes shining. 'Abigail pink and pretty,' he murmured surprisingly, and spoilt that too by adding, 'My registrar will be in the seventh heaven!'

The dance had already started, by the time they had arrived the dance floor was crowded and everyone, in Abigail's feverish imagination, knew everyone else, except her. The professor waited for her while she disposed of the sables and then danced with her. He danced very well, but with a remoteness which was decidedly chilling, so that after one or two attempts at conversation, successfully squashed by his gravely polite replies, she took refuge in silence and was relieved when the dance finished and she was introduced to the junior registrar—a young man of a most friendly disposition even if he was a little on the short side and inclined to be fat. He in his turn introduced her to friends of his own so that presently she began to enjoy herself despite the lack of interest shown by the professor. It was all the more surprising, therefore, when he sought her out and asked her to go in to supper with him. She had already been asked by Henk, the registrar, and was on the point of saying so, for the professor didn't look over-enthusiastic at the prospect of partnering her anyway, when Henk said, 'That's OK by me, Abigail—Professor van Wijkelen has first pick, since he brought you. We'll dance again after supper.'

The professor led her away towards the supper room, chose

a small table for two, and only when he had seated her and fetched two plates of food did he speak. 'That was a little unfair of me, I'm afraid,' he observed coolly, 'but I haven't seen you for some time.'

'I've been here all the evening,' stated Abigail flatly, 'and it was very unfair.'

'Meaning that you prefer Henk's company to mine? I can well believe it, Miss Trent—he's still a young man and good fun, I should imagine, do you not agree?'

Abigail bit into a small sausage on a stick. 'Quite nice,' she answered. 'Why do you pretend to be Methuselah? I've no intention of pitying you.' She watched his eyebrows lift and went on recklessly, 'You really had no need to bring me in to supper, you know—I didn't expect it.'

His voice was all silk. 'The reason I did so was because I have something to say to you and this seems a good opportunity to say it.'

Abigail finished the sausage and started on a minute vol-au-vent. Surely he wasn't going to tell her she looked nice, or was being a success or something of that sort? Hardly twice in one evening. She took another bite and asked, 'Yes, sir?' She added the sir from sheer naughtiness because he looked so remote, just as though they were on a ward, discussing a patient and she in uniform. If he preferred her in her cap then she would wear it, metaphorically speaking.

'You leave Mrs Macklin in three days' time,' it was a statement, not a question. 'Unless you are committed to returning to England, you would oblige me greatly by remaining for a further week or so and working in the hospital. There is an outbreak of salmonella on the children's ward, both nurses and patients, I am afraid. We are short of nursing staff as a consequence just when they are most needed. I have a number of beds on the ward and we—that is, I and my colleagues agreed that it would be a good idea if you would be kind enough to help fill the gap while the emergency lasts. You will be paid your usual fee. As to where you will live, I am of the opinion that Mrs Macklin would be delighted if you were to remain with her as a paying guest—and it would be excellent for her to have an interest in life after her long illness.'

How like him, thought Abigail, everything worked out beforehand. She wondered what he would say if she refused. She chose a cheese straw and nibbled at it while she studied him across the table. He looked as impassive as ever, although he was staring at her in a rather disconcerting way. He said suddenly, 'Please, Abigail,' and she gave him a reassuring, almost motherly smile because she sensed anxiety behind the blandness of his face and she loved him far too much to allow him to be worried or anxious even when he was annoying her so excessively.

'Of course I'll come. I like children—besides, it will do me good to do some work for a change. Do you want me to come straight from Mrs Macklin's?'

'Thank you, Abigail. Yes, if you could manage it—I don't know about your days off.'

She shrugged. 'I have plenty of free time and I shall get two days each week in hospital, shan't I? If you will tell me the name of the ward to go to and what time.'

'The Beatrix ward, it's in the oldest part of the hospital, on the top floor. Could you manage ten o'clock? I'll see Zuster Ritsma—you will do staff nurse's duties, of course.' And when she nodded briefly, he went on:

'Can I get you anything else to eat?'

She shook her head; he had got what he wanted—he hadn't eaten anything himself, probably he was waiting to take one of the pretty girls she had seen him dancing with down to supper—it had been an excuse to get her alone and pin her down. 'When did the epidemic start?' she asked him.

He looked faintly surprised. 'Six days ago.'

The day before he had invited her to the dance. She managed a smile as she got up and her voice was a little high. 'Well, I think I'll go and find Henk—he'll be looking for me...' Which wasn't quite true but saved her pride a little, only to have it trampled upon a moment later by the professor.

'You look charming, that dress is most becoming.' He smiled a little as he spoke and she was conscious of a stab of humiliation. As they went back to the dance floor she said a little unsteadily, 'You didn't have to say that—I would have come to the hospital without any—any softening up.'

It wasn't until that moment the idea took shape that the whole thing had been a softening-up process—the invitation to the dance and the interest in what she would wear, being fetched by him and danced with and supped with. She went a little white and said in a voice that was almost shrill:

'Oh, there's Henk—I daresay I shall see you later.' She smiled with forced gaiety, ignoring the fact that the professor was about to say something, and lost herself in the crowd.

She danced for the rest of the evening and once more with the professor, with whom she kept up such a steady flow of chatter that he was hard put to it to get in a yes or no. He did indeed manage to say: 'There is something I should make clear...' before she interrupted him with: 'Oh, please need we talk shop—I'm having such fun.' She spoke to his shirt front in a brittle voice and avoided his eye, fearful that he was going to pay her another insincere compliment or launch into her hospital duties, neither of which she felt she could bear at that moment.

She had spent some time with Professor de Wit, sitting in a good deal of state, surrounded by friends and admirers and watching the dancing with a good deal of amusement. He welcomed Abigail with a delighted smile and urged her to sit with him. 'You look delightful my dear,' he said happily. 'What a pretty girl you are, to be sure—that pink dress is just your colour,' and he spoke with such sincerity that she very nearly believed him. 'You have danced with Dominic?' he asked, and she said yes, she had, and wasn't it a fab dance and how was he feeling. They talked cosily together until several elderly gentlemen, heavily bespectacled and delightfully mannered, presented themselves with the wish to spend a little time with their old friend, but on no account must the young lady feel called upon to desert them. Which she rightly interpreted as a flowery way of hinting that she should go. Which she did, leaving them prosing gently over Professor de Wit's book, oblivious of the gay scene around them. She was dancing the last dance with Henk when he remarked:

'We shall be seeing you in a day or two, so the Prof tells me. He's got beds in the other wards as well, but Children's is his pet. Very soft-hearted is our Prof, though you wouldn't think it sometimes—got a tongue like a razor and a voice like a deep freeze most of the time.' He glanced at her and added, 'He's a fine man, though. I wouldn't like to work for anyone else.'

Abigail nodded understandingly. 'I'm sure you wouldn't. I've seen some of his kindness.'

There wasn't much kindness evident in the professor's face when they met presently, however. She was wrapped once more in the sables, her plain little face radiant with the pleasures of the evening and her modest success. She saw him waiting by the entrance and exclaimed as she reached his side,

'Oh, it was fun. Thank you very much for inviting me.'

'You thank me when you believe that I did it merely to— what was the expression? Soften you up? How generous of you, Miss Trent!'

He led the way to the car and she got in silently and sat, still silent, while he drove through the quiet streets of the city to the Begijnsteeg. They didn't speak as they got out of the car either. They were half way across the square when at length he broke the silence, at the same time coming to a halt in the dim light of the street lamps.

'I wished to say something to you, to explain, while we were dancing, but I was unable to get a word in edgeways for your ceaseless chatter. I shall do so now, at the risk of us both catching a chill, but as the cold will doubtless preclude you from either interrupting me or answering me back, I feel the risk is worth taking.'

Abigail, from the depths of the sables, eyed him with her mouth open. She had become used, in the last few weeks, to the professor's deliberate way of expressing himself, and indeed, could not imagine him doing anything else, but she hadn't liked that bit about the ceaseless chatter, although she was fair enough to own that it was perfectly true. 'Yes, sir?' she prompted him encouragingly.

'Stop calling me sir,' said the professor nastily. 'You do not need to throw my age at me every time you open your mouth.'

Abigail, perhaps because it was darkish and his face was in shadow so that she couldn't see its usual harsh expression, said boldly:

'Don't talk rubbish! You're far too sensitive about your age—you're in your prime and extremely handsome and you must know that women adore men who are a little bit older.' She stopped, appalled at her own words, and hastened to rectify her mistake by adding belatedly, 'Well, most women.'

'Are you toadying to me?' he asked her in a dangerously quiet voice.

'Toadying?' She was breathless with rage now. 'Why should I toady to you? You—you...' the rage went as suddenly as it had come. 'I was trying to help you,' she said sadly, 'but I see I've made a mess of it.' She moved away a few steps, towards Mrs Macklin's house. 'I'll say good night.'

'No, you won't, not until I've done. You were wrong this evening. I wasn't—er—softening you up, I wouldn't stoop to such a trick. I meant what I said too—you do look pretty in that pink gown, it becomes you and you are charming. You're charming in whatever you wear.'

She couldn't see his face properly, but it didn't matter. She could hear the sincerity in his deep voice and her heart sang, she wanted to throw her arms around his neck and hug him, but all she said was: 'Thank you, Professor' in a voice devoid of all expression. 'I'm glad I was wrong.'

They walked on and at the door he took the key and opened it for her, then with it still in his hand stood looking down at her.

'Thank you for coming,' he said, and now his voice wasn't cold or austere but warm. 'I told you, did I not, that you had almost restored my faith in women. You have done more than that; you have restored my faith in human nature.'

He bent his head and kissed her on her mouth, a little awkwardly as though he hadn't had much practice at it lately. She longed to return his kiss, but didn't; with a murmured good night she slipped inside.

She had a great deal to think about, she decided, as she crept up to her room—the professor's contradictory behaviour for a start. Why was it that at times he looked at her as though he disliked her—no, it wasn't dislike, it was disquiet, as though he expected her to do something which would upset him, and on the other hand, at times he was charming and more than that. She paused on the top step of the precipitous staircase and remembered his kiss. Out of gratitude perhaps, her common sense urged her, and indeed, when she got to her room and viewed herself in the mirror she had to admit that common sense was right; the sables were magnificent, but her face was still unremarkable and her hair had become loose. She lacked glamour or whatever it was that made a man kiss a girl. It had of course been almost dark—she smiled a little bitterly; in daylight she would have stood no chance at all.

CHAPTER FIVE

THREE DAYS LATER she reported for duty at the hospital. Mrs Macklin had received her news with glee and an instant offer of her room. 'Because, my dear,' she explained, 'it would be so very pleasant to have you living here. I know I'm perfectly able to manage for myself now, but I do so enjoy your company.' She added that Abigail was to consider the house as her own home and if she wanted to ask Bolly round at any time, she was to do so, and anyone else she liked to invite.

'I don't know anyone else,' Abigail pointed out.

'That nice surgeon you were telling me about?' enquired Mrs Macklin, 'or perhaps one of the nurses—or Dominic.'

Abigail had made some sort of a reply, trying to imagine herself inviting the professor round for tea. He had paid his usual visits during the three days, of course, and he had been pleasant enough, though a little distant, and she had caught him eyeing her warily; probably wondering to himself what on earth had possessed him to kiss her; wondering too how she would react to it. Well, she had no intention of reacting at all, she resolutely buried the memory of it under the activities relative to her removal to hospital, and if her thoughts were wistful, she took care that they didn't show.

She had paid a visit to Bolly, of course, carefully choosing a day when she knew the professor to be operating and therefore away from home. She and Bolly, in company with Annie and Colossus, had tea in the little sitting room and discussed the turn of events.

'Things are looking up,' declared Bollinger, well content. 'I must say I like this city, Miss Abby, and you look pretty bobbish yourself. I hope you stay a week or two at the hospital.'

A sentiment to which Abigail heartily subscribed!

The sister of the children's ward was glad to see her; her staff had been severely depleted by salmonella, and worse, several of the small patients were ill with it too. The ward was closed to outsiders; a great effort was being made to find the source of the infection, but as Zuster Ritsma explained, it wasn't so easy, for this wasn't the salmonella due to infected food, which would have been comparatively easy to trace, but an insidious type so that a nurse would be working on the ward, unaware that she was already infected.

'I hope,' she continued in her excellent English, 'that you are a strong girl, Nurse Trent.' She eyed Abigail's small, nicely plump frame with some uncertainty, and Abigail made haste to assure her that she was as strong as a horse and very healthy. Zuster Ritsma took her word for it. 'At least I am grateful to have another nurse on the ward,' she observed with relief, and proceeded to delve into the report, carefully explaining each case as she went. It took some time, and when she had finished, Abigail followed her round the ward and in and out of the glass-partitioned cubicles.

The ward was full, with the infected children away from the rest at the end of the ward—six of them, in various stages of illness, three with drips up and the other three, Zuster Ritsma said, getting better. There were four more suspects in the next two cubicles, and in the last large cubicle there were four babies, each isolated and each very ill. They were post-operative and all were infected. They lay making no sound, dangerously lethargic. Zuster Ritsma adjusted a drip and said, 'We shall save them all, but it will be much hard work.'

She smiled at Abigail as she spoke, and Abigail, who liked her and sensed her anxiety, agreed bracingly. 'What do you want me to do?' she asked.

'These babies. There are four, you see. It will be a heavy task, but if you would stay here, in these cubicles, then the other nurses can stay in the ward.' She picked up a chart and they bent over it together while she explained what had to be done. 'If you need help, I will come—there is a bell and an intercom—also a red light. The night nurse comes on duty at ten o'clock—we work in three shifts.' She hesitated. 'Would you work until then, do you think? Just for today—I have no nurse until tomorrow, and the professor insists that there are *gediplomeerd* nurses.'

'Yes, of course I will, and if this doesn't go on for too long surely two of us could manage between us—I'm quite willing if the night nurse is.'

Zuster Ritsma brightened. 'Oh, that would be excellent. But I do not know if Professor van Wijkelen will allow it.'

'Does he have to know?' asked Abigail. 'As long as there's a nurse here—we can have the time made up to us later. After all, we shall each get twelve hours off and the sick nurses will be coming back in a few days, won't they?'

'It is, how do you say? emergency,' mused Zuster Ritsma. 'You do not dislike?'

'No, I don't dislike,' Abigail agreed quietly, 'and I don't suppose he'll notice.'

But her companion shook her head at this rash statement. 'The professor notices everything.' She was very positive about it.

He came half an hour later, looking thunderous, but not, Abigail guessed, because he was annoyed, rather because he was deeply worried about the infection on the ward, especially the babies, each of whom he had operated upon for pyloric stenosis and who should have by now been on the way to recovery. He ground to a halt beside Abigail and wished her a good morning in a voice which implied that as far as he was concerned there was no such thing, and then, with Zuster Ritsma by his side, examined the babies one by one with meticulous care, throwing suggestions and orders at Henk as he did so. Abigail stood silently by, wishing that she could understand even a quarter of what he said; and in the end she had worried unnecessarily, for he repeated everything he had said to the other two in clear and concise English as he dealt with each baby.

When he had finished he came and stood beside her, looming large in his gown and mask. 'You're quite happy to be doing this work?' he wanted to know, and he sounded so irritable that she wouldn't have dared to say anything but yes, though that was the truth anyway.

'You're off duty,' he snapped at her. 'There is a grave shortage of nurses for a few days, but I have asked for extra staff. You will take your usual time off, Nurse.'

Abigail said, 'Yes, sir,' before Zuster Ritsma, who was looking guilty, could speak; if there were extra nurses, well and good, otherwise they would carry on as she had suggested and he would be none the wiser. This thought allowed a look of complacency to cross her grave face and he was quick to see it. 'Why do you look like that?' he demanded, 'as though you had been clever about something.'

Abigail gave him an innocent look. 'Me?' she asked. 'What have I to be clever about?'

He grunted, nodded briefly and went away, followed by Henk, who winked cheerfully at her as he passed. She was left on her own then, busy with the babies—their drips, their charts, their tiny, feeble pulses, their unhappy vomiting and the continuous cleaning up and comforting. When Zuster Ritsma did appear again she looked as agitated as someone so calm could look.

'The nurses—the professor asked for them, you know? Two

of them have the first symptoms...the other one has gone home at a moment's notice because her mother is ill.'

'That's OK—we'll carry on as we said we would, shall we, Zuster? Provided the night nurse doesn't mind, I certainly don't.'

The professor came again in the afternoon, looking preoccupied, but beyond studying the babies' charts and altering his instructions accordingly, had nothing to say to her. And early in the evening Henk came and stayed for ten minutes or so and, unlike the professor, asked her if she was managing and was there anything she needed. She was feeling a little tired by now and longing to get out of her enveloping gown and mask; she hadn't had them off since she had been relieved for her dinner; tea had been brought to her on a tray and she had had it while she wrote up the charts.

It was a quarter to ten when the professor came again. Only his eyes showed above the mask, staring at her coldly, although he had nothing to say until he had examined the babies at some length. But presently he straightened himself, professed satisfaction that they were at least holding their own, and then in a voice of withering chill demanded to know when she had been off duty.

'Well,' said Abigail carefully, 'you see, it's like this—I haven't. It seemed a good idea.'

'You disregarded my instructions, Nurse Trent?' His eyes narrowed. 'No, don't interrupt me. I am not in the habit of having my wishes ignored.' He went on disagreeably but without heat, 'I asked you to come to this ward to help out temporarily, nothing more. When I need advice from you concerning its management, I shall no doubt ask you. Until then, be good enough to refrain from interfering.'

Abigail adjusted a drip to a nicety and said kindly, as though she were reasoning with a bad-tempered child, 'There's no need for you to get into a nasty temper, Professor. You know very well that everyone here falls over their own feet to satisfy your every whim, and don't pretend you don't. Zuster Ritsma carried out your orders to the letter, but she couldn't prevent two of the nurses due on duty from sickening with salmonella, nor could she stop the third one from going home to look after her ill mother. She was so worried that I suggested that the night nurse and I should do a twelve-hour stint each until there are more nurses. That's all—nothing to lose your cool over.'

She stopped abruptly; she had said much more than she had intended, and none of it very polite. He was, after all, a consultant in the hospital and a well-known surgeon. She met the stare from his blue eyes and tried not to feel nervous.

'I have not—er—lost my cool, Miss Trent—it is not in my nature to give way to my feelings, although I am bound to plead guilty to a bad temper.' His eyes gleamed above the mask and she wondered if he was laughing, but decided that it was most unlikely. 'I am indebted to you for your help and I apologise for jumping to conclusions. I will see that your off-duty is made up to you as soon as it can be arranged.' He turned and walked away as silently as he had come, leaving her feeling bewildered. She had expected a good telling off at the very least; instead he had been—what had he been? It was difficult to know, but she suspected that he had been amused at her outburst.

The night nurse came and they spent the next twenty minutes poring over charts and studying the babies together, until finally Abigail was free to leave the ward. She tore off her gown and mask, threw them in the bin and hurried to the changing room where she took off her uniform and cap and tugged on a skirt and sweater without much attention as to how she looked, bundled her hair up under the woolly beret, flung on her coat and made her way to the front entrance of the hospital. It was very dark outside and the wind seemed, if anything, more bitter than a month ago when she had first arrived in Amsterdam. The winter was lasting a long time; she tucked her chin into her scarf and started down the steps.

The Rolls was at the bottom of them and the professor was at the wheel. He got out when he saw her and she made to pass him with a cheerful good night, but he put out a hand and stopped her. 'Get in,' he said.

There was nothing she would have liked more than to have sunk into the comfort of its leather-covered interior, but perversely she replied, 'The walk will do me good, thank you, sir. I need the exercise.'

Wasted breath. He urged her gently towards the open door. 'This is hardly the time of day to go walking around,' he said testily. 'As for exercise, we shall consider that presently.'

She saw that she had no chance against him. She got in and sat silent, fuming at his arrogance and wondering what he had meant about exercise. The journey was a short one. He turned the car silently into the Begijnsteeg and stopped and ushered her out, to fall into step beside her. 'I also need exercise,' he stated, and took her arm to lead her across the silent square. Abigail thought at first that he would stop at Mrs Macklin's door, but he didn't pause, striding briskly along, and she, perforce, keeping pace with his large well-shod feet. He didn't speak for a few minutes and nor did she; for one thing she had been surprised into speechlessness by his action and for another she was far too busy with her thoughts. She had been rude to him in the ward, so probably he was going to give her a telling-off. She sighed without knowing it and braced her tired shoulders.

He spoke at length. 'Have you the door key?' and when she said that yes, she had, he fell silent again. It must have been five minutes later before he asked her, 'How much terramycin are we giving Jantje Blom?'

Jantje was the smallest and the frailest baby. She told him the amount and they went on walking briskly over the cobbles, the wind creeping meanly through her coat so that she shivered.

The professor stopped and peered down at her in the dim light. 'I haven't done this for a long time,' he remarked thoughtfully, and she, thinking that he was talking to himself, said soothingly: 'No, I don't suppose many people do,' and was amazed when he burst into a bellow of laughter so that she said: 'Oh, hush, you'll wake all the old ladies!'

She shouldn't have spoken like that, she supposed, she stood still, waiting for him to snarl something nasty about young women being pert, but all he said was: 'That isn't what I meant, but you don't understand, it doesn't matter at the moment. I'm sorry I was ill-tempered this evening.'

'You had every right to be,' said Abigail fairly. 'I was abominably rude.'

'Yes. I didn't mind—at least you're honest.' His voice sounded bitter and she made haste to say, 'I expect it's worrying for you,' and he laughed again softly; she wondered why, shivering with cold, and he said at once,

'God, I'm thoughtless—you're cold.'

'Yes, but I enjoyed it.'

'Not if you catch a chill.'

She shook her head in the dark. 'I'm very tough.'

He walked her briskly to Mrs Macklin's house. 'Your spirit's tough,' he corrected her.

The house was in darkness. They stood very close in the hall while she found the light switch and then led the way to the kitchen, where, to her surprise, he said, 'I'll get the tea,' and sat her down by the table against the wall. Presently, with the teapot between them, sitting opposite her in one of the narrow wooden chairs, he began to discuss her small patients, and although she was very tired by now, she listened intelligently and even ventured one or two opinions of her own as to their treatment. It was a surprise to her when the Friese clock on the wall chimed midnight, and it surprised the professor as well. He got to his feet with the remark that he should be shot for keeping her from her bed, and although she protested, he washed the cups and saucers and tidied everything away before putting on his topcoat and going to the door. Abigail got up too, because she would have to lock it after him, and followed him out into the hall, but when she put out a hand to switch on the light his large one came down on hers and prevented it. 'No need,' he said very quietly, then caught her close and kissed her, and this time, she thought confusedly, he must have been putting in some practice. He was through the door and down the steps with a muttered good night before she could utter a word.

She went on duty the next morning with her thoughts in confusion—she had been too tired to do more than tumble into bed and fall asleep the night before, and there had been no time to think in the morning for Mrs Macklin had been full of questions about her work as they sat at breakfast together. Only at the end of Abigail's recital of the day's happenings had she said with something like complacency, 'I heard you come in last night, my dear, but Dominic was with you, wasn't he, so I knew you would look after yourselves and there was no need for me to come down.'

'Professor van Wijkelen was kind enough to bring me home,' said Abigail, with a composure she didn't feel. 'He came in for a cup of tea. It was very cold yesterday, wasn't it?'

Her companion ignored this red herring. 'He works too hard,' she observed, 'and I daresay he's worried about this infection—whatever it is. I hope you won't catch it, Abigail.'

Abigail assured her that she wouldn't, cleared the table, washed up, wished Mrs Macklin goodbye and set off for hospital. She went the long way round so that she could have a quiet think as she went, but somehow only one thing occupied her thoughts and that was the professor's kiss. As she went through the hospital gates she wondered how it would be when they met.

It needed only one look at his face as he came towards her in the ward to see that they were back to square one. He looked withdrawn and tired; she wasn't sure how old he was, but today there were lines she had never noticed before. He bade her good morning with the austere good manners which so daunted her, and went at once to work on the four babies.

They were a little better, she reported, her disappointment well hidden behind a professional manner not to be faulted gave chapter and verse of their progress during the night and since she had been on duty, adding that Jantje was not responding quite as well as the other three. His mother, she informed the professor, was waiting in the visitors' room on the landing and hoped for a word with him. He nodded without looking at her, got out his stethoscope and when he spoke again it was only to give her further instructions, and presently when Henk joined them, the two men talked together in their own language and it was Henk who turned to her at last and detailed the new treatment the professor had decided upon for Jantje. They went away together, with a cheerful wink and smile from Henk and the briefest of nods from the professor.

It wasn't until after the list that the professor came and then it was almost six o'clock, and although they discussed Jantje together he had little else to say. After he had gone she wondered sorrowfully what it was she had done to cause him to change so towards her. She had actually believed that at last he was beginning to like her, or at least to tolerate her, but she had been wrong. She tended the babies carefully and tried not to think about him.

Off duty at last, she changed rapidly, a little uneasy about the walk back to the Begijnhof; there was no bus going near enough to make it worth while to take one; it was only ten minutes' walk, but it was dark outside and looking out of the window she could see sleet beating upon it. She would get wet. She hurried through the hospital, her mind busy trying to remember some other way home which would save her going through the narrow dark lanes.

Long before she had reached the front hall she had given up the idea; the day had been long and she was tired and the effort was too great. She went through the door and down the steps and the sleet bit into her face like miniature knives and forced her to close her eyes. When she opened them a few seconds later, the Rolls was within a few feet of her and Jan was already getting out and holding the door open for her to get in.

He said cheerfully, 'Good evening, miss, I am to bring you to Mrs Macklin's house.'

'Oh, Jan, how lovely! But who…? Did Professor van Wijkelen tell you…?'

'Yes, miss.'

His tone was fatherly and final, and indeed Abigail was too tired to argue. She sat back in her seat beside him, wondering why the professor should take care of someone he could barely greet civilly; perhaps he was afraid that if she was out in the rain and caught cold, she would be of no further use to him—but that hadn't bothered him the previous night. Because she was tired and rather unhappy the memory of it brought tears to her eyes, and when the car stopped she thanked him in a quiet, normal voice and would have got out, but he got out too and started to walk with her across the cobbles. When she protested, he said merely, 'The professor told me to, miss,' and waited while she went up the steps before he wished her good night and walked away, back to the car.

She hadn't expected Mrs Macklin to be up, but that lady popped her head out of the sitting room as she went into the house and without appearing to notice her woebegone expression, said cheerfully, 'There you are, dear—I didn't feel like going to bed, so I've made a jug of cocoa for us both. You're tired—come in by the stove and be warm and comfortable for half an hour.'

She turned her back and went and sat down again, leaving Abigail to take off her outdoor things and brush away the tears. When she was sitting opposite Mrs Macklin in the comfortable warmth of the little room, her companion asked, 'A bad day?'

'No, not really,' Abigail admitted. 'Three of the babies are much better and the fourth will do, I think, and there aren't any fresh cases today and none of the contacts are proved positive—I should think the worst's over. Henk seemed to think so—they've found the source—one of the porters.'

'Did you see Dominic?'

'Yes, he came to see the babies.'

'I heard the car—he didn't come in this evening.'

'No, Jan brought me home, actually. I hadn't expected...he was waiting for me...the professor had sent him.' Abigail drew a determined breath. 'Mrs Macklin, why is he so—so considerate of me, and yet he doesn't like me at all?' She sighed, took a sip of cocoa and looked enquiringly at the older woman.

'I've been hoping you would ask me that,' said Mrs Macklin surprisingly. 'I didn't feel I could tell you, but now that you've asked—' she nodded her grey head in satisfaction. 'One can't gossip about one's friends, but there comes a time... The reason Dominic dislikes women is because he mistrusts them—young women, that is.' She waited expectantly for Abigail to say something.

Abigail poured more cocoa for them both; all she said was: 'You're sure you want to tell me?'

'Oh, yes, I'm going to tell you, my dear—he's far too nice a man to be misjudged, especially by you, Abigail.'

Abigail let that pass. Mrs Macklin went on: 'He's—let me see turned forty now. When he was a young man, in his early twenties, he married—a lovely girl, tall and dark, I remember she was most arresting. I don't think that for one moment he loved her—infatuated perhaps, and that passes for love for a little while, doesn't it? She was the kind of girl men fall for, and because Dominic was young and handsome and knew everyone, as well as being a wealthy man—you knew that, Abigail?—she married him. Within a few weeks he discovered that she was having affairs; before six months were out she was killed in a car crash with her current boy-friend. Dominic changed from that day—oh, he wasn't brokenhearted, he had long since lost all feeling for her, but his pride was hurt. He was still charming to the girls of his acquaintance, but it was as though he had resolved to live his life without them. He had—still has—his work. It absorbs him, doesn't it, and always will. Mind you, he keeps his true feelings well hidden,' she paused, 'at least I always thought so, but now I'm not so sure—he goes out a great deal, because he has many friends and he's well liked. He's still a very good-looking man, of course, he has almost everything; looks, brains, an excellent position in life, more money than he knows what to do with—but no love.'

Abigail's hands were clasped so tightly round her cup that the knuckles showed white. She said in a tight little voice, 'Yes,' and went on inconsequently, 'He loves little children, and he's good to his patients; they trust him. It's very sad that he has no one to love and won't allow anyone to love him.'

Mrs Macklin gave her a long thoughtful stare. 'Very,' she agreed, 'especially as every female under forty who can get within striking distance of him has done her best to remedy that fact.'

Abigail, who seldom blushed, went becomingly pink. 'Oh, is that why he?—surely he would never think that I—he gets irritated with me, all the time—well, almost all the time,' she amended truthfully. 'I didn't know—I'll try and keep out of his way as much as possible. Perhaps he'll meet some girl who can make him happy. I hope so.'

She got up and went to the kitchen with the cups on a tray. 'You could make him happy,' her heart urged her silently, 'because you love him.' She drowned the lunatic thought with a gush of water from the tap and washed the cups and saucers with a deliberately empty mind, and when she went back to the sitting room, beyond thanking Mrs Macklin for her confidence, made no reference to their conversation. Instead she enquired how her companion felt and listened sympathetically to Mrs Macklin's small grumbles about her health. They went to bed soon after that, and Abigail lay trying not to think about the future, because it would be without Dominic and she couldn't imagine it without him, even though, because he had been let down once, so long ago, he wouldn't even allow himself to like her. After all, she told herself wryly, she had got used to his irritable manner and cold voice by now; they made no difference to her feelings, and now that she knew their reason, she wouldn't mind any more—well, not very much.

The days, with their strict routine and small crises, came and went. The weather became steadily worse, with little flurries of wet snow and leaden skies. Abigail's boots leaked and she didn't dare to buy another pair, since she had, as yet, had no money for her first week's work at the hospital and paying Mrs Macklin had made a hole in what she had. Possibly she would be paid when she had finished working for them, and borrowing from Bolly was out of the question, anyway. She didn't intend seeing him until the salmonella scare was over. The situation was improving fast now, although there were still a number of nurses off duty, but there had been no fresh infection for some days. The babies were out of danger too, although they still had a long way to go and needed a great deal of care. She had become very fond of them and delighted in their progress; even little Jantje was improving at last.

It was in the middle of the second week of her job at the hospital that the professor arrived alone one afternoon. He examined the babies, studied their charts and path lab reports, expressed his satisfaction and then asked her: 'When do you intend to revert to your normal working hours, Nurse Trent?'

She kept her voice coolly friendly. 'Tomorrow, sir. Zuster Ritsma may have told you that there are two more nurses returning to duty, and another one at the end of the week. Is it true that the ward is to come out of isolation in a day or two?'

'Yes. Which duty will you be taking?'

She knew that too, but she wasn't going to tell him. 'I'm not sure—Zuster Ritsma has it all arranged.'

'Your days off?' he persisted.

'I'm to have those as soon as possible. Zuster Ritsma has kindly said that I may choose.'

'Have you any plans for them? Do you wish to go away, or spend some time with Bollinger? He can be spared.'

'That's very kind of you. I hadn't begun to think about it. I think I should like to take him out for the afternoon—he loves the cinema.'

He looked at her unsmilingly, his eyes thoughtful, and she was hopeful that he had remembered that she was owed a week's salary, but all he said was, 'I see,' and stalked away.

She was to do an early shift; half past seven until four each day, and as the professor invariably came before noon and after five, it meant she would see him only once a day, and not at all on operating days. Which, she told herself, was all for the best. It would leave her evenings free to keep Mrs Macklin company too and she could call and see Bolly on her way off duty. An excellent arrangement for all concerned, she reiterated, and began to wonder how much longer they would need her in the hospital.

She had mentioned it tentatively to Zuster Ritsma over coffee and had been told kindly that the professor had arranged that she should work there and would doubtless tell her when he no longer needed her. 'Although,' Zuster Ritsma had added, 'I hope it won't be just yet, for we shall be short-staffed for another week or so yet.' Abigail hugged that fact to her as she went about her work.

It had surprised her that Jan came to fetch her each evening; she had thanked the professor on the day following the first occasion and he had looked down his nose at her and remarked rather testily that as there were so many nurses off sick, it behoved him to take care of those who weren't. So she hadn't mentioned it again, but it was nice to find Jan waiting for her in the cold dark and she was secretly glad that she didn't need to walk alone through the dim, deserted lanes around the hospital.

She was a little tired on the morning of her new shift; it had meant getting up at six o'clock to get her breakfast and take Mrs Macklin a cup of tea before she left the house, and she had been late off duty the evening before, but she cheered up as she walked along the familiar little back ways in the semi-dark, replying to the milkmen and postmen and paper boys' cheerful *Goeden Morgen,* as she hurried by. The night nurse was cheerful too, for the night had been without worries. The babies were asleep, so Abigail helped with the older children's breakfasts, laughing a good deal with them because half the time she couldn't understand what they were saying and when she spoke herself they found her accent so comical. Jantje woke up presently and she went to give him his bottle. He was very slow still; she sat on the low chair by his cot, cuddling him close and encouraging him while he blinked up at her with eyes still lacklustre from his illness. 'Beautiful boy,' she urged him, 'drink up like a good lad.' She kissed the top of his small bald head. 'I wish you were mine.'

'You like babies—children?' The professor's voice sounded harshly from behind her and the bottle jerked in her hand so that Jantje, sucking half-heartedly, stopped altogether.

'Yes,' said Abigail, and hoped that he couldn't hear the uneven thud of her heart, and then to Jantje, 'Come along, my lovely boy, it's good for you.'

'No,' said Henk from the doorway, 'it's Guinness that's good for you, is that not so?' It sounded funny in his strongly accented English and she gave a chortle of laughter and laughed again when he said, 'Since he seems to understand English, can you not also say, "'Time, gentlemen, please?'"'

'That's an idea, he's such a slowcoach.' They were both standing by her now and she looked up and smiled, to meet Henk's cheerful face and the professor's bleak stare, which she ignored, saying cheerfully, 'He's better, isn't he, sir?'

'Yes, Nurse Trent.' He turned away to examine the other babies as Zuster Ritsma joined them and they all talked babies for a few minutes while Abigail coaxed the last of Jantje's feed into him and popped him back into his cot. She was about to pick up the next baby when Zuster Ritsma said, 'Nurse Trent, there are nurses returning, is it not good? Today at one o'clock there will be two, one will work here tomorrow and you will take a day off. There are three days due to you, is it not, but the others you shall have when you wish. The professor wishes it so.'

Abigail looked at the professor who was frowning at nothing in particular. When he looked at her the frown turned into a scowl. 'We are still not fully staffed,' his voice was stiff. 'I do not wish you to be overtired, otherwise you will be of no use here. Also it is convenient.'

'Charming!' Abigail's voice rang with annoyance. 'Such thoughtfulness does you credit, I must say.' Her usually soft voice had an edge of sarcasm. 'It's nice to know I'm useful, even if only as a cog in your machine.'

She would have liked him to have looked uncomfortable or even ashamed—had she not, only the day before, told him that she was to choose her days off?—and now they were being thrust upon her without a by-your-leave. He appeared to be neither; there was a gleam in his blue eyes which might have suppressed temper, but his expression remained bland; beyond a faint lift of the eyebrows he might not have heard her. She turned her back, picked up the baby she was going to feed and bore it away to change its nappy. She hated him! The hate lasted a good five minutes and was then wiped out by a flood of love which made nonsense of her own bad temper and his own disregard of her as a person. She fed the baby and thought of all the good reasons why he should be so horrible, then forgave him for all of them.

He didn't come again that day. The two nurses, Zuster Vinke and Zuster Snel, came on at noon; the three of them worked together until it was time for Abigail to go off duty.

It was still cold and it didn't seem to have got light all day and now that was fading, making the lighted shops she passed seem very cheerful. Almost home, she stopped at a *banketbakkerij* and bought some crisp little biscuits, which would be nice for tea, for she had no doubt that Mrs Macklin would be waiting for her. She couldn't afford the biscuits, her store of money was now so low that even that small luxury was an extravagance, but she was feeling reckless and a little defiant. She turned into the square with the windows of its little houses shining a welcome, her head full of plans for the next day. She wouldn't be able to do much—visit Bolly, naturally, and perhaps take Mrs Macklin to see Professor de Wit. He didn't live very far away; she wondered uneasily if it was too far for the old lady, or would she have to have a taxi? She decided to break into her fare which she still had saved; after all, she would be paid soon, especially as she made up her mind, there and then, to ask about it at the hospital the moment she returned.

She opened the little house door and shut it thankfully upon the dark outside, calling, 'It's me, Mrs Macklin,' as she cast her outdoor things on to the banister of the little staircase. 'I'll get the...' she began as she went into the sitting room, and stopped, because the professor was standing before the stove.

His 'Good evening, Miss Trent,' was very stiff. 'I am just about to go—I am already late. I called to see how Mrs Macklin does and find her very well, so well, in fact, that she is going on a small outing tomorrow. There is a concert of Viennese music tomorrow evening in the Concertgebouw which she is anxious not to miss. Perhaps you would care to accompany her?' he added carelessly. 'I don't suppose you are interested.'

'Why should you suppose that?' enquired Abigail, falling neatly and unwittingly into his trap. 'I should enjoy it very much!'

'Yes?' If she had any doubts about accepting, the one syllable would have decided her; it contained enough faint mocking disbelief to furnish a whole scathing sentence.

'Yes,' she reiterated, and realised too late why he had been so adamant about her day off—she would be company for Mrs Macklin who he would not wish to go alone. If it hadn't been that she liked her erstwhile patient far too much to disappoint her, she would have said a decided no. She gave the professor a smouldering look and saw that he knew exactly what she was thinking. She said hastily before her temper got the better of her, 'Shall I get the tea, Mrs Macklin? And does the professor intend to stay?'

It seemed that he didn't. She showed him to the door, wished him a chilly goodbye and went to put the kettle on.

They had almost finished tea, talking trivialities in which the professor had no part, when Mrs Macklin observed, 'Dear me, Abigail, I almost forgot. Dominic asked me to tell you that Jan would be here with the car at ten o'clock tomorrow morning and he will take you wherever you wish. Dominic will be away all day and if you would care to lunch with Bollinger at his house, he hopes that you will do so—he has already mentioned it to Bollinger, I believe.'

Which meant, thought Abigail, that Bollinger would be expecting her and she couldn't disappoint him. She might as well go straight there in the morning; it would be pleasant to have a long talk to him and having lunch there would solve the vexed question of her shortage of cash. Perhaps the professor was making amends, although he hadn't seemed particularly friendly just now. On the contrary; he had got his own way again. She said aloud, 'That will be very nice. I would have gone to see Bolly anyway, but I had thought that perhaps you and I could have gone round to see Professor de Wit in the afternoon.'

'A very kind thought, Abigail, but as it happens, he will be at the concert with us, so we shall be able to have a good chat there. I'm greatly looking forward to it. What will you wear?'

'Oh, lord,' exclaimed Abigail, dismayed, 'I haven't got anything—at least only a very plain velvet dress—it's brown and I've never liked it. I only packed it at the last minute because I thought it might be useful—it's that sort of a dress. Will it do, you think?'

'I'm sure it will. You're not a girl to need frills and flounces. Look how well that pink dress becomes you, and that's simple enough.'

Abigail agreed reluctantly and wished wholeheartedly for a new dress, although no one would see her at the concert and her two patients were much too kind to criticise her appearance.

'What will you wear?' she asked in her turn. The two ladies spent a delightful evening discussing clothes.

By the time Jan came she had breakfasted, taken Mrs Macklin hers on a tray, tidied her own room and dressed herself ready to go out. The weather showed no signs of improving, but in the comfort of the big car, it didn't matter. She spent the short journey practising her Dutch upon Jan, who obligingly corrected her many mistakes and helped out when she lacked a word. She thanked him nicely, as she always did, when they arrived at the professor's house and got out, to be admitted by a delighted Bollinger.

It was only a week or so since she had seen him, but it seemed much longer than that. He led her into the small sitting room and poked up the bright fire in the grate, then went away to return a few minutes later with a tray of coffee and with Colossus and Annie at his heels. They made much of her and then planted themselves side by side before the fire.

'Regular little charmer, is our Annie,' observed Bollinger, 'makes rings round the boss, she does, sits on his lap the instant he takes a chair. Lucky Colossus don't mind—fair spoils the little beast does that dog.'

'I'm glad. She's quite a beauty now she's plump and well fed. And now tell me, Bolly, how are you getting on?'

She listened patiently to the recital of his days. Not exciting, but she could see that he had enjoyed every minute of them, and when he had finished she explained carefully about not getting her pay and why she couldn't give him any money. As she had known he would, he offered to lend her all he had, but she refused gently and with gratitude, telling him that she would certainly be paid at the end of the week. And that awkward fact negotiated, she went on to give him a lighthearted account of her own week, making it out to have been much easier than it was.

Bolly, who was no fool, shook his elderly head and said, 'It can't have been much fun, Miss Abby—the boss told me each evening how you was getting on—real hard work, he said it was, and you not saying a word of complaint.'

'Well,' Abigail replied reasonably, 'I really didn't have much to complain about, you know,' at the same time swallowing surprise because the professor should have said that.

There was a great deal to talk about. Somehow sitting there in the comfortable room, life seemed suddenly secure and pleasant, with the dog and kitten between them and the cheerful firelight turning the silver coffee service to gold; for all the world as though it were home, thought Abigail wistfully.

Presently Bolly went away to return with Mevrouw Boot, both carrying loaded trays, the contents of which they proceeded to arrange on the small rent table under the window, and when, after a short chat, the housekeeper went away, Bolly said diffidently: 'Miss Abby, here's your lunch. The boss said you was to have it here. I usually eat with Mevrouw Boot, but the boss, he suggested you might like me to stay with you.'

'Well, of course I should love you to stay,' Abigail went round the table to give the old man a hug. 'You're my friend, Bolly, I don't know what I'd do without you.'

He beamed at her. 'That's the very words the boss used,' he commented, and pulled out a chair for her to sit down.

'Oh?' she tried not to sound interested. 'Did he?'

Bollinger placed a pipkin of soup before her and removed its lid, and its fragrance caused her small nose to twitch in anticipation of it.

'That's right,' he agreed. 'He's a fine gentleman, is the boss, once you get to know him.'

And that was something in which Bolly had been more successful than she—for she didn't know him at all and it didn't seem likely that she ever would. She sighed, dismissed the unhappy thought and applied herself to her soup.

They went for a walk when they had finished lunch, taking Colossus with them and leaving Annie curled up before the fire, and although it was cold and windy, Abigail enjoyed it, just as she enjoyed the tea they found waiting for them when they got back, for it was like the teas she remembered when she was a child—hot buttered muffins in a silver dish, tiny sandwiches and a sponge cake as light as a feather.

'What a marvellous cook Mevrouw Boot is,' she commented, licking a jammy finger.

'You're right there, Miss Abby—made the muffins, she did. The boss said you was to have a good English tea—muffins, he says, and an English cake, and see there's plenty of milk in the jug. We done our best.'

'It's marvellous,' Abigail praised him, much struck by the professor's attention to detail—for instance, knowing that there was never enough, if any, milk served with tea in Holland. 'I must go to the kitchen and thank Mevrouw Boot.'

Which she did before setting out for the Begijnhof once more, after promising that she would meet Bolly for coffee in a day or two's time.

She found Mrs Macklin in her bedroom, doing things to her hair.

'Heavens, am I late?—it's not till eight o'clock, is it?—there's still supper...!'

'Yes, dear,' said Mrs Macklin, 'there's plenty of time. I thought I'd get all ready except for my dress; I can put that on after supper. *Erwten* soup—it's been on all the afternoon—and yoghurt for afters.'

'Very nice.' Abigail, who wasn't fond of pea soup, remembered her splendid lunch, went downstairs again to lay the supper table.

She dressed after supper when everything had been tidied away and she had laid her breakfast ready for the morning, but first she fastened Mrs Macklin into the handsome black dress, laid the table wrap ready and then went to her own room. Twenty minutes later she was standing before her mirror, eyeing her reflection with distaste, intent on her face and quite failing to see that the brown dress matched her eyes exactly and showed off her pretty figure to advantage. She had made up her face with care and had done her hair with even more attention to detail; now she put on her tweed coat over the despised brown velvet and went downstairs. She found Mrs Macklin already there, looking very *grande dame,* even though, as she pointed out to Abigail, she had lost so much weight that the dress was loose-fitting.

'And mine's a little too tight,' said Abigail, 'which is far worse.' She looked down at her person rather anxiously. 'I hope the seams don't pop. How lucky there won't be anyone there to see, though I expect you'll be bound to meet someone.'

'Certainly,' said Mrs Macklin, and her dark eyes snapped with amusement, but Abigail, with her head twisted over one shoulder trying to see if she looked all right from the back, missed that.

They were to be fetched by Jan, who would collect Professor de Wit first, Mrs Macklin told her and at ten to eight, Jan rang the door bell and escorted the older lady to the car, while Abigail made a few last-minute arrangements for Jude's comfort, she hurried after them and got into the seat beside Jan, leaving the two older members of the party to greet each other on the back seat and then talk non-stop throughout the entire short journey.

Jan seemed to know exactly where they were to go. He gave Mrs Macklin an arm up the stairs in the Concertgebouw, and Abigail, her arm tucked protectively in Professor de Wit's, followed him happily. They had a box and once the party was seated Abigail looked around her with a good deal of interest.

The auditorium was full and, from what she could see of the audience, it was smartly dressed. It was all much more splendid than she had anticipated and she thanked heaven silently that the brown dress, although not exciting, was at least passable, but she forgot that presently when the music started. She was sitting beside Mrs Macklin with an empty chair beside her, but she forgot her companions too, leaning forward, her elbows on the red plush of the box, her chin in her hands, staring down at the orchestra. It was the faintest of sounds which caused her to turn her head. Dominic van Wijkelen was sitting beside her in the chair which had been empty; he nodded briefly into her surprised face and became at once absorbed in the music, and most unreasonably the thought that she might just as well not be there for all the notice he had taken of her crossed her mind, then she stifled a laugh, because she herself had been completely absorbed not a minute since, and anyway, what was there about her to rival the music? She focused her attention once more and found that although the magic was still there it was tempered by the presence of the professor, sitting so close and so withdrawn.

The music came to an end and the lights went up and in the general buzz of clapping and talk the professor got up and went to bend over Mrs Macklin's chair; he didn't take his seat again until the lights were lowered and he hadn't spoken one word to Abigail. She sat like a statue, wondering if she hadn't been meant to come with Mrs Macklin—whether she had misunderstood, and this, mixed with a rising hatred of the miserable brown dress, caused her calm face to assume an expression of extreme disquiet, which was perhaps the reason for the professor to place a hand quietly over her own, clasped in her lap. The expression on her face turned to one of great surprise; she turned her head slowly to look at him, her mouth a little open, her eyes saucer-round, and met a look to melt her bones, a look she had only seen on his face when he had been bending over a patient—kind and gentle and faintly smiling, and when she attempted to pull her hand away, he merely held it in a firmer grip, and the smile widened. There was nothing to do but leave it where it was, tear her gaze away from his and stare at the orchestra below.

He gave her her hand back when the lights went up and asked, still smiling: 'You are enjoying your day off, Abigail?'

She found her voice, a little high and squeaky. 'Yes, thank you. It was lovely to see Bolly—thank you for letting me spend the day at your house and giving me lunch and tea.'

'A pleasure which I was unfortunately prevented from sharing,' he replied. 'What do you think of our Annie?'

They talked about commonplace things and soon her heart stopped its absurd racing, and she was able to tell herself that probably the music had made him feel romantic and she was the nearest woman—a tale which held no water at all when presently the lights went out and he possessed himself of her hand again.

The evening was like a dream—a dream from which she had no desire to waken, but the concert came to an end and Abigail put on the serviceable winter coat once more, took Professor de Wit's old arm and walked slowly in the wake of the others, down to the car. Jan wasn't there this time. The professor stowed his passengers comfortably and got behind the wheel himself, disentangled the Rolls with remarkable patience from the multitude of cars around them and drove without haste through the city. They had stopped before his house before Abigail had even begun to wonder where they were going, and she found herself, in company with the two older members of the party, being ushered into the welcoming warmth of the hall, where Bolly, who had opened the door to them, took their coats and invited them to enter the drawing room—a room Abigail had not yet seen. She smiled at Bolly and paused a moment to have a word with him before following the others inside, and became aware that the professor was beside her, but beyond giving her a quick glance he didn't speak to her but to his guests in general.

'It seemed a good idea if we had a drink and a sandwich before we part,' he said pleasantly, and piloted them to the chairs scattered around the great fireplace, and as though she had been given her cue Mevrouw Boot came in with a trolley and Bollinger behind her.

Abigail, eating tiny hot sausages, *bitterballen* and vol-au-vents and drinking the Cinzano she had asked for, made conversation with Professor de Wit and contrived at the same time to look around her. The room was large and lofty with an ornate plaster ceiling and panelled walls painted white, divided by gilded columns. The floor was completely covered by a fine carpet of a delicate, almost faded pink, and the chairs, of which there were a considerable number, were upholstered in a variety of shades in that colour, as well as muted blues and greens. There was a chandelier hanging from the ceiling's centre, reflecting light into every corner, and a number of matching wall chandeliers. The curtains were of the same dull pink as the carpet, and the only dark colours in the room came from the paintings on the walls, family portraits and landscapes for the most part. It was a delightful room, restful as well as beautiful; it made her feel dowdy, and the knowledge that her host's eyes were upon her did little to make her feel anything else; she and her brown dress stuck out like a sore thumb in the beautiful pastel-tinted room. She turned her shoulder to the professor and listened attentively to the old man's dissertation on the music they had been listening to.

They stayed an hour before the professor drove them home, Professor de Wit first, to be handed over carefully to the ministrations of Juffrouw Valk and then on to Mrs Macklin's house. The professor accepted Mrs Macklin's offer of a cup of coffee with the air of a man who had had no refreshment for a considerable time, and sat down to talk to her while Abigail went to the kitchen to make it. But Mrs Macklin took only a few sips, declaring that she was now too tired to enjoy it and would go to bed at once, but despite this she refused Abigail's help, merely allowing her to help her off with her dress when she got to her room and then sending her downstairs again. Abigail had expected the professor to be on his feet, coated and ready to go home, but he was still sitting where she had left him, and now as she entered he got to his feet and fetched the coffee pot from the top of the stove and refilled their cups. Abigail sipped in silence, while her thoughts, like mice on a wheel, spun round, trying to find a suitable topic of conversation.

There was no need. The professor put his cup down and said

in the kind of voice he used when he was giving her details of a patient: 'You look very pretty, Abigail.'

He was of course either being kind or joking—she thought the former. She was not in the least pretty, certainly not in the brown velvet. Probably her nose was shining too. She said in a small voice:

'Thank you, I don't know why you said that because it's not true, but thank you all the same.'

She gasped when he answered her blandly, 'No, it's not true. You're not pretty, you're beautiful, because you're honest and kind. I told you, did I not, that you had restored my faith in women, and now I'm a little afraid.'

'Why?'

'Because it may not be true...'

She got to her feet and walked over to him. 'It's quite true,' she assured him, and smiled up into his face. She only just stopped herself in time from telling him how much she loved him. But perhaps he didn't want love—not from her—perhaps she was just a stepping stone to some other girl, a girl who really was pretty and led his kind of life. She kept the smile there, though, and he smiled slowly back, towering over her. For the third time he kissed her, and this time it was a kiss to keep her awake for a very long time after he had gone.

CHAPTER SIX

SHE WAS TALKING to Henk when the professor came on to the ward the next morning. They had been laughing about something or other together and she turned a still smiling face to him, and although her good morning was quiet, her eyes were warm; a warmth dispelled instantly by the austerity of his face and his own dry, 'Good morning, Miss Trent.' He looked as though he had been up all night, she thought, which might account for his withdrawn air. When he asked for the reports on the babies, she gave them in a brisk friendly voice, not smiling at all. Perhaps when Henk went… Henk didn't go; he suggested it, for he was wanted on another ward, but the professor told him rather sharply to remain where he was, so that it was impossible to say anything, even if Abigail had known what to say. Which she didn't.

After a night of thinking, sometimes very muddled because she had dozed off from time to time and the thoughts became dreamlike and quite unmanageable, she had come to the conclusion that in some way she had been the means of making him realise that not all women were like the girl he had so disastrously married. She doubted if he had any feeling for her—gratitude perhaps, a slow dawning friendship which was destined to come to a premature end once she was back in England, and right at the back of her mind, hardly to be thought of, was the possibility that he had, much against his will, fallen a little in love with her.

She watched him stalk away from the ward after a blandly polite goodbye and admitted that the possibility of him entertaining any feelings for her was so slight as to be non-existent. She picked up Jantje and put him on the scales. He was beginning to gain weight now and looked like a baby once more. He smiled windily at her and she said aloud:

'He's going to send me away, dear boy. I'll bet you my month's money on it, for either he has set his sights on some blonde lovely and wants me out of the way, or I embarrass him.'

She was right, of course. She didn't see him the next day and the following afternoon, just before she was due off duty, he turned up, with Henk and Zuster Ritsma. The babies were examined, a fairly short business now, and then he turned round to address Abigail.

'We seem to be over our emergency, Nurse. I must thank you for your help, we are all deeply appreciative of it. Shall we say that you can go at midday tomorrow?'

She had expected it, and now it had happened it wasn't as bad as she had thought it would be. She said matter-of-factly, 'That suits me very well, thank you.' She glanced at him and managed to smile briefly, then found his eyes upon her in a thoughtful stare. But when he spoke it was abruptly. 'I'll say goodbye, Nurse.' He offered his hand and she took it and remembered vividly how he had held it at the concert and how, later, he had kissed her. She smiled again, too brightly, quite unable to speak.

Mrs Macklin, when she was told, was so astonished that she could think of nothing to say for several seconds. 'I thought you would be here for weeks—months even,' she managed at last. 'I knew you wouldn't be at the hospital for ever, but Dominic always has so many private patients and he has often told me how difficult it is to get a nurse for those who want to stay at home. You're not mistaken, my dear?'

'No, I expected it—at least for the last two days I've been expecting it.'

'Since we went to the concert,' commented Mrs Macklin sharply.

'Well, more or less.' Abigail got up from her chair, 'If I'm to leave at midday I'll go back to England by the night boat, if I can get a ticket.'

It would be better that way, for she would be able to sleep on board and when she got to London she could go straight to the agency and get another job. She went up to her room and started to pack in a halfhearted fashion. She would have liked a good weep, but there was really no time; she had to see Bolly before she went and got her ticket and say goodbye to Professor de Wit, and what was the use of crying anyway? She screwed up the brown velvet dress into an untidy bundle and rammed it into her case. She didn't care if she never wore it again, but the pink dress she folded carefully in tissue paper and tucked it away, out of sight, under her spare uniform. It was a pity, she told herself, that she couldn't tuck her dreams away as easily.

She left the hospital the next day, handing over to the nurse who was to relieve her before going to say goodbye to Zuster Ritsma, who shook her fervently by the hand, wished her well and told her that any papers concerning her work would be posted on and what was her address.

Abigail gave the name of the agency, and when Zuster Ritsma, not quite understanding, persisted that she wanted Abigail's home address, explained that just for the time being she had no home. Zuster Ritsma, the eldest of a large family to whose welcoming bosom she retired on her days off, gave her a deeply pitying look, and Abigail, to forestall the sympathy she could see in the sister's eye, asked for her money.

Her companion looked blank. She knew nothing about it,

she said. She had understood that the professor would be paying her as he had engaged her in the first place.

'I think you had better ask him, Nurse Trent—if you would like to go to the consultants' room and see if he is there?'

Abigail liked no such thing; to ask him meekly for her salary after he had so thankfully wished her goodbye was more than enough. She had just sufficient money to get to London and a pound or two besides; she would manage until he sent it on to her. In any case, she consoled herself, Mrs Morgan's money would have arrived at the agency by now. There remained only Bolly to worry about; she was glad now that they had already discussed her return to England, leaving him behind for a little while. She made her way to the house on the *gracht,* doing hopeful, inaccurate sums in her head.

Bolly was surprised and disconcerted at her news. 'A bit quick,' he observed. 'I don't like the idea, Miss Abby—you on your own.'

'But, Bolly,' she made her voice reasonable and cheerful too, 'we did agree that it was the best thing, remember? I shall be quite all right, with any luck I'll get a job straight away and then I can start looking for a flat. I shall be much happier knowing that you're here while I'm doing it.'

And seeing Dominic each day, she added silently. Still determinedly cheerful, she went on: 'I must go now, Bolly dear. I'll write to you the minute I get fixed up, I promise.' She gave him an affectionate hug, bade farewell to Annie and Colossus and went round to Professor de Wit's house, where she told him her news and wished him goodbye. Unlike Bollinger, the old man didn't seem in the least surprised to hear that she was leaving.

'A natural sequence of events,' he called it, and when she enquired what he meant he told her she would have to wait and see, but she could mark his words. Abigail smiled and murmured and decided he didn't mean anything at all; he was old and so clever as to be a little eccentric at times. She kissed him goodbye with real affection.

She had plenty of time when she got back to Mrs Macklin's. The boat train didn't leave until the late evening. She ate a simple supper with Mrs Macklin, who was frankly tearful at the prospect of her leaving and only cheered up when Abigail pointed out that she would most certainly return one day, 'For if I can come once I can come again,' she pointed out, knowing that she never would, because then she might meet the professor again and she wouldn't be able to bear it. A clean break, she told herself silently, was by far the best.

She cleared the supper things away and made coffee, then sat by the stove, chatting with false gaiety until it was time for her to put on her outdoor things and fetch her case. She had refused Bolly's offer to take her to the station; he was an old man and she didn't like the idea of him being out in the cold darkness. She would go to the Spui and find a taxi. She told Mrs Macklin what she was going to do as she went to the door. It opened as she got to it and the professor, looking more irritable than ever, came in. He said without preamble, 'I intended to take you to the boat, but I'm expected in theatre in an hour. I'll take you to the station.'

Abigail frowned. How like him to be so awkward; they had said goodbye—not a very pleasant one, but still goodbye, and here he was again, just as she had schooled herself to be sensible about the whole wretched business.

'Please don't bother,' she told him, a little stiffly, and noticed as she said it how tired he looked. 'I was just on my way to get a taxi.'

He couldn't have been listening, for he took her by the arm and walked her back to where their mutual friend was sitting, calmly knitting as though she had the house to herself. The professor greeted her briefly and said smoothly, 'I was just telling Abigail that we must leave in five minutes.'

'Clever,' thought Abigail. 'Now he's got her on his side', but aloud she said, 'I'm most grateful, sir,' in the kind of voice she used on the wards when she addressed consultants. She saw him wince, which quite pleased her, and brightened still more when the idea that he might be going to pay her crossed her mind. She bade Mrs Macklin goodbye and followed him out on to the cobbles to the waiting car. The drive would take five minutes, perhaps a little longer, so there would be no need to talk—a view, apparently, not shared by her companion, however, for once he was behind the wheel he began testily:

'I find it impossible to talk to you, but there is something I must make clear. I have been deeply appreciative of your work for me—you are an excellent nurse, I can think of no one I would rather have to care for anyone I—loved. I should like you to remember that, Abigail.' He halted the car at the traffic lights. 'There is another thing I must say. My behaviour may have taken you by surprise—indeed, I am surprised at myself. I haven't been—sentimental for years. I intend to forget it and I hope that you will too.'

They had arrived at the Centrale Station. Before he could do anything, Abigail got out of the car, beckoned a porter, opened the car's door, hauled out her case, gave it to the man and then thrust her head through the window. She spoke in a voice thick with tears, and a little wildly.

'What a lot of fuss you make about nothing—nothing, do you understand?' and marched away without looking at him once.

London looked bleak and grey when she arrived the following morning. She got up early and went along to the restaurant and made an early breakfast; she wasn't hungry, but it was cheaper than having it on the train.

She took a bus from Liverpool Street to the agency and sat down thankfully in the waiting room. There weren't many other people there—the two girls who went in ahead of her came out looking so cheerful that she took it as a good omen when her own turn came. The stern woman hadn't changed in the least, unless it was to look rather more stern. She gave Abigail a sharp glance, said 'Good morning, Miss Trent,' and handed her a bill. 'I understand that after the case you accepted from us you worked independently in Amsterdam.'

Abigail, a little overcome by so much efficiency, said a polite good morning and that yes, she had, and took a look at the bill. It wasn't much, Mrs Morgan had only lasted three weeks, but seven pounds and fifty pence would just about take all the money she had. With commendable calm she asked, 'Is there a letter for me? Mrs Morgan—my patient—said she would forward my fare...but she forgot.'

The severe woman smiled thinly. 'Yes, I have a letter for you here.' She opened a drawer and handed Abigail an envelope and waited while she opened it. The cheque was inside. 'Perhaps you would like us to put it through the bank for you?' she enquired.

'Oh, please,' said Abigail thankfully. All at once the woman looked quite human. She paid the commission at once and stuffed what was over into her purse; it was amazing how much better she felt. She still had only enough to live on for a week, but a lot could happen in that time.

'Have you a case for me straight away?' she asked.

The woman shook her head. 'I'm not sure, but I think not,' she got up and thumbed through the filing cabinet. 'There are several nurses wanted urgently for mental—you're not trained for that?'

'No, only general.'

'A pity. It's most unusual for us not to have a number of cases waiting.' She resumed her seat and picked up her pen. 'Come in again tomorrow morning, Miss Trent,' she advised, 'there will probably be something.' Her gaze swept over Abigail. 'You don't mind where you go?'

Abigail thought of Bolly. 'London or somewhere not too far away,' she said slowly, and added a polite good morning as she went out.

She went to the Golden Egg again because her case was heavy, and ordered a cup of coffee. She could of course apply for a job in hospital—her own training school would take her back, she supposed, but then what about Bolly? It was impossible, after seeing his happiness in Amsterdam, to condemn him to some back room again; besides, if she went back into hospital she wouldn't be paid for a month and how was she to manage in the meantime? She brooded over her coffee and then went out into the street once more. She had to find somewhere to sleep for the night—one night, she told herself bravely, there would be a job for her in the morning. She found a small hotel not too far away and left her case in her room, then spent the rest of the day looking in shop windows and eating as economically as she could at Woolworth's cafeteria.

She was early the next morning and the first to go in. She could hardly believe her luck when she was asked if she would go to Virginia Water as a companion nurse to a widowed lady who was, most regrettably, suffering from delirium tremens. It would involve some night work, but there was daily help for the rough; the pay was twelve pounds a week, all found. It sounded ghastly, and Abigail had her mouth open to say an emphatic no when the woman behind the desk got in first with the news that there was nothing else at present and she was under the impression that Abigail wanted work as soon as possible. 'You can always give it up after two weeks,' she told Abigail. 'If you leave before that time, I'm afraid we take you off our books.'

Abigail thought rapidly. It would certainly be an awful job, and very underpaid, but it would be a roof over her head. On the other hand, something much better might turn up in a day or two and she would miss it.

The woman at the desk tapped her fingers impatiently on the desk. She asked sharply: 'Well?'

Abigail started to get up. She ignored the other woman's frown and began 'I...' but was interrupted by the telephone.

She stood patiently while her companion lifted the receiver and stated who she was. After a minute she took the receiver from her ear. Her voice was frigid. 'This call is for you, Miss

Trent. Most irregular, I cannot think what made you give this number.'

'But I haven't! I don't know who would want to...' Bolly? the professor? Hardly. She took the receiver and said worriedly, 'Hullo.'

The professor—and speaking as though they were on the ward, together by a patient's bed while she listened to his instructions. 'Abigail? How fortunate that you should be there. You have no case yet?'

She shook her head, just as though he were there to see, and then said faintly: 'No.'

'Good. I want you for someone special—my niece, in Spain with her parents.'

'Your niece?'

'My niece—kindly don't interrupt me. Two weeks ago she swallowed three coins, pesetas. She was X-rayed and my sister was assured that nature would take its course. Unfortunately this has proved to have been too hopeful a view. She is now vomiting and dehydrated, and an operation is necessary. My sister refuses to have anyone touch Nina but myself. I intend going to Spain and bringing her back with me to hospital here. I should like you to come with me. You would be expected to remain in hospital with her until she is fit enough for her father to come and fetch her back. You will be paid expenses and your usual fees.'

The silence between them was profound until Abigail heard him explode with: 'My God, I haven't paid you!'

She said, 'No,' and waited, listening to the rush of her heartbeats; she was so happy at that moment that she would gladly have agreed to work for nothing.

His voice again; unhurried, concise. 'Abigail, you will go to Coutts' Bank,' he gave her the address, 'and ask for Mr Cross. Take your passport with you. He will pay your expenses for the journey and the salary which I owe you. It is Wednesday— there is a Swedish Lloyd ship sailing for Bilbao at six o'clock this evening from Southampton, you will have plenty of time to catch it. I will arrange to have your ticket ready for you. I will meet you when you dock in Spain. Is there anything else you wish to know?'

There was a great deal; she remembered that she hadn't agreed to go. Of course she would, but it would have been nice if he hadn't taken it for granted that she would come running.

'Abigail?'

'Yes, Professor.'

'Will you do this for me? Nina is very dear to me—she must have only the best—you remember what I said?'

High praise indeed and, she supposed, better than nothing.

'You have no other case?' he asked again.

'No—that is, I was just going to accept one, but I hadn't actually said that I would.' She looked across at the severe woman, silently fuming behind her desk, and watched her close the folder containing the widow with delirium tremens. She said, 'I'll be glad to help,' and heard him sigh.

His voice sounded very clearly. 'Abigail? I'm sorry—about your salary. I should have remembered—I was worried. Why didn't you ask me?'

She didn't answer but asked instead, 'Would you do something for me, please?' She heard his grunt and took it for yes. 'Tell Bollinger.'

'I have already done so—it was he who furnished me with the address of the agency. I will see you on Friday morning about seven o'clock.'

He rang off with a brief goodbye which she had no time to answer and she looked across at the severe woman, who looked positively grim. 'The idea,' said that lady, 'you have been on that telephone for more than five minutes! Heaven knows how many calls…'

'I'm sorry,' said Abigail, finding it impossible to feel anything else for the poor creature, condemned no doubt to spend the rest of her days at a dreary desk instead of going off to

Spain to meet the only person in the world who really mattered. 'They'll ring again,' said Abigil kindly.

'I take it that you have accepted a post not connected with this agency?'

'Yes—I worked for a Professor van Wijkelen in Amsterdam—there is a case in Spain which he has asked me to take.'

The older woman stared at her. 'At least you're a sensible girl,' she offered. She meant plain, both she and Abigail knew it, but there was no point in being rude.

Abigail smiled, not minding in the least, and bade the woman good morning, then skipped out of the agency, still smiling. She went back to the hotel, told the desk clerk that she wouldn't want her room for another night and went upstairs to review her wardrobe. She had left her trunk at Bolly's lodgings, so presumably it was still there. She repacked her case; she would go and forage through her clothes, leave the pink dress in the trunk and then go to the bank. During the bus ride she occupied herself trying to guess what the professor would have done if she hadn't been at the agency when he had telephoned. Presumably he would have gone on telephoning at intervals throughout the day. She wondered, too, how long it would take him to go to wherever it was they were to meet in Spain. Bilbao was in the north, she knew that, he would drive through France and return that way. She hoped the little girl wasn't too ill, and became engrossed in trying to remember the treatment for such cases. As far as she knew they could be serious but not fatal; once the coins were removed the child should recover rapidly. She wondered why the mother didn't take the child to Amsterdam herself—after all, the professor was a busy man and it was quite a journey. She got off the bus pondering, and rang the bell of the shabby little house where Bollinger had lived.

Her trunk had been stored in a cupboard-like room, too small to take a bed. She sorted out what she wanted to take with her, packed the pink dress away in the trunk, gave the brown velvet to the daughter of the house, and left again. It was ten past twelve when she reached the bank, by now beset with the fear that no one there would know anything about her and what on earth was she to do if they didn't?

She was wrong—she had only to mention her name to the imposing messenger at the door to be whisked into an enormous room, occupied by a small, bewhiskered man who leaped to his feet as she was ushered in and offered her a chair.

He gave only a cursory glance at her passport and embarked at once upon the matter in hand. 'Professor van Wijkelen is an old and valued client of ours,' he said by way of opening, 'we are only too glad to oblige him in any way.' He rang a bell and a clerk slid in, laid a folder before him and slid out again.

'We have arranged for you to collect your ticket at the Southampton Docks office,' he began. 'Take a taxi from the station, Miss Trent, the driver will know where to take you. Here is your train ticket from Waterloo, and I have been asked by Professor van Wijkelen to remind you to take tea on the journey. Here also are the expenses for your journey and the salary due to you. If you would be so kind as to check the amount?'

Abigail, a little overawed by such smooth, effortless efficiency, did as he asked. There seemed to be much too much money. She said so and the bewhiskered gentleman smiled kindly at her. 'No, no, dear young lady—your salary, money in lieu of days off and spending money for your journey. There are bound to be a few comforts you will require on the journey.'

Champagne with my early morning tea, for instance, thought Abigail, feeling lightheaded. The professor must have extravagant girl-friends if that was the amount he found necessary for a two-day journey. She frowned, uneasy about the girl-friends. She put the money carefully into her handbag, promising herself to keep strict account of what she spent and to return the surplus when she met the professor, wished her new-found friend goodbye and was ushered out with grave courtesy.

She spent the next two hours shopping. Over a slightly extravagant lunch she made a list of things she needed and then made a beeline for Marks and Spencers. She had prudently left her case at Waterloo Station; now she wandered uncluttered from one counter to the next, making her choice. She settled finally for a pleated tweed skirt in a warm brown and oatmeal with a matching brown sweater and a gay little neck scarf. She bought a plain wool dress too, a soft blue, nicely cut and easily packed, as well as some undies. Lastly she bought an overnight bag with a wide zippered mouth so that she would be able to get at things easily while they travelled. She went back to Waterloo then, had a cup of tea, fetched her case and joined the queue for the train. It wasn't until she was handing her ticket to the collector at the barrier that she noticed it was for the first class.

It was pleasant to travel in such comfort and when the steward came along and asked her if she would like tea, mindful of the professor's instructions, she said yes. She had barely finished it when the train was at Southampton. It was in the taxi that she realised that she knew very little about the journey and still less about her destination. The professor hadn't bothered to tell her where they were going or how long they would stay, nor indeed, if her memory served her right, had he told her anything other than the bare bones of the case. But at the ticket office she found that she had underestimated him, for with her ticket was a long envelope addressed to herself. Abigail put it into her handbag and once inside her cabin, sat down on the bed to read it.

It was, naturally enough, typed and signed by Mr Cross and obviously made up from the professor's instructions. She was not to stint money upon her enjoyment during the short sea journey, it was stated. She would be met at Santurce at half past seven on Friday morning and she would be good enough to leave the ship at this hour, go through the Customs and contact the professor, who would be waiting for her. If by any chance he was not there, she was to go to the waiting room and remain there until he was. Their destination was his sister's house, situated some kilometres from Baquio, a small seaside resort half an hour's run from Bilbao. Probably they would stay the night there, but it might be necessary to leave before this; it depended on the child's condition. The return journey would take two days, if all went well. She was wished a pleasant journey.

She read the message through twice, then folded it neatly and returned it to her handbag. Presently, when she had unpacked, she would find a map and find out exactly where she was going. In the meantime she explored her cabin, a large and airy one on the promenade deck with its own tiny shower, and most adequately furnished. Even if she had been a fussy girl, which she was not, she would have had a job to find any fault in it. She put away her few things and went along to find out about table reservations, then wandered about the ship. It seemed half empty, which in mid-February was to be expected, but the restaurant, when she went along for dinner, seemed comfortably full. She shared a table with a young married couple and a man of about her own age, on his way out to Guernica where, he informed her, he had something to do with the tourist trade. And when she mentioned, almost apologetically, that she had never heard of that city, he spent the rest of the meal describing it to her, and a host of other, smaller towns besides, and when they adjourned to the bar for their coffee he obligingly found a map and explained exactly where she was going. It seemed natural enough to dance for a little while after that and they parted on excellent terms, with an agreement to meet before breakfast and walk the decks. All the same, it was of the professor Abigail thought as she got ready for bed.

The sun was shining the next morning and although the sea looked cold and the ship was rolling a little, the idea of exercise was inviting. Her companion of the evening before was waiting for her, and they walked briskly, arm-in-arm, pausing every now and then to view the vast, empty sea around them before going down to breakfast. They spent the rest of the morning lounging about on the comfortable promenade deck, reading and talking and playing the fruit machines. Abigail wasn't quite sure if she wasn't wasting the professor's money on them, although he had told her to have anything she wanted; when she won a minor jackpot, her relief was profound.

They went to the cinema after lunch and Abigail watched the film without seeing it because the professor's handsome, remote, ill-tempered face was printed indelibly beneath her eyelids. And the evening, although pleasant, went on for ever. She retired to her cabin as early as she decently could and hardly slept for excitement.

There were quite a number of people at breakfast, for some of the passengers were to spend the day ashore. She ate little, one eye on the clock, and presently, accompanied by the young man in the tourist trade, she walked along the deck for the last time, bade her companion goodbye and went down the gangway, paused briefly in the Customs shed and walked out of the door at its end, the porter with her cases hard on her heels. The professor appeared with such suddenness that she was strongly put in mind of a genie in a bottle. He said briefly, 'Good morning, Abigail,' tipped the porter, took her case, whisked her into the Rolls and got in beside her. 'You had a good journey, I hope?' His voice was cool and its chill swallowed up the warmth of her excitement at seeing him again.

She said pleasantly: 'Yes, thank you—I met some people...'

'I saw him as you left the ship,' his voice was dry. 'You must have been disappointed that the voyage didn't last longer.'

He was in a bad mood; probably he had been driving all night, or had slept badly, so she took care to make her voice sound reasonable.

'I don't wish that at all. He was a nice young man. He's going to marry a Spanish girl in a few weeks, he told me all about her. I expect,' she went on in a matter-of-fact voice, 'it's my lack of looks that makes people confide in me—people always pick plain confidantes, you know.'

She was rewarded by a faint twitch of the corner of his mouth. 'Have you been driving all night?' she wanted to know.

'No, since about four o'clock this morning. We'll go if you're ready.'

An unfair remark. She had been sitting, composed and unfidgeting, for the length of their conversation. She stole a look at his profile; it looked stern and a little bad-tempered and although he was freshly shaved and as immaculate as he always was, his face was grey with fatigue. He had driven himself too hard. If he had a wife…she snapped off the thought before she became too immersed in it, and waited until they had left the quayside behind them and were on the road to Bilbao before she suggested that they should stop for coffee. 'It's twenty odd miles to Baquio, isn't it? Have we time to stop for a little while so that you could tell me a little more about your niece?'

He might have been tired, but he was driving superbly. The road was narrow and the traffic, even so early in the day, was dense. Abigail, gazing out of the window, could see that they were running through shipyards and a muddled mass of factories, modern flats and tumbledown little houses. She was disappointed, but probably it would get better later on. The professor hadn't answered her. Only after he had negotiated a crossing jammed with traffic and sent the Rolls purring ahead once more did he remark, 'A good idea. We'll stop, there's a place in Bilbao which may be open.'

It was hard to see where Bilbao started and the shipyards and factories ceased, but presently the blocks of flats grew larger and more affluent-looking and the shops, although small, looked more interesting. They passed a modern hospital and then a much older one and at last reached the centre of the city.

The main streets were broad and tree-lined with imposing buildings on either side and a good deal of traffic. The professor, who seemed to know his way about, turned the car into a side street and nodded ahead. 'Behind that store,' he said briefly. It looked like Selfridges on a small scale, with gaily dressed windows which she would dearly have loved to look at, but he drove round the block and parked the car at the back and led her to a row of shops on the opposite side. The café they entered was empty, indeed, only just open, but they were greeted with smiles and an unintelligible flow of words which the professor answered without apparent effort.

The coffee, when it came, was dark and rich and a little bitter, and Abigail was intrigued to find that the milk came in the form of a powder in decorative little sachets. She looked up, her face alight with interest and caught him looking at her with an expression which, although she couldn't decide what it meant, caused her to say quickly:

'About your niece, Professor...'

He went on staring at her. 'You understand why I asked you to come?' He spoke quickly, as though the subject was distasteful and he wanted to get it over with. 'I am sorry if I have interfered in any way with your plans, but I cannot take chances with Nina and I can trust you as a nurse.'

'And not as a woman?' Abigail hadn't meant to say that, and she was appalled at the frozen expression on his face.

'That is hardly a relevant question.' His tone implied rebuke. 'Nina is high-spirited and three years old. My sister is awaiting the birth of their second child, that is why I have made this journey; it was quite out of the question that she should travel that distance at such a time. Her husband is attached to the Netherlands Consulate in Bilbao. They have lived there for more than a year now, but Odilia remains very Dutch in her outlook. The idea of allowing Nina to go into any hospital other than the one in which I work is quite abhorrent to her, absurd though this may seem. I have no choice other than to come for Nina myself and bring a nurse with me.' He paused, his voice was suddenly curt. 'That is my only reason for asking you to return, Abigail.'

She said sensibly, 'Yes, of course, Professor, what other reason could there be?' and was pleased to hear that her voice sounded exactly as it always did, which was surprising, because she was engulfed in a wave of disappointment all the more bitter because she had been buoyed up by the false hope that there might be another reason. Despite his abrupt greeting when they had met, she had taken heart from his evident annoyance at seeing her with the tourist agent, but now it was apparent that his annoyance hadn't been for that reason at all, much more likely that he had considered she had been wasting precious minutes of his time while she said goodbye.

She drank the rest of her coffee in silence and said rather defiantly that she was going to powder her nose. She had gone some steps from the table when she realised that she had no idea what to look for. She paused, trying to remember the Spanish for Ladies, but perhaps they didn't... She glanced over her shoulder at the professor, who said gently:

'You should look for flowers on the door, Abigail.'

She returned some five minutes later and he said at once, 'I see that you are big with information of some sort—am I to be told?'

'Well—there's no one else to tell,' began Abigail, 'but I'm not sure if it's quite...'

'My dear good girl, in this day and age? And you forget that I have a sister—a most outspoken woman, I might add. Further, I am completely unshockable.'

'Oh, it's nothing shocking,' said Abigail with endearing forthrightness. 'It's just that it was all so grand—like being on one of those Hollywood film sets.' She watched the corners of his mouth twitch. 'Powder blue velvet walls and little upholstered chairs and gilt wall lamps, and a carpet I got lost in, and I washed my hands in a gilded shell. I don't feel I shall ever get over it!'

The twitch came and went again. 'It sounds incredible and a little vulgar,' said the professor. He added gravely, 'I expect they do a roaring trade during the tourist season.'

Abigail laughed, her ordinary little face transformed, so that it wasn't ordinary at all, but very attractive. Then she became grave again. 'I'm sorry, I'm holding you up, Professor.'

They drove uphill out of Bilbao, and because it was now a

bright, cloudless morning, she was able to see the mountains around them, with little green fields, each with its red-tiled house, shutters closed and rather shabby but delightfully picturesque with red peppers drying in colourful strings from the windows, and occasionally a man working in the fields and once a pair of oxen drawing a plough. She exclaimed at each new sight until she remembered that he had seen it all before and apologised for being tiresome. She turned in her seat and smiled at him, but he didn't reply, nor did he smile. It was as though he wished she weren't there beside him—but she was and, she reminded herself, at his invitation. Perhaps it was the Spanish air or the strength of the coffee which emboldened her to ask:

'Why do you sometimes call me Miss Trent and sometimes Abigail?'

They were approaching a town and he slowed the car's rush. 'I forget.'

She stared around her while she pondered this brief answer. It made no sense, for what had he to forget—but he gave her little time to think about it; they were approaching Munguia, he told her, where there was an interesting church of the Gothic period and the old tower of the Palacio de Abajo, and she obediently gazed in the directions to which he pointed as they passed through the small place, and then, because the silence was so heavy between them, she asked, 'Are we nearly there?'

'Yes. We go to Plenzia next and then take the coast road to Baquio. My sister lives a mile or so beyond the village.'

She sat quietly, not speaking until they reached Plenzia, and although she had promised herself that she wouldn't annoy him with any more comments, she exclaimed with delight as they entered the little town and turned on to the coast road, cut into the towering hills which ran down to the sea.

The road followed the hills bulging into the sea and began to descend. Baquio lay beyond and below them, and even the blocks of new flats along its sandy bay couldn't spoil its beauty. The Rolls tiptoed round a hairpin bend and tore happily down the hill into the village, along its shore and then up the hill on its other side. The road curved presently so that the houses were hidden behind them and only the sweep of the rugged coast was before them. They slowed momentarily while an old man in the flat cap of the Basque country, and carrying a rolled umbrella, trudged past them, urging along a donkey almost hidden under a load of wood.

'He doesn't look strong enough,' said Abigail.

'They live long lives here—hard work and a good climate—they walk a great deal too.'

'I meant the donkey. I'm sorry for it, it should be free in one of those fields.' She sighed. 'I've heard that they aren't very kind...they eat horses and they like bullfights.'

'Are you showing me yet another side to your many-sided nature, Miss Trent? kind Miss Trent, gentle Miss Trent—the rescuer of kittens from gutters and old men from attics, the nurse who tends old ladies and grizzling babies.' He sounded so savage that she was struck to dumbness, and when she forced herself to look at him she could see that his mouth was curved in a sneer. He had made her sound a prig, a do-gooder, and she wasn't, just an ordinary girl, with her living to earn and doing a job she liked. She concentrated on hating him, but that didn't seem to help much, so she tried despising him instead, but her companion snapped, 'Up here,' and turned the car, with inches to spare, through an open gate on to a narrow, well surfaced road, leading, as far as Abigail's apprehensive eyes could see, straight up the side of the mountain, to lose itself in the trees which crowned its summit. She had decided that even the Rolls wouldn't be able to manage it when the professor swung the car round a right-angled bend and continued uphill, but now less steeply, but now she could see the sea again, only to lose it as they turned once more, this time into the trees, to emerge on to a wide sweep of tarmac before a modern and very large bungalow. They had arrived.

The front door stood open and even before they were out of

the car a girl was coming towards them—the professor's sister, quite obviously, for she had his good looks, softened into beauty. She flung herself at him and he suffered her rather tearful embrace for a few moments with commendable calm and then spoke to her in Dutch, and she laughed a little as she turned to Abigail.

'Nurse Trent,' said the professor, 'my sister, Mevrouw de Graaff,' he turned back to her. 'Odilia, you do not need to worry any more, we will take Nina back with us and you will have no need to cry about her.' He patted her shoulder in a brotherly fashion and turned to greet a thickset, fair-haired man coming out of the house towards them.

'Dirk—I didn't expect to see you.' The two men shook hands and the professor went on, 'Nurse Trent, this is my brother-in-law, Dirk de Graaff.'

Abigail shook hands and stood quietly while the professor enquired after his niece. 'Nina? She's here? No worse?'

'She's in bed,' it was his sister who answered him. 'The nursemaid's with her for a minute or two, but she doesn't want anyone else but Dirk or me—it makes it difficult.' She glanced at Abigail. 'I hope she will like you, Nurse.'

Abigail murmured that she hoped so too and smiled reassuringly at Nina's mother because she looked so worried, as they followed her into the bungalow.

It was a roomy dwelling and most elegantly furnished. They crossed the wide hall and entered a room at one side of the bungalow with a wide window overlooking the sea and with a magnificent view of the coastline stretching away into the distance. The nursery, and a very nice one too, thought Abigail. There was a small white bed in one corner and the girl sitting beside it got up as they went in. She said something in Spanish and went away and the small creature in the bed cried 'Mama!' in a whining voice and began to grizzle. Her mother went to sit on the bed and spoke softly to the child, and presently said:

'She would like to know your name. She understands a little English—she speaks Dutch, of course, and Spanish too.'

Abigail looked with something like awe at this three-year-old who had already mastered more than her mother tongue and smiled at the pinched white face on the pillow. The child was ill, that was obvious, and despite her peevish greeting Abigail thought that when she was well again she would be a delightful small girl. She was blonde like her father, with enormous blue eyes. She had a distinct likeness to her uncle too; Abigail loved her on sight because of that.

'I only speak English, I'm afraid, and about a dozen words of Dutch. My name's Abigail.'

She smiled and Nina smiled faintly in return. 'Why?' she demanded.

Abigail thought it wise to ignore this question. Foreseeing language difficulties ahead, she said instead, 'I'm going to look after you for a day or two.'

The small mouth turned down ominously. 'Oom Dominic...'

'He'll be with us.' Abigail had the satisfaction of seeing the mouth right itself and marvelled anew that the child could understand her.

'Speak Dutch,' demanded the moppet, and added please because her mother told her to.

'Oom Dominic...' began Abigail slowly, not in the least sure what she was going to say.

'Is right behind you,' said the professor from the doorway, and passed her as he spoke to swoop down on his niece. It was obvious that they were devoted to each other, for the small face lighted up as Nina gabbled away to him, her two arms clutching him tightly round his neck.

Presently he disentangled himself and sat down on the side of her bed, still talking—explaining, Abigail thought, why he had come. When he had finished he listened patiently while Nina argued shrilly, and then said:

'Nina wants to leave now—this minute. I've told her we must

wait until I have seen the doctor and studied the X-rays—it will give us the chance to pump some fluids into her before we go. Today, I think, from the look of her.'

He went on to give instructions and Abigail said, 'Yes, sir,' then he got up off the bed and went away, presumably to telephone the doctor. When the door had closed behind him, his sister asked, 'Do you always call Dominic sir?'

'Not always. Sometimes I call him Professor, although I suppose while Nina is with us I had better address him as Oom Dominic.'

Odilia smiled. 'And I suppose he calls you Nurse. I'm going to call you Abigail, if I may, and will you call me Odilia? What a pity you can't stay longer, but Dominic says he wants to get Nina to hospital as soon as he can, and he's bound to be right, he always is.' She sighed. 'I've been a dreadful nuisance, haven't I, but the baby will be here in another week and I simply will not let Nina go into a hospital here. Oh, they're very good, but I'm a dyed-in-the-wool Dutchwoman and if she's got to have something done then Dominic is the only one who must do it, and there was no other way; Dirk would have taken Nina to Amsterdam, but who could have gone with him to look after her? The nursemaid's a good girl, but she's not trained and she gets excited, and I'm no use either, I get so upset each time Nina's sick.'

The word had an unfortunate effect upon her small daughter. Abigail caught up a bowl and reached her just in time. She was sponging Nina's face and hands when the professor put his head round the door to speak to his sister and then in English, 'Oh, lord, at it again? No pesetas, I suppose?'

He strolled over to the bed and pulled a hideous face at his niece, who giggled weakly, but when he spoke to Abigail it was in his usual austere fashion. 'Glucose and water, Nurse—as much as you can get into her—getting a bit dehydrated, isn't she?'

He looked at Odilia enquiringly. 'Her things are packed?

She had better travel in her nightie and dressing gown—we'll wrap her in blankets and she can sit on Nurse Trent's lap. We'll want several things with us,' he began to list them and Odilia interrupted him to say, 'I've got most of them. Abigail's going to sit with you?'

'Yes.' He stared across the room to where Abigail was sitting with her small patient, coaxing her to drink.

'I'll send Rosa in,' began Odilia, but he interrupted her. 'Nurse Trent will, I know, be glad to stay here and get to know Nina.' He took his sister's arm. 'Let's find those odds and ends and you can tell me how life's treating you—I must say you look prettier than ever.'

His sister smiled, she looked much happier now he had come. Abigail guessed that she had been in the habit of leaning on him whenever she wanted help.

They went out of the room together and Odilia said as she went:

'We'll have lunch together presently, all of us.'

'Thank you, that would be nice.' Abigail was still busy with the glucose drink and smarting under the professor's manner towards her. She would, she promised herself, say as little as possible to him on the journey back, and that would be of a professional nature.

The doctor came, held a consultation with Dominic and went again. Abigail had been present, because as it was pointed out to her, it would save time if she was told the results of their talk as they went along, so she sat between the two men, listening to the professor speaking Spanish with almost as much ease as he spoke English; it made her feel inferior until he said in English:

'How fortunate that you can't understand Spanish, for mine is so shockingly bad, I wonder Doctor Diaz can understand a word of it and I should be ashamed to speak it before you.'

She thought it was rather nice of him, but the idea of him being ashamed of anything he did was so amusing that she smiled and then straightened her face to gravity because she had discovered that whenever she smiled he seemed to dislike her more.

They were to leave at three o'clock, the professor informed her after Doctor Diaz had gone. They would spend the first night some two hundred and twenty miles away, midway between Biarritz and Limoges, and they would leave early on the following morning again, provided that Nina was well enough, and get as far as possible; if necessary he would drive on to Amsterdam, a matter of seven hundred miles, but only if it was advisable because of Nina. As it was he considered that they should be able to do the journey in two days. 'Indeed,' he went on, 'we must, for I have a number of engagements I cannot miss. I rely upon you, Nurse Trent, to take such good care of Nina that I shall be free to devote my attention entirely to driving, nor do I want any display of nerves, as I intend to drive fast when it is safe to do so.'

'I'm not given to nerves.' Abigail's voice was tart even while she wondered just how fast a Rolls-Royce went when pushed.

She lunched with Odilia and her husband and, of course, the professor, who when he did speak to her at all, engaged in the detached conversation of someone who had met her for the first time and didn't much care if he never saw her again. But Odilia was nice, Abigail liked her and she believed the liking was reciprocated. Abigail went back to her small charge after that and prepared her for the journey, and at the last minute Nina burst into loud sobs, shrieking her intention of staying with her mama in the three languages at her command. It was her uncle who picked her up out of her bed, whispering something or other as he did so, causing the shrieks to turn to an occasional snivel. Her mother, almost in tears herself, demanded, half laughing:

'Dominic, what are you saying—what are you promising, something wildly extravagant?'

'A bicycle—a Dutch bicycle, and I'll come down in the summer and watch her ride it.' He smiled very kindly at her. 'Don't worry, *lieveling,* everything will be all right, she will be safe with us. Abigail is a splendid nurse—I trust her, so can you. I didn't bring her all this way without good reason, you know. I'll telephone you this evening and again tomorrow and as soon as she's well enough I'll have her home with me and Dirk can come up to Amsterdam and fetch her back.'

Odilia smiled then and kissed him, then went over to where Abigail was standing, holding blankets and thermos flasks and all the impedimenta of a long journey. 'I'm so glad it's you,' she said, and kissed Abigail too. 'We shall see each other again. Have a good trip.'

'We will, I'm sure, and I'll take care of Nina for you. Good luck with the baby.'

The two girls smiled at each other and Abigail said goodbye to Dirk, got into the car, and the professor arranged his niece on her lap. When he had tucked the child around with a variety of wraps, he asked:

'Anything else?'

'The bowl and that packet of Kleenex tissues,' Abigail begged him, still practical even though he was so close that his cheek brushed hers. She wasn't sure what the journey was going to be like; perhaps Nina would get worse, perhaps the professor would be bad-tempered for the whole way, she didn't really mind; a thousand miles, or nearly that, her heart sang, as he got in beside her, even if he didn't speak more than a dozen words in those two days, he would be there, beside her. She smiled out of the window at Odilia and held Nina close as the professor waved too, then began a headlong dive down the road towards the gate and the road back.

CHAPTER SEVEN

ABIGAIL'S VAGUE FEARS about the road were justified; it looked a great deal worse too by reason of the angry black clouds racing towards them from the sea. It was barely three o'clock, but the day was already darkening, the road reeled from one bend to the next and the professor drove along it as though it were a motorway with no traffic in sight. Presently the road turned inland, following the river, with its wide, peaceful mouth ringed by a picturesque village before it changed to a turbulent stream tumbling between the rocks below them. 'Guernica,' said the professor briefly. 'We cross the bridge in the centre of the town and turn back to the coast.' A piece of news Abigail took with resignation; probably, she consoled herself, the coast road wasn't half as bad as the roads through the mountains crowding in on them as they approached the town—if there were any roads. They hadn't gone very far when the rain started, a fierce, heavy downpour which washed away any views there might have been. They passed through several villages, dismal in the wetness and with not a soul to be seen in their single streets, and streaked up towards the mountains Abigail sensed were in front of them.

'Lovely scenery here on a fine day,' observed her companion laconically. 'Is Nina all right?'

'Dozing,' said Abigail, 'worn out with excitement, I fancy. You know this road, Professor?'

'Yes—it's a good one—rather a lot of bends, but we're not likely to meet much traffic in this weather.'

He sent the Rolls swooping round a curve at the top of a small ravine running down to the sea on their left. 'We reach Lequeito shortly. There is a thirteenth-century basilica there—it is also famous for the tuna fishing championships each summer.'

He offered her these titbits of information rather impatiently, as though he found it a nuisance to say anything at all and her answer was a little cool in consequence.

'You have no need to talk if you don't wish to. I can read it up in a guide book when I get back,' and was disconcerted by his low laugh. He didn't bother to answer her, though.

He was driving very fast and, she suspected, in an ill-humour despite the laugh when, in response to Nina's urgent and plaintive whisper, Abigail asked him to stop. He shot her a baleful glance and she met it firmly.

'It is awkward, isn't it? but Nina's the one to consider, I imagine. Perhaps there's somewhere where we could pull in...?'

She said it with more hope than certainty, for it wasn't that sort of a road; it snaked in breathtaking curves, mountains on one side, plunging ravines tumbling down to the sea on the other. Nevertheless the professor slid to a stop between one bend and the next. He got out, saying, 'Make it as quick as you can,' as he made for the side of the road in the pouring rain, adding as an afterthought, 'Do you need any help?'

'No, thank you. Give us three minutes.' She was already busy unwrapping Nina.

He gave them five, which, in view of the weather, was generous of him.

'You're very wet.' Abigail's soft voice sounded almost motherly as he got in beside her again. She went pink under the ferocity of his look.

'A singularly apt remark,' he commented. His voice had a bite in it, but as his glance fell upon Nina his face softened and Abigail felt a pang of envy that he would never look at her like that.

'She's all right?'

'Yes, she was a little sick as well, but she's had a drink. I'll cuddle her up and perhaps she'll go to sleep again.'

'Yes—you're all right until we can find somewhere where we can get tea?'

'Yes, thanks.' She spoke cheerfully and smiled at him, but all she got was a frowning glance as he started the car.

They came to an hotel on the side of the road, perched rather uneasily on the side of the cliffs above the sea, and although it looked deserted there was a light burning dimly from somewhere inside, despite its closed shutters.

'This will do,' said the professor, and drew up before its door. 'I'll carry Nina inside, you follow me in.'

She did so, pausing to catch a glimpse of the bay directly below them, fringed with rocks and the grey sea boiling past them to reach the sand. Inside she found herself in a small dark room, half café, half bar, rather smoky and smelling of the day's meal. But it was pleasant enough, with little tables scattered around, covered with red and white checked cloths. She sat down and took Nina into her arms while the professor went over to the bar. He came back after a minute.

'There's only coffee—do you mind?'

'Not a bit,' she answered readily, and longed for tea.

'What about Nina?'

'I've got milk and water for her. I brought the thermos with me.'

'Sensible girl!'

They drank their coffee in almost total silence; it was warm in the room and after a little while one didn't notice the smell of food.

Refreshed and warmed, they set off again; the road seemed even worse than before; now and again the clouds would lift just long enough for Abigail to glimpse the spectacular scenery on either side of them, but the rain still fell steadily, forcing the professor to slow his pace. He slowed even more as they went through Deva's narrow streets, with its harbour full of fishing boats and the sea breaking against the grim, grey cliffs. The road climbed out of the little town and wound its way towards San Sebastian, the sea still in view and the foothills of the Pyrenees ahead of them. Only in Zarauz did they leave the sea briefly as they passed through the town's main street, lined with a mixture of picturesque old houses, ornate villas and modern hotels. The professor hadn't spoken for a long time, and although Nina was awake she was content to lie quietly in Abigail's arms. She looked pale and listless, and Abigail, thinking of the long journey ahead of them, hoped that she would get no worse. She offered the child a drink, speaking in her clumsy Dutch, and Nina rewarded her with a weak giggle. 'Do you want me to stop?' The professor spoke without taking his eyes off the road, and when she answered that no, she thought she could manage, he didn't speak again, not until they reached San Sebastian, where, he told her, he would stop for a few minutes. 'For I don't intend to stop again until we reach Marmande,' he advised her, 'and that's just over a hundred miles away.'

It was a bare ten minutes before they were on their way again. As Abigail settled herself in the car once more and put out her arms to take Nina, the professor gave her a long searching glance, as though he had expected her to say something, and when she didn't he turned away and got into his own seat. As he started the car he said, 'There's chocolate in the pocket beside you—I imagine you must be getting hungry.'

'I'm perfectly all right, thank you, and so will Nina be until we reach Marmande,' her eyes searched around her and she nodded to herself, 'and if she's not, we've everything we need within reach. I rather think she'll go to sleep for a while, sir.'

He muttered a reply which she scarcely heard, but she did hear him when he said suddenly: 'Be good enough not to address me as sir at every other breath, Abigail,' and she spent the next five minutes or so wondering what she should call him. All in all, Oom Dominic seemed both suitable and blameless.

They crossed into France with hardly a pause, and Abigail, who had been considering that they had been travelling quite fast, discovered how wrong she was. The road was a good one, and the Rolls, as though aware that speed was essential, tore, silent and powerful, along it, with the professor, just as silent, at the wheel. And when Nina piped up that she felt sick Abigail said at once, 'Don't slacken speed, we're perfectly able to manage.' And manage she did.

They reached Marmande just after seven o'clock, to Abigail's relief, for Nina had been awake for the last hour of the journey, lying silent—too silent for a moppet of three. The professor had barely opened his lips and she, for her part, was heartily sick of her own thoughts, for they had been far from happy. From the comfort of the big car she had looked ahead into a future which, in its very uncertainty, was unsatisfactory. It was a good thing they had arrived, she told herself bracingly, for now she would have something to do other than think.

The hotel wasn't a large one; it looked old and very clean, though, and the foyer was comfortably furnished. Abigail sat down once more and took Nina from the professor and listened to him talking to the reception clerk. Her French was quite good; the boarding school had taken care of that. It amused her to hear the professor, in glacial, perfect French, refusing a double room and explaining that she was the nurse, that the child was his niece and that it was necessary for them to have two rooms, each with a bathroom. The clerk smiled and shrugged and beckoned the porter, apologising as he did so. On their way upstairs, Abigail, just behind the professor with Nina in his arms, said soberly, 'It would have been better if I had worn uniform, you know—I never thought…'

'You have a knowledge of French?'

'Quite a good one, as it happens.' She heard the tartness of her voice and was disconcerted by his chuckle.

The room she was shown into was well furnished and warm and the bathroom was more than adequate. She got Nina ready for bed, gave her a drink she didn't want, took her temperature, which was quite high, and tucked her up for the night. A few minutes later the professor tapped on the door to spend ten minutes with his small niece, studying her carefully as he laughed and joked with her. Presently, he asked Abigail: 'You're comfortable?'

'Yes, thank you. Perhaps I might have something here on a tray…'

'Certainly not. I have arranged for the chambermaid, a sensible woman, to sit with Nina while we have dinner. You will have it with me downstairs.'

'An invitation or an order?' she wanted to know quietly, and saw his unwilling smile.

'An invitation.'

'On the assumption that any company is better than none?'

The smile had gone; perhaps she had imagined it. 'If you wish, Nurse Trent.' He turned away. 'I'll be back to see Nina in half an hour, I will bring the maid with me.'

He was as good as his word. He walked in with a middle-aged woman with a kind, sensible face, and such was the strength of his niece's affection for him that she closed her eyes and promised to go to sleep at once when he bade her to do so.

They dined in an empty restaurant, which on a summer's evening must have been a very pleasant place. Abigail was hungry. She chose the soup, which the waiter assured her had been made in the hotel's kitchen—the asparagus tips and herbs, thickened with tapioca and piping hot, followed by cutlets with an orange sauce, and while the professor contented himself with cheese she allowed herself to be tempted by the little something the chef had whipped up for her; a delicious concoction of Chantilly cream, fruit, nuts and liqueur brandy, which, combined with the dry white wine the professor had chosen, had the effect of combining with the table lamps to give everything around her a rosy hue. Not that the professor made much effort to entertain her; he talked, it was true, at great length and with great attention to detail, of the local customs, and when he had exhausted those, he embarked on the customs of the Basque country. Abigail, listening politely, was strongly put in mind of her student days, when with rows of other nurses she had sat listening to lectures delivered by the various honoraries of the hospital. The professor's manner was exactly similar.

They had their coffee at the table and when they had finished she suggested that she should return upstairs and went scarlet in the face when he asked, 'Dear me, was I so dull?'

'Of course not,' she said hastily, 'I enjoyed it very much, but I don't like to leave Nina too long.' She frowned. 'She's...it will be a good thing when she's safely in hospital.'

His smile was mocking, and the scarlet, which had just faded, flamed anew. 'I didn't mean—that is...' She paused and added carefully, 'She's in safe hands with you, but we're an awful long way from home.'

'You think that she will get worse?'

'I don't know—it's just an idea, a feeling...' She looked at him helplessly. How could she explain the premonitions all nurses had from time to time? As it turned out there was no need for her to explain, for the waiter came hurrying over to their table to ask if they would go upstairs immediately.

Nina was being sick again. The maid had coped without worrying overmuch to begin with, but the child seemed unable to stop. The professor thanked her calmly, tipped her with discretion and sent her away, then went over to the bed where Abigail was doing all the necessary things which had to be done with a complete absence of fuss, and even though the child couldn't have understood the half of what she was saying, her gentle, placid talk and unhurried movements, which nevertheless got things done, calmed the child, so that she stopped crying and listened to what her uncle was telling her. He made it sound amusing; he fetched his case from his room, took off his jacket, and made preparations for putting up a saline infusion. He did it without haste, talking all the time, so that presently Nina laughed a little and laughed a little more when Abigail, swathed in a towel to protect her blue dress, joined in the conversation in her own halting Dutch, not minding at all when the little girl giggled at her comic way of pronouncing the words. The drip was up and running with a minimum of fuss, for the professor had shamelessly used all his powers of persuasion upon his small niece as well as promising her a bell to go on the bicycle and a little gold chain with a pearl on the end of it for her birthday, as well as ice-cream every day as soon as she could eat again. 'And heaven alone knows what your mother will say to me when she's told,' he observed in English.

'She won't care a fig,' Abigail assured him as she cleared away his mess and tidied things away in his case. 'She'll be so glad to have Nina well and home again.' She shut the case on an unconscious sigh. 'How fast is this to run in? There's to be a second vacolitre, isn't there?'

He nodded. 'If she has a good night's sleep, I think we had better press on tomorrow.' He handed her a bottle. 'Largactil syrup. Give her a dose, will you?'

Abigail did as she was bid, tidied the room, pulled up a chair to the side of the bed and was on the point of sitting in it when his hand hauled her to her feet again.

'No,' he said firmly, 'go and have your bath and get into bed—use my room. I'll call you about three, have a bath myself and an hour or two's sleep; that way we'll both be rested. I'll get them to send breakfast up here at eight o'clock and if everything's all right we'll get away soon after. It rather depends on Nina.'

'But you've got to drive—I shall be quite comfortable here, truly—I can always doze in the car tomorrow.'

'Why do women argue?' he wanted to know pleasantly. 'Do as you're told, Nurse Trent.' He smiled suddenly. 'Please.'

There was no further use in argument. She collected her night things and went away to the bathroom, then to his room and got into bed; she was asleep immediately.

She wakened at once to the touch of his hand on her shoulder, and sat up instantly. 'Nina's all right?' she wanted to know.

'Hasn't stirred,' was his reassuring answer. 'I've just changed the drip—it should be through by seven. Take it down if I'm not about.'

He went away leaving her to scramble into her dressing gown and slippers and pad back to her own room. A minute later he had wished her good night and disappeared.

The rest of the night passed uneventfully. Nina hardly moved, even when the drip had run through and Abigail took the needle out of the small thin arm and covered the tiny puncture with strapping, and when she opened her eyes, frowning a little, Abigail said:

'It's all right, darling, you're much better, aren't you?' and the moppet nodded and, obedient to Abigail's suggestion that she should go to sleep again, closed her eyes.

The professor came in a few minutes later, with his hair ruffled and an unshaven chin, but his eyes were as calm and untroubled as a child who had slept the night long. He nodded his satisfaction, patted Abigail on the shoulder, said 'Good girl' and then: 'How about some tea—I'm dying of thirst.'

Abigail rang the bell and waited to see what would happen. The maid who had looked after Nina came in answer to it, smiled a good morning and promised tea within five minutes.

The child slept peacefully while they drank it, sitting side by side on the other bed with the tray between them. Abigail poured second cups and enquired of the professor if he had slept well. 'You must have been tired,' she added.

His blue eyes swept lazily over her and she became aware that her hair was hanging in a mousy curtain around her shoulders, and her dressing gown, warm as it was, was hardly glamorous. To cover her discomfiture she asked, 'Do you intend to leave directly after breakfast, Professor?'

'Yes, as things are I think perhaps we should try and reach Amsterdam as quickly as possible. It's roughly six hundred and seventy miles.'

She thought. 'About fourteen hours' driving.'

He laughed. 'Less, with luck. There are some splendid stretches of road where I can give the car her head.'

'A hundred miles an hour?'

She wasn't looking at him, so she missed the engaging twinkle in his eyes.

'Probably more—are you nervous?'

'Not in the least.'

'Am I to take that as a compliment?'

'As you wish,' she forced her voice to casualness. 'Which of us shall dress first?'

'Would you like to? I imagine there isn't much to do for Nina, but if you will, perhaps you can do whatever needs doing before breakfast. She might have some tea—no milk.'

When Abigail got back to the bedroom, very neat as to hair and dress, and with her face nicely made up, it was to find the professor stretched out on the second bed with his eyes closed. She stood looking down at him, studying every line of his handsome face. He looked more approachable with a bristly chin, she considered, and lonely. He opened his eyes with a suddenness which took her completely by surprise and asked:

'Why do you look at me like that?'

'Like what?' She took a step backwards, and he got off the bed and stretched hugely, but all he said was: 'You have a very expressive face, Abigail, did you know?'

At least the rain had stopped. They got off to a good start soon after eight o'clock with a wide-awake Nina on Abigail's lap. For the time being at least she seemed a great deal better, a fact amply demonstrated by her chatter, which for the first hour at least was ceaseless. They stopped briefly at Limoges, having covered over a hundred and thirty miles in two hours. Refreshed by coffee and a glucose drink for Nina, they took to the road again, at first running through high country. But this didn't last long. Once more on level ground, the professor urged the Rolls forward, and they reached Châteauroux in time for a hasty lunch, more glucose for Nina, who had by now become silent and rather sleepy, and tore on towards Orleans and Paris.

South of Paris the professor broke the long silence to say, 'We'll stop for tea, and get through Paris before dark. What do you think about going straight on?'

She was surprised that he should ask her. He had seemed remote the entire morning; when he had spoken, he had been civil and that was all.

'It depends entirely on how tired you are. There's a great distance to go, isn't there? More than three hundred miles, and you've already driven more than that.'

'I'm thinking of Nina,' he reminded her coldly, and she saw that he wanted—probably intended—to drive through the night. She looked at the child on her lap, awake once more and looking decidedly sickly. 'Let's go on—you intended to anyway, didn't you?'

'Discerning of you—but you are the child's nurse—I needed your opinion.'

They stopped shortly after that at a roadside hotel and Abigail tried not to look as if she had understood when the waiter referred to her as the professor's wife, but her faint astonishment at his not denying it betrayed her. He said shortly: 'If you have no objection, I'm sure that I have not—it is a waste of time to correct such a ridiculous mistake.'

Several telling replies to this piece of arrogance bubbled upon Abigail's lips. She longed to utter them, but suppressed her feelings, outraged though they were, sternly; now was not the time nor the place to have words with the professor.

It took some time to get through Paris even though the professor knew the way. It was obvious to her that her companion was concentrating on his driving to the exclusion of all else. She thanked heaven that Nina was still quiet; the child was running a temperature again; she could feel the heat of the little body through the blankets and Nina's small face had become even paler. They still had three hundred miles to drive, a long way still, but there was a motorway into Belgium; presumably the professor would make good time once he got on to it. She was perfectly right. He hadn't looked at Nina for some time and she had said nothing to him, but he seemed to sense that she was uneasy about her, for he sent the car tearing along at a great speed, and yet, thought Abigail, looking at him stealthily, he seemed quite relaxed; his hands rested lightly on the wheel; he wasn't frowning. Without looking at her, he said, 'Not long now, Abigail.'

An hour and a half later, going through Bapaume, he asked her how Nina was.

'Dozing, but her pulse is up. She's got a temp. too.'

'Roughly two hundred miles to go—I'm going via Antwerp and on to Tilberg and Utrecht.'

A name which sounded reassuringly Dutch in Abigail's ears, it made home seem very near.

They had travelled quite some distance before he spoke again. 'Can you last out until we reach Amsterdam?'

'Easily.' Her voice was steady; even at the speed they were travelling at, the journey seemed endless and she was worried about Nina. Her relief when later, he said briefly, 'Holland,' was so great she could have cried.

'How is she?' he wanted to know.

'Asleep. I think when she wakes she'll probably be sick again.'

To her surprise he laughed, a normal, relaxed sound with no

sound of tiredness in it. 'My dear Abigail, what a sensible girl you are! I should like to have you with me in a tight corner—although this one's tight enough—I can't think of any girl of my acquaintance who wouldn't have been in tears or hysterics long ago. Aren't you tired?'

'Yes,' said Abigail, smarting under his good opinion. Who wanted to be called sensible? That was twice in twenty-four hours! 'Aren't you?'

'Yes, but it's worth it.'

They lapsed into silence again until it was broken by the professor's forceful opinion of the rain which began to beat against the windscreen. After a little while he asked, 'Are you prepared for Nina; in case she's sick?'

'Yes.' Her answer was brief because she sensed that he didn't want to talk. They were through Utrecht, on the motorway and only a few miles from Amsterdam, when Nina woke up and did exactly as they had expected, and in the ensuing minutes which followed, Abigail had no time to feel relief as they slid through Amsterdam's lighted streets and at last stopped before the hospital entrance. It was almost midnight.

The professor wasted no time but carried his small niece into the hospital and Abigail, left on her own, got out too, much more slowly because she was cramped and stiff, and now that they had arrived, deathly tired.

The entrance hall was empty, although she could see the night porter in his small office, but he had his back to her, telephoning; she decided to wait. She had no idea where she should be or what the professor wanted of her. Nina would go to the children's ward, but there would be a nurse on duty there.

It was quiet in the hall, the night sounds of hospital reached her ears faintly, but she was so familiar with them that she hardly heeded the far-off rustles and thumps and door shuttings and clanging of metal as some nurse cleared a trolley. Presently she peered through the porter's lodge window again; he had disappeared altogether now—there was a small inner room, so probably he had retired to eat his meal. She felt shy about disturbing him; besides, her tired brain felt unable to cope with asking questions in Dutch. The professor wouldn't be very long; he would have to go home and go to bed, he needed rest before he operated upon Nina, and the child needed a night's sleep in a proper bed too. Somewhere close by a clock chimed twelve and she went to the door and stood looking at the Rolls, still majestic despite its deplorably dusty condition. It was a pity her case was in the boot and that the boot was locked, otherwise she could have taken it and been in bed by now, although that wouldn't have been very polite, she supposed.

She shivered and went back inside and walked round once more. 'If ever I'm rich,' she said to herself as she walked, 'I shall give a bench—two benches, to this place. There must be a waiting room.' But she couldn't see one, only corridors, disappearing into gloom on either side. She hadn't been in this part of the hospital before, only to pass through it on her way in or out when she had been working there. She yawned widely and sat down on the floor, her back to the wall. It was a dark corner and she was almost hidden. She closed her eyes.

And opened them again almost immediately, because the professor was bellowing her name in a furious voice, which to her mind was far too loud for that time of night in a hospital, even though he was an important surgeon. She called hastily. 'I'm here, in this corner,' and before she could get up he was towering over her.

'Good God, girl, what in the hell are you lying there for?'

He was in a bad temper; he wasn't his usual cool, bland self at all, his voice was almost a snarl. He bent down and plucked her to her feet, keeping his hands on her shoulders, and she had a strong feeling that he would have liked to have shaken her. Before he could do so she spoke, her voice low and reasonable.

'I wasn't sure what you wanted me to do and I'm tired. If I could have my case I'll go over to the Home. How's Nina?'

The hands lost their ferocious grip and became gentle. 'Nina's asleep. Henk's with her, I'm too tired to be of much use. My poor girl, what a thoughtless brute you must think me!'

She looked up into his grey weary face. He looked every day of his age and a year or two besides, but she loved him a little more because of it. She would have liked to have told him what she did think of him, but that was something she would have to keep a secret, probably for ever and ever.

'No,' she said gently, 'I don't think anything of the sort. It's Nina who matters, and I'm perfectly all right. If I could just have my case—you could get home to bed.'

'Didn't I tell you? You're coming back to my house for the night. I shall want you on duty tomorrow morning at eight—you can move into the Home during the day.'

'But I can't—it's past midnight...'

'Don't tell me the conventions worry you,' he paused, 'although I daresay they do; you're that kind of girl.'

'No,' she snapped, very ruffled, 'I'm not in the least worried. Why should I be—even if you expected it? I was thinking of someone having to get a bed ready at this hour of night.'

'My dear good girl, Bollinger and Mevrouw Boot will have prepared a room. I told them I expected to be back at some ungodly hour.'

There seemed nothing more to say, he took her arm and they went out to the car again, and in five minutes had arrived outside his house on the *gracht*. Bollinger and Mevrouw Boot were still up. Bolly had the door open before the professor could get his key out and Abigail, quite forgetting him, flung herself at the old man.

'Oh, Bolly dear, how lovely to see you!' she cried, and hugged him fiercely before saying good evening to the housekeeper, who smiled and nodded and said a great deal, none of which made any sense to Abigail at all.

'A bath and bed, and Mevrouw Boot will bring up your supper,' ordered the professor, and when she would have protested, said:

'Please do as I say, Abigail. I want you on your toes tomorrow morning. We leave the house at a quarter to eight.'

Bolly had gone to get their cases, Mevrouw Boot was on the stairs, on her way to run a bath. Abigail said meekly: 'Very well. Good night. I hope you sleep well, you must be very tired.'

'Not so tired that I cannot find the time to thank you for your share in this whole business.' He stared at her from under frowning brows. 'You didn't complain once; you must have wanted to.'

A dimple appeared in her cheek. 'Oh, a dozen times.' She turned away as Bollinger reappeared with the cases, and started up the stairs after him. As her foot was on the first tread the professor said: 'Abigail,' and she turned round again. Bolly turned round too and watched from the top of the stairs. The professor had followed her across the hall; she turned round into his arms, and they held her with a gentleness she had never imagined as he bent to kiss her.

Abigail ran upstairs without a word or a backward glance and tried not to see Bollinger's delighted smirk. She refused to think about it while she undressed and had her bath and got her uniform ready for the morning, and then, warm in the little canopied bed, ate the delicious supper Mevrouw Boot brought her. She looked about her room as she ate. Not very large, but furnished with excellent taste with dainty Regency furniture as well as an ultra-comfortable easy chair and a soft carpet underfoot, it was exactly the kind of room she would have chosen for herself. She pushed the bedtable away and lay back on the pillows, drowsily contemplating the flower painting over the fireplace. The housekeeper would be back for the tray presently and she must stay awake and thank her. She closed her eyes and went to sleep even as she thought it.

She was called at seven and told that breakfast would be in exactly half an hour, and with five minutes to spare she went down the staircase, very trim and crisp in her uniform, her starched cap perched on her bun of hair, her packed case in her hand. Half way down the stairs she remembered that she had no idea where to go. There were several doors—she knew where the little sitting room was and she knew the great drawing room too, but there were other doors, all shut. One of these was flung open as she stood hesitating, and the professor said, 'In here, Nurse Trent. Good morning.'

He had already been at the table, with papers, letters and an open notebook before him. There was some coffee, half drunk, and a slice of toast half eaten. She sat down opposite him and gave him a wary greeting, and he lifted his eyes to hers briefly and asked her how she had slept.

He looked rested himself, she saw that at once, and as bland and cool as ever he had been. Abigail sighed and he said at once, 'Oh, would you rather have tea—I'll ring...'

'I like coffee, thank you.' She poured herself a cup and took a slice of toast. 'I see that you have slept well too, Professor,' and some small imp of mischief prompted her to add, 'Things that happened yesterday seem so different after a good night's rest, don't they?'

He put down the letter he was reading and stared at her with faint suspicion. 'And just what does that mean?' he wanted to know.

'Why, nothing—would you pass me the sugar? I expect you're one of those people who prefer not to talk at breakfast, I don't mind in the least if you want to go on with your letters.' She smiled kindly at him and helped herself to toast and marmalade, and although she knew that he was staring at her, she didn't look up; after a moment he picked up his letters again.

In the car, driving to the hospital, he told her:

'I telephoned Odilia last night—she asked me to thank you for taking such care of Nina. She sent her love too and hopes that she will see you again. She hopes too that you will find time to write to her.'

'Of course I will. She'll want to hear about Nina—all the little things, you know,' she explained, 'that mothers worry about.'

Nina was awake and quiet after a restful night—she had a

little room to herself for the time being, but later, when she had recovered from the operation she was to have in an hour's time, she would be able to go into the ward with the other children. She kissed her uncle with childish fervour and kissed Abigail too, and presently the professor went away and Abigail busied herself getting the little girl ready for the theatre. She was to go with her, she had been told, and afterwards nurse her on day duty until she was fit to leave hospital. Zuster Ritsma had told her too that there was a room ready for her in the Nurses' Home, and would she mind taking her off-day each afternoon so that the day shift could cover her. Abigail, still thinking about the professor, said that she didn't mind in the least, and went off to X-ray with her little patient, so that her uncle could have a last-minute check of the three pesetas.

The operation was a complete success. The professor, with no difficulty at all, removed the coins through the smallest of incisions which would leave only the faintest of scars, and when the wound had been clipped, peered down his little niece's gullet with his gastroscope to make sure that nothing had been left behind, a state of affairs confirmed by the portable X-ray machine, trundled into the theatre before Nina was lifted on to the trolley ready to take her back to her bed. Abigail had stood by the anaesthetist during the operation, doing what was asked of her quickly and competently, her mind deliberately closed to any thought other than those connected with the job on hand, and back in the small hospital room once more, with Nina in bed, there was plenty for her to do and no time to think of her own affairs.

She had regulated the drip, taken Nina's pulse and charted it, inspected the tiny wound and written up the chart by the time the professor came in. He had Henk with him, and that young man, who had had no chance to speak to her that morning, said, 'Hullo, Abigail, nice to see you again. We must get together...' and Abigail murmured something, conscious of the professor's eyes upon her and wishing Henk wasn't quite so pleased to see her. But when the two men had gone she brightened a little, cheered by the thought that a little competition was supposed to be a good thing, and then chided herself for being a fanciful fool; the professor didn't care anything at all for her; she was a useful nurse, probably he knew how she felt about him and took advantage of it. It had been stupid of her to come running the moment he called...and as for his kisses, there were a dozen good reasons why a man kissed a girl, and none of them necessarily because he loved her.

She was kept busy for the rest of the morning, for Nina, once she was conscious, was rather cross and inclined to cry as well. Abigail, watching her drop off to sleep after she had given her an injection, was glad to go off duty for a few hours.

She had the same room in the Home as she had had previously. She unpacked her case, changed rapidly into her outdoor clothes and hurried through the well-remembered streets to Mrs Macklin's house. It would be nice to see that lady again; they would have time for a chat and a cup of tea before she was due back on duty. She stopped at the baker's shop and bought some cakes before turning into the peace and quiet of the Begijnhof.

Mrs Macklin received her with rapturous surprise. 'My dear,' she exclaimed as Abigail took off her coat, 'I knew you would be back, but I didn't expect you as soon as this—what has happened?'

Abigail told her while they had tea, toasting themselves round the little stove and drinking cup after cup of the strong brew Mrs Macklin liked.

'Dear Dominic,' she declared when Abigail had finished her tale, 'how like him to go tearing off for hundreds of miles to help someone. He adores Nina, of course, you'll have seen that for yourself, my dear, and he's devoted to Odilia—she's fifteen years younger than he is, you know, and they've always been very close. He missed her very much when Dirk was appointed to Bilbao—Dirk's a good man too, did you meet him?'

'Yes—I liked him too, and I thought Odilia was charming.'

'You say Dirk's coming up to fetch Nina?'

'Yes, I think so, though I think it all depends on the baby—when it arrives. Nina won't take long to get over this.'

'No. I suppose Dominic will take her back with him to his house when she can be moved, until her father can come for her. He'll need someone to look after her, though.' She gave Abigail a shrewd look and Abigail, aware of what her companion was thinking, said nothing. It wasn't very likely that the professor would ask her to go back to his house with Nina; a couple of weeks and she would be on her way back to England.

Nina was still sleeping when she got back and there was little to do but sit by the bed getting up from time to time to do the small tasks necessary for the little girl's treatment. The professor had come in again just after she had got back and gone again, well satisfied with his small relative's progress. He had hardly spoken to Abigail beyond leaving her fresh instructions and asking her to tell the night nurse that he would come again about ten o'clock. He scarcely looked at her as he bade her a quiet good night.

Nina recovered rapidly; long before she was able to eat them, she was demanding impossible and unsuitable meals of sausages and chips, pea soup and *pofferjes,* delicious, indigestible fried dough balls. Abigail, plying her with suitably milky foods, heaved a sigh of relief when ice-cream, often demanded, was allowed.

Nina was getting up each day now, sitting in a chair, swathed in blankets and wearing the new dressing-gown her uncle had bought her. It was pale pink and frilly and quilted and there were slippers to match. She was a pretty child and as beguiling as most small girls of that age, it was no wonder that he was fond of her. In a few more days she would be able to play with the children in the ward; the only reason she didn't do so now was because she might be tempted to eat the sweets and cakes their mothers brought in for them. And during these days, the professor came and went, saying little to Abigail that wasn't to do with her work until one evening when he walked in just before the children's bedtime, to find Abigail, with Nina and several other children from the ward.

Nina was curled up on Abigail's lap, the other children lay about her feet, rolled up or stretched out according to their several whims, each of them had a bulging cheek as they sucked on a bedtime sweet. Abigail was singing to them; she had a voice like a little girl's, rather high and breathy and sometimes off key. She was singing them nursery rhymes and children's songs which she had almost forgotten so that she had to sing da-de-da from time to time, but as none of them understood a word she was singing anyway, it really didn't matter. She was half way through 'Cry Baby Bunting' for the second time when Nina lifted her head from her shoulder and cried: 'Oom Dominic!'

Abigail stopped singing, as though the thread of her voice had been cut by the professor's scissors. He advanced into the centre of the small room, while the children, quite prepared to accept him as their uncle too, all began to talk at once. It was strange, thought Abigail, watching him, how they saw through his austere look and took no notice of his frown at all; he waved to them now and pulled a hideous face so that they roared with laughter as he came to a halt before her and bent to kiss his niece.

'I liked the one about the king in his counting house,' he remarked.

She had sung that one quite five minutes previously. 'Have you been here all that while?' she wanted to know. 'I would have stopped...'

'Yes, I thought you would have done.'

She said miserably, 'I wish you hadn't—I can't sing.'

'No, but it sounded charming, all the same.'

He picked Nina up and enquired of her how she was and left Abigail to meditate on sounding charming even when one sang habitually out of tune. Just then Zuster Ritsma came in and he went away with her to look at a sick child, leaving Abigail to shoo the children back into the ward and Nina into her bed.

It was two mornings later that he told Nina that she would be going home with him the next day. Abigail was making the bed, and Nina, sprawled on the floor, was playing with a doll, which she threw down to rush at her uncle and embrace his knees, shouting rapturously.

'Noisy little brat,' said her uncle fondly. 'You will accompany her, if you please, Abigail. Mevrouw Boot and Bollinger have enough to do without having this imp to look after—besides, they're a little elderly.'

Abigail folded a blanket with precise, neat movements. 'For how long, sir?'

'I can't tell you that. Why do you want to know? Have you another case?'

'No. I was just curious. Of course I'll come.'

'Odilia had a son last night, so as soon as she is up and about, Dirk will come and fetch Nina.'

Abigail smiled widely. 'Oh, I am glad, how lovely for them—Odilia is quite well?'

'Yes, she telephoned me an hour after he was born. Dirk is naturally delighted.'

'I can well imagine it. I suppose men want sons...' She could have bitten out her tongue when she saw the bleakness of his face. He turned away and when he spoke again his voice was without expression. 'I'll see the Directice about you leaving tomorrow, Nurse Trent—Zuster Ritsma will give you all the details.'

He walked away without another word.

She didn't pretend to herself that she hadn't hoped to go with Nina when the little girl left the hospital; she allowed herself to feel happy about it, but only in moderation, for the professor hadn't shown himself particularly pleased to have her. She supposed that she would stay ten days at the most, and then Nina would go back to Spain and she would be back in London again, looking for another case. Professor de Wit, when she had gone to see him one afternoon, had urged her to remain in Amsterdam. 'For,' he had said, 'Dominic must have any number of patients who require a nurse, you could be employed for months to come,' and she had taken heart from his words, hoping each time that she saw the professor that he might suggest this, but he never had done so. She packed her case with the few clothes she had with her and which she now heartily hated, and prepared to leave the hospital. There was another thing—she had received no salary, and because the professor had been so irritable when she had offered to pay back the surplus from her travelling expenses, she hesitated to say anything about it now. Perhaps he intended to pay her when she left Amsterdam. In the meantime, she was running low again, and Bolly had had nothing for some weeks.

They left after lunch the next day, with a jubilant Nina, her clips out, carried through the hospital in the professor's arms, and when he set her down in the entrance hall and she began to jig around with excitement, he exclaimed, laughing:

'No one would believe that I carved you open such a short time ago,' to which sally she screamed with laughter and asked to be told, for the hundredth time, how exactly he had done it.

He was called away on some urgent business or other soon after that, and they went home with Jan in a Mercedes she hadn't seen before, to be welcomed by Mevrouw Boot and Bollinger, but of the professor there was no sign for the rest of the afternoon.

CHAPTER EIGHT

SHE WAS TAKEN to the room she had had before and Nina had the room next to it; a room as charming as Abigail's and thoughtfully provided with a miniature chair to accommodate Nina's smallness, and a table to go with it. It took most of the afternoon to arrange her toys and dolls in exactly the positions she wished and by the time she had had her tea she was tired. Abigail carried her off to her room with the promise of a bedtime story if she was a good girl, then undressed the small creature and bathed her with a good deal of giggling and chatter, for they understood each other very well by now, even though they mostly spoke different languages. She was in bed, with a bowl of bread and milk, nicely flavoured with sugar and cinnamon, by way of supper, and Abigail sitting on the bed beside her, telling her, in English of course, all about the old woman who lived in a shoe, by seven o'clock. The tale took a long time to tell, because almost every word had to be explained, which meant searching for it in Abigail's dictionary. They were hugging each other with merriment over Abigail's peculiar way of pronouncing even the simplest Dutch word, when the door opened and the professor came in.

He said pleasantly enough, 'Good evening, Nurse Trent, I see that you have settled in,' and went to bend over his niece, to be hugged and kissed and chatted to while Abigail got up and went to the pillow cupboard against one wall and busied herself putting away Nina's clothes.

It was to be a 'Nurse Trent' evening, she supposed a little sourly. Come to that, it would probably be no evening at all; she hadn't the least idea if she was to take her meals with him or have them served alone, or if she was to have them with Bolly and Mevrouw Boot. She decided not, remembering how annoyed he had been when she had used the tradesmen's entrance. She shut the cupboard door in time to hear him say:

'I dine at seven, Abigail. I hope you will keep me company.'

She said thank you in a polite voice which hid her pleasure, while she brooded over the difficulty of falling in with his moods. In the space of ten minutes she had been both Miss Trent and Abigail; she found it a little wearing on her nerves.

They were half way through their soup—hare soup and home-made, as Bollinger informed her as he served it, and they were alone in the elegant dining room. Bollinger had gone back to the kitchen to see about the next course, and the professor, making polite conversation, had fallen silent, and she, who had been turning over in her mind his insistence on calling her Miss Trent, found herself voicing her thoughts.

'I can't think why you will persist in calling me Miss Trent with one breath and Abigail with the next,' she remarked suddenly. She looked at him as she spoke and he was neither frowning nor smiling the faint sneering smile she so disliked.

He said simply, 'I told you once before. I forget.'

'Forget what?' she persisted.

'You may have restored my faith in women, Abigail, but it's been so long—I'm not quite used to it, perhaps I haven't quite learned to trust.' He paused and smiled at her across the table, and for fear that she would give herself away she said a little shortly, 'I haven't the least idea what you mean,' and wished that she had never started the conversation, while at the same time longing for him to go on. It was a pity that Bollinger came back just then with the *Boeuf Bourguignonne,* served, as it should be, in a brown glazed casserole; it smelled delicious and she was hungry, and so, she expected, was her host. Abigail ate with appetite and abandoned her questions for just sufficient polite conversation to make for good manners.

There was fruit tart next; an elaborate dish which not only contained fruit but cream and eggs and cream cheese. When the professor pressed her to a second helping, she hesitated. 'It was delicious…' she began.

'Then have some more—I don't think you've been eating enough, you've got thinner.'

He was right; she had been eating as sparingly as possible because she had had to pay for her meals in hospital and she was counting every cent now. She had told herself bracingly that it was a good thing, for she was far too plump, but she had sometimes been a little hungry. She passed her plate; in a week or two she would probably be on short commons again.

They had their coffee in the little room where she had had tea with Bollinger and when she had handed him the delicate Meissen cup and saucer he said blandly:

'We were talking about you.'

'No, not really.' She spoke too quickly, but it made no difference, for he went on just as though she hadn't spoken.

'You didn't understand what I meant, Abigail. Will it help if I call you Abigail all the time?'

'You mean you don't dislike me any more?'

She was unprepared for his explosive, 'Dislike you? My dear girl, I have never…'

She cut in ruthlessly, 'Oh yes, you have, from the very first time we met. I don't know why—perhaps you're one of those men who can't bear plain girls. I don't mind being plain—not any more, now I'm used to it, but you don't have to make it so obvious…'

He was looking at her gravely, his eyebrows arched, and she sensed that he was laughing silently, which irked her.

'Your eyes are lovely—you have a dimple, did you know? and the sweetest smile.'

'Which hardly adds up to good looks,' she answered him crisply. 'If you don't mind, we won't talk about me. How is your sister?'

He followed her lead without apparent regret and presently excused himself on the grounds of work to do. She sat on alone for another hour or two, staring into the fire, deep in thought. She had won his friendship; she was almost sure about that, and perhaps, just a little, his regard.

She saw him only briefly the following day; just long enough to be told his wishes concerning Nina. There was little enough nursing to do, for the little girl was almost well again and full of life and mischief—it was largely a question of keeping her amused and making sure that she didn't tire herself out. As he left the room, the professor said:

'I'll be away for a day or so, Abigail, so please feel free to go wherever you wish in my house. Bollinger will look after you. Nina will need more clothes, I imagine, take her to 't Kleuterhuis in P. C. Hooftstraat and get what you need and have the account sent to me—if she needs shoes, there's a good shop in the same street—Pennocks; they can send in their account too. Jan will take you if you wish it.'

They shopped two days later, with Jan driving them in the Mercedes, for the professor had taken the Rolls, spending the morning in the most agreeable fashion to them both, buying, without bothering too much about the prices, a new outfit for Nina and some red shoes which she had set her heart on. They went back to the house for lunch and afterwards Abigail tucked her small charge up for a nap, left Bollinger on guard, and went out for her hour or two's off-duty.

She went to Mrs Macklin's, and that lady was delighted to see her.

'Sit down,' she invited, 'and tell me all your news,' and Abigail took the chair opposite the old lady's in the small, overwarm room.

'Dominic told me that he intended asking you to remain with Nina until her father could come to fetch her, and I told him he was wise to do so, after all, what would he do with a three-year-old to look after and your Bollinger and Mevrouw Boot would spoil her hopelessly—besides,' she added dryly, 'his well-ordered household would have been chaos. He spends most of his days working, but that doesn't prevent him from expecting—and getting—a perfection of comfort which most of us only dream about. You like his house, my dear?'

'What I've seen of it—it's a great deal bigger than one would suppose from the outside, and the furnishings are beautiful.'

Mrs Macklin nodded agreement. 'It's been in the family for hundreds of years. Such a pity if Dominic doesn't marry again, because if he doesn't everything will go to a distant cousin of his, who farms his lands somewhere in Gelderland and dislikes city life, which means that the house here would be neglected, or worse, sold. No, Dominic needs a wife, Abigail, and children too.'

Abigail stirred in her chair, rocked by a brief, glorious daydream. She got up. 'I'll get tea, shall I?' she offered, anxious to have something to do, and as she went to the door: 'I expect he'll find a wife sooner or later. He has a lot of friends in Friesland, hasn't he?'

'Dozens. He's there now—I expect you know that.'

She hadn't known, and after all, there was no reason why he should have told her. She murmured something which meant nothing as she went through the door to the kitchen. Neither of them mentioned him again for the rest of her visit.

He came home that evening. Nina, tired out from trying on her new clothes, not once, but several times, had had her bath and was tucked up in bed, already half asleep. Abigail arranged the nightlight where the child could see it if she wakened, and prepared to go to her room. She left the door open as she always did so that she would hear if Nina called, and sat down in the easy chair by the window. She had meant to do her hair and her face and then count her money, something she had done several times in the last few days, as if by doing so she would increase the small sum left in her purse. Instead, she sat idle, thinking about the professor and wondering where he was and what he was doing.

He was on his way up his own staircase, having let himself into his house with surprising quietness, considering his size. She had heard nothing at all until he asked from the door, 'Is Nina asleep?' and then, when she turned round, 'Hullo, Abigail.'

He looked so pleased to see her that she forgot how untidy she was and that her face needed doing, and smiled warmly at him.

'Oh, nice to see you, Professor,' she spoke impulsively. 'Did you have a good time? Nina's been such a very good girl.'

He leaned against the wall, his hands in his pockets, smiling faintly.

'I'm glad to hear that. May I come in?'

'Of course—but don't you want to see her? She's not been in bed long, I daresay she's still awake. I put her to bed a little early because we went shopping this morning and she was excited and tired.'

He made himself comfortable on the side of the bed. 'What did you buy?'

'Oh, a zipper suit—a nylon one with ribbed cuffs and a high neck; she likes to play in the garden in the morning and she can't do that properly if she's wearing something she has to be careful of. And another dress—she only had two with her, you know, and a pair of red shoes and a little fur bonnet.' She paused, then added guiltily, 'I do hope I haven't been extravagant... you did say...'

He shrugged wide shoulders. 'I don't think we need worry about that. You're not out of pocket? You must let me know if you are.'

Here was a splendid opportunity to bring up the matter of her salary. She said, 'No…' but was interrupted by the entrance of Bollinger, who knocked on the open door and came in with a cheerful air. 'Nice to see you back, boss,' he remarked, 'I seen the car below and there's a Doctor Leesward on the phone for you. He says it's urgent.'

The professor, with a brief word of excuse, went out of the room and Bolly with him; Abigail was left to take off her cap and do her hair and her face, wondering the while if she would have the chance again that evening of bringing up the subject. No chance at all, as it turned out, for when she went downstairs for dinner, a few minutes early, it was to learn from Bollinger that the professor had gone to the hospital and was likely to be late home. She ate the meal as quickly as she could, trying not to feel lonely, then sat by the fire, knitting a pair of red mitts for Nina to match the new red shoes. She had been in bed for more than an hour when she heard the professor come in.

He had gone when she and Nina got down in the morning. They were eating their simple lunch together when he came in. He took his seat at the table to Nina's delight and after glancing at their plates, exclaimed:

'In heaven's name—fish, steamed fish and potato purée!' He looked so horrified that Abigail burst out laughing.

'It's very good,' she said, 'and it's good for Nina's tummy. Besides, there's ice-cream for afters.'

'Good God, who perpetrated this menu?'

'Me,' said Abigail, paying no attention to her grammar. 'It's nourishing and easy to digest.'

'Are you eating it too?'

'Of course—it would be the height of extravagance to have something different—besides, think of Mevrouw Boot.'

'Very commendable. I hope you don't expect me to join you.' He spoke a little absentmindedly and with a muttered word of excuse, pulled some papers out of a pocket and became engrossed in them; Abigail could see that he had other more important things on his mind than his companions at table, so she urged Nina to eat up like a good girl, and went back to her own lunch.

Bollinger came in presently, bearing a magnificent steak, which the professor ate with the same absentminded air, while Abigail, who didn't care for steamed fish at all, tried to keep her nose from twitching at the appetising aroma from his side of the table. She ate the rest of her fish as a good example to Nina, and went on to the ice-cream, while the professor, with every sign of enjoyment, ate hugely of the apple pie and cream Bollinger had brought for him. The cream he shared with his small relative, who had asked, with a good deal of vehemence, if she might have some, but when he offered the dish to Abigail she refused with such promptness that he asked her if she didn't care for it—a singularly annoying question, for they had shared enough meals together by now for him to have noticed that she had never refused it before.

He caught her smouldering gaze and said coolly, 'Ah—I think I understand. I'm breaking my own rules, aren't I? I must say you look very ill-tempered about it.'

A remark calculated to stoke her ill humour, so that she said sharply:

'Yes, you are. You told me exactly what Nina was to eat and I've kept strictly to your wishes. She's clever enough to remember this the next time I give her rice pudding or egg custard. And I don't like steamed fish.'

He shook with laughter. 'My poor dear girl, how tiresome I have been! Excuse me while I explain to my niece.' Which he did, amidst a good deal of giggling from Nina and a bellow of laughter from himself, so rare a sound that Abigail stared.

'It's all right, Abigail, we're not laughing at you. Well, I must go back, I suppose. Would you walk round to Professor de Wit's for me this afternoon? There's a book I particularly want him to have.'

He smiled at her and her heart beat a little faster, and after he had gone she wondered if he could possibly be the same irritable, cold-seeming man she had first met. Probably Nina's company, she thought; he was so fond of the child, and she was indeed a dear little creature. Abigail was fond of her too; she would miss her when she returned home to Spain, and that would be very soon now.

The professor joined her for dinner that evening, and because she could see that he was tired, Abigail, beyond answering his brief enquiries as to the afternoon, made no attempt at conversation. They were eating Mevrouw Boot's perfectly turned out chocolate soufflée when he said:

'Anyone else would have chattered—how did you know that I didn't want to talk?'

'Well,' said Abigail frankly, 'you looked a little forbidding, you know, and weary. I daresay you had something on your mind you wanted to think out quietly, and in that case you would hardly wish to make conversation, would you?'

'Do I usually make conversation with you, Abigail?'

She nodded her neat head at him. 'Oh, yes, but mostly you don't talk at all.' She smiled at him as she spoke, but he remained unsmiling, until:

'Do you find me a bad-tempered man, Abigail?'

She put down her fork and thought before she answered this. He was asking awkward questions again and if she gave the wrong answer he might change back into the same cold, irritable man she had always thought him. On the other hand it would be of no use to fib to him. She said finally:

'No, not bad-tempered—that is, not bad-tempered underneath, are you? otherwise the children would be afraid of you, and they're not, they're sold on you, aren't they? You have always been,' she hesitated, 'abrupt, as though…no, that's not quite right. I think you were annoyed at having to meet me; I had the strong impression that you disliked me, that you still do, but not always, and I can't understand that. Is it because I'm

English? or perhaps because I'm nothing to look at, although you said it wasn't...'

'I'll say it again, if only to convince you. But you are right, I didn't want to meet you, I've had no interest in women—girls—for a long time, but after I had met you I found myself arranging for you to take over a case so that I could see you every day. Do you not find that strange?'

She shook her head, for it seemed no stranger than her own acceptance of his offer for the very same reason. She longed to tell him so, but something warned her not to say anything—not yet.

'Contradictory behaviour, was it not? And you know why?' His blue eyes searched hers, he looked suddenly grim. 'I was once married. It was a long time ago.' The bleakness of his voice hurt her.

'Yes, I know about that.'

He looked suddenly ferocious. 'Who told you? Not the servants—they know better.'

'No, it wasn't the servants, and it wasn't gossip either. It was the only way someone could answer a question I had asked.' She went on hurriedly, trying not to see the arrogantly arched brows, 'You see, I couldn't understand why you were sometimes... just as though you hated me...and others...' she became a trifle incoherent, remembering the other times. 'I got upset once or twice and—and angry, and to make me understand better, this—person told me about you—just that you had been married and had lost your wife. I didn't ask any questions, it wasn't my business.' She added with a little flare-up of feeling, 'It isn't my business now; you started telling me—I should never have dreamed of mentioning it.'

'It's something I don't talk about. I'm surprised that I'm talking about it now, but I wanted to tell you, Abigail—I had to tell you, before...' He paused as Bollinger came into the room to enquire where they would have their coffee.

'Oh, here,' said the professor impatiently. 'We'll ring when we're ready for you to clear, thank you, Bollinger.'

Bollinger was back very quickly, and a good thing too from Abigail's point of view, for in the deep silence in which they sat her thoughts were racing round and round inside her head, thoughts she hardly dared to think. If she had been a cool, poised girl, she would have used those few minutes to good purpose instead of allowing her brain to seethe with nonsense.

She poured the coffee when it came and handed him his cup across the table and met his eyes as she did so, her own troubled and bewildered.

He said thoughtfully, 'It's strange, Abigail, but in all these years I have never wanted to tell anyone—and I must admit to several—er—friendships in that time—about my marriage, but I want to tell you, because you're different; you know what it is to be unhappy and you're honest too and I think that you would keep a confidence. But you see, my dear, I have grown wary of women, and I found it difficult.'

'You're sure you want to tell me? You're not going to feel awful about it in the morning?'

He laughed a little and shook his head, then passed his cup for more coffee and she busied herself filling it, then put the cup down, forgetting to give it back to him, her eyes upon his as he began to speak.

'I married when I was twenty-five—fifteen years ago. Did you know that I am almost forty-one, Abigail? She was very pretty and gay too, she loved clothes and jewels and furs and fast cars and she was the kind of girl men like to be seen about with—I counted myself very fortunate when she agreed to marry me. It took me just six weeks to discover that she didn't love me, and another six weeks for me to find out that I didn't love her. Perhaps if I had loved her I could have forgiven her the affairs she had. She was killed in a car crash, together with the current boy-friend, five months after we were married. I swore I would never love another woman again, for although

I had no feeling for her, my pride suffered, and although, as I said just now, I became—involved, shall we say, from time to time, it meant nothing to me.' He put out his hand for his coffee cup. 'Now you know why I have never allowed anything—any woman, to interfere with my life.'

Abigail emptied the cooling coffee from his cup and poured fresh with a steady hand, which was surprising, for inside she was trembling. It seemed to her that she had been warned that, even though he liked her, he had no intention of allowing his feelings to take over from the life he had decided upon. What other reason could he have had for telling her something he admitted he had never discussed with anyone? The only good reason would be because he loved her, and he had had plenty of opportunity of saying so; it could be dismissed without a thought. He had felt the urge to talk; he was used to her by now and presumably, as she was a suitable recipient of his confidences, he felt himself able to talk to her. She summoned a smile.

'Thank you for telling me, Professor. It was a truly awful thing to happen to you and I can well imagine that it's made you wary of women. But it's a long time ago. I'm sure you will find someone who will change your views for you. Perhaps you don't get out enough to meet people; you work so hard, don't you? There are a great many nice girls in the world, you know.'

'You suggest that I should find one and marry her?'

'Yes, why not? Just because there's one rotten apple in the barrel doesn't mean that the whole barrelful is bad.' She made her voice as matter-of-fact as she could.

'But I enjoy working hard. If I took a wife she might try to change that.'

'But she wouldn't—not if she loved you, she would want to help you in every way she could.'

He looked amused. 'How?'

She was suddenly out of patience with him. 'How should I know? She's the one to answer that question.'

'I must remember to ask her when the time comes.' He spoke gravely, although there was a gleam in his eyes. 'And now, much as I have enjoyed this conversation, I have to go back to the hospital. There is a case...'

He told her about it and she listened with interest and asked questions too; it was another ten minutes before he got to his feet.

And as for Abigail, she rang the bell for poor patient Bollinger and went to sit by the fire, and when he came into the room, said how sorry she was that they had been so desultory over their dinner.

'That's OK, Miss Abby,' said Bollinger, busy with the table, 'I was right glad to see you having such a nice chat. The boss don't often talk. He must like you.'

Abigail swallowed from a throat thick with the tears she would have liked to shed. 'I do believe he does, Bolly,' she agreed sadly.

The professor was at breakfast when she and Nina went down the following morning. He lifted his niece into her chair, tied her bib, urged her to eat up her porridge and then turned his attention to Abigail, who had sat down silently after a quiet good morning. Unlike her, he seemed in the best of spirits.

'I'm going to Friesland tomorrow; Bollinger will be going with me, for he has to see about bulbs for the garden there. I think it would be nice if Nina were to accompany us—you too, naturally, Abigail.' He gave her a bright glance. 'I feel that Nina has deserved a treat, do you not agree?'

'Yes, she's been as good as gold, but are you sure you want me to come?' She coloured faintly and added hastily, 'She doesn't really need a nurse now.'

'No? Bollinger and I love her dearly, but I believe we should both be mentally deranged by the end of the day if there wasn't someone to take her off our hands for at least part of the time. I have business to attend to and Bollinger takes his bulbs seriously.'

Abigail couldn't help smiling at him. She had never seen him look so relaxed. 'Then I'll come, I should like to. What time do you want us to be ready?'

'Could you manage eight o'clock? We could make it later if you like—it's barely a hundred miles.'

'I'm sure we can be ready by then. Nina wakes early, you know.'

'Does she? She keeps very quiet about it.'

'Well, she gets into my bed and I tell her a story.'

'In English?' He was laughing again.

'A little of both. She understands quite a lot, don't you, poppet?' She turned to look at the small girl beside her, tucking into a boiled egg and fingers of bread and butter with remarkable energy. 'Yes,' said the poppet from a full mouth, adding rapidly, 'No—Mary, Mary, quite con...con...' a frown marred the small features, to be replaced by a rapturous smile. 'Little Boy Blue...' she began.

'Lovely, darling,' said Abigail fondly, 'you're a clever girl, but eat up that nice egg and Oom Dominic will tell you something very exciting.'

The egg was forgotten. 'Oom Dominic,' she smiled eggily up at him, 'tell,' she commanded in an imperious pipe.

Her uncle told her and rather unfairly left a few minutes later, leaving Abigail to calm a very excited little girl. He didn't come back all day and Abigail ate her dinner alone, not sure whether to be relieved or not. She had spent a good part of the night and most of the day persuading herself that the only way possible to her was to forget most of what the professor had said and to remember that within a very short time she would be going away and would never see him again, and in the meantime to behave exactly as she always had done. Breakfast had been a test; she considered she had come out of it rather well. She talked to Bollinger as she ate, glad of the opportunity of explaining that she would be able to pay him some more money very soon—quite a lot of money, she pointed out; she hadn't been paid for three weeks, and there would be some money over, even after that, for she still had her fare intact. After her old friend had gone, she curled up by the fire. There would be enough left to buy some clothes; she occupied herself deciding what she would buy when she got back to London.

They were ready as she had promised by eight o'clock, with Nina in the fur bonnet and the red shoes to match the zipper suit. Abigail, standing beside her in the hall, wore the tweed coat, which she now loathed, her knitted beret and the scarf to match. She hated those almost as much; only the gloves Professor de Wit had given her gave her pleasure. Her boots still leaked, but Bolly, bless him, had cleaned them beautifully and no one knew about the leak. But she felt shabby beside her small charge and she had an uneasy feeling that the professor shared her feelings as he came into the hall, for the look he gave her was a leisurely and searching one, starting at the pompom of her beret, and going slowly down to her feet. The little smile he gave her did nothing to mollify her ruffled feelings.

There had been some late snow during the night, just sufficient to turn the roads to slush and powder the bare trees, but once out of the city, the flat country on either side of the motorway was blanketed in white; only the road ahead of them gleamed blackly. Abigail, sitting comfortably in the warmth of the big car, with Nina cuddled close to her and Colossus beside her, felt sorry for the drivers of the slow-moving farm carts drawn by plodding horses, but Nina, untroubled by this aspect of the winter's morning, wanted to know about the horses; she wanted to know about the cows and the canals and the windmills and bridges too; Abigail's Dutch was strained to breaking point and the professor, helping her out from time to time with the right words laughed a good deal, and Bollinger glanced at him several times, surprise all over his wrinkled face.

They went by way of the sea dyke, over the Ijsselmeer, and there was nothing to see because the snow blotted out the view on either side and the road ahead was straight, fading into an unseen horizon. Abigail scarcely noticed when they reached the mainland and the professor told her that they were in Friesland. They went down the coast of the great inland water and then turned inland to Bolsward and on to Sneek, both of which small towns Abigail had but the briefest glimpse of, but what she saw enchanted her, for despite the snow and the grey sky and the lack of people about the streets, they were picturesque.

They turned off the main road presently, and then again, this time into a much narrower road, running between fields with no villages to be seen. They could, thought Abigail, be in the middle of a snow-covered desert, and had her thought answered by the professor, who remarked easily:

'A little bleak today, I'm afraid, but when it is clear weather, the country is charming.'

The road gave way to a still narrower one, made of bricks and uneven, with a signpost pointing to Eernewoude, but before they reached there the professor swung the car into a side lane lined with bare trees, and almost at once through an open gateway. The lane ended abruptly in a wide sweep of cobblestones and before them was the house.

It was an old house, with a multitude of gables, and built of rose bricks, and while not large, appeared roomy enough. Its windows were small and arched and its panelled door studded with nails. The door swung open as they got out of the car, Nina was whisked up into her uncle's arms, and with an invitation to follow him, Abigail went inside, with Bollinger behind.

It was similar to the house in Amsterdam, with the same square hall with its black and white flagged floor and its lovely linenfold panelling, but this hall extended back a good deal further and the staircase rose out of its centre and divided from a little landing half way up it. It smelled of wax polish and pot-pourri and was pleasantly warm. Abigail's coat was taken from her and she was invited to go into one of the rooms on the right of the entrance, but not before the professor had introduced the old woman who had opened the door. Joke, he called her, and it was apparent that he and she had known each other for a long time.

The room they went into was quite large and a little dark by reason of the weather outside and the small windows, but the lamps in their wall brackets gave it a cheerful air, as did the fire burning briskly in the old-fashioned cast-iron fireplace. It was furnished in much the same style as the small sitting room in Amsterdam; a happy blend of comfort and antiques.

The professor offered Abigail an easy chair by the fire and Nina immediately perched on her lap. Bollinger had disappeared. 'To see to those bulbs of his,' explained the professor. 'My gardener, the man Bollinger has replaced so well, is convalescing here, they will no doubt have a most interesting talk over their coffee.'

'However can they talk?' Abigail wanted to know, 'unless your gardener knows any English.'

'He does. He was in England during the war. Besides, they both know the Latin names of everything that grows, which makes it easy.'

The idea of Bollinger being so clever hadn't entered Abigail's head. She said in astonishment, 'How extraordinary, Bolly speaking Latin.'

'He's a clever old man when it comes to gardens,' replied the professor, and went to take the coffee tray from Joke.

Over coffee he said, 'I shall be busy for an hour or two. Can you amuse yourselves, do you think? The garden is quite large. It's stopped snowing again. I daresay if Nina's sufficiently wrapped up, she might like to make a snowman—there's just about enough for that.'

Abigail, thinking uneasily of her leaking boots, agreed because Nina wanted to go outside so badly, and moreover, the professor had finished his coffee and she sensed that he wanted to be gone. There was a wide stretch of lawn behind the house and plenty of snow to make the promised snowman. Between them they made a magnificent specimen and then snowballed each other and Colossus until they were warm and Nina was tired.

'Time to go indoors,' said Abigail firmly, and scooped up the little girl and bore her inside. Even after they had tidied themselves in the cloakroom surprisingly hidden in the hall panelling, there was still an hour till lunch. They went back to sit by the fire, and Nina, on Abigail's lap, recited her jumble of nursery rhymes. She was giving her own version of Baa Baa, Black Sheep when the professor joined them. He listened gravely to his niece's efforts, congratulated her with suitable enthusiasm and offered Abigail a drink before stretching himself out in the chair on the opposite side of the hearth. It was pleasant sitting there in the warm, delightfully furnished room. Abigail sipped her sherry, on the edge of a daydream, and was brought back to reality by his voice.

'Nina's going home in two days' time, Abigail. Dirk telephoned me. We shall miss her, shan't we?'

'Yes, very much.' She contrived to make her voice normal. 'Will she go by car?'

'Yes, Dirk will be here tomorrow evening and will spend the night, and they will leave the next morning. You will wish to return to England as soon as possible?'

She could only say yes to that and add: 'Is Bollinger to come with me?'

'Not unless you want him to, but it's entirely up to you—and him—to decide.'

Abigail looked relieved without knowing it. 'Oh, well, if he could stay—you see I shall have to find another job and—and somewhere to live, and if it's a case where I have to live in, I must find a room for Bolly. It would be nice if I could have it all settled before he goes back to England.'

'It would be nicer still,' said the professor, not looking at her at all but into his glass, 'if you would stay on for a while and work in the hospital.'

Her heart rocketed into her throat, she swallowed it back,

staring at his downbent head. 'Oh, yes, it would, but is there a job for me there?'

'My dear good girl, we are as short of nurses here as they are in England. I can think of half a dozen vacancies...you don't mind where you work?'

'No—at least, I know Zuster Ritsma already and she speaks English, which makes it easier for me, and I prefer surgery.'

'Theatre?'

'Yes—I did six months.'

He nodded and put down his glass, half smiling. 'Good, that's settled then—how about having your room at Mrs Macklin's again?'

'Do you suppose she would let me? I should like that very much.'

'So will she.' He got up and lifted Nina into his arms. 'Shall we have lunch, and then while this young lady is having her nap, I'll show you round the house.'

Lunch was a gay meal and the food so good that Abigail felt constrained to mention it.

'Joke's daughter,' the professor told her. 'It's her husband who does the garden. Joke attends to the housekeeping although she has retired, but she's lived here all her life and it's home to her. She lives with Arie and her daughter in the little cottage behind the garage.'

They ate thick pea soup, followed by grilled sole and a salad; the sweet, as a concession to Nina's youthful appetite, was a pile of waffles and a great dish of whipped cream. They drank a dry white wine with it and the professor poured Nina's orangeade with the same care as he poured the wine. Abigail, watching the two of them, thought what a splendid father he would make, for he was surprisingly patient with children. Only with himself, she thought sadly, was he impatient.

When they had finished, he led the way upstairs to a small room on the first floor, where Joke was turning down the coverlet of a narrow bed with a carved headboard.

'Odilia used to sleep here when she was little,' the professor told Abigail. 'I've never changed it, it seemed so right for a little girl. It hasn't been used for a long time...' He frowned a little and Abigail busied herself with Nina because she could guess why he was frowning—there might have been a small daughter of his own in that room. Out on the landing after tucking Nina up under the pink eiderdown she asked, 'Have you really got the time to take me round? I shall be quite happy on my own if there's something else you want to do.'

'There's nothing else I want to do,' he spoke briskly. 'Let's go downstairs first, shall we?'

There were two other rooms besides the sitting room and the darkly splendid dining room; one a vast drawing room, hung with silk panels in a faded strawberry pink, with an Aubusson carpet on its floor and dark green curtains of velvet. Its walls were lined with cabinets displaying china and silver and glass and on either side of its vast fireplace were velvet-covered sofas flanked by rosewood sofa tables. Here too the chairs were a happy mixture of modern comfort and antiques and what paintings there were were light flower studies or pastoral scenes.

The other room was the library, its walls crowded with books, and from the look of it, frequently used. The furniture was heavy and smelled faintly of tobacco and leather, and Abigail wrinkled her nose. 'Nice,' she commented. 'What a marvellous collection of books. I suppose most of them are in Dutch.'

'Some—there are quite a number in English, though, and German and a few in French.' He gave her a sidelong glance and smiled. 'I have to keep up with my studies, you know.'

She agreed gravely, 'Yes, of course, but I expect you write too, don't you?'

'Only when I have something worthwhile to say.'

He led her back into the hall and up the staircase to the bedrooms, more numerous than she would have supposed, each with its narrow windows and each too, with its own colour scheme, pale vague blues and pinks and greens which acted as magnificent foils to the beautiful old furniture, and was echoed again in the thick carpeting.

Abigail sighed gently as they went downstairs again. 'It's a beautiful house, as beautiful as your house in Amsterdam—have your family lived here for a long time?'

They were back in the sitting room, facing each other across the fireplace with Colossus between them. The professor eased himself into his chair and answered her in a leisurely fashion.

'Yes, three hundred years or so. My family are Friesian, you know, with strong ties with Amsterdam. While I was married we came here very seldom. My—wife disliked it, it is so quiet, you see. Only the country around us and a handful of small houses, but I find it delightful.'

Abigail nodded. 'And Amsterdam—surely you love your house there?'

'Yes, equally, I suppose—but here I can escape, you see.'

She saw very well. Away from the bustle of the hospital and his eternal round of patients and still more patients, this old house would be like a quiet heaven. She said so and was rewarded by his smile. 'You see how you have changed me,' he said quietly. 'Before I came to know you I should have suspected you of saying that merely to please me.'

'Isn't that a little conceited of you?'

'Yes—but perhaps you don't know that for a number of years I have been regarded in the light of a good—what is the word?—catch, I believe. I have come to regard any girl who agreed too readily with me or said something obviously meant to attract my attention or win my approval as highly suspect.'

'So that's why you accused me of toadying. But they may have meant it—they might have been charming…'

'Just as my wife was charming?' He gave her a bitter little smile. 'Do you not say in your own language: Once bitten, twice shy? I am very shy, Abigail.'

She eyed him warily. He looked irritable again and all set to say something ill-tempered. Perhaps it would be a good idea to talk about something else.

'You have a lovely garden,' she told him brightly. 'Do roses do well here?'

The look of bitterness left his face; he looked as though he was going to laugh. 'Excellently—there is a large bed in the centre of the lawn at the back of the house, and there's a rose walk besides, at one side.'

'I should have loved to have seen it,' said Abigail regretfully. 'We had a rose garden, when we lived in the country. Bolly was very good with them and my mother had great bowls of them around the house.'

He said deliberately, 'Tell me about your parents, Abigail.'

'I don't think I want to...'

'Yes, you do, only you have buried them deep down, haven't you? You shouldn't, you know. Happy times are for remembering. When did you move to London?'

She found herself telling him about her childhood and her parents, and Bolly and the pleasant house they had lived in, and he scarcely interrupted her, sitting in his chair, smoking a pipe and staring at the ceiling and not at her at all. When she had finished she felt as though she had talked all the sadness away for ever and left only happy memories. She sat up straight, aware that she had been talking for a long time. 'I'm sorry,' she said shyly, 'I didn't mean... I must have bored you...'

He got up and pulled her to her feet and stood in front of her, her hands still in his. 'No, never that. You deserve a happier future, Abigail.'

She reddened. 'I don't pity myself in the least; I'm very fortunate to have a job—and there's Bolly...'

'Don't you have other friends?'

She answered reluctantly. 'Yes—quite a number, but one doesn't burden friends, they have their own lives.' She fidgeted under his steady gaze. 'Shall I go and fetch Nina down?'

'By all means. I have to work for half an hour or so.'

He sounded aloof, even annoyed, perhaps because she had refused to talk about herself; indeed, thinking about it she thought that perhaps she had snubbed him although she hadn't meant to do so. She went slowly from the room and up the lovely staircase to where Nina was waiting impatiently to be got up.

They went back after tea, and Abigail, half hoping that the professor might suggest that she and Nina should sit beside him, was disappointed. The two men talked about gardens and gardening for the whole of the journey. Nina had dropped off to sleep, curled up like a kitten in her lap, Colossus slept too, and Abigail was left with her thoughts again, and they weren't very happy.

She dined alone, for the professor, Bollinger informed her, had gone out. 'Some big do or other,' he confided. 'All got up, he is, and very handsome too. Must give the ladies a treat. I hear you're to work in the hospital for a while, Miss Abby, and very nice too, if I may say so. You'll be living with that nice Mrs Macklin again?'

'Yes, Bolly, though I don't know for how long. I'm so glad for you—you're happy here, aren't you?'

'Not half! Lovely bit of garden in that house where we went today, and no one breathing down your neck—I missed me garden, Miss Abby.'

'Oh, Bolly dear, I know, and I'll never be able to repay you for giving it all up when Father died. What should we have done without you? You've been a real friend. I hope I stay for ages, just to make you happy.'

'Won't you be happy too, Miss Abby?' He sounded wistful and full of curiosity all at once.

'Yes, I shall, actually, Bolly.' She didn't look at him. 'I think I'll go to bed early, I'm almost as tired as Nina.' She gave him a sweet smile and presently wandered through the quiet house and up to her room.

She didn't hurry over her bath and it was an hour or more before she was ready for bed, and when she went into Nina's room as she always did at bedtime, it was to find the child awake. It took only a few minutes for her to discover that Nina wasn't ill, only excited. She had slept and wakened and remembered that she was to go home in a day's time and she wanted to talk about it. Abigail fetched her some warm milk from the kitchen and then curled up beside her on the bed while she sipped it, very slowly and with pauses for excited chatter. But presently she had said it all and the milk was nearly finished. She edged nearer Abigail. 'Not pretty,' she informed her, fingering Abigail's dressing gown, a serviceable one she had received from her aunt and uncle at Christmas. Nina was right, it wasn't in the least pretty; a dim red, thick and woolly, it made Abigail's plumpness assume enormous proportions and the colour merely emphasized the mediocrity of her features.

'Hideous,' she agreed, and Nina cheerfully echoed her. 'But it's warm,' Abigail went on, just as though Nina could understand every word she said, 'and it covers me up. I hate it.'

'What do you hate with such vehemence?' asked the professor from the door, and Abigail jumped and said crossly, 'Don't you know that you shouldn't creep up on people. It's most upsetting.'

He advanced into the room, looking twice his usual size in his tails. Definitely a reception, thought Abigail, eyeing his snowy waistcoat and white tie. He bowed his head in mock humility. 'My apologies, Abigail. I had no intention of frightening you, only to make sure that my niece was sleeping.'

He looked at her enquiringly as he spoke and she made haste to explain.

'She's had some milk, and now we've had a little talk, she'll go back to sleep. I'll stay with her until she does.'

He said nothing to this, merely bent to kiss Nina and be hugged before going to sit in a rocking chair in a corner of the room, blandly ignoring Abigail's look of enquiry in her turn.

'Baa, baa, black sheep,' demanded Nina sleepily, and Abigail obediently repeated the verses; she did so several times until she saw that the child was asleep again, and got up quietly to leave the room. On the way to the door she paused. 'Good night, Professor,' she whispered to the silent man sitting so still, and was shocked into a gasp, for he was beside her, going through the door almost before the words were out of her mouth.

The landing was dim and warm, through the half open door of her room she could see the cheerful glow of the bedside lamp. Somewhere downstairs Bollinger was tramping about, closing windows and shutting doors. For a moment she had the illusion that she lived in a safe, secure world which she shared with the professor, a world where she was cherished and loved and even, absurdly, admired. She tightened her mouth to prevent her lips quivering with the sudden horrid threat of tears, and with a nod in the general direction of the professor, who was behind her, started towards her room. But he wasn't behind her, he was beside her, in front of her. His arms were round her and all so quickly that she had no means of eluding him, and anyway, she didn't want to. He asked: 'What were you hating?'

The question was a surprise, all the same she answered it truthfully.

'My dressing gown—it's hideous.'

He held her away from him and surveyed her slowly. 'Indeed it is—not your own choosing, surely?'

'No.'

'Then go out and buy yourself the most glamorous garment you can find,' he advised her.

Perhaps not quite the right moment to mention her salary, but probably as good as any; at least they were alone and uninterrupted. She opened her mouth and began: 'I wonder...'

'Don't talk,' said the professor with a touch of his old imperious manner, and kissed her. He kissed her several times, and with a fine disregard for good sense, she kissed him back.

It was only when, five minutes later, she was in her room again, that she remembered that he had said nothing at all and she, to her chagrin, had. Not much, but enough. It had, at the time, seemed quite natural to address him as Dominic darling.

CHAPTER NINE

She went down to breakfast the next morning, with Nina holding her hand; she looked as calm as was her habit and her neat appearance gave no indication of the sleepless night she had passed. Most of it she had spent reassuring herself. The professor might not have heard her, she had told herself over and over again, and even if he had, it didn't really matter, but these brave thoughts were reduced to meaningless nonsense by the certain knowledge that although she hadn't spoken loudly, she had certainly repeated herself several times—there was nothing wrong with the professor's hearing either. Her pale cheeks reddened painfully as she entered the dining room with the gaily chattering Nina dancing beside her, a prey to a variety of expectations, all of them unthinkable.

None of them materialised. The professor was sitting on the side of the table, with a cup of coffee in one hand and the telephone in the other. He lifted his eyes from the thoughtful contemplation of his elegantly shod feet, met Abigail's look with a vague one of his own, said 'Morning,' and broke into a lengthy monologue in Dutch. When he had finished he listened for a moment, frowned, said something loud and rather violent, which she was glad she couldn't understand, gulped his coffee and said:

'I must go, Abigail—something's turned up. Tell Dirk to come to the hospital as soon as he arrives.'

He dropped a hand on to Nina's small head and ruffled her hair, nodded to Abigail and left the room, and very shortly afterwards, the house, banging the house door after him quite unnecessarily.

Abigail drank coffee while Nina munched her way through her breakfast. She felt a little let down, just as one would feel when, having screwed up courage to go to the dentist to have a tooth pulled, one was told that there was no need. The professor couldn't have heard her. Perhaps he was a little drunk; after all, he had been to a banquet or something similar. It was a pity that this comforting theory was quite shattered by her complete certainty that he wasn't the sort of man to get drunk, not even slightly. All that remained was that he had heard her, and—mortifying thought—had dismissed the incident as so trivial as to be beneath his notice.

Dirk arrived a couple of hours later, had coffee with them, an enraptured Nina on his knee, gave Abigail a brief account of his wife and son's health, and departed for the hospital. She saw neither him nor the professor until dinner that evening, when the conversation was of Spain, Odilia, the new baby and his journey back the following morning.

The professor had talked to her, from time to time, with his usual faint aloofness; he certainly hadn't bothered to look at her overmuch. She retired to her room early, pleading packing for Nina, wishing the two gentlemen a cool goodnight as she went.

She was getting ready for bed when she remembered that although she was to go to the hospital on the following day, no one had told her how or when she was to go and the professor would either be gone or on the point of going by the time she and Nina got down in the morning; she decided to pack her own case too, so that, if necessary, she could leave at a moment's notice—she went down the back stairs too, and explained to Bollinger. She then returned to her room, slightly out of temper, to sleep fitfully and be awakened much too early by a joyful Nina wanting to get up and dress and go with her papa on the instant.

They were early for breakfast, only to find that the professor had left the house at six o'clock that morning to undertake an emergency operation. There was still no sign of him by the time Dirk and his small daughter were ready to leave in the former's Mercedes-Benz 350 SL; they were making their final farewells when the telephone rang and Abigail answered it. The professor's voice sounded quietly in her ear. 'Abigail? Ask Dirk to come to the telephone, will you? And Nina.'

It was a short conversation; Nina gave Abigail a last hug, Dirk wrung her hand and they had gone. She went back into the house with Bollinger and Mevrouw Boot, wondering what she was supposed to do. At the end of an hour she decided to go to the hospital. She couldn't stay in the house without a patient and she had a job to go to anyway—besides, she still had to find out if Mrs Macklin would have her again. She put on her outdoor clothes, fetched her case downstairs, said a temporary goodbye to Bollinger and went to the front door. The professor opened it as she put her hand on its massive brass knob.

He said instantly, 'Running away?'

The unfairness of this remark stung her to snap, 'Don't be ridiculous! I'm on my way to the hospital. You asked me to work there, if you remember, and there's no reason for me to remain here any longer.'

He answered this logical remark by shutting the door firmly behind him and leading her by the arm across the hall to his study. He shut this door too before taking off his coat and tossing it untidily over a chair, then he caught hold of her arm again and propelled her across the room, so that she was standing by a window with the cold, unkind March light on her face.

'Did you sleep?' The question was unexpected and she was taken off her guard. She faltered: 'Well, not...' she looked up at him, aware that her face wasn't at its best in the harsh grey morning. He didn't look tired, nor did he look aloof, and the little irritable frown had gone completely, and his eyes, which had looked at her so coldly on so many occasions, were warm and twinkling. She began again: 'Not very...' to be interrupted:

'I heard you, dear Abigail, did you think that I did not?' He put a hand lightly on her shoulder. 'You and I, we have to talk, but not now. Zuster Ritsma wants you on duty at midday; it seemed quicker to come and fetch you than telephoning.' A smile touched the corners of his mouth. 'That's not true, I wanted to see you—that's why I came. I didn't know that you would be packed and ready, but as you are, we had better go. Will you come with me?'

Abigail smiled at him; she felt happy and excited and intensely curious as to what they would talk about. 'I'm quite ready,' she told him, in a voice which shook very slightly with these feelings. He took his hand from her shoulder and ushered her out into the hall. Bollinger was there, standing by her case. He carried it out to the car for her, his face alight with smiles. He shut the car door on her, wished her goodbye, admonished her not to work too hard and then stood on the steps to watch them go. Abigail turned to wave as they reached the corner of the *gracht*.

They were almost at the hospital when the professor spoke.

'I have a great deal of work which must be done,' he sighed, 'and this evening I have to go to Brussels for two days. When I return, there are things to tell you, Abigail, dear girl.'

She turned her head to look at him and for a fleeting moment his eyes met hers and he smiled. Two days seemed a very long time, but if that was what he wanted, she would wait. She said rather breathlessly, 'Very well, Professor,' and when he said on a laugh, 'Did you not call me Dominic?' she repeated obediently, 'Dominic.'

They parted in the front hall of the hospital and she didn't see him to speak to alone after that. True, he did a round in the children's ward where she had been sent to work, but beyond asking her one or two questions about the baby she was bottle-feeding, he said nothing. He hardly looked at her—indeed, she had the strong impression that he was deliberately avoiding her eye. Only as he came to a halt at the ward door did he turn round to look back at her, a look, brief though it was, to destroy the ridiculous doubts which had edged into her mind during the day.

The two days were endless, even though they had been busy ones on the ward, and her off-duty had been fully occupied settling in again with a delighted Mrs Macklin. She had visited Professor de Wit too, who seemed to take it for granted that she would remain permanently in Amsterdam and invited her for tea the following week. The day the professor was to return was a renewal of winter. Abigail walked to work through the bleak coldness of the city streets, sure that, despite the fact that it was the first week of March, it would snow before nightfall—not that she minded, for Dominic was coming. Within a few hours she would see him again, and the world, despite a regrettable shortage of money and her still leaking boots, seemed a lovely place.

She looked at the clock as she went to feed the first of the babies. Even now he might be getting on the plane although it was early enough—too early perhaps, but some time that day... beyond that delightful thought she was careful not to think; there was a good deal of work to get through, and she would need all her wits about her to get done. She dismissed the delights of the future and picked up an urgently crying baby.

It was a tiresome morning; Zuster Ritsma was off duty, the other two nurses spoke only the most basic of English, and it was a relief when Henk strolled on to the ward and after doing a round stopped for a chat. They were standing with their backs to the door and he was telling her in his inaccurate unidiomatic English about his latest girl-friend—a lady, it seemed, of many charms but a good deal older than he. He asked anxiously of Abigail: 'Too old, you think?'

Abigail laughed at him. 'Of course it's too old,' she spoke gaily. 'A gap of how many? fifteen years, isn't it? It's absurd—but of course it's not serious—just a passing fancy and a chance to have a good time.'

He rolled his eyes at her and said dramatically, 'My *lieveling...*' and Abigail, trying not to laugh at him said, 'No, no—your darling,' and laughed then because he looked so funny and she was so happy she could have laughed at anything. The slight sound behind her caused her to turn her head. The professor was standing behind them, in the doorway, only a foot or so away, staring at her; her smile faded before the iciness of his eyes.

He said with a cool blandness which hurt her, 'Good morning, Nurse Trent. Henk, I want you in the theatre in ten minutes.' As he turned away he added in a voice like a razor's edge, 'I'm sorry to interrupt your—er—conversation.'

He didn't wait for Henk, who, preparing to follow him, exclaimed, 'And what's he in a rage for? And he's back hours earlier than he said. Perhaps he missed his dollybird in Brussels.' He saw the stricken look on Abigail's face as he said it and added hurriedly, 'I joke, Abigail—he has no dollybird. *Dag.*'

He hurried away after his chief and Abigail, left alone, went to see why the baby in the first cubicle was crying. She had no idea what had come over the professor; he hadn't looked like that for a long time now and she had been quite unprepared for it. She tended the baby with gentle, competent hands, telling herself that something must have happened in Brussels to have upset him, trying to ignore the fact that he wasn't a man who was easily upset.

He did a round in the afternoon, surrounded by students, with his senior registrar and Henk flanking his every movement. He was delightful with the children and curt with everyone else. Abigail, trailing along behind Zuster Ritsma, felt sorry for the students, who, unless they came up with the right answers to the professor's barked questions, were subjected to a withering fire from his tongue and a look of such irritation that the most stout-hearted of them were quailed. From the safety of Zuster Ritsma's rear, she watched him; not only did he look ill-tempered, he looked weary too. Perhaps when they were alone together he would tell her what the matter was. He glanced round and she caught his eye and gave him a small loving smile which stiffened on her face as he looked through her. She felt her cheeks pale and for the rest of the round didn't look at him at all. Only after he had gone, and it was time for her to go off duty, she made her way down to the porter's lodge and asked where he was and if she could see him. The porter looked surprised, but he went to the switchboard and after a few minutes he shook his head. 'Professor van Wijkelen is *weg*,' he told her.

She walked slowly back to the changing room. Why had he gone without leaving a message? She stopped in the middle of the corridor. Surely she hadn't imagined all that he had said to her—worse still, mistaken his meaning?

She had cheered up a little by the time she reached Mrs Macklin's house, having persuaded herself that Dominic would come that evening. She stayed in the little sitting room, her ears strained for his footsteps, and when Mrs Macklin wanted to know if he was back, explained in a colourless voice that yes, he was but that he seemed to be busy.

'Not too busy to see you,' stated Mrs Macklin decidedly, and when Abigail gave her an enquiring look, 'He's a different man since he met you, my dear. It's amazing what love will do.'

'Love?' faltered Abigail.

'You love him, don't you? He needs someone to love him and to love. He has become so embittered over the years that I was beginning to think that he would never allow himself to love another woman, but I think you have changed that. I wonder why he doesn't come.'

Abigail looked up from the contemplation of her nails. 'I don't know. When he went away, he said—he said there was no time to talk then, but when he came back…he came back this morning, but he's…something's happened. He's not coming.'

She was sure of that now. 'Perhaps tomorrow.' She looked appealingly at her companion. 'I expect he's tired.'

The old lady eyed her thoughtfully. 'You're tired too, Abigail. Go to bed, my dear. Things are always better in the morning.'

Abigail did as she was told for the simple reason that she didn't much care what she did and bed was as good as anywhere else; contrary to her expectations, she slept all night.

She was off duty at four-thirty the next day too. The morning passed quickly enough; there were two cases for theatre and she went with both of them; tiny babies with pyloric stenosis and the professor operating. If he saw her in the theatre he gave no sign, but she hadn't expected him to. She stayed by the anaesthetist, performing the small duties he required of her throughout the two operations. When she got back from her dinner it was to discover from Zuster Ritsma that the professor had been to see his patients and since he would be operating for the rest of the afternoon, the chance of seeing him was slight. She went off duty a little late, spinning out the minutes in case he should come; she even went a long way round to the hospital entrance in the hope of seeing him, despising herself for doing so—she had never thought much of girls who chased men, and here she was doing just that. There was no sign of him, so she went back to the Begijnhof and after tea went for a long walk. Let him telephone and find her out, she told herself bracingly, it would serve him right if she wasn't there at his beck and call. Only he didn't telephone. She went to bed early and cried herself to sleep.

She was on at one o'clock the next day and would work until nine in the evening. Zuster Ritsma was on too and a couple of student nurses, and because the ward was full and some of the children and babies were very ill, they were kept busy. It was well after three o'clock when Abigail went to the office to pour the tea for Zuster Ritsma and herself. They had barely sat down to drink it when the professor walked in.

Zuster Ritsma looked at him with resignation. She had been

on her feet for a long time and now here he was, wanting to do a round, she supposed. Before she could speak he said, 'No, no round.'

'A cup of tea?' she smiled her relief.

'Thank you, no.' He hadn't looked at Abigail, but he gave her the briefest of glances now, a look of cool enquiry which prompted her to ask:

'You would like me to go, sir?'

'Since it concerns you, Nurse Trent, I see no need for that.' He smiled thinly. 'We are now fully staffed, or nearly so; it only remains for me to thank you for the help you have given us and tell you that there is now no further need of your services. I am sure that we are all most grateful to you for the way in which you helped out, but I am sure you will be glad to be free to arrange your own future.'

Abigail listened to this speech with absolute amazement; she wasn't even sure if half of it were true to begin with, but she could hardly challenge him on that score. She was a freelance nurse, under no obligation to give or receive a month's notice, so presumably the hospital could terminate her job when they wished. She found her voice and filled the awkward pause with an over-hearty, 'Oh, splendid, I shall be able to go back...' Her voice petered away, because unless someone paid her, she couldn't go back to England; she hadn't got her fare any more, for she had paid Mrs Macklin for her room, and she had been paying for her meals in hospital too. She could borrow from Bolly, but that was something she wasn't prepared to do; she had leaned on Bolly enough in the last few years.

Neither Zuster Ritsma nor the professor appeared to notice her hesitancy.

'We shall miss you, Nurse Trent,' said Zuster Ritsma kindly. 'You are good with the children, is that not so, Professor?'

'Very good.' He spoke shortly and turned to go, his face blandly polite, no more. 'You will leave tonight, Nurse Trent.'

It was a command, no less, and she seethed, but she didn't

bother to answer him, nor did she look up as he went. He could at least have wished her goodbye. She blinked back tears and said shakily, 'I'll make a fresh pot of tea, shall I? This lot's cold.'

And Zuster Ritsma, after one look at her face, sat down at her desk, instantly absorbed in the papers on it, so that Abigail had time to compose herself and subdue the searing misery and bewilderment and rage which worked so strongly beneath her starched apron.

It was a good thing that the rest of the day proved to be so busy she had no time to think at all, and when at length it was nine o'clock and she was free to go, she made her farewells as quickly as possible before hurrying through the hospital which had suddenly become alien ground. She couldn't get away faster, she told herself.

She had told Zuster Ritsma about her delayed pay and that kind soul had been sympathetic but quite unable to do much about it. She had sent Abigail down to the hospital office where they dealt with such things and she had been met with blank looks and shrugged shoulders. As far as she could understand from the clerk she wasn't on the hospital pay roll at all; Professor van Wijkelen had engaged her to work for him and had made himself responsible for her salary, and beyond suggesting that she should find him and ask for herself, the clerk had no advice to give.

She went past the porter's lodge without hearing the man on duty wishing her good night and plunged outside into the dark. The desultory snow had ceased again, the pavements were wet under her feet and she shivered as she ran across the forecourt. She was totally unprepared for Jan's voice calling, 'Miss, miss!' from the car which slid silently alongside her. He smiled and opened the door, saying in his heavily accented English, 'I am to take you home, so please to get in.'

Abigail shook her head. 'Thank you, Jan, but there must be some mistake—Does the professor know that you've come to fetch me? And anyway I don't want to.'

Jan looked at his most fatherly. 'I am just this minute told by the professor to take you home, miss,' he contrived to look worried. 'He will be angry if I return and say that you would not go with me.'

She got in beside him, answering his polite remarks absent-mindedly while her mind ran on and on, trying to decide what she would do. To remain in Amsterdam was unthinkable, to go back to England was impossible for the moment. She would have to get a job until she had enough money. When they arrived at the Begijnhof she thanked Jan and asked if he would take a message for her. 'To Bollinger,' she explained. 'Just tell him that I've gone away for a few days and he's not to worry, Mrs Macklin will let him know more about it later.' It sounded harmless enough like that, by the time Bollinger got worried enough to ask Mrs Macklin, she would certainly have another job, and she could always think of something to tell him when the time came. It was all a little vague, but it would have to do. She wished Jan goodbye and reminded him not to tell anyone else but Bollinger what she had said, and he agreed cheerfully, wishing her *Tot ziens* as he went back to the car, a hopeful form of farewell to which she was unable to subscribe. She wished him goodbye and went soberly indoors.

Mrs Macklin was in the kitchen making their bedtime drinks. She turned and smiled as Abigail walked in, saying, 'There you are, child—how nice and early. You must have been walking fast.'

'Jan brought me in the car.'

'Dear Dominic, what care he takes of you.' Mrs Macklin spoke with a satisfied pride which sparked off Abigail's held-down feelings.

'He does nothing of the kind,' she declared hotly. 'He doesn't care a brass farthing for anyone but himself! He's cold and heartless and I detest him. He's given me the sack, today—this very afternoon—just like that—he said...' she choked. 'He owes me weeks of salary too...' She burst into tears.

The whole story came out; in fragments which didn't make sense at first, but Mrs Macklin had patience. Slowly she sorted out the facts from the fiery condemnation of the professor's character, the bewilderment as to why it had happened and determination, repeated many times, never, never to see him again. 'And I would rather die,' declared Abigail in far too loud a voice, 'than take a penny from the man!' She turned a tear-blotched face to her listener. 'I love him so,' she said miserably.

'There is, of course, a mistake somewhere,' said Mrs Macklin with kind firmness. 'Someone or something has caused him to behave like this.'

Abigail took a drink of cooling cocoa which she didn't want. 'But why didn't he at least tell me? I thought he trusted me, I even thought that he was beginning to love me a little—that's absurd, of course. Look at me, no one ever looks at me more than once—no man, that is.' Which wasn't quite true, but she was in the mood to exaggerate. 'And Dominic least of all.' She put down her cup. 'I'm going away, Mrs Macklin.'

'Yes, dear. Where to? England?'

'I can't—I haven't any money, at least, not enough.'

'I will gladly lend...'

'You're a dear, Mrs Macklin, but no, thank you, I won't borrow unless I'm quite desperate. If I could get a job somewhere away from Amsterdam, just long enough to save my fare. I must get away.'

'You're sure that's the right thing to do, Abigail?'

Abigail got up and took the cups and saucers over to the tray on the table. 'Yes, I'm sure. I couldn't stay, you see, I might see him. I haven't known him long, I should be able to forget him.'

Both ladies knew that this was a silly remark, but neither of them said so. Mrs Macklin nodded her head and offered:

'In that case, I believe I can help you. I have a friend, a Mevrouw Hagesma. She lives in Friesland, in a tiny village north of Leeuwarden. She's had a stroke and although she can get about, she finds it difficult on her own. Her daughter is going home to be with her, but not for a week or so. I think she would be delighted if you would go and stay with her and help her. The only thing is, she's very poor.'

Abigail said quickly, 'She need not pay me; as long as I could have a room and some food, it would give me a chance to decide what to do—there must be some work I can do, I don't care what. Even if it's only a few gulden a week—I don't need much to make up the money for my fare.'

'I still think you should borrow from me, my dear.'

Abigail crossed the little room and planted a kiss on the smooth, elderly cheek. 'What a kind person you are, Mrs Macklin, but I won't. I'll go to your friend if she'll have me, at least I'll be out of the way.' She gulped, determined to put a bright face on things. 'I'll go back to England just as soon as I can and get a job and then Bolly can come back.'

'He's very happy at Dominic's house,' Mrs Macklin reminded her.

'You think he'd like to stay? If—if Dominic would keep him and he'd be happy, then that would be wonderful. He deserves better than I can offer him.' She sighed. 'Could I write to your friend tomorrow and ask...?'

'She sits up till all hours,' Mrs Macklin interrupted her to say. 'I'll telephone her now.'

Ten minutes later Abigail said wonderingly, 'Well, I can hardly believe it—all fixed up so quickly. I'll pack tonight and leave on that early train—you're sure it runs?'

'Yes, my dear,' Mrs Macklin smiled at her. 'I shall miss you. What am I to say if—when Dominic calls?'

'He won't. He's—he's finished with me, I think. Perhaps he remembered his wife and thinks I should get like her—he must be mad,' Abigail's voice rose a little, 'if he thinks that. His wife was lovely, wasn't she? with lots of men-friends. I couldn't be more different—perhaps that's why. I mean, I'd be such a safe, unexciting sort of wife, wouldn't I, because he would never need to be jealous of me.'

Mrs Macklin quite rightly took no notice of this diatribe. 'What shall I tell him?' she repeated.

'That I've gone to another job; he'll not want to know more than that, if he asks. And please don't tell him where I am or about the money.'

Her companion gave her an understanding look. 'No, dear. Now go to bed, you have to be up early in the morning. What about Bollinger?'

Abigail explained about him. 'I don't think he'll worry, not for a little while, and if he comes to see you, if you'll just tell him that I'm working—another case—and that I'll write.'

She said goodnight and went away to pack and then to go to bed and lie awake until it was time for her to get up. The night had been very long. She dressed with relief, had a sketchy breakfast, took Mrs Macklin a cup of tea, wished her goodbye and left the house.

The train journey to Leeuwarden was uneventful. Abigail, watching the flat, wintry fields as they flashed along, saw nothing. Because of her sleepless night she was quite unable to think; wisps of conversation flitted in and out of her tired mind, snatches of things she had said and done in the last few weeks since she had met Dominic, came and went, tangling themselves into a frenzied, half-remembered muddle which did nothing to improve a rapidly worsening headache. She got out at Leeuwarden and a kindly ticket collector sent her to the station café to have a cup of coffee while she waited for the bus, which wasn't due for an hour. There was a map on the café wall, and she studied it, glad to discover that the village she was going to was a long way away from Dominic's home. As far as she could make out, it was on a side road, half way between Leeuwarden and Holwerd on the coast. The side road, according to the map, ended at Molenum, which was the place she was going to. For the first time since she had accepted the job, she wondered what sort of a house she was going to, and what kind of a village it was in.

Molenum, when she reached it, was small; one shop, a post office in the front room of a small house in its main street and a very large church. The landscape was rolling and wide and there weren't many trees. There was a chill, damp wind blowing in from the sea, some miles away, and absolutely no one to be seen. She watched the bus lumber away and went into the shop.

The woman behind the counter was tall and gaunt and middle-aged, dressed severely in black. She stared at Abigail in a disconcerting way which she found a little daunting as she said: *'Dag, mevrouw,'* and then, 'Mevrouw Hagesma?'

The stare melted into a nice smile. The village was so small, probably everyone in it knew she was coming; she smiled back as the woman came from behind the counter and pointed up the narrow cobbled road, past a row of dollshouse-sized cottages, to a house standing alone; it was just as small as the others, but it had a garden all round it. Abigail said *'Dank U'* and picked up her case and started towards it, aware that, as she passed, the spotless white curtains at the little front windows were stirred by invisible fingers. She opened the gate and walked up the narrow brick path and knocked on the old-fashioned wooden door; it had a small square shutter in it which opened to allow an eye to examine her before the door was opened.

Mevrouw Hagesma was tall and gaunt too, and quite old, but her face was kind and her eyes were as bright and blue as a little girl's. It was then that Abigail realised that she would have to speak Dutch, something she hadn't thought about before. She embarked on a few muddled phrases to which the old lady listened with grave courtesy, and then said slowly, her speech thickened by her stroke, 'A friend of Mrs Macklin's is a friend of mine,' and led the way into the living room. She walked with a stick and very slowly and one arm hung, not quite uselessly, at her side.

The room was comfortably furnished and tidy, but the pristine cleanliness Abigail knew was a Dutchwoman's pride was absent. The old lady waved an arm clumsily around her and shrugged her shoulders, and Abigail understood the gesture to be one of apology because not everything was exactly in its place, nor was it quite spotless.

It was surprising how, after those first few minutes, they managed to understand each other. Abigail had a room like a cupboard at the top of the ladder-like stairs—she unpacked her few things and went down again to find Mevrouw Hagesma making coffee. While they drank it, and with the aid of the little dictionary Abigail always carried with her, she found out all she needed to know about the old lady as well as telling her as much as she thought necessary about herself. Mevrouw Hagesma nodded and smiled her slightly lopsided smile when Abigail had finished. 'We shall be friends,' she told her, and although she spoke in Dutch, Abigail understood her very well.

Abigail had expected the days to drag, but surprisingly they didn't. There was so much to do in the little house, and once Mevrouw Hagesma saw that she was a good housewife, able to sweep and dust and polish and not grumble about it, she was content to leave a great deal to her. Not that Abigail allowed the old lady to be idle. She had her exercises to do each day, and her reading, and Abigail was helping her to write once more with her still partly paralysed hand. Mrs Macklin had telephoned several times too and Abigail had longed to ask about Dominic but didn't, and Mrs Macklin didn't mention him.

Each morning, just before dinner time, Abigail took Mevrouw Hagesma for a walk, a very short one, down to the village shop, where she rested for a little while and then back home again. It was a slow clumsy business, but the old lady looked forward to a gossip with Mevrouw Beeksma in the shop and most mornings there were customers there too so that the gossip became half an hour's chat, something which the old lady enjoyed very much although Abigail found the elderly, soberly clad ladies unexciting. They spoke Fries, which made it impossible for her to understand them, and when they spoke to her in careful, slow Dutch, she still had difficulty in understanding them. She got into the habit of wandering round the little shop, examining the crowded shelves, looking at the tins and packets, learning their prices for the sake of something to do, and when she found that Mevrouw Hagesma enjoyed correcting her wild attempts to speak Dutch, she suggested that they should spend a little time each evening struggling with that language and improving her deplorable accent. It passed the long hours before bedtime and the old lady, now that she had something to occupy her mind, began to improve rapidly.

Abigail had been there ten days when Mevrouw Beeksma told her that her daughter had been taken ill and had been taken to hospital in Leeuwarden. Abigail, wrestling with the shopkeeper's pantomime of screwed-up face, hands clasped to back and urgent bendings, tried to guess what complaint the poor girl had. Renal colic, perhaps, or even a slipped disc—she made a sympathetic murmur and listened to Mevrouw Beeksma bemoaning the fact that she wouldn't be able to go and see her each afternoon, because there was no one to mind the shop. If only there was someone to take the place over for an hour or so each afternoon, said poor Mevrouw Beeksma, looking gaunter than ever.

'I will,' said Abigail, not stopping to think.

'Wel, neen,' declared Mevrouw Beeksma, and then: *'Waarom niet?'*

Why not indeed, thought Abigail, she had been wanting a job—here it was. For the first week it hadn't mattered too much because deep down inside her she had hoped that Dominic would come thundering after her. But of course he hadn't, and now it was urgent that she should earn some money; she would have to go when Mevrouw Hagesma's daughter came, it would be splendid if she could earn enough money to go straight back to England before that time.

'Three hours each afternoon,' said Mevrouw Beeksma, 'and I pay two gulden an hour.'

Abigail did sums—six gulden a day for six days, that would

be thirty-six gulden. She needed more than that, but perhaps she could sell something.

'Yes,' said Abigail.

She was slow that first day. The ladies of the village who came for their groceries had to help her with their change and point out just what they wanted, but Abigail, who considered the job as a gift from heaven, didn't make the same mistake twice. By the fourth afternoon she was managing very well and Mevrouw Beeksma pronounced herself satisfied. 'Another week,' she told Abigail, 'and my daughter will be home.' She smiled and nodded and strode out into the windy street to catch the bus.

It was cold again, just like winter, as indeed it still was. A few snowflakes, blown by the sea wind, settled on the window ledges of the shop. Abigail watched the bus disappear into the empty countryside beyond the village and went back into the shop. She had been working hard all the morning, turning the little house upside down for the weekly clean Mevrouw Hagesma considered absolutely necessary, and today, for the first time, the old lady had helped a little and talked cheerfully about her future, so that Abigail felt heartened by her progress. There had been a letter from Mrs Macklin too, full of messages from Bollinger, who was a little puzzled but quite content to take Mrs Macklin's word for it that Abigail was happy. She took the letter out of her pocket now and read it through as though she might have missed something in it—something, some news of Dominic, but he wasn't mentioned.

She put the letter away with a little sigh, put on the white apron, much too large, which was Mevrouw Beeksma's concession to hygiene in her shop, and got out the stepladder. The apron got terribly in the way and Abigail muttered rudely; it wasn't as though it was necessary—the shop was cleaner than anything she had ever seen in her life, there couldn't be a germ in the place; still, as her employer wished her to dress up in it, she supposed she should. She hitched it up round her pretty legs and climbed the steps.

She had been up there perhaps ten minutes, dusting bottles of pickles and gherkins and onions, when the door opened, allowing a draught of cold air, a few persistent snowflakes and the professor to enter.

Abigail put the pot of gherkins she was holding carefully back on the shelf, for her hands felt strangely incapable of holding anything. Her heart had leapt, stopped and then begun to hammer at her ribs in a most unnerving fashion. She had no breath; all she could do was to sit and stare down at the top of his head, until he looked up and saw her. They stared at each other for a timeless age before she asked idiotically, 'Is there something you want?' just as though he was a housewife come to buy tea or coffee or a few slices of cheese.

'You,' he said in a rough voice, and went on staring. 'Come down, Abigail.'

Somewhere at some time she remembered she had read that one should always begin as one meant to go on, especially when it concerned matters of the heart. It seemed to her a sound idea. She stayed where she was.

After a silence which she found unendurable the professor said in quite a different voice, 'Please come down, Abby, I want to talk to you,' and when she still didn't move because truth to tell she found herself incapable of doing so, he began again, but this time in a loud rough voice.

'I can no longer sleep because of you, nor can I eat—presently I shall be unable to do my work. It is intolerable that a small mouse of a girl like you can reduce me to this miserable state. Each time that I have sent you away I have racked my brains for an excuse to get you back; I thought at first that I could hold out against you, but I find that there is nothing to hold out against, only gentleness and kindness and honesty and a smile to twist my heart, my dearest darling.'

'You have behaved abominably,' said Abigail severely, 'and I will not be your dearest darling until I know why you did.' She watched the rueful smile touch his mouth.

'I came back from Brussels hell for leather, longing to see you again. I found you with Henk, laughing up at him—you are so pretty when you laugh, my darling—I listened to you talking and it seemed to me that it was I whom you were discussing. I wanted to hurt you then as I was hurt.' He sighed, he went on humbly, 'It has taken me all this while to swallow my pride, for I have to know...'

He was interrupted by the opening of the door. Old Mevrouw Henninga from one of the houses across the street shook the snow off her cap, bade them good day and asked for tea. Abigail had to descend her steps then. She found the tea, served her customer, gave her, for once, the right change and wished her a polite good day, while the professor, not to be outdone when it came to manners, opened the door and closed it after her.

When he spoke he forgot to be humble. 'And why in the name of heaven are you serving behind a counter?' His voice a snarl.

Abigail prudently climbed her ladder again; there was a distinct advantage in being a little above him. 'I'm earning my living,' she explained haughtily.

He glared at her under lowered brows. 'Why here in this back-of-beyond place? Why aren't you in England? I went after you and you weren't there.'

Abigail's heart began to beat its own happy little tune, spreading a tingle of excitement over her.

'I'll tell you why I wasn't there,' she said, and struggled to keep her voice cool and calm and slow. But it came out in an excited babble. 'I had no money—no money to go back to England, and do you know why? Because you haven't paid me—not for weeks,' her voice rose a little. 'You sent me away without references and didn't even bother to ask if I had somewhere to go, just like a Victorian servant girl; for all you cared I might have gone on the streets!'

'On the streets?' he looked thunderstruck. 'My dear little love, what a brute I have been! Can you ever forgive me? You see I could think of nothing else but you and Henk, laughing together—and you are so young...' he was leaning on the counter now, looking up at her. 'For years now I believed that I had built myself a new life, a nice safe life in which women didn't matter, in which I could work without getting involved with anyone—any girl. And then I saw you and lost my heart, my lovely girl, but not without a fight. I told myself that you were clever and scheming with your quiet voice and your friendliness and kindness. I fought very hard, my darling, but then I discovered that I didn't want to fight any more. I have used you very ill, haven't I?'

Abigail smiled. 'Indeed you have.' She paused. 'We weren't talking about you at all, only about Henk's latest girl-friend.' She went on primly, 'Listeners never hear any good of themselves.' She frowned quite fiercely at the professor. 'There is something else. I am considered quite old for my age.'

'Abby...' The door opened once more and a small boy sidled in and demanded *bischuiten*. The professor, curbing impatience with a visible effort, handed him a packet from the counter, took his money and put it in the till.

'He wants three cents change,' advised Abigail from her observation post, and watched while the professor rang up the till to the manner born and proffered the coins.

'Give him a sweetie,' and when the boy had gone, his cheek bulging with a toffee, she explained, 'It's good business to give the children sweeties when they come on an errand.'

She didn't say any more because the professor was looking at her with such tenderness and love that her breath deserted her. He said now, very firmly, 'Abigail, I have never proposed to a girl on top of a stepladder before, but that's what I intend doing unless you come down.'

He held out his arms and she jumped straight into them; they held her so tightly that she could feel his heart beating under her cheek. Her voice a whisper, muffled by the thickness of his jacket, she said:

'Only Mrs Macklin knew where I was, and I asked her not to tell.'

'And she kept her word. Bollinger and I put our heads together when I got back from England and I went to see her, but all she would tell me was that an old friend of hers needed help until her daughter could go to her.'

She felt his kiss on her hair. 'Abby, my darling girl, if you wish to tell me off I promise you that I will be very meek.'

'Don't be ridiculous!' She looked up into his face, smiling, and he bent his head to kiss her.

'Will you marry me, Abby?'

'Yes, dear Dominic, of course I will.' She would have said more, but the professor's hold tightened so that she had no breath, or almost none, and when she at last essayed to speak, he kissed her silent. It was an enjoyable silence which at length Abigail broke.

'Dominic—wait a minute, there's something important—what about Bolly?'

The professor loosened his grasp very slightly so that he could see her face. 'A useful addition to our household, wouldn't you think, my darling? He's terrific with animals and gardens and, I've no doubt, children too.'

'Oh, he will be pleased—he's splendid with them.'

'Then we must do our utmost to give him every opportunity to be splendid, mustn't we?'

She smiled, and the dimple came and went. 'A bad-tempered little boy just like his father,' she murmured.

'And an adorable mousy little girl just like her beautiful mother.'

They stared at each other happily, contemplating a blissful future, and for good measure the professor kissed her again.

'What shall we do?' asked Abigail, feeling that one of them at least should be practical, but it seemed that Dominic had everything arranged.

'You're coming back with me to Amsterdam, my love. Arie's

sister is on her way over to take your place with Mevrouw Hagesma—Jan's fetching her, I'm sure she'll understand when we explain.'

'About Amsterdam,' said Abigail. 'Where…?'

'Bollinger and Mevrouw Boot will have everything ready for you—and before you protest, Mrs Macklin is already at my house. You will stay there until I can arrange our wedding, my dearest—in the church in the Begijnhof, don't you agree?'

Abigail nodded, savouring the delight of being loved, indeed her ordinary face had become quite transformed by it so that the professor exclaimed,

'How very pretty you are, Abby,' and since it was obvious that he really believed it she smiled at him with delight and lifted her face for his kiss.

Presently: 'How long do we have to play at shop?' Dominic wanted to know.

'Until the bus gets in at half past four—and it's not playing at shop. I get paid—two gulden an hour.'

The horrified incredulity on the professor's face would have satisfied any girl who might have considered herself to have been badly treated, but Abigail wasn't any girl; she loved him. Looking into his stricken face she remembered that she hadn't yet told him this indisputable fact, and did so there and then, and the professor, holding her with powerful gentleness, kissed her at great length until she reminded him that she should get behind the counter, 'Just in case someone should come, dear Dominic.'

He glanced over her head at the snowflakes whirling past the shop window in a last wintry onslaught before spring made nonsense of them. 'Anyone coming out on a day like this would be mad,' he declared, 'and if they do I will serve them for you, my dearest heart.'

'Well,' conceded Abigail, 'you managed to sell the *bischuiten* very nicely. All the same I just can't stand here…'

'Oh, yes, you can,' said Dominic in a voice which sounded

so certain of this that she found no point in arguing with him about it, and it was, after all, quite delightful with her head on his shoulder and his arms around her.

'If you say so, dear Dominic,' she said meekly, and kissed him.

* * * * *

Hilltop Tryst

CHAPTER ONE

THE SUN, rising gloriously on the morning of Midsummer's Day, turned the swelling Dorset hills into a wide vista of golden green fields and clumps of trees under a blue sky. Miles away, traffic along the dual carriageway thundered on its way to the west, unheard and unheeded in the quiet countryside around the village of Hindley, its inhabitants for the most part still sleeping in their beds. Farm workers were already about their work, though; the bleating of sheep and the sounds of horses and cattle were blotted out from time to time by the sound of a tractor being started up; but on the brow of the hill rising behind the village these sounds were faint, the bird-song was louder.

Half-way up the hill a girl sat, leaning comfortably against the trunk of a fallen tree, a shaggy dog sprawled beside her. She had drawn up her knees, clasped her arms around them and rested her chin on them—a pretty, rounded chin, but determined too, belying the wide, gentle mouth and the soft brown eyes with their thick black lashes. Her hair was long and brown, plaited and hanging over one shoulder. She flung it back with a well-shaped hand and spoke to the dog.

'There—the sun's rising on the longest day of the year,

Knotty. Midsummer Madness—the high tide of the year, a day for fairies and elves, a day for making a wish. Do you suppose if I made one it might come true?'

Knotty, usually obliging with his replies, took no notice, but growled softly, cocked his large, drooping ears and allowed his teeth to show. He got to his feet and she put a restraining hand on his collar, turning to look behind her as she caught the sound of steady feet and someone coming along, whistling.

Knotty barked as a man left the line of trees and came towards them. A giant of a man, dressed in an open-necked shirt and elderly trousers, his pale hair shone in the sunlight and he walked with an easy self-assurance. Tucked under one arm was a small dog, a Jack Russell, looking bedraggled.

He stopped by the girl, towering over her so that she was forced to crane her neck to see his face. 'Good morning. Perhaps you can help me?' He had put down a balled fist for Knotty to examine, ignoring the teeth.

'I found this little chap down a rabbit-hole—couldn't get out and probably been there for some time. Is there a vet around here?' He smiled at her. 'The name's Latimer—Oliver Latimer.'

The girl got to her feet, glad for once that she was a tall girl, and very nearly able to look him in the face. 'Beatrice Browning. That's Nobby—Miss Mead's dog. She'll be so very glad, he's been missing for a couple of days—everyone has been out looking for him. Where was he?'

'About a mile on the other side of these woods—there's a stretch of common land... The vet?'

'You'd better come with me. Father will be up by now; he's leaving early to visit a couple of farms.'

She started down the hill towards the village below. 'You're out early,' she observed.

'Yes. You too. It's the best time of the day, isn't it?'

She nodded. They had left the hill behind them and were in a narrow rutted lane, the roofs of the village very close.

'You live here?' he wanted to know. He spoke so casually that she decided that he was merely making polite conversation.

'My home is here; I live with an aunt in Wilton.' She turned to look at him. 'Well, not all the time—I'm staying with her until she can get another companion.' She went on walking. 'Actually she's a great-aunt.'

She frowned; here she was, handing out information which couldn't be of the slightest interest to this man. She said austerely, 'What a splendid day it is. Here we are.' Her father's house was of a comfortable size surrounded by a large, overgrown garden, and with a paddock alongside for any animals he might need to take under his care. She led the way around the side of the house, so in through the back door, and found her father sitting on the doorstep drinking tea. He wished her good morning and looked enquiringly at her companion. 'A patient already—bless me, that's Nobby! Hurt?'

'Nothing broken, I fancy. Hungry and dehydrated, I should imagine.'

'Mr Latimer found him down a rabbit-hole the other side of Billings Wood,' said Beatrice. 'My father,' she added rather unnecessarily.

The two men shook hands, and Nobby was handed over to be examined by her father. Presently he said, 'He seems to have got off very lightly. There's no reason why he shouldn't go straight back to Miss Mead.'

'If you will tell me where to go, I'll take him as I walk back.'

Beatrice had poured the tea into two mugs. 'Have some tea first,' she offered. 'Do you want to phone anyone? This must have delayed you...'

'Stay for breakfast?' suggested her father. 'My wife will be down directly—I want to be well away before eight o'clock.' He glanced up. 'Far to go?'

'Telfont Evias—I'm staying with the Elliotts.'

'George Elliott? My dear chap, give him a ring and say you're staying for breakfast. It's all of three miles. Beatrice, will you show him where the telephone is? You can take Nobby back while breakfast is being cooked.'

Miss Mead lived right in the village in one of the charming cottages which stood on either side of the main street. Trees edged the cobbled pavement and the small front gardens were a blaze of colour. Mr Latimer strolled along beside Beatrice, Nobby tucked under one arm, talking of this and that in his deep voice. Quite nice, but a bit placid, Beatrice decided silently, peeping sideways at his profile. He was undoubtedly good-looking as well as being extremely large. Much, much larger than James, the eldest son of Dr Forbes, who had for some time now taken it for granted that she would marry him when he asked her…

She decided not to think about him for the moment, and instead pointed out the ancient and famous inn on the corner of the street and suggested that they might cross over, since Miss Mead's little cottage was on the other side.

Miss Mead answered their knock on her door. She was tall and thin and elderly, and very ladylike. She wore well-made skirts and blouses, and covered them with cardigans of a suitable weight according to the time of year, and drove a small car. She was liked in the village, but guardedly so, for she had an acid tongue if annoyed.

But now her stern face crumpled into tearful delight. 'Nobby—where have you been?' She took him from Mr Latimer and hugged him close.

'You found him. Oh, I'm so grateful, I can never thank you enough—I've hardly slept…'

She looked at them in turn. 'He's not hurt? Has your father seen him, Beatrice?'

'Yes, Miss Mead. Mr Latimer found him down a rabbit-hole and carried him here.'

'He seems to have come to no harm,' interpolated Mr Latimer in his calm voice. 'Tired and hungry and thirsty—a couple of days and he'll be quite fit again.'

'You're so kind—really, I don't know how to thank you...'

'No need, Miss Mead. He's a nice little chap.' He turned to Beatrice. 'Should we be getting back? I don't want to keep your father waiting.'

A bit cool, she thought, agreeing politely, wishing Miss Mead goodbye and waiting while she shook hands with her companion and thanked him once again. Perhaps his placid manner hid arrogance. Not that it mattered, she reflected, walking back with him and responding politely to his gentle flow of talk; they were most unlikely to meet again. A friend of the Elliotts, staying for a day or two, she supposed.

He proved to be a delightful guest. Her mother sat him down beside her and plied him with breakfast and a steady flow of nicely veiled questions, which he answered without telling her anything at all about himself. That he knew the Elliotts was a fact, but where he came from and what he did somehow remained obscure. All the same, Mrs Browning liked him, and Beatrice's three sisters liked him too, taking it in turns to engage him in conversation. And he was charming to them; Ella, fifteen and still at school, Carol, on holiday from the stockbroker's office where she worked in Salisbury, and Kathy, getting married in a few weeks' time...

They were all so pretty, thought Beatrice without rancour; she was pretty herself, but at twenty-six and as the eldest she tended to regard them as very much younger than herself, partly because they were all cast in a smaller mould and could get into each other's size tens, while she was forced to clothe her splendid proportions in a size fourteen.

Mr Latimer didn't overstay his welcome; when her father got up from the table he got up too, saying that he must be on his way. He thanked Mrs Browning for his breakfast, bade her daughters goodbye and left the house with Mr Browning, bidding him goodbye too as they reached the Land Rover parked by the gate and setting off at a leisurely pace in the direction of Telfont Evias.

'What a very nice man,' observed Mrs Browning, peering at his retreating back from the kitchen window. 'I do wonder...' She sighed silently and glanced at Beatrice, busy clearing the breakfast-table. 'I don't suppose we shall see him again—I mean, Lorna Elliott has never mentioned him.'

'Perhaps he's not a close friend.' Ella, on her way to get the school bus, kissed her mother and ran down the drive.

And after that no one had much more to say about him; there was the washing-up to do, beds to make, rooms to Hoover and dust and lunch to plan, and as well as that there were the dogs and cats to feed and the old pony in the paddock to groom.

Mr Browning came back during the morning, saw several patients, just had his coffee and then dashed away again to see a sick cow; and at lunch the talk was largely about Great-Aunt Sybil who lived in Wilton and to whom Beatrice was acting as a companion until some luckless woman would be fool enough to answer her advertisement. Beatrice had been there three weeks already, and that, she pointed out with some heat, was three weeks too long. She was only at home now because the old lady had taken herself off to London to be given her yearly check-up by the particular doctor she favoured. She was due back the next day, and Beatrice had been told to present herself at her aunt's house in the early afternoon.

'If it wasn't for the fact that she's family, I wouldn't go,' declared Beatrice.

'It can't be for much longer, dear,' soothed her mother, 'and I know it's asking a lot of you, but who else is there? Ella's too young, Carol's due back in two days' time and Kathy has such a lot to do before the wedding.'

Beatrice cast her fine eyes to the ceiling. 'If the worst comes to the worst, and no one applies for the job, I'd better get married myself.'

There was an instant chorus of, 'Oh, has James proposed?'

And Kathy added, 'I mean properly, and not just taking you for granted.'

'He's not said a word,' said Beatrice cheerfully, 'and even if he did I wouldn't...' She paused, quite surprised that she had meant exactly that.

Until that very moment she hadn't bothered too much about James, while at the back of her mind was the knowledge that when he felt like it he would ask her to marry him, or at least allow his intentions to show, but now she was quite sure that she wouldn't marry him if he were the last man on earth.

'Oh, good,' said Kathy. 'He's not at all your sort, you know.'

'No. I wonder why I didn't see that?'

'Well, dear—he may never ask you,' observed her mother.

'That's just what I mean,' went on Kathy, 'you would have dwindled into a long engagement while he deliberated about the future, and then got married without a scrap of romance.'

'Great-Aunt Sybil offers an alternative, doesn't she?' Beatrice laughed. 'I only hope she liked this doctor she went to see. And wouldn't it be wonderful if there were dozens of replies to her advert for a companion? Then I can come back home and help Father.'

Her father drove her over to Wilton the next day after an early lunch. 'I'm sorry about this, love,' he said as they drove the few miles to the town, 'but your great-aunt is my mother's sister, and I did promise that I'd keep an eye on her.'

'And quite right too,' said Beatrice stoutly. 'Families should stick together.'

Her aunt's house was Georgian, its front door opening on to the street which divided a square, tree-lined and ringed around by similar roomy old houses. Beatrice kissed her father goodbye, picked up her case and pulled the bell by the door. Mrs Shadwell, the sour-faced housekeeper, answered it and stood aside so that she might go in, and with a final wave to her father Beatrice went into the dim and gloomy hall.

Her aunt hadn't returned yet; she went to her room and unpacked her few things, and went downstairs again to open the windows and the glass doors on to the garden at the back of the house; her aunt would order them all closed again the moment she came into the house, but for the moment the warm sun lit the heavily furnished room. Too nice to stay indoors, decided Beatrice, and skipped outside. The garden was quite large and mostly lawn bordered by shrubs and a few trees. She went and sat down with her back to one of them and allowed her thoughts to turn to Mr Latimer. A nice man, she decided; a thought dreamy, perhaps, and probably he had a bad temper once roused. She wondered what he did for a living—a bank manager? A solicitor? Something to do with television? Her idle thoughts were interrupted by a sudden surge of movement within the house. Her aunt had returned.

Beatrice stayed where she was; she could hear her aunt's voice raised in umbrage and she sighed. It wouldn't have been so bad if she were paid for her companionship—if one could call it that: finding things, running up and down stairs with knitting, books, a scarf, answering the telephone, reading aloud to her aunt until that lady dozed off, only to wake a few minutes later and demand that she should continue reading and why had she stopped? Companion, Beatrice decided after a few days of this, wasn't the right word—there was no time to be a companion—who should have been someone to chat to and share jokes with and take little jaunts with on fine days. The word was slave.

Her aunt's voice, demanding to know where Miss Beatrice was, got her slowly to her feet and into the drawing-room.

'I'm here, Aunt.' She had a nice, quiet voice and a pleasant, calm manner. 'Did you have a good trip?'

'No, I did not. It was a waste of my time and my money—that old fool who saw me told me that I was as sound as a bell.'

She glared at Beatrice, who took no notice, but merely asked, 'But why don't you believe him, Aunt?'

'Because I know better; I am in constant pain, but I'm not one to moan and groan; I suffer in silence. You cannot possibly understand, a great healthy girl like you. I suppose you've been at home, idling away the days.'

'That's right, Aunt,' said Beatrice cheerfully. 'Nothing to do but help Father in the surgery, feed the animals, groom the pony and do some of the housework and the cooking...'

'Don't be impertinent, Beatrice! You may go upstairs to my room and make sure that Alice is unpacking my case correctly, and when you come down I wish you to get the telephone number of a heart specialist— No, on second thoughts you had better open the letters. There are bound to be answers to my advertisement.'

But from the little pile of letters Beatrice opened there were only three, and they didn't sound at all hopeful. The first one made it a condition that she should bring her cat with her, the second stipulated that she should have every other weekend free and the third expected the use of a car.

Beatrice offered them to her aunt without comment, and after they had been read and consigned to the wastepaper basket she observed, 'Perhaps if you offered a larger salary...?'

Her aunt's majestic bosom swelled alarmingly. 'The salary I offer is ample. What does my companion need other than a comfortable home and good food?'

'Clothes,' suggested Beatrice, 'make-up and so on, money for presents, probably they have a mother or father they have to help out, holidays...'

'Rubbish. Be good enough to take these letters to the post.'

A respite, even though brief; Beatrice lingered in the little town for as long as she dared, and when she got back she was rebuked for loitering. 'And I have made an appointment with this heart specialist. I shall see him on Wednesday next and you will accompany me. He has rooms in Harley Street.' She added in her loud, commanding voice, 'Jenkins will drive us, and I intend to visit several of these agencies in the hope that I may find someone suitable to be my companion.'

'What a good idea. There's bound to be someone on their books. Will you interview them here or there, Aunt?'

'You may safely leave such decisions to me.' Great-Aunt

Sybil turned a quelling eye upon her, only Beatrice took no notice of it; she was a sensible girl as well as a pretty one and had quickly learnt to ignore her aunt's worse moments. There were plenty of Great-Aunt Sybils in the world and, tiresome though they were, they had families who felt it their duty to keep an eye on them. Only she hoped it wouldn't be too long before she could go back home again, which thought led to her wondering how Miss Mead's Nobby was doing and that led naturally to Mr Latimer. An interesting man, she reflected, if only because of his great size and good looks; she speculated as to his age and quickly married him off to a willowy blonde, small and dainty with everybody doing everything they could for her because of her clinging nature. There would be children too, a little girl and an older boy—two perhaps... She was forced to return to her prosaic world then, because her aunt wished for a glass of sherry. 'And surely you can do that for me,' she grumbled in her overpowering voice, 'although you don't look capable of anything, sitting there daydreaming.'

Beatrice poured the sherry, handed it to her aunt, then gave herself one, tossed it off and, feeling reckless, poured a second one. Great-Aunt Sybil vibrated with indignation. 'Well, really, upon my word, Beatrice, what would your father say if he could see you now? Worse, what would that young man of yours think or say?'

'James? He's not my young man, Aunt Sybil, and I have no intention of marrying him, and I expect that Father would offer me a third glass,' she answered politely and in a reasonable voice, which gave her aunt no opportunity to accuse her of impertinence...

That lady gave her a fulminating look; a paid companion would have been dismissed on the spot, but Beatrice was family and had every right to return home. She said in a conciliatory voice, 'I dare say that you have had several opportunities to marry. You were a very pretty young girl and are still a pretty woman.'

'Twenty-six on my last birthday, Aunt.'

Beatrice spoke lightly, but just lately faint doubts about her future were getting harder to ignore. Somehow the years were slipping by; until her sudden certainty that she couldn't possibly marry James, she supposed that she had rather taken it for granted that she and James would marry, but now she knew that that wouldn't do at all. She didn't love him and she didn't think he loved her. Perhaps she was never to meet a man who would love her and whom she could love. It was getting a bit late in the day, she thought wryly.

'Time you were married and bringing up a family,' declared Aunt Sybil tartly. 'A woman's work...'

And one which her aunt had never had to do, reflected Beatrice. Perhaps if she had had a husband and a handful of children, she might not have become such a trying old lady: always right, always advising people how to do things she knew nothing about, always criticising and correcting, expecting everyone to do what she wanted at a moment's notice...

'Well,' said Beatrice naughtily, 'when you find another companion and I can go home again, perhaps I'll start looking for a husband.'

'Do not be impertinent, Beatrice,' was all her aunt said quellingly...

Wednesday came to break the monotony of the days, and since it was a lovely summer morning Beatrice got into a rather nice silky two-piece in a pale pearly pink, brushed her hair into a shining chignon, thrust her feet into high-heeled sandals and got into the elderly Daimler beside her aunt.

Her aunt eyed her with disapproval. 'Really, my dear, you are dressed more in the manner of someone going to a garden party than a companion.'

'But I'm not a companion,' observed Beatrice sweetly. 'I'm staying with you because you asked me to. And it's a lovely day,' she added, to clinch the matter.

'We will lunch,' stated Great-Aunt Sybil in a cross voice, 'and visit some of these agencies. The sooner I can approve of a companion the better. You are becoming frivolous, Beatrice.'

Beatrice said meekly, 'Yes, Aunt Sybil, perhaps I'm having a last fling before I dwindle into being an old maid.'

Jenkins drove them sedately Londonwards, and at exactly the right time deposited them outside a narrow Regency house in a row of similar narrow houses. Beatrice rang the bell and then followed her aunt's majestic progress into a pleasant waiting-room, where they were greeted by an elderly receptionist and asked to sit down.

'My appointment is for half-past eleven,' pointed out Aunt Sybil, 'and it is exactly that hour.' She drew an indignant breath so that her corsets creaked.

'That's right, Miss Browning.' The receptionist spoke smoothly. 'But the doctor is engaged for the moment.'

'I do not expect to be kept waiting.'

The receptionist smiled politely, picked up the telephone and became immersed in conversation. She was putting it down again when a door at the end of the room opened and a woman came out. Beatrice could hear her saying goodbye to someone on the other side of the door and sighed thankfully; any minute now and her aunt would be whisked away by the nurse who had come into the room.

'You will accompany me,' decreed her aunt. 'I may need your support.' She sailed in the wake of the nurse and was ushered through the door, and Beatrice, walking reluctantly behind her, came to a sudden halt. The eminent doctor, a cardiologist of the first rank, according to her aunt, coming forward to shake her aunt's hand, was Mr Latimer.

A rather different Mr Latimer, though; this elegant man in his sober grey suit and spotless linen was a far cry from the casual walker in his old trousers and shirt. He showed no surprise at the sight of her, but greeted her aunt quietly and then waited with a slightly lifted eyebrow until Great-Aunt Sybil said testily, 'Oh, this is a great-niece of mine. I have a delicate constitution and may require her support.'

Mr Latimer said 'How do you do?' to Beatrice with a blandness which led her to suppose that he had forgotten her completely, observed that he had an excellent nurse in attendance and asked in what way could he advise his patient?

'You are a very young man,' observed Miss Browning in a suspicious voice. 'I trust that you are adequately trained to diagnose illness?'

Beatrice blushed and looked at her feet; her aunt was going to be awful.

'If I might know the nature of your illness?' asked Mr Latimer with just the right amount of professional dignity. He glanced at the folder on his desk, containing letters from various colleagues on the subject of Miss Browning.

Miss Browning fixed him with a cold stare. 'I suffer great pain in my chest. It is at times unendurable, but I do not wish to bother those around me with complaints: I have learnt to conceal my suffering. I think I may say that I have more than my share of courage and patience. The pain is here,' she patted her massive bosom gently, 'and I will explain exactly...'

Which she did at great length, while Dr Latimer sat quietly watching her, though now and again he took a quick look at Beatrice, still examining her feet and wishing the ground would open beneath her.

Presently he interrupted her aunt's flow of talk. 'Yes. Well, Miss Browning, I think the best thing is for me to examine you. If you will go with Nurse, she will prepare you.'

Miss Browning swept out, pausing by Beatrice to beg her in ringing tones to come to her aid of she were to fall faint. 'For this will be an ordeal.'

Beatrice mumbled and peeped across the room to where Dr Latimer sat behind his desk. He was looking at her and smiling, and after a moment she smiled back.

'Don't you miss your green fields and hills?' he asked.

She nodded. After a moment she said, 'I didn't expect to see you again.'

'No? I rather feel it was inevitable that somehow we should meet.'

He got up in response to the buzzer on his desk and went to the examination-room, leaving her to wonder what on earth he meant.

She had plenty of time to ponder his words, for it was quite fifteen minutes before he came back, and there was nothing in his face to tell her what his examination had revealed. He sat down and began to write until after another five minutes his patient came back.

Miss Browning swept in on a tide of ill temper, sat herself down and addressed herself in quelling tones to the impassive man sitting behind his desk.

'I very much doubt,' began Great-Aunt Sybil, 'if you are qualified to diagnose my particular illness. It seems to me that you have failed to appreciate my suffering.'

Dr Latimer appeared unworried. He said smoothly, 'Miss Browning, you have a sound heart; your pain is caused by indigestion. I will give you a diet which, if you choose to follow it, will dispel the pain. From what you have told me, your diet is too rich. I will write to your doctor and inform him of my diagnosis.'

He stood up and went to her chair. 'What a relief it must be to you that you are so splendidly healthy.' He offered a hand, and she had perforce to take it. 'Nurse will give you the diet sheet.'

He accompanied her to the door, and Beatrice was relieved to see that for once her aunt had met her match: Dr Latimer's silky manners screened a steely intention to be in command of the situation. They were ushered out without Miss Browning having the time to utter any of the telling replies she might have had in mind.

The nurse had gone ahead to open the waiting-room door, and for a moment Beatrice and Dr Latimer were alone.

He held out a large, firm hand. 'Goodbye for the present,' he said.

'Oh, do you intend to see my aunt again?'

'Er—no—but we shall meet again.' He gave her a charming smile. 'You don't live with your aunt?'

'Heavens, no! Her companion left and I'm staying with her until we can find another one.' She paused. 'I did tell you.'

Aunt Sybil had turned at the doorway and was looking back at them. 'Come at once, Beatrice. I am exhausted.'

'Dear, oh, dear,' murmured Dr Latimer at his most soothing, 'we must see about that companion, mustn't we?'

She thought that he was merely being comforting, but then, she didn't know him well.

Lunch was a stormy meal, taken at her aunt's favourite restaurant. Naturally it consisted of all the things Miss Browning had been advised not to eat, and while they ate she gave her opinion of doctors in general and Dr Latimer in particular. 'He should be struck off,' she declared.

'Whatever for?' asked Beatrice. 'I thought he had beautiful manners.'

'Pooh—any silly woman could have her head turned by the professional civility these men employ—I am able to see through such tricks.'

Beatrice poured the coffee. 'Aunt Sybil, I think you might at least give his advice an airing…'

'I shall do just as I see fit. We will go now to that agency I have written to; there must be any number of women needing work. Just look at the unemployment…'

But there was no one suitable, nor was there at the other two agencies they visited. Beatrice, a cheerful girl by nature, allowed herself to get despondent at the prospect of weeks of Great-Aunt Sybil's irascible company.

Only it wasn't to be weeks, after all. Three days after her aunt's visit to Dr Latimer, a letter came. The writer, having seen Miss Browning's advertisement, begged to apply for the post of companion, and was willing to present herself at an interview whenever it was convenient.

'Let her come this afternoon,' said Great-Aunt Sybil grandly. 'She sounds a sensible woman.'

'Well, she could hardly get here and back again today,' Beatrice pointed out. 'It's a London address—besides, there's the fare, she might not have it.'

'I cannot think what these people do with their money.'

'They don't have any—or not much to do anything with.'

Her aunt frowned. 'You have this habit of answering back, Beatrice—most unbecoming. Write a letter and tell her to come the day after tomorrow in the early afternoon. You had better take some money from my desk and enclose it.'

Beatrice, addressing the envelope to Miss Jane Moore, hoped fervently that she would be suitable.

It was obvious from the moment that she faced Great-Aunt Sybil in the drawing-room that she was not only suitable but quite capable of holding her own with the old lady. Polite but firm, she allowed Miss Browning to see that she had no intention of being a doormat—indeed, she stipulated that she should have regular hours of freedom and a day off each week—but she sweetened this by pointing out that she was able to undertake all secretarial duties, keep accounts, drive the car, and read aloud. 'I also have some nursing skills,' she added composedly.

Beatrice thought she looked exactly the right person to live with her aunt. Middle-aged, small and wiry, with her pepper and salt hair and a severe bun, Miss Moore exuded competence, good nature and firmness.

Whether she would be able to stand up to her great-aunt's peevish ill humours was another matter. At the moment, at any rate, her aunt seemed more than satisfied. Miss Moore was engaged with the option of a month's notice on either side, and agreed to come in two days' time, Miss Browning's good humour lasting long enough for her to arrange for Miss Moore to be collected with her luggage at the station.

'So now you can go home,' said Miss Browning ungratefully as she and Beatrice sat at dinner that evening. If Beatrice expected thanks, she got none, but that didn't worry her; she telephoned her mother, packed her bag, and at the end of the next day returned home.

It was lovely to be back in her own room again, to unpack and then go down to the kitchen and help her mother get the supper.

'Do you think she'll last, this Miss Moore?' asked her mother.

'I think she might. I mean, Great-Aunt Sybil's other companions have always been so timid, but not Miss Moore—one could think of her as a ward sister used to geriatrics—you know—quite unflustered, but very firm and kind.'

She paused in the enjoyable task of hulling strawberries. 'I shall get up early tomorrow and take Knotty for a long walk before breakfast.'

'Yes, dear. Your father will be glad to have you back to give a hand. Carol's back in Salisbury and Kathy's staying with the in-laws. Ella will be glad, too. You always help her so nicely with her Latin.'

Beatrice woke as the sun, not yet visible, began to lighten the cloudless sky. She was out of bed, had washed her face, got into an old cotton dress she kept for cleaning out the chicken house, tied back her hair and was in the kitchen within minutes. Knotty was waiting, and together they left the house and started to climb the hill. Knotty had bounded on ahead, and Beatrice, almost at the top, looked up to see why he was barking.

She wasn't alone on the hill; Dr Latimer was there too, waiting for her.

CHAPTER TWO

BEATRICE GAPED, half a dozen questions rushing to her tongue.

'Later,' said Dr Latimer. 'Let us watch the sunrise first.'

They sat side by side with Knotty panting between them, while the sky in the east turned pink and gold, and the sun rose slowly between the distant hills. Only when the whole of its shining splendour was visible did Beatrice speak. 'You don't live here...?' And then, 'But it's only just gone five o'clock.'

'Miss Moore told me that you had returned home, and I knew that you would be here.'

How did he know? She let that pass for the moment. 'Miss Moore—do you know her? She's gone as companion to Great-Aunt Sybil.'

She turned her head to look at him, sweeping her hair over her shoulders out of the way. 'Did you tell her about the job?'

He said placidly, 'Yes. She is a retired ward sister who worked for me for several years. Not quite ready to sit back and do nothing much—it suits her to live with your aunt for the time being. She will be able to save every penny of the salary she gets—and I must admit that I found it remarkably poor. She intends to share a small house with a widowed sister, but it won't be vacant for some months.'

'She seemed awfully capable.'

'Oh, indeed she is.'

He sat back with nothing more to say, and presently she asked, 'Have you a day off?'

'No, but no patients until noon. Do you suppose your mother would give me breakfast?'

'I'm sure she will. There's only Ella home, and unless Father's been called out he hasn't a surgery until half-past eight.'

'You're glad to be home?'

She nodded. 'Oh, yes. I don't think I'm cut out to be a companion...'

'You have no ambition to take up a career?'

She shook her head. 'I suppose that years ago, when I was eighteen and full of ideas, I would have liked to train as a vet, but Father taught me a great deal and I like helping him. Ella's too young, and anyway she's not made up her mind what she wants to do, and Carol—she's the brainy one and works in an office, and Kathy will be getting married in a month.' She was silent for a moment, then, 'I'm almost twenty-seven, a bit old to start on a career.'

'But not too old to marry?' He paused. 'I feel sure that you must have had several opportunities. Dr Forbes did mention that his son and you...'

'People make things up to suit themselves,' declared Beatrice crossly. 'James and I have known each other forever, but I have no wish to marry him. I keep saying so, too.'

'Very tiresome for you,' agreed her companion, and gave her a kindly smile, so that her ill humour went as quickly as it had come. 'We had better go if we want breakfast...'

They went unhurriedly down the hill with Knotty cavorting around them, and so to the village and her home, carrying on a desultory conversation and on the best of terms with each other.

Early though it was, the village was stirring; Beatrice called cheerful good mornings as they went, not noticing the smiling, knowing looks exchanged behind her back. She was liked in the village, and although no one had actually said so it was generally thought that she was far too good for Dr Forbes's son. Her companion, aware of the glances, gave no hint of having seen them, although his eyes danced with amusement.

Mrs Browning was breaking eggs into a large frying pan on the Aga, and bacon sizzled under the grill. She looked up as they went into the kitchen, added two more eggs and said happily, 'Good morning. I do hope you've come to breakfast—such a satisfying meal. A lovely day again, isn't it? Beatrice, make the toast, will you? Ella's finishing her maths, and your father will be here directly.' She dished the eggs expertly and put them to keep warm. 'Are you on holiday, Dr Latimer?'

'I only wish I were. I must be back in town by noon...'

'Good heavens! All that way.'

'I had a fancy to watch the sunrise.'

He took the knife from Beatrice and began to slice the loaf, and Mrs Browning, bursting with curiosity, sliced mushrooms into the frying pan, reflecting that he couldn't possibly have driven down from London in time to see the sunrise, in which case, he must have spent the night somewhere nearby. After breakfast, when everyone had gone, she would phone the Elliotts... Lorna would surely know something about him. But her curiosity wasn't to be satisfied; when everyone was out of the way Mrs Browning phoned her friend, only to discover that she was on the point of going out and had to leave the house on the instant. Mrs Browning put down the receiver with something of a thump.

Beatrice, helping her father with his morning surgery, was wondering about Dr Latimer too; it was two hours' hard driving to get to London, and he had said that he had patients to see at noon. There had been no sign of a car; he must have had one, though, parked somewhere nearby—or did he live close by?

She had to hold a large, very cross cat while her father gave it an injection, her thoughts far away so that her father asked mildly, 'Will you take Shakespeare back, my dear? Mrs Thorpe will be waiting for him... I want to see him in two weeks, so make an appointment, will you?'

She bore Shakespeare away to his doting mistress, made an appointment in her neat hand and went back to the surgery where a small boy was standing, clutching a pet rat. She didn't care for rats or mice, but years of helping her father had inured her to them. All the same, she shuddered slightly as she took the animal from its anxious owner. There was nothing much wrong; advice as to diet and a few words of encouragement, and the small boy went away happy to be replaced by Major Digby with his Labrador. Since he and her father were old friends, a good deal of time was spent in talking about the good fishing locally, the chances against Farmer Bates planting sugar beet instead of winter greens and the vagaries of the weather. Beatrice, aware that she was no longer needed, left the two gentlemen, tidied the waiting-room and went along to the kitchen, where her mother was putting a batch of loaves to rise.

'I wonder where he lives?' she asked as Beatrice walked in.

'I have no idea, Mother. London, I would suppose, since that was where Great-Aunt Sybil went to see him. Probably he likes driving long distances.'

Beatrice spoke rather tartly, and Mrs Browning gave her a quick look.

'Oh, well,' she observed, 'we aren't likely to see him again.'

She was wrong. It was exactly a week later that Mr Browning had a heart attack—very early in the morning, on his way back from checking Lady Lamborne's pet donkey. Beatrice, coming down to make early morning tea, found him lying at the kitchen door. He was conscious, but cold and clammy and a dreadful grey colour, and when she felt for his pulse it was fast and faint. She wasn't a girl to lose her head in an emergency; she put a cushion under his head, covered him with the old rug which was draped over one of the Windsor chairs, told him bracingly that he was going to be all right and went to phone Dr Forbes, fetched her mother and then went back to crouch beside her father.

Dr Forbes was there within ten minutes, listened to Beatrice's calm voice, examined his old friend and told her to ring for an ambulance. 'We'll have to go to Salisbury,' he told Mrs Browning. 'I'll give him an injection and we'll keep him on oxygen.' He patted her arm. 'I think he'll do, but it's hard to tell for the moment. Thank heaven that Beatrice found him when she did.'

'You stay with him while I put some things in a bag for him,' said Beatrice. Her voice was quite steady, but her hands shook. 'You'll go with him? I'll stay and sort things out here.'

She was back with the bag within minutes, and urged her mother to get what she needed, ready to go in the ambulance. Her father was quiet now, but he looked so ill that she felt sick with fright, although nothing showed of that upon her pale face. She held one limp hand in hers, and stared down at her father, oblivious of everything else, so that she didn't see Dr Latimer get out of his car at the same time as the ambulance drew up.

A large, gentle hand on her shoulder made her look up. 'Tell me what has happened, Beatrice.' His voice was calm and matter of fact, so that she answered him readily.

'Father—I found him here—Dr Forbes says he's had a coronary thrombosis.' She saw the ambulance for the first time. 'He's to go to Salisbury. Mother's going with him.'

Her voice had been steady enough, only it didn't sound like hers.

Dr Forbes had been talking to the ambulancemen; now he came to his patient. He paused when he saw Dr Latimer. 'We've met,' he said at once. 'You gave a talk at the seminar in Bristol last year... Latimer—Dr Latimer, isn't it?'

He launched into a brief description of Mr Browning's collapse, and Dr Latimer said, 'Do you mind if I come to Salisbury and take a look? I know Dr Stevens, we were students together...'

'I'll be glad of your advice—I suppose Dr Stevens will be in charge of him?'

'Oh, yes, but Mr Browning is a friend...'

He bent down and plucked Beatrice on to her feet to make way for the ambulancemen with their stretcher. 'Beatrice, find your mother, will you? I'll drive her into Salisbury; we'll get there ahead of the ambulance. Will you stay here?'

She said in a wispy voice, 'I must let several people know—farmers, mostly. The small stuff I can manage on my own... Will—will you telephone me if you go to the hospital with Father? I expect Mother will want to stay there.'

'As soon as we know what's happening I'll give you a ring, but stay here, Beatrice, until you hear from me.'

She nodded and went upstairs to find her mother. Mrs Browning, usually so matter of fact and competent, had gone to pieces for the moment. Beatrice took off the pinny she was wearing, got a jacket from the wardrobe, found her handbag and shoes and tidied her hair. 'Dr Latimer is here, he's driving you to the hospital so that you'll be there when Father gets there. He knows the consultant there too, so Father is going to get the best possible care.'

Her mother gave her a blank look. 'Your father's never been ill in his life. It's like a dream—a bad dream.'

Beatrice agreed silently and led her downstairs. The ambulance was just about ready to leave, and Dr Forbes was getting into it to be with his patient. Dr Latimer was waiting patiently at the door, and as they reached him Beatrice said urgently, 'You will let me know?'

'Yes. Come along, Mrs Browning.' He put an arm round her shoulders as he smiled at Beatrice and walked to the dark grey Rolls-Royce parked to one side of the drive. He opened its door and urged Mrs Browning inside, got in himself and, with a wave of the hand, was gone.

Beatrice went slowly inside. There was a great deal to do, but just for a minute she was bewildered by the speed of it all, and the suddenness. It was a blessing that Ella had spent the night with a schoolfriend, but she would have to let Carol and Kathy know. As she went into the house, Mrs Perry, the elderly woman who came each morning to help in the house, caught up with her.

'I saw an ambulance, Miss Beatrice. 'as one of them dogs bitten your dad?'

'Dogs?' Beatrice gave her a blank look. 'Dogs—oh, no, Mrs Perry, my father has had a heart attack. My mother has gone with him to the hospital.'

'Oh, you poor love. I'll make a cuppa, it'll pull you together. And don't you fret, he'll be fine—them doctors are clever old fellows.'

She bustled into the kitchen and Beatrice went along to her father's study and opened his appointments book. Miss Scott, who acted as his receptionist-cum-secretary, would be in presently, but in the meantime there were several people expecting him that morning—farmers mostly. They would just have to get hold of another vet.

She began to telephone, drank the tea Mrs Perry brought her, and went along to the surgery. Her father's practice was mostly widespread among the estates and farms round the village, but there was always a handful of family pets needing pills or injections and occasionally a stitch. The small patients in the surgery now were easily dealt with, and she attended to them with her usual calm; she had helped her father for years and no one thought of disputing her skill. The last patient, old Miss Thom's elderly cat with ear trouble, was borne away, and Beatrice put the surgery to rights, tidied the waiting-room and started off towards her father's study. Miss Scott would be there by now and she would have to talk to her. The phone ringing stopped her, and she raced back to the waiting-room and snatched up the receiver.

The voice at the other end sounded reassuring and, at the same time, bracing. 'Beatrice? Your father's in intensive care and is holding his own nicely. Don't leave the house, I'll be with you in half an hour.'

He rang off before she could say a word. Just as well, as she found that she was crying.

She felt better after a good weep, and with a washed face, well made-up to cover her red nose and puffy eyelids, she went to find Miss Scott. That lady was sensible and middle-aged and could be relied upon to cope with any emergency, and she was sorting the post, bringing the books up to date and going through the appointments book. She looked up as Beatrice went in, and said with real sympathy, 'I'm so sorry, Beatrice—what a dreadful shock for you all. Your father will be all right, of course; he's very fit and he'll have the best of care. Mrs Forbes told me that Dr Latimer has been called in for consultations—a splendid man, it seems. How fortunate that he happened to be here.'

For the first time Beatrice paused to wonder why he had been there, anyway. 'He phoned a few minutes ago. Father's holding his own. I waited to phone Carol and Kathy and Ella...'

'Quite right, my dear. You'd like to do it now? I'll go and have my coffee with Mrs Perry.'

Carol and Kathy took the news with commendable calm, and both said at once that they would come home just as soon as they could arrange it. Ella wasn't easy; Beatrice spoke to her headmistress first, so that she was half prepared to hear Beatrice's news. All the same, she burst into tears and demanded to come home at once.

'Of course you shall,' promised Beatrice, 'just as soon as I get some kind of transport. Be a good girl, darling, and try to be patient, just as Father would expect you to be. I'll ring you just as soon as I've fixed something up—there's rather a lot to do.'

Her sister's voice came, penitent in her ear. 'Sorry, Beatrice. I'll wait and not fuss. But you won't forget?'

'No, love.'

Miss Scott came back then and they set to work ringing

round neighbours and neighbouring vets, fitting in the patients already booked by her father. They had almost finished when Dr Latimer joined them.

Beatrice jumped to her feet. 'Father—how is he?'

'Holding his own, as I told you; if he can hang on a little longer, he'll be out of the wood.' He bade Miss Scott a polite good morning and Beatrice introduced them. 'We're handing over most of father's patients for the moment—I've dealt with the minor stuff in surgery this morning.' She lifted unhappy eyes to his. 'I'm not sure what we should do...'

'Get a locum,' he told her promptly. 'Your father will need an assistant for a few months. I know you do a great deal to help him, but it will have to be someone qualified if he's to keep his contacts with the local farmers.'

She could have hugged him for his matter-of-fact acceptance of her father's recovery. 'Of course, I'll get in touch with the agency he uses sometimes—if he's on holiday or something...'

She smiled for the first time that day, and Dr Latimer studied her unhappy face without appearing to do so. 'Your father will be in hospital for a week or two, and when he's home he won't be able to do much for a time. Do you know of anyone he might like to work for him?'

She shook her head. 'No. They've always been different, and they've never been here for longer than three weeks.'

'Well, see what you can do. Get him here for an interview; it may make things much easier if you like him. Did you ring your sisters?'

'Yes. Carol and Kathy are driving back, they should be here quite soon. Ella's at school; I promised her I'd fetch her as soon as I could. I dare say Carol will fetch her.'

'Where does she go to school?'

'Wilton...'

'We'll go and get her now, shall we? Perhaps I should explain things to her...'

'Oh, would you? She's got her exams, and Father was anxious that she should pass well; if she could be reassured it would help a lot.'

Sitting in the soft leather comfort of his car, she said rather shyly, 'You're being very kind, and I'm most grateful. I know Mother will be too when she knows. You do think Father will be all right? Dr Stevens is very good, isn't he? Did he think he would recover?' She stopped and the bright colour washed over her face. 'Oh, I do beg your pardon, you're much cleverer than he is, aren't you? I mean, you're very well-known—Mrs Forbes said so. I expect Dr Stevens does what you suggest, doesn't he?'

A small sound escaped Dr Latimer's lips. 'Well, more or less—we pool our knowledge, as it were; he was good enough to allow me to take a look at your father. Is your Miss Scott reliable? Could she be left for a couple of hours while I take you to the hospital? Your mother wants to stay the night, and asked me to fetch some things for her. There is no reason why all of you shouldn't see him for a moment.'

'Thank you, I know we would all like to do that. But don't you have to work? Don't you have patients in London and hospital rounds and—and things?'

He said gravely, 'I take an occasional day off.'

'Oh, yes, of course. If you turn down the next street, the school's half-way down.'

Ella was waiting, red-eyed and restless. When she saw Dr Latimer she rushed to him and flung her arms around him. 'It's you. Oh, I'm so glad, now Father will be all right. How did you know? Had you come for breakfast?'

He didn't answer her questions, but said cheerfully, 'I'm going to take you to see your father, but first Beatrice has to put a few things together for your mother. She will stay at the hospital for a day or two while you help Beatrice to look after the house and the animals.'

He stowed her in the seat beside him and Beatrice got into the back, relieved at the placid way in which he had dealt with Ella, and once they were back home again he exhibited the same placid manner with Carol and Kathy, prevailed upon Miss Scott to stay until they returned, piled them all back into the car and drove back to Salisbury. And Beatrice sat in front beside him, listening to his advice, given in a diffident voice but sound none the less, so that, when he suggested that it might help if he were to be present when she interviewed any applicant for the post of assistant at the surgery, she agreed without a second thought.

'And it should be as soon as possible,' he reminded her, 'so that whoever comes has settled in nicely before your father returns.'

'I'll phone as soon as we get home,' she promised him. 'How shall I let you know if someone comes for an interview?'

'I'll leave you my phone number.' He drew up before the hospital entrance and they all got out. Ella was crying again, and he paused to mop her face. 'Your father is on a life-support machine, so there are a number of tubes and wires attached to him; don't let that frighten you. And you may only stay a few moments. Come along.'

Mrs Browning was sitting on a chair outside intensive care; she looked as pale as her daughters, but gave them a cheerful smile. She looked at Dr Latimer then. 'I'm eternally grateful,' she said. 'I don't know what we would have done without your help. And I do believe you when you say that Tom is going to get better.' She gave him a sweet smile. 'May the girls see him?'

'Certainly. Two at a time, I think. I'll just make sure that they won't be in the way...'

He disappeared, to return presently with a white-gowned Sister. 'Carol and Kathy?' he suggested. 'You'll have to put on white gowns. Sister will show you.'

They were only gone for a minute or two, and then it was Beatrice's and Ella's turn. 'And not so much as a snuffle from you,' warned Dr Latimer, giving Ella a gentle push.

Beatrice had steeled herself to see her father's grey face once more, but despite the tubes and wires he looked more like her father again, with colour in his face, and apparently asleep.

The sight of him acted like a tonic upon her; he was alive and he was going to get better. Dr Latimer had said so. She quelled a great desire to burst into tears, and urged Ella back into the waiting-room.

Dr Latimer went away presently, excusing himself on the grounds of a brief consultation with Dr Stevens, leaving them to drink coffee a nursing aide had brought them.

They said goodbye to their mother when he returned, and he drove them back to Hindley, to share the sandwiches which Mrs Perry had made and write his phone number down for Beatrice, with the reminder that she was to phone him as soon as she had an applicant to be interviewed. He wished them all a cheerful goodbye, and for Beatrice at least the house seemed very empty when he had gone.

But she had little time to sit and be sorry for herself; the most pressing necessity was for someone to carry on the practice while her father was away. While her sisters scattered to do the various jobs around the house, she went to the study, found the address of the agency her father had always used and phoned them.

It had been a miserable day so far, now lightened somewhat by the news that there was a newly qualified vet on their books who might be exactly what Beatrice was looking for. An appointment was made for the following day, and she went to find her sisters and tell them the good news.

'If he can come straight away, we shan't need to hand over too many of father's regular accounts. I can manage the surgery for a few more days, and we'll just have to go on as usual. I expect Mother will come home as soon as Father is out of danger.'

She spoke with a confidence she didn't feel, although Dr Latimer had told her with quiet certainty that her father would recover.

Dr Latimer phoned again around teatime; Mr Browning was showing a steady improvement, their mother would stay the night at the hospital, but if everything was satisfactory in the morning she would return home by lunchtime. 'Everything all right your end?' he wanted to know.

'Yes, oh, yes, we're managing. There's someone coming from the agency tomorrow morning, about eleven o'clock.'

'I'll be with you before then.' He hung up with a brief goodbye.

Tired out with anxiety and worry, they all slept soundly, but Beatrice was up soon after six o'clock, to let Knotty out into the garden, feed the cat, Wilbur, and make a cup of tea. Perhaps it was too early to ring the hospital, she decided, and then changed her mind, knowing that she wouldn't be content until she had news of her father.

He was continuing to improve, said Night Sister; they hoped to take him off the life-support machine very shortly, and perhaps Beatrice would like to telephone later in the day.

Beatrice drank her tea and set about the day's chores. There were several cats and dogs convalescing behind the surgery; she attended to them, fed Knotty a dish of tea and the bread and butter he fancied for his breakfast, and then went to wake the others.

Breakfast was almost a cheerful meal. 'I'll wait and see Mother,' said Carol, 'and then if everything is all right I'll go back—I can go straight to the hospital if—if I have to.'

'And I'd better go back, too,' decided Kathy, 'but you'll let me know at once if I'm wanted?'

Beatrice looked at Ella. 'You'd better go to school, love—Father will be disappointed if you don't do well in your exams. Yes, I know you don't want to—supposing we wait until Mother gets here and I drive you back in time for this afternoon's paper—biology, isn't it? Father would be so proud if you got good marks for that.'

Beatrice was clearing away after surgery when her mother arrived, and with her Dr Latimer. Her mother kissed her and said quickly, 'Oliver brought me back—such a good man and so clever. Your father's going to be all right, and we have Oliver to thank for that. He'll stay if you want him to just to cast an eye over this locum you've arranged to see.'

'You didn't mind me seeing to that, Mother? We must keep the practice going well until Father can take over once again.'

'I'm only too thankful that you were here to deal with everything.'

She turned round as Dr Latimer came in with her case, and Beatrice said, 'I'll get Mrs Perry to bring in the coffee; there's still half an hour before that man comes.'

She smiled at him and thought how tired he looked—she had thought of him as a youngish man, but he looked pale and lined in the morning light. She was too worried about her father to bother much about the doctor; she went off to the kitchen and laid a tray while Mrs Perry made the coffee and got out the biscuits. By the time Beatrice got back, the other three were there as well as Miss Scott, and since everyone had a good deal to say and a great many questions to ask no one noticed that the doctor was rather quiet.

The doorbell interrupted them. 'You go, dear,' said Mrs Browning. 'You know as much about the practice as your father. Do what you think best.'

By the time Beatrice had reached the front door, Dr Latimer was beside her. 'The study?' he asked, and went there while she went to the front door.

Worried though she was, she couldn't help but be pleasantly surprised by the sight of the young man on the doorstep. James Forbes was young, too, but thick-set and slow and pompous; and Dr Latimer, regretfully, seemed a lot older than she had at first thought. This man was splendidly different. She blushed faintly at allowing her thoughts to stray so frivolously. Guilt made her voice stiff. 'Mr Wood? Will you come in?'

He smiled at her, self-possessed and charming. 'Miss Browning? The agency did explain...' They shook hands and she led the way across the hall to her father's study, where Dr Latimer stood looking out of the window.

He turned round as they went in, and she introduced them. 'Please sit down, Mr Wood—would you like a cup of coffee?'

'I stopped in Salisbury, thanks.' He glanced quickly at the doctor, who met his look with a bland one of his own. 'I understand your father needs a locum for a month or two. I'm planning to go to Canada in the near future, so perhaps we might suit each other.'

He smiled at Beatrice, who smiled back; he was really rather nice and they might get on well together... She explained about the practice. 'I have been helping my father for several years; I'm not trained, but I do a good deal round the surgery and help with operations.'

He asked all the right questions and she had time to study him. He was good-looking, with dark hair curling over his collar, pale blue eyes and a delightful smile. She found herself hoping very much that he would take the job.

Dr Latimer had said almost nothing, and she thought pettishly that he might just as well not be there; he was certainly giving her no advice. Not that she would have taken it; when Colin Wood suggested that he might start in two days' time, she agreed with a readiness which made the doctor raise his eyebrows, but since she wasn't looking at him that escaped her notice.

Only as she was explaining the working hours and when he might expect to have some free time did the doctor ask gently, 'References?'

'Oh, of course.' Colin Wood shot him an annoyed look, and turned it into a smile as Beatrice looked up. He fished in a pocket and produced an envelope which the doctor took from him before Beatrice could do so. He read the small sheaf of papers closely, murmured, 'Entirely satisfactory,' and handed them back again. 'Were you thinking of a contract of any sort?' he asked casually.

'That won't be necessary,' said Beatrice sharply, 'if we have a gentleman's agreement.' She looked at Colin Wood. 'You are prepared to work here until my father can manage without help?'

'Oh, of course,' he said easily, and laughed. 'There, I've said that before a witness—what more can you want?'

'Would you like to see over the clinic?' offered Beatrice. 'And your room—there's a small sitting-room you can have, too.'

He rose with alacrity. 'May I?' He turned to Dr Latimer. 'I'll say goodbye, sir. I'll have to go straight back and pack my things.'

They didn't shake hands; the doctor bade him a grave goodbye and stood watching them from the window as they crossed the wide sweep of gravel to the surgery on its far side.

Presently he went back to the drawing-room where Mrs Browning was sitting with the three girls.

'You approve?' asked Mrs Browning.

'He has excellent credentials and, what is more important, Beatrice likes him. He can come in two days' time.'

'You'll stay for lunch?'

He shook his head. 'I would very much like to, but I want to take another look at Mr Browning before I go back to town. But I'll be down again and I will keep in touch with Dr Stevens.'

'You'll wait to say goodbye to Beatrice?'

'Will you do that for me? I'm glad that things have been settled so quickly.' He shook hands and within a few minutes had driven away; a few minutes later Beatrice came in with Colin Wood, who was introduced to them all before saying that he simply had to go but looked forward to seeing them again in a couple of days.

Beatrice saw him away in his showy little sports car, and went back to her mother and sisters.

'Where's Dr Latimer?' she asked, and in the same breath, 'Well, did you like him? I think he'll be splendid—'

'Oliver,' said Mrs Browning gently, 'has gone back to check on your father's condition, then he is driving up to London, presumably to work at one of the hospitals. I only hope that he gets a rest during the day; he was up all night...'

'All night? Oh, I didn't know; that must have been why he was so quiet.'

Her mother said drily, 'Probably. You're satisfied that Mr Wood will do all right, darling?'

Beatrice nodded. 'Oh, yes, Mother. I'm sure he will, and he doesn't want a contract or agreement or anything in writing; he plans to go to Canada in a few months and wouldn't want to stay anyway. He says there aren't many good openings for a man without capital. He's ambitious.'

'I didn't like him,' said Ella suddenly.

'Why ever not?'

'I don't know—I just didn't like him.'

'Well, that doesn't really matter, for you'll not see much of him.' Beatrice spoke with unusual tartness. 'There's the phone—Father...'

It was Dr Stevens. 'Your father is recovering well, phone here for news some time in the evening. There is no need for your mother to come again today; she needs a rest anyway. Dr Latimer will be down to see him tomorrow afternoon. I suggest your mother comes then, and she can talk to him then about your father.'

'I'll tell her. Thank you for all you are doing, Dr Stevens.'

'It's Dr Latimer that you should thank—we had a very anxious few hours during the night, but he dealt with the complications. He's a very sound man, you know; you were lucky to have him.'

'We are very grateful,' said Beatrice, and put down the receiver slowly. Of course they were grateful, and she felt suddenly guilty because, in the pleasure of meeting Colin Wood, she had forgotten the doctor.

She did her best to make up for it the following afternoon. She and her mother had visited her father, who was conscious now and feebly cheerful, and then they were ushered into Sister's office, where Dr Latimer and Dr Stevens were murmuring thoughtfully together. They turned impassive faces towards them as they went in, shook hands and offered chairs.

'Well,' began Dr Latimer, 'your husband is coming along very nicely, Mrs Browning, but it will be a slow job—you do realise that? We'll keep him here for a week or two, and when you get him home he will have to take things easily for some time.' He smiled then, and Beatrice thought once again what a very nice man he was.

She said, 'We are truly grateful to you, Dr Latimer. We can never repay you...'

'My patient's recovery is payment enough, Beatrice,' he told her coolly, and for some reason she felt snubbed, not by his words but by his manner—perhaps in hospital he was impersonal to everyone, but he wasn't the man who had watched the sunrise with her on Midsummer's morning, or if he were he was taking care to hide it.

She accompanied her mother back home, and after they had all had tea Carol left to go back to her rooms in Salisbury and Kathy went off with her fiancé. 'In the morning you can go back to school, Ella,' said Mrs Browning. 'The house will seem empty.'

'Mr Wood will be here,' observed Beatrice, and felt a little surge of excitement.

CHAPTER THREE

COLIN WOOD ARRIVED the following morning with a great deal of luggage, several tennis rackets and a set of golf clubs. He was charming, too, and offered to start work at once.

'Well,' said Beatrice, 'I must say that's nice of you—I saw to morning surgery—there wasn't anything I couldn't manage by myself, but Mr Dobson—he has a big farm a mile or two down the road—wants someone this afternoon. He's not quite happy about a cow due to calve. I told him you might be here in time to go.'

'Splendid, that gives us time to go through the appointments book. I'll unpack, shall I?'

He breezed away to his room and Mrs Browning watched him go with a faint frown. 'He's very—very self-assured...'

'A good thing, Mother dear. We must keep this practice going until Father can get back.' She gave her parent a comforting hug. 'And he will be; this morning's report was very reassuring. I'll get the coffee, then Mr Wood and I can get down to the books.'

She went to bed tired that night, but satisfied with the day. She had driven her mother to the hospital that afternoon, and there was no doubt that her father was better. When they got home again it was to find Mr Wood back from the Dobson's farm, sitting at her father's desk in the surgery, checking the appointments for the evening surgery. He had had tea with them but hadn't sat over it, declaring that he wanted to go through the files and get to know as much as possible quickly. So Beatrice had joined him, showing him as much as she could before surgery started, and then stayed with him to give him a hand with the ease of long competence. And after supper she spent half an hour with him while he looked over the next day's appointments.

She closed her eyes, happier than she had been for several days. Colin Wood was the perfect answer to their difficulties; what was more, she liked him.

The days fell into a regular pattern again: morning surgery, outside calls, taking Knotty for his walk, helping around the house and taking her mother to see her father each afternoon, and then evening surgery and more work, going through the next day's appointments. Her father's practice was a large one, and scattered, and she could see now that he would have to have a partner or at least an assistant other than herself—indeed, he should have had one months ago, for although she acted as his right hand she had no qualifications. She began to hope that when eventually her father came home he would take to the idea of keeping Colin Wood as his partner.

Dr Latimer had come to see them, arriving quietly just as they had finished the afternoon clinic; he didn't stay long. 'Mr Browning is doing very well indeed,' he told Mrs Browning. 'Another week or ten days and you will have him home again, although you do understand that he must do very little? But there is no reason why he shouldn't do some desk work if he feels like it.'

He had smiled kindly at Mrs Browning, and added, 'Of course, Beatrice and Mr Wood will bear the bulk of the work for the moment.'

Beatrice said quickly, 'Of course, Colin has taken everything over without a hitch.' She glanced warmly at the young man, and the doctor watched her without appearing to do so.

He said placidly, 'I'm sure you must feel very grateful to Mr Wood. I take it that everything goes smoothly with your father's practice?'

Beatrice beamed at him. 'Oh, yes, thank you.' And then, feeling that she should show some interest in him as well, 'Are you very busy? Would you like to stay for supper?'

'I should like very much to stay,' he told her, 'but I must get back to town this evening; I never quite catch up with my work, I'm afraid.'

Colin Wood laughed. 'You need someone to organise you, like Beatrice, sir. She keeps my nose to the grindstone...' He smiled across the room at her. It was full of charm, and held a hint of possessiveness.

The doctor got up to go. 'I shall be seeing Mr Browning in a few days' time; I hope I shall have good news for you then.'

He bade Mrs Browning goodbye, nodded to Beatrice and Colin Wood and went away, accompanied by Mrs Browning.

'Seems a nice enough old boy,' said Colin when they had gone. 'A bit slow, but I dare say he's good at his job.'

Beatrice said sharply, 'He's not old, and he's quick enough when someone's ill...'

Colin gave her a quick glance. 'I'm not criticising him; he's quite famous, isn't he? I must say he's been wonderful in his care of your father.' He added contritely, 'I shouldn't have said that he was old—he's not. Somewhere in his thirties, I should suppose.' He smiled disarmingly and she forgave him at once. She liked him; that was, she liked him almost all the time. Sometimes he said or did something which struck a note of doubt in her mind, but she forgot that quickly enough. He was beginning to fill her thoughts, so much so that James, when he had encountered her in the village, had been given short shrift and told once and for all that she had no wish to marry him.

'I've been saying so for months,' she told him reasonably, 'but you never would listen. But I do mean it, James. We wouldn't suit, you know you don't really love me. It's only because we have seen each other on and off for years and years. And there isn't anyone else, so you don't have to mind...'

He hadn't minded all that much, either, and she felt free at last. Free for what? she asked herself, and immediately thought of Colin.

He was very efficient and he wanted to know as much as possible about the practice. Indeed, one morning after surgery she had gone into her father's study to fetch something and found him sitting at the desk, looking through the accounts for the previous year with a neat summary made by Miss Scott showing just what the income for the year had been.

She had shown her surprise, and he had said quickly, 'I wanted to look up the treatment for Mr Gregg's pigs—I seem to have got hold of the wrong file.' He gave her an apologetic smile. 'Sorry about that, but there is rather a lot to cope with all at once...'

Her sudden feeling of suspicion faded. 'That's all right; I think you're managing beautifully. It must be very difficult, taking over at a moment's notice. The treatment files are on the second shelf. You'll find the pigs under G—Miss Scott is a wizard at keeping things in order.'

'It's a large practice, too,' he observed as he put the file back. 'I can't think how your father managed on his own; there's work enough for two at least. Of course, he had you, and I must say you're as good as any vet.'

She pinkened delightfully and shook her head. 'But not qualified. When he's home again he will have to have someone besides myself.'

He said lightly, 'Well, I might decide that I don't want to go to Canada, after all.' He smiled. 'There's more than one reason why I might want to stay.' He was looking at her very intently. 'A man wants to settle down, you know. I thought that I was footloose and fancy free, and Canada for a year or so seemed the answer, but now I'm not so sure.'

She didn't pretend not to understand him; it never entered her head to do so. Her colour deepened, but she returned his look honestly.

'You have only been here a week or so. It's too soon for you to decide anything.'

He had crossed the room and taken her hand. 'Dear Beatrice, some things don't need deciding—they just happen.'

She had lain awake that night for quite some time thinking about him. She had her daydreams like any other young woman, now she was allowing them free rein. Colin liked her, perhaps more than liked; what could be better than a partnership with her father? The practice would stay in the family, they could live nearby, and when her father retired they could stay on in the house and her parents could move to a smaller house in the village. It was almost too good to be true. She allowed common sense to take over for a moment. She wasn't quite sure that her feeling for Colin was anything stronger than liking; he attracted her, she liked to be with him and she thought about him a lot, but she was still uncertain. She had, naturally enough, fallen in love several times, but she had fallen out of it again without either pain or regret; she wasn't, truth to tell, quite sure how one was certain that one was in love. She had always imagined that one was quite sure with not a single doubt, but at the back of her mind she had to admit to herself that there were vague doubts she couldn't put a finger on. Perhaps, she decided, on the edge of sleep, one was never absolutely sure...

The days slid into a week, and then two, and her father was coming home again. Dr Latimer had been to see them again, confident that her father would be almost as good as new, provided he took things easy.

'And no worry of any kind,' he advised. 'No accounts or finance for the moment, and don't let him get tired. He can advise from his desk, see patients if he wants to, provided that there is someone to do the actual work. But no night calls or sudden emergencies. I'm sure you and Mr Wood will be able to arrange that between you.'

He was in the drawing-room, sitting opposite Beatrice and her mother. 'He's settled down nicely?' He looked at Mrs Browning.

'Yes.' Mrs Browning sounded hesitant. 'In fact he seems to have taken over completely, if you know what I mean, although I'm sure that's just my fancy.' She glanced at Beatrice. 'Beatrice tells me that he's splendid in the job, and I'm sure we're very lucky to have him.' She paused. 'Only I hope that when Tom gets back home Colin will understand that he will want to take charge again...he behaves rather as though the practice is his.'

Beatrice frowned. 'I think you're worrying about nothing, Mother.' She spoke gently, but there was an edge to her voice. 'Colin wouldn't dream of usurping Father's place.'

She looked at Dr Latimer and found his intent gaze fixed on her and went red. 'I don't know what we should have done without him,' she spoke defensively. 'I like him—we get on very well.'

She looked away crossly because Dr Latimer was smiling and the smile held mockery.

He went presently with the promise that he would examine Mr Browning at the hospital three weeks later. 'Dr Stevens knows everything there is to know; if you're at all worried, let him know, he will deal with any problem and Dr Forbes is close by. I think that you have no further need to worry, provided Mr Browning takes care.' He shook hands. 'And remember, no worries or sudden surprises.'

Two days later Mr Browning came home, looking almost as good as new. Dr Forbes called almost as soon as he was home, checked that he hadn't suffered from the journey, advised him to go slow for a week or two, and told him to be sure and call him if he were needed. On the way out, he stopped to speak to

Beatrice. 'I'm sorry that you and James...' He coughed. 'Known each other all your lives; rather took it for granted...'

She came to his rescue. 'That's why,' she told him gently. 'We're more like brother and sister, you know; James will realise that when he meets the right girl.'

'I'm sure you're right, my dear; I hope that you meet the right man, too.'

Beatrice was almost sure that she had, but she wasn't going to say so.

Colin was a tower of strength during the next few days. Indeed, she thought worriedly, too much so, for her father was inclined to be irritable at Colin's assumption of so much of the practice. At least, it wasn't so much that he had shouldered the major share of it, it was his satisfied air at taking everything upon his shoulders... She longed to tell him this, but she was afraid that if she did he might resent it and leave; something which was the last thing she wished for. He was beginning to fill her life and her thoughts, and it worried her that no one else shared her opinion of him. True, her mother was unfailingly polite and thoughtful for his comfort, but Ella made no secret of her dislike of him, and after the first few days it was only too apparent that her father, while agreeing that he was very good at his job, had no liking for him. This was something which Colin smoothly ignored, for he never mentioned it to her and she had to admire him for that; indeed, in her eyes, he could do very little wrong. He was always charming and kind to her, letting her know in a dozen ways that she mattered. She wished that there was someone who would lend a sympathetic ear to her worries. Dr Latimer would have done very well, she reflected, only he seemed to have disappeared into his own particular busy world, and when her father would go to hospital for an examination, even if he were there, there would be no chance to talk.

But she had her chance. A week or so after her father had returned home, she came in from feeding the animals convalescing behind the surgery, and found him sitting in the garden, stretched out in one of the garden chairs, talking to her father. It was a warm day, and she had been up early to attend to a litter of puppies before she had started on her usual chores. She was hot and tired, her nose shone and her mane of hair had come loose of its plait. Over and above that, her father had been annoyed because Colin had altered a treatment which he had been in the habit of using for years. Life was getting complicated, and now here was Dr Latimer, looking cool and immaculate and faintly amused.

She wished him good morning in a cross voice, which he chose to ignore. 'Busy?' he asked unnecessarily. 'And on such a lovely day, too. Have you been up the hill lately?'

'I haven't had the time.' She bent to pat Knotty's head as he sat by her father. 'Have you come to see Father?' She frowned at his amused look. 'I mean, to examine him?'

'No, that will come in a week's time. Besides, he looks pretty fit to me. I was coming this way and I had half an hour to spare.'

They had had coffee; she longed for a cup herself and said, still cross, 'It's a lovely day, as you said. I dare say you will be gone before I get back...'

'You have surely finished for the morning in the surgery?' asked her father. 'We always had half an hour to ourselves before I did my rounds. I see no reason to change my ways—'

Dr Latimer interposed smoothly, 'Come back here when you've done your hair or whatever; we might take a stroll. You look as though you need a little time to yourself.' He met her vexed look with a placid blue stare, so that she found herself agreeing...

She felt more in tune with her world when she had done her face and brushed her hair. She ran down to the kitchen and drank a glass of lemonade her mother was making, and, much refreshed, went into the garden again.

'That's better,' observed Dr Latimer. 'Shall we go and look at the world from the top of the hill? Knotty is dying for a walk. So is Mabel.'

'Mabel?' Beatrice just stopped herself in time from asking who is Mabel? She followed him out into the lane. His wife? A small daughter? A girlfriend? Not possible, he would never have left them sitting in the car.

Mabel, she discovered as they reached the car, was an amiable Labrador, lolling on the front seat by the open window.

'Oh, why didn't you bring her in?' cried Beatrice.

'She hasn't met Knotty, and they might have romped around and disturbed your father. Besides, she rather fancies herself guarding the steering-wheel...'

He let the dog out and Mabel was made much of before trotting off ahead of them with the amiable Knotty at her heels. The doctor strolled along in a comfortable silence, and Beatrice's ill temper left her. They had begun their climb up the hill before he asked, 'Something's wrong? Tell me about it.'

It seemed the most natural thing in the world to unburden herself to him, and it all came out in a muddle of doubts: her father's scarcely concealed antipathy towards Colin, Ella's frank dislike. 'And it's all so unfair,' she mumbled. 'He works so hard—you have no idea...' The doctor, who had a very good idea of what hard work was like, merely made a soothing sound, and she went on, 'He manages so well, he's even gone through the books with Miss Scott. She didn't want him to, but he said he had to know as much about the practice as possible.'

'The books? You mean the appointments and the various cases?'

'Oh, those too—no, the account books. Just to get some idea, he explained; he's very conscientious...'

'And you like him.' It was a statement, not a question.

She said defiantly, 'Yes, I do—he's—he's young and alive and he's—well—fun.'

'Of course,' the doctor's voice was just sufficiently sympathetic. 'I dare say he's ambitious too.'

'Oh, yes—he wants his own practice, but of course he's only been qualified for two years and he hasn't the capital.'

Dr Latimer was surveying the landscape below them. 'He's young enough to work for that,' he commented, 'and he'll be the better for it.'

She agreed doubtfully; Colin wasn't a man to wait for what he wanted, but it seemed disloyal to say so.

The silence between them lengthened, until she said slowly, 'I did wonder if Father would make him a partner...'

The doctor's gaze was still on the scenery. 'It's early days yet,' he counselled. 'Give him time to—er—er—discover Colin's worth.'

She said gratefully, 'You're such a nice person to talk to. I've been wanting to talk to someone; I can't worry Mother, Ella's too young—besides, she doesn't like Colin—and Kathy and Carol aren't at home.' She added quickly, 'I don't want advice...'

'Regard me as an uncle or an elder brother—I'll promise never to advise you, Beatrice. But for what it's worth, I'll listen.'

She gave him a grateful look. 'Thank you. I think I'm a bit muddled.'

'Things have a way of sorting themselves out,' he pointed out comfortably. He whistled to the dogs. 'I would like to stay longer, but I must get back to town.'

'To the hospital?'

They started down the hill with the dogs racing ahead. 'I have an out-patients session this afternoon...'

She asked, for something to say, 'You don't work in the evenings?'

'Sometimes.' He smiled. 'This evening I'm giving myself the pleasure of dining out.'

'Is she pretty?'

He cast her a sidelong glance. 'Yes, extremely so.'

For some reason his answer annoyed her: she said pettishly, 'Oh, that's nice; I dare say she has lots of time to buy lovely clothes and have her hair done...'

His smile was instantly suppressed. 'Indeed, yes. She is one of the lilies of the field—neither toils nor spins.' He added blandly, 'She dances delightfully.'

'Then I expect you will have a simply wonderful time.' Beatrice spoke with something of a snap.

They were turning into the drive and she said, 'I must check on Mrs Sim's cat; there should be kittens some time today.' She stopped and held out a hand. 'Thank you for letting me talk. It must all seem very petty to you after your life and death work.'

'No. Life is never petty, Beatrice.' He put up a finger and gently tapped her cheek. 'I hope the kittens arrive safely.'

He went on towards the house, leaving her feeling that she had had something taken away from her.

But she forgot that almost at once. Mrs Sim's Siamese was about to produce her kittens and Beatrice stayed with her until four tiny creatures were tucked up against their proud mother, who squinted at Beatrice and purred her delight before accepting the milk and chopped liver she was offered. By the time Beatrice got back to the house there was no sign of Dr Latimer. She hadn't expected him to be there; all the same, she felt disappointment, quickly forgotten when Colin got back from his visit to an outlying farm.

The afternoon clinic was short; she cleared up after it, and since there was an hour or so in which there was little to do she suggested to Colin that they might go for a walk.

'My dear, I have a mass of paperwork to get through—Miss Scott overlooked some accounts, and I'm trying to sort them out.'

'Accounts? That's not like her.' Beatrice leaned over the desk and took a look. 'Oh, you don't have to bother about those—Father won't send those in for a few months—Bruton's Farm had bad luck with their sheep this year and the bill is enormous; they'll pick up again, but they've got to live in the meantime. And these—' she sorted through a handful '—they're all smallholders who are only just beginning to make things pay. They won't get their accounts for another six months.'

She picked up the small sheaf of papers and put them tidily back on the shelf.

Colin frowned. 'But that's not the way to run a successful practice; if they use the vet, they must pay for him.'

'And so they do, the moment that they can afford to.' She added coolly, 'It's Father's practice, Colin.'

He got up from behind the desk and came to stand by her. 'My dear girl, I had no intention of interfering. I'm sorry—I wanted to help.'

He smiled at her apologetically and she forgave him at once; she was half in love with him, she supposed, and it was difficult to resist his charm. She said, 'That's all right—come and see the kittens. They're a nice little bunch. Mrs Sims will be delighted—she relies on breeding them to help out her pension.'

She forgot, or almost forgot, the small episode, and a week went by like most weeks; plenty of work mitigated by her father's rapid recovery and glorious weather. Kathy's wedding was only a few days away, and the whole house was in cheerful turmoil, with Mrs Perry polishing and helping out in the kitchen, a marquee erected in the garden and a great deal of toing and froing by the ladies of the household, trying on their wedding outfits and experimenting with hair-styles. But somehow they managed to create a quiet oasis around Mr Browning, who was left to sit peacefully in the garden or his study. He was beginning to take an interest in the practice once more, and expected Colin to see him each day so that they might discuss the various animals to be seen and treated. And outwardly, at least, Colin appeared to welcome this, although several times he changed the treatment Mr Browning had ordered and did what he wished to do. He was careful not to let this be known, and since he was a good vet no harm came to his patients, but he derived satisfaction from edging his way deeper and deeper into the practice. Another few months and he hoped Mr Browning might accept him as a partner, even though he had no money to put into the practice. In the meantime he was pleasant to everyone, worked hard and remained the best of friends with Beatrice.

The weather held, and Mrs Browning's secret nightmare, that it might rain on the wedding day and spoil all her careful arrangements, melted before blue sky and bright sunshine. The caterers arrived, the wedding cake was carefully set on its stand and the bouquets were delivered.

Beatrice had got up earlier than usual; wedding or no wedding, the animals needed attention. She had a hurried breakfast in the kitchen and went to her room, poking her head round Kathy's door as she went.

Kathy looked beautiful, and Beatrice said so before tearing off to have a shower and get into her bridesmaid's dress, which was of pale rose wild silk, the long skirt veiled with chiffon, the bodice quite plain, the ballooning sleeves ending at the elbow in tight bands. It was a style which suited Carol and Ella as well as herself. She took pains with her hair, winding it into a chignon and fastening the little wreath of silk roses around it. Surveying herself in the pier glass in her mother's room, she hoped that Colin would approve...

There were a lot of guests; the Brownings had lived in the village for several generations and they were liked; besides, Kathy's bridegroom came from a large family. The village church, half-way up the main street, was packed with best summer dresses and morning-suits with a fair sprinkling of villagers in new hats and stiff white collars. Beatrice, with Ella and Carol, waiting in the porch for her sister and her father to arrive, was gratified to see that all those who had the use of their legs had come to watch the bride go to her wedding.

Kathy looked a little pale, but her father looked remarkably well as they went up the path to the church. Beatrice rearranged her sister's train and followed them up the aisle, and a whisper of sound went through the church at the sight of the four pretty girls, quite serious now, looking ahead of them to where the bridegroom stood. However, Beatrice allowed her eyes to wander to the pews on her family's side, looking for Colin. He was there, well turned out, quite sure of himself—and standing beside him was Dr Latimer. She hadn't expected that; true, she hadn't sent out many of the invitations for she had been busy for the greater part of each day, but no one had said that he would be a guest. But there he was, rather larger than life on account of his great size, wearing his morning coat as though he were in the habit of doing so frequently—and it was certainly not hired from Moss Bros, Beatrice reflected as she glided slowly past the pew, for it fitted to perfection. He turned his head and looked at her, and she felt her cheeks pinken most annoyingly. They were at the altar now, and she realised that she hadn't looked at Colin at all; she must remember to smile at him as they left the church.

She did, smiling into his rather sulky face and ignoring the doctor, and once they were back at the house she wandered around the marquee, greeting friends and family, and edged her way to where he was standing. If she had hoped for a compliment about her appearance, she was to be disappointed; she didn't know why he was so sullen, it was a side of him she hadn't encountered, and she asked him, without mincing matters, what was the matter. 'It's Kathy's wedding. You should at least look as though you were enjoying yourself...'

He caught her hand. 'Oh, my dear, I'm sorry. You see, I've been sort of wishing that I was the bridegroom, and you...' He paused and smiled. 'I mustn't say more, not yet.'

And in any case he hadn't the chance; an elderly uncle Beatrice hadn't seen in years appeared at her elbow and marched her off to have what he called a cosy little chat, and which lasted until it was time to toast the bridal pair. It was then that he disappeared from her side and Dr Latimer took his place, a glass of champagne in each hand. He offered her one, and said, 'Hello, Beatrice. You look very fetching in that pink thing.'

She thanked him gravely. 'I didn't know that you would be here.'

'No—well, I don't suppose it would have made much difference if you had. When do we hear the next peal of wedding bells?'

She took a sip of champagne. 'I don't know what you mean,' she observed coldly.

'Don't be coy. Not ten minutes ago you and young Wood were holding hands.'

'I'm not coy,' she snapped, and then, 'I liked it—having my hand held.' She smiled at him. 'I'm sorry if I snapped. You have always been so kind to all of us, and I'm very glad you could come today.'

'So am I. Kathy is a beautiful bride and they look very happy. Your father has stood up to all this very well. I've asked him to Salisbury tomorrow, and I'll have a look at him before I go away.'

'Away? Where to? For a long time?'

He smiled faintly. 'I have a short lecture tour: Paris, Brussels and the Hague. I shall be gone for a week.'

She beamed her relief. 'Oh, that's all right, then—I—we all feel safe about Father while you're looking after him.' She added frankly, 'I had no idea that you were so important. Dr Forbes was telling me.' She smiled suddenly. 'Have you seen Great-Aunt Sybil?'

'Oh, yes, indeed. She addressed me as "young man", which did a great deal for my ego.'

'I shouldn't think your ego needed anything done for it—oh, Father's going to make a speech…'

She didn't speak to him again, only exchanged a brief goodbye as he left later. And as Dr Forbes had said that he would drive her father into Salisbury since he had to go there himself, she wouldn't see Dr Latimer there; she was aware of a vague regret about that.

Her father came back the next day feeling very pleased with himself. He had passed Dr Latimer's meticulous examination with flying colours, and provided that he was sensible there was no reason why he shouldn't take on the less heavy work of the practice.

'What I shall do,' he observed to Beatrice and her mother, as they sat in the drawing-room after supper, 'is get hold of an older chap; he can deal with the night work and the more distant farms until I'm up to it again. There's that empty house at the other end of the village—it belongs to Forbes, and he wants to rent it out, not sell it. It would do nicely for a man with a small family.'

Mr Browning puffed at his pipe and looked pleased with himself.

'What about Colin?' Beatrice made her voice casual.

'I'll give him a month's notice—he's a locum and he came on that understanding, did he not?'

'He's worked very hard,' persisted Beatrice. 'He knows a great deal about the practice.'

'Good experience for him. I'll see him in the morning.'

Beatrice went to bed presently, but not to sleep. Somehow she had taken it for granted that Colin would stay on, perhaps as a partner. The future, still vague in her mind, had been full of exciting possibilities, and it had suddenly become empty. She got up early and took Knotty for his walk before having her breakfast and plunging into her busy day. The house was still in a state of upheaval after the wedding; there were things to pack up and return, the caterers to collect the leftovers, a posse of men to take down the marquee. No one had time to speak to anyone, and since Colin had been called out to an injured horse Mr Browning had no opportunity to talk to him.

They met at lunch, all of them edgy from the excitement of the wedding and its aftermath of muddle, and no one talked much, but as they got up from the table Mr Browning said, 'Colin, will you come to my study? There is something I should like to discuss with you.'

Colin jumped to his feet, smiling, and Beatrice thought how boyish he looked and how willing he was to please. The two men went away and she started to clear the table and carry the dishes to the kitchen for Mrs Perry to wash. Colin, she felt sure, would be able to persuade her father to let him stay. She wandered off to one of the paddocks to cast an eye over the old donkey abandoned by a party of tinkers. His hoofs were in a sorry state, but good food and rest would give the beast a new lease of life. Her father had accepted him without demur, knowing that he would never be paid for his treatment, and she remembered with a small frown that Colin had voiced the opinion that the donkey should have been turned over to the RSPCA, or failing that, sent to the knackers. Then, seeing her look of horror at his suggestion, he had made haste to tell her that he was only joking. He had caught her hand, smiled into her eyes and told her that she was soft-hearted and that he loved her for it.

She did her usual afternoon chores, made sure that everything was ready for the early evening clinic and went along to the surgery. Colin was there, sitting at the desk, writing. The face he turned to her was, as usual, smiling. 'There you are. When you are not around I feel lost! Come and sit down; I've almost finished this letter. What a bore all this paperwork is...'

'You should let Miss Scott do it; she knows everything about the practice and she's marvellous at letter-writing.'

'Oh, I like to keep my hand in.' He put his pen down. 'It's such a glorious day. Do you suppose we might sneak off for a walk after tea?'

Her heart sang. 'Why not? I've seen to the sick animals and got the surgery ready—we could spare half an hour. Father wanted to see Dr Forbes's dog and he's the first case.'

So after tea, a rather silent meal in the drawing-room, she accompanied Colin across the paddocks and into the narrow lane running behind the garden. At first they talked trivialities, but presently Colin took her arm. 'You know, Beatrice, we get on awfully well, don't we? We're friends?' And, when she nodded, 'I'd like it to be something more than that—I've nothing much to offer, but I intend to make my way to the top in record time. I'll not say any more now, that wouldn't be fair, but think about it, darling—you're everything a man could want, and so beautiful.'

Before she could speak, he added, 'Don't say anything, just remember what I've said.'

And he began to talk about the good results he had had from a new drug he had been using on a nearby pig farm.

Beatrice passed the next week or two in a state of dreaminess, interlarded by vague doubts which she couldn't put a name to but which persisted at the back of her mind. Her father had said nothing more about Colin going, and she hadn't asked. Surely if Colin had been going to leave he would have told her? She allowed herself to dwell in a state of euphoria and ignored the niggling doubts.

Which made it all the more nightmarish when the doubts became certainty. Pure unlucky chance had sent her back to the surgery after the short afternoon session. Colin had told her that he was going out to one of the farms, her father was resting and her mother was in the kitchen with Mrs Perry, making jam. Beatrice went unhurriedly across the garden which separated the surgery from the house, intent on collecting the towels they had used. The door to the surgery was open and she walked in, her sandalled feet making no noise, and stopped doubtfully when she heard Colin's voice. He was on the phone, and the door to the office was half-open. She took a step forward to see why he was still there and then she heard her name.

'Beatrice? I've got her eating out of my hand. No, I haven't told her I'm going; I've a couple of weeks still, time enough to persuade her to marry me—her old man can't do much if his daughter marries me, can he? Only offer me the partnership.' He laughed. 'Oh, she's OK. Not my type, but I can't have everything, can I?'

He was silent, apparently listening to someone at the other end of the phone, and Beatrice stood like a statue, her world slowly tumbling around her, not quite believing her ears. A great wave of humiliation seemed to sweep over her, doused by indignation and rage as he spoke again, 'I've been through the books—it's a first-class practice, plenty of lolly; I shan't be able to get my hands on it at once, but after a few months, once we're married, I'll get my besotted Beatrice to hand some of it over.'

He laughed again. 'No, I'm not a rogue, just a man with an eye to the main chance. Besides, she thinks I'm the only man in the world...'

Beatrice had been frozen to the spot, now suddenly she turned and sped out of the door, running blindly to get away. She had no idea that the tears were streaming down her face, and she couldn't have cared less if she had known. She could hardly believe it, and she couldn't see where she was going, so when she ran full tilt into Dr Latimer, she let out a breathy yelp and tried to pull away from him.

He caught her neatly and made no effort to let her go. 'Dear, oh, dear.' His voice was disarmingly gentle. 'No, don't talk for a moment. Let me mop you up, and then presently you shall tell me all about it.'

CHAPTER FOUR

BEATRICE CHOKED, sniffed and allowed him to dry her sopping cheeks, but presently she took the handkerchief from him, blew her nose in a no-nonsense fashion and mumbled, 'Could we go away from here—please?'

He flung an arm around her shoulders, where it lay as solid as an oak and just as heavy but strangely comforting. 'My car. I've only just driven up, no one knows I'm here—we'll go for a drive.'

He drove unhurriedly through the narrow lanes, going towards Tisbury and then tooling around the maze of still narrower lanes; no distance from Hindley, but to all intents and purposes buried in remote country.

'Nice here,' he observed. 'Restful and delightfully green.'

Beatrice sat quietly beside him, his hanky screwed up in a wet ball in her hands, and she said politely, 'Yes, it is lovely. You know your way around here; but of course, you stay with the Elliotts, don't you?'

He didn't answer directly. 'I know them very well.'

They had come to a widening in the lane and a gap in the trees on either side of it. He stopped the car. 'A pity there's a hill in the way, otherwise we would get a splendid view of Wardour Castle.'

She turned obediently to look, and heard his gentle sigh. 'And now, are you going to tell me what happened?'

'No—oh, no,' said Beatrice, and instantly contradicted herself. 'He wants the practice—I heard him telephoning. I didn't mean to eavesdrop, but the door was open and I heard my name.' She gave a sniff. 'That's why he was looking through the books, but he said he'd got them off the shelf by mistake. Father's getting a partner and Colin is to go, and I thought...he said—he said that he could easily get a partnership if he m-married me, only he doesn't love me.'

The doctor sat quietly beside her, sorting out her mutterings and making sense of them. He asked quietly, 'Did Colin tell you that he was leaving?'

'No. And Father didn't either. I asked Father if Colin couldn't stay as his partner, but he wants an older man, only I thought that Colin—he said that he hoped he could stay and I... I've been such a fool, haven't I?'

'No. You may feel one, but you aren't one. If he gave you to understand that he was in love with you and hoped one day to marry you, you had every reason to believe him.'

'But he was only pretending because he knows Father's practice is a good one, and it would have been so easy for him to take over in time and have all the benefit of Father's hard work without having done much towards it himself. He wanted the money, I suppose.' She gave a shuddering breath. 'I thought he wanted me.'

She hadn't looked at the doctor once, which was just as well, for his usually placid expression had been replaced by a look of ferocity, but his voice was as calm as usual. 'And how fortunate that you discovered that he didn't before any harm was done. Just think, if you hadn't heard him just now, you might possibly have married him and been unhappy ever after.'

She said in a woebegone voice, 'Yes, I'm sure you are right. But I don't know what to do.'

'Do? Why, behave as though you know nothing of this conversation of Colin's. Of course, he will—er—make overtures of a romantic nature; but forewarned is forarmed, my dear, and I'm perfectly certain that you will be able to deal with those as they occur.'

'Oh, will I?'

'But of course—all women have an inborn instinct for frustrating a man in his intentions. I have no doubt that you are well equipped to do this just as well as any other.'

He watched her reluctant smile and said, 'That's better. You're hurt and upset, but believe me, you will get over it, although that's cold comfort now, isn't it? But you have your father to think of as well—on no account must he be worried or bothered. Can you carry on as usual, do you suppose? You have become very friendly with Colin, have you not? Perhaps there is rather more than friendship on your part?' He took no notice of her quick breath. 'He goes in two weeks, doesn't he? Not long, and you're a level-headed girl, not given to hysterics.'

'I don't feel at all level-headed at the moment,' declared Beatrice in a tear-clogged voice.

He turned to look at her, his blue eyes impersonal, just as though he were examining a patient. 'Not quite your usual self, perhaps,' he conceded. 'If I drive you back, can you manage to get to your room and repair the damage?'

Sensible advice, and yet she found herself wishing peevishly that he wasn't quite so sensible.

She said with something of a snap, 'Yes, of course.' And after a moment, 'Thank you for listening to me and giving me advice. You're quite right, and I'll do what you suggest.'

He started the car again. 'If you need help, give me a ring. You know my London number, and if I'm not there I can be reached.'

'You're very kind. It's only two weeks...'

Not long, but how she dreaded them.

Back at home, he opened her door. 'Off you go,' he urged her. 'I'm going to see your father and mother, and no one need know that I arrived half an hour ago.' He gave her an encouraging pat on her shoulders and she said goodbye and ran indoors. No one was about, and she gained her room and spent twenty minutes getting her face back to normal. Only then did she go back downstairs, to meet Dr Latimer in the hall, bidding her mother and father goodbye. His suave, 'Ah, Beatrice, how are you? I'm so sorry that I have to go just as we meet again,' disconcerted her for a moment.

However, after only a tiny pause, she said in her usual calm way, 'Oh, I'm sorry, I was in my room cleaning up after seeing to the kittens. But you'll be down again? Are you pleased with Father?'

'Yes, indeed I am, but no excitement or exertion, from what he tells me he is doing enough for the moment.'

He smiled at her, shook hands with her mother and father and drove himself away.

'So good of him to call,' said her mother. 'He seems to come this way a great deal. Perhaps he visits someone...he's not engaged, is he? I mean, he could be coming to see a fiancée, couldn't he?' She looked at Beatrice. 'I know he doesn't stay with the Elliotts, not lately, anyhow. I wonder where he goes?'

'I dare say he has other friends than the Elliotts, Mother; he might even have other patients in this part of the world.'

'Yes, dear. Oh, Colin popped in to say that he'd gone over to Muston's Farm, and if he's not back could you get the clinic organised?'

Beatrice bent to pat Knotty. 'Yes, of course. Father, did you want to see Dr Forbes's dog again? He's due for another injection.'

Her father nodded. 'Yes—I'll take the clinic too. There aren't many booked, are there?' And, at her questioning look, 'Dr Latimer suggested that I should do so and see how I felt.'

She wouldn't have to see Colin again then until the evening. She sighed with relief.

He was at supper, of course, entertaining them with a light-hearted account of his visit to Muston's Farm, and at the end of it suggesting that Beatrice might go over the patients booked for the next day. It was something they had done several times, sitting in the clinic, discussing each case at length and finding time to talk about other things as well. But this evening that was something Beatrice just couldn't do. She made the excuse that she had several phone calls to make to friends, and a letter she simply had to write to a friend who had gone to live in Canada.

Immediately she had said that, she worried that Colin might think it strange, for she had been more than willing to go with him on several occasions. She would have been furious if she had known that he wasn't in the least put out; his conceit allowed him to suppose that it was because she was shy of him since he had allowed her to see his supposedly real feeling for her.

It was her mother who remarked upon it as they were clearing the table after supper. 'Are you sure you didn't want to go with Colin, dear? You usually do.'

And at breakfast the next morning Mr Browning, who had got up early, remarked, 'Beatrice, when Mr Sharpe—Mr Cedric Sharpe—comes this morning, about ten o'clock, bring him to my study, will you?' At her questioning look he went on, 'He sounds very suitable as a partner, but of course we need to talk about it.'

Beatrice couldn't stop herself looking at Colin, but he was looking down at his plate. 'Colin is going in rather less than two weeks,' went on her father. He looked across at his assistant. 'I dare say you will find Canada rather different from here.'

Colin looked up. 'I'm not sure that I'm going,' he said. His smile was disarming. 'In fact, I have great hopes of staying in England.'

He looked across at Beatrice as he spoke and, mindful of Dr

Latimer's advice, she smiled back rather vaguely and said, 'Oh, really? I feel sure there are plenty of jobs going.'

The morning clinic was busy, and she was kept hard at work, but, when the last four-legged patient had been borne away and she began on the clearing up, Colin strolled over to where she was washing instruments.

'Are you wondering why I didn't tell you that I was leaving?'

She made her voice as non-commital as possible. 'Well, no, I wasn't. You were only a locum; I knew you would be going as soon as Father felt he could get back into the practice.'

'With a partner.' He sighed loudly. 'That was a bitter blow to me, Beatrice. I had hoped that he would offer a partnership to me. I know I have no capital, but I have brought a lot of up-to-date ideas into the practice, and eventually I could have taken over completely.'

Beatrice began to lay out clean towels. 'Oh, I don't think Father would ever retire; he's not all that old, you know, and he'd die of boredom. I dare say you would do much better in Canada—there must be an enormous scope for vets out there.'

Colin came a little nearer, and she whisked away to the sink and began to wash the bowls they had used.

'You must know why I want to stay.' He sounded so sincere that if she hadn't listened to his conversation on the phone she would have believed him. 'We get on so well together, Beatrice, you can't pretend that you don't know how I feel...'

It was fortunate that the phone rang then, for it saved her from having to answer him. She pounced on the instrument like the proverbial man clutching at a straw, and said 'Hello,' so heartily that Dr Latimer at the other end observed softly in her ear, 'Am I right in thinking that I have phoned at exactly the right moment? In a tight corner, are you? Could you be free on Saturday? I'd like to take you out.'

'Oh, would you? How nice.' She was aware that she sounded inane, but she had been taken by surprise. 'Why?' she asked.

'A whim—a breath of fresh air, preferably in company. I'll pick you up about nine o'clock.'

'I haven't said...'

'No. I know. I dare say Ella will do your chores for you. Bring Knotty with you, if you like.'

She put down the phone and Colin asked sharply, 'Who was that?'

'A private call. I must go up to the house and see if Mr Sharpe has arrived.'

He was on the doorstep as she reached the front of the house; a stocky, middle-aged man with a mild, craggy face and wispy, greying hair.

'Just right for Father,' muttered Beatrice, making herself known and showing him indoors. She left the two men together and went along to the kitchen to make coffee for them. Her mother and Mrs Perry were there, debating the advantages of a steamed jam pudding over treacle tart for supper.

'He's here,' said Beatrice. 'Mr Sharpe. He looks nice.'

'So Oliver says,' said her mother.

'Oliver? Who's Oliver?'

'Dr Latimer, dear. It seems silly to be so formal with him, doesn't it?'

'Yes. Well, I suppose so. But how did you you know about Mr Sharpe?'

'Oh, he recommended him to your father in the first place.'

'Did he, indeed?' Beatrice assembled the coffee-tray and bore it to her father's study, and when she got back to the kitchen Colin was there, exerting his charm on the two ladies. He turned it on Beatrice as she went in.

'I was just saying how I shall miss you all when I finally go. I feel so completely at home here.' He pulled a wistful face. 'Life is going to be very empty.'

'Not if you get a job, it won't,' observed Beatrice cheerfully. It was surprising, she thought, how she could be so casual with him while all the time her heart was—if not broken—severely cracked. In a day or two, she was sure, when she had got over her indignation and shock, she would feel unhappy; she had been almost but not quite in love with him...and she had never doubted that he was attracted to her, had fallen in love with her. Hurt pride was a splendid thing to stiffen one's backbone.

After a day or two, she got rather good at keeping Colin at a distance. Several times he had hinted strongly that he couldn't bear the thought of leaving her, but she had never given him a chance to get any further than that, although it had been tempting to do so—just once, to see what he would say—but pride forbade her.

Her father had accepted Mr Sharpe as a partner, and it was no longer possible for Colin to put off his arrangements for leaving with only a week left before Mr Sharpe and his family moved into the house in the village. He had become reticent as to his future plans, hinting to Beatrice when they were alone that he had no intention of going out of her life. She took no notice of this; she was honest enough to know that she was going to miss him, although she despised him for his pretence. All she wanted now was for him to be gone.

Ella was perfectly willing to do Beatrice's chores on Saturday; she disliked Colin, but she was good with the animals. It was a pity that at supper on the Friday evening she should have remarked upon Beatrice's outing with Dr Latimer. Mr and Mrs Browning knew of it, but had remained discreetly silent, so that it was left for Ella to let the cat out of the bag.

'You'll have to put up with me in the morning,' she told Colin. 'Beatrice is having a day off—Dr Latimer is taking her off somewhere.'

Colin's face had darkened, and after a moment he pushed back his chair. 'I've just remembered a prescription I had to have ready,' he said to no one in particular. 'You'll excuse me?' He cast Beatrice a long, reproachful look as he went.

'Didn't he know?' asked Ella innocently.

* * *

It had rained overnight, but the sky was a clear blue when Beatrice got up the next morning. She spent a good deal of time going through her wardrobe; Dr Latimer hadn't said where they were going. How like a man, she thought, wondering whether a blue linen dress and a little jacket would be more suitable than a pale pink cotton dress with a demure collar. Ella, who had wandered in, eating an apple, said, 'Wear the pink; men like pink.' She added as she sidled across to the bed and perched on it, 'I'm sorry I let Colin know about you going out with Oliver—I didn't know he didn't know, cross my heart.'

'No harm done. Who said you could call Dr Latimer Oliver?'

'Well, Oliver did. Dr Latimer is so stuffy; he must get awfully sick of all the nurses bending the knee and calling him Dr Latimer with every other breath.'

Beatrice poked her head through the pink dress. 'I believe they call consultants "sir" in hospital.'

'Really? That makes him sound like a stuffed shirt, and that he most certainly is not.' Ella tossed the core into the wastepaper basket. 'I shall probably marry him when I'm grown up.'

'Does he know?'

'I don't think I'll even tell him, in case I meet someone I like better.'

'Sound thinking,' observed Beatrice, and started throwing things into her good leather handbag. 'I wish he'd said where we were going.'

'Well, you look all right,' said Ella kindly, 'and it isn't as if you're going out to dinner, is it? Will you be gone all day?'

'I don't know. He didn't say.'

'I expect you will go into Salisbury and have lunch in some stuffy restaurant.'

Beatrice gave her face a last-minute survey. 'He said he wanted a breath of fresh air.'

'A picnic on Salisbury Plain,' said Ella.

'I'd like that.' Beatrice went downstairs and found Colin in the hall, obviously waiting for her.

'If only I'd been free today,' he began in an aggrieved voice, 'we could have spent the day together. But I'll make up for it once I've left here.'

Beatrice wasn't paying much attention, for she had heard the doctor's car coming up the drive; it came to a whispering halt and she went to open the door, saying over her shoulder, 'Yes, you'll take a holiday, I expect.'

Dr Latimer had got out of his car and was strolling round to the kitchen door, but he stopped when he saw her.

'I didn't expect you to be ready,' he told her. 'I was going to say hello to your mother. I dare say your father is at the clinic.'

'Well, no—he'll be with Mother. It's Colin's Saturday duty.' She frowned as she spoke; he should have been in the clinic, seeing his patients, instead of mooning round the hall. The frown cleared when she heard Ella's voice shouting for him, her clear young voice raised impatiently.

'You've several patients and it's five past nine already.'

The doctor lifted an eyebrow, but continued on his way, although he spent barely five minutes with Beatrice's parents before urging her, quite unnecessarily, to hurry up.

'But I've been ready for ages,' she protested, and blushed at his,

'I'm flattered.'

In the car she asked, 'Where are we going?'

'Not far. Would it bore you to loll around in the sun for an hour or so? And perhaps a swim?'

'It sounds lovely, but I haven't my swimsuit with me.'

'Oh, I dare say one can be found for you.' He began to talk in a pleasant rambling fashion about nothing much, and she sat back and let all the small worries of the week melt away. Colin had been very tiresome once or twice, almost as though he were quite happy to be leaving, and yet hinting that he would still be able to see her...

'Only another five days,' said Dr Latimer suddenly. 'Has it been difficult?'

It was such a comfort to have her thoughts read. 'Yes. At least, I don't know why, but Colin makes me feel uneasy; he behaves as though we shall go on seeing each other even though he's leaving.'

'Does he, now? A pity you can't go and stay with your great-aunt, but then you would have to leave your father—your mother looks after him quite splendidly, but I don't think she could cope with young Wood, and your father must be protected from anything likely to raise his blood pressure.'

'Oh, I'll be all right.'

They were on a country road she knew well, going in the direction of Phillip's House, a large estate only a few miles away, and she wondered where they were going, but she didn't like to ask again for he hadn't answered her the first time, only talked about swimming and lying in the sun.

They entered the village just short of the estate, and he slowed the car and turned down a narrow country lane, away from the few houses in its main street.

'There's a lovely old house along here,' said Beatrice chattily, 'with a red-tiled roof, and it's all shapes and sizes, just as though whoever lived there needed to add a room or so from time to time. I expect you've seen it?'

They were almost level with its open gate, and he slowed the car. 'Well, yes. I live here.'

She shot round in her seat to look at him. 'You do? I thought you lived in London.'

'Well, I do for a good deal of each week, but this is my home. It's been my family's home for a long time.'

He drew up in front of the solid door, undid her seat-belt and leaned across to open her door; and when she got out he put a hand under her elbow and ushered her into the house. There was an elderly man standing by the open door.

'This is Jennings—he and Mrs Jennings look after me.'

She shook hands, aware that a pair of very shrewd blue eyes were studying her. Jennings' voice held satisfaction. 'Welcome, Miss Browning.'

He stood aside to let them pass, and it wasn't until much later that she wondered how he had known her name—the doctor hadn't mentioned it...

The hall was wide, low-ceilinged and panelled; an oak dower chest against one wall held a bowl of roses, and against the opposite wall there was a solid oak table flanked by two high-backed, cane-seated oak chairs. There were flowers here too, and wall sconces with pale rose-coloured shades. There were doors on either side, and passages leading off left and right with an uncarpeted staircase, its wooden treads worn with age, at the back of the hall.

'In here,' said the doctor, and opened a door and swept her before him. The sitting-room was low-ceilinged like the hall, but with plain white walls hung with paintings. There was a bow window at one end with a window-seat beneath it, piled high with cushions, and the fireplace was wide and deep. The chairs and sofas were velvet-covered and looked comfortable, and Mabel got out of one of them to bounce across the floor and greet them. Beatrice bent to pat her and took the opportunity to take a good look around her. She liked what she saw; it was a lived-in room despite the splendid glass-fronted cabinets along its walls, which were filled with porcelain and silver, and the magnificent crimson brocade curtains at the window. The window-panes were latticed and old, but at some time or other a door had been made to open into the garden beyond. She wandered over to look through it and the doctor opened it.

'The garden's rather nice,' he observed. 'We'll go round it presently if you would care to.'

'Oh, I would.'

'Coffee first, though. Come and sit here and tell me how your father is.'

She thought for a moment. 'I think he's improving fast, especially now that he's arranged for Mr Sharpe to take up a partnership.' She hesitated. 'I think he will be glad when Colin's gone.'

'Can you tell me why?'

'I think he feels that he's being edged out, if you see what I mean.'

'And you, Beatrice? I understand that you will be glad to see Wood go, but perhaps in your heart you are hoping that there has been a misunderstanding. Have you spoken to him? Asked him to explain his conversation on the phone?' He paused. 'Let him see that you are a little in love with him?'

Beatrice raised her lovely eyes to his. 'I think I'd rather die,' she said quietly, which somehow made the words all the more dramatic. She went on. 'I—I shall miss him, and I think I've been hoping that he would explain, but he hasn't, because of course he doesn't know that I heard him in the first place.'

The doctor agreed gravely, a gleam of amusement in his eyes. 'Then things should be left as they are, don't you agree? He will be gone in another few days, and in time you will mend your cracked heart.'

This sensible speech cheered her up; they drank their coffee and presently wandered out into the garden. The grounds were large and beautifully laid out, and when they came to a high, old brick wall the doctor opened a wicket gate and ushered her into the kitchen garden with its rows of orderly vegetables, fruit bushes and raspberry canes. The walls were lined with apricot and peach trees, and there were apple and pear trees growing haphazardly between the beds of peas and beans and beetroots.

'Oh, this is fabulous,' cried Beatrice. 'It must be looked after by several gardeners.'

'Old Trott, who's been with us, man and boy, and his two grandsons, and I like gardening too when I have the time.'

They strolled around in the bright sunshine, and she felt happy for the first time in days—a gentle happiness, very soothing to her trampled ego and gently stoked by her companion's manner towards her: a well-balanced mixture of casual friendliness and pleasure in her company.

The swimming pool looked inviting, hidden away behind a screen of trees, with lounger chairs arranged invitingly around it. There were small changing-rooms at one end too, and the doctor said placidly, 'Mrs Jennings found some swimsuits; I dare say one might fit you. Shall we have a swim before lunch?'

There were half a dozen swimsuits in as many sizes. Beatrice, weighing the charm of a dark blue one-piece against the spectacular stripes of a bikini, chose the blue; it did more for her splendid figure than any bikini, but she hadn't thought about that.

The doctor was already in the water; she slipped in feet first and began a sedate breast-stroke, but by the time she had swum the length of the pool the warmth of the water and the bright sun encouraged her to alter her speed, and in no time at all she was racing her companion up and down its length until they cried a truce and got out to lie in the sun.

The doctor was an undemanding companion; Beatrice lay half asleep, speculating idly as to who else had a choice of the wonderful swimming-suits he had provided. It was a pity, she reflected, that she didn't know him well enough to ask. She turned her head to look at him, lying on the lounger next to her. He looked even larger in swimming trunks than he did in his formal grey suits; his eyes were closed and she felt a faint flicker of annoyance that he was actually asleep, but at least it gave her the opportunity of studying him at length. Very good-looking, but, now she came to notice, the good looks were etched with lines of weariness. Six feet, five inches at least, she guessed, and a pair of shoulders which wouldn't disgrace a prize fighter. She lifted her head a little in order to get a better view of his commanding nose, and then drew in her breath sharply when he opened one eye.

'How very discourteous of me. I had rather a disturbed night.'

'Why?'

'Oh, a patient I have been looking after.'

'You had to go to him in the middle of the night? I thought specialists didn't do that.' She frowned. 'Don't you have a registrar at the hospital?'

'Oh, yes, but specialists get up in the middle of the night too. It's all part of the job.'

'Do have another nap,' she begged. 'I'm very happy just lying here doing nothing.'

He rolled over to look at her. 'How nice of you to say that. But that would be a waste of time. Shall we dress? I'll show you the horses before lunch.'

'Horses? You ride?'

'Whenever I can. You do, too?' He had got to his feet and bent to pull her to hers. 'There's still half an hour before lunch.'

There were two chestnuts in the paddock beyond the kitchen garden, and with them an elderly donkey. They came to the gate and took the sugar they were offered, and Beatrice stroked their soft noses. 'Nice beasts—do you hunt?'

'No. I like to ride wherever the fancy takes me.'

'And the donkey?'

'Kate? Oh, happy enough to live here with the horses.'

'A pity there aren't any children to ride her...'

'Yes, but that can be remedied in the future.'

Beatrice had her mouth open to ask him if he was about to marry, but stopped herself just in time. 'She looks very fit,' she observed.

The doctor whistled to Mabel. 'Time we went back for lunch. What would you like to do this afternoon?'

'Lie in the sun,' said Beatrice promptly, 'and you can tell me about your work.' They were strolling back towards the house. 'No, that wouldn't be fair. You must want to get away from it at weekends.'

He smiled a little. 'And you? What do you intend to do, Beatrice?'

'Me? Well, stay and help Father, I suppose...'

'And then?' he prompted.

She said uncertainly, 'I don't know; I suppose I haven't thought about it a great deal. That is—' She went pink, but turned her candid eyes on his. 'I suppose I thought that Colin would ask me to marry him.'

The doctor stared down at her. 'He probably still will do so.'

'But he's going...'

'He is leaving the practice, which is an entirely different matter.'

They had reached the house, and Jennings came to meet them. 'I've put drinks on the terrace, sir—if the young lady wishes to tidy herself, Mrs Jennings will show her the cloakroom.'

So Beatrice did her hair and her face and used the charming cloakroom beside the staircase; Ella had been quite right, the pink dress looked nice. Feeling light-hearted, she drank her sherry and listened to the doctor's placid voice talking about nothing in particular, and presently was led across the hall to the dining-room; it was panelled like the hall, and furnished with a rectangular table in mahogany and a beautiful bow-fronted sideboard. There were eight ribbon-backed chairs, but lunch had been laid at one end of the table and they sat facing each other, eating iced watercress soup, chicken salad and raspberries and cream, and drinking Chablis. Afterwards they went back to the terrace and had their coffee. Thinking about it later, Beatrice couldn't remember what they had talked about, only that she had enjoyed every minute of it.

And presently, stretched out on a swinging hammock in a shady corner of the garden, with the doctor lying on the grass beside her, she drifted off into a vague daydream, very much influenced by her surroundings. To be able to live in such a lovely house would be a delight in itself; she tried to fit Colin into the picture, but somehow he didn't seem right. She must forget him; perhaps if she went away for a week or two?

'I'll give two guesses,' murmured the doctor, his eyes half shut, watching her face. 'Colin...'

'Well, yes, partly. I can't help it, although I do try. It'll be all right once he's gone.' She rolled over in order to see him better. 'Oliver, it will be all right, won't it?'

'Of course. That is the first time you have called me Oliver.'

'Oh, is it? You see, most of the time I have seen you, you've been a doctor.'

'I see what you mean. Don't forget I am a friend as well, Beatrice.'

'I won't. Has Ella told you that she intends to marry you when she grows up? You'll be in the family.'

'A pleasant thought, but a pity that in another five years or so I shall be fortyish. I fancy she may have changed her mind by then. She's a nice child.'

'Haven't you any brothers or sisters?'

'Four sisters, all married with children, and a younger brother. He's a houseman up in Edinburgh, and just got himself engaged to a very pretty little nurse.'

'So you're the only one...' began Beatrice, and went red. 'Sorry, I didn't mean to pry.'

'Not married,' he finished for her. 'Although I rather fancy I shall achieve that state in the near future.'

She longed to find out more, but he began to talk about the garden and what he planned to do that autumn. Not quite a snub, but almost, she reflected while they discussed Christmas roses and chrysanthemums; she must take care not to let her tongue run away with her.

They had tea presently—sandwiches and fruitcake and tea poured from a silver teapot, all brought out to them by Jennings, with a strapping girl carrying a folding table to put everything on. Beatrice munched cake and reviewed a safe topic of conversation. 'Have you had your holiday yet?'

'In the spring. I went to Madeira; it's a splendid place for walking. It rather depends on various things as to when I shall take another week or two. And you?'

'Oh, I don't expect so. I'm hoping Mother and Father will go away somewhere quiet, just as soon as he feels that the practice is his, if you see what I mean, and that Mr Sharpe is able to cope. I'll stay at home and look after things. Ella is going on one of these school trips—climbing in Cumbria—and Carol is going to Paris to stay with some friends of hers.'

'So the house will be empty; you and Knotty will have time to climb the hill every morning if you want to.'

They went indoors presently, still talking in a desultory way while he showed her the library and urged her to roam the bookshelves and take anything she fancied. She settled for a history of Dorset, a very old edition, and a book on the Greek Islands.

He drove her home fairly soon after dinner, spent ten minutes or so chatting to her parents, smiled nicely at her when she thanked him for her lovely day, and a little to her chagrin didn't suggest that they might do the same thing again. But later, thinking about it, she had to acknowledge that, if he was intending to marry, his future wife might not approve.

Colin had been in the sitting-room when they had gone in, but he had greeted them with perfect good humour, remarked upon the weather and took himself off in a cheerful manner. Perhaps he had become reconciled to leaving, after all, thought Beatrice, and forgot about him while she recounted her day to her mother and presently took herself off to bed feeling happy. Although just before she slept she was conscious that behind the happiness was a tinge of sadness.

CHAPTER FIVE

BEATRICE MANAGED NOT to be alone with Colin during the next few days, something made much easier by reason of her father's increasingly active part in the running of the practice. As yet, he spent only short periods at the clinic, but this meant that Colin had more visits to pay, so that he was seldom for any length of time at the clinics when they were held. And, when the actual day of his departure came, Beatrice was agreeably surprised that he made no mention of seeing her again, but bade them all a friendly goodbye, got into his sports car and drove himself away.

'I must say,' observed Mrs Browning, 'that I'm quite glad to see him go; your father wasn't all that happy about him. He did his work well, but there was always this feeling that he was encroaching, gradually pushing his way in. He did want a partnership, but he couldn't have expected one without some capital. Besides, he's young; a few years as an assistant won't hurt him.'

She took Beatrice's arm. 'I wonder when we shall see Oliver again. Such a busy man, but perhaps he'll find time to come and see us next time he goes to his home. So strange that he lives only a short drive away. His home must be lovely...'

'It is.' Beatrice was conscious of a great wish to see it again, although she very much doubted if she would. 'Would Father like me to go down to the village and make sure the house is ready for the Sharpes? They'll be here this evening, won't they?'

The next two or three days passed peacefully. Mr Sharpe proved to be exactly what Mr Browning wanted: unassuming, pleasant and hard-working. And, being a Dorset man himself, he was able to get on very well with the local farmers. Beatrice, helping at the clinics, found him easy to get on with too, and, although she missed Colin more than she had thought she would, it was a relief to return to the mundane way of life she had known before he came.

Only it didn't stay mundane for long. Towards the end of the week she had gone down to the village shop for her mother. The fine weather had broken and she had cycled there, wrapped against the weather, propped her bike against the wall outside the shop and gone inside. The shop was unusual in that it sold groceries which wouldn't have shamed Fortnum and Mason, and at the same time it did a nice line in knitting wools and local pottery; and since it was just across the street from the village's famous pub it did a splendid trade, especially in the tourist season. But today, since the weather was bad, the shop was empty, and Beatrice, having passed the time of day with the proprietor, took her time over choosing bacon and cheese and the kind of biscuits her father preferred. It was while waiting for Mr Drew to fetch the particular brand of chutney her mother wanted that she glanced out of the window. Crossing the road was Colin, making for the shop.

He came in quietly and shut the door behind him. 'Hello, Beatrice. I saw your bike. I thought you would be down sooner or later.'

'You're still here,' she said stupidly.

'Of course, and I don't intend to go until we've had a talk.' He came and stood close to her, and she edged away until her back was against the counter. 'There wasn't much chance before; you kept out of my way, didn't you? But you can't really have thought that I would just go without seeing you. Beatrice, I shall stay here in the village until you say that you will marry me; then your father will have to offer me a partnership. He's far too fond of you to let you marry a penniless man.' He put out a hand and laid it on her arm. 'And if he doesn't want me in the practice, he would give us the money to get started on our own.'

Beatrice struggled to find words. She lifted his hand from her arm, and said, 'I'm a means to an end, aren't I? Well, I shall say this once: if you were the last man on earth I wouldn't marry you; you're wasting your time. I suggest that you go away and find yourself a job—preferably on the other side of the world.'

Colin's smile turned ugly, but Mr Drew, coming back with the chutney, gave her the chance to turn away from him and finish giving her order. She barely heard Colin's whispered, 'I shall stay here; don't think you can get rid of me so easily. After all, there's no one else, is there? You told me that once.'

She bitterly regretted that now as she cycled back home.

And he was as good as his word. Whenever she went to the village or took the dogs for a walk, he contrived to meet her; and after a day or two, when she reluctantly stayed away from the village and took the dogs in different directions, he wrote to her—impassioned letters, declaring his love and outlining a brilliant future for them both if she would marry him.

Oliver had said that her father wasn't to be worried, and that applied to her mother, who had worry enough; Carol was still away and Ella was too young; Beatrice said nothing to anyone, and began to look a little pale and worried, as well as becoming unusually short-tempered. When she wanted him, she thought crossly, the doctor wasn't there; there had been no sign of him for days. He could at least have phoned.

She came back from exercising the dogs, hot and tired and hardly at her best, and was putting the last of them back in its kennel when Oliver spoke from the door. She turned to look at him, not answering his cheerful 'hello' at once.

'Where have you been?' she wanted to know peevishly. 'It's almost a week...'

He said mildly, 'I've been over in West Germany—a consultation. What's the matter, Beatrice?'

She came out of the shed which housed the dogs and closed the door. 'I'm sorry I snapped. I've so wanted to talk to someone...'

'About Colin?'

'Yes. How did you guess? He's making a great nuisance of himself. I can't make him understand that it's quite hopeless expecting to—to marry me so that he can get a partnership. He's still in the village, at the Lamb. Whenever I go out, he's there.'

'How tiresome for you,' observed the doctor, and she said crossly,

'Of course it's tiresome; I hardly dare show my nose outside the clinic. What's more, there is no one to talk to about it.'

'There is now, I'm here.'

'Yes, but you'll go again as soon as you've seen Father, and I want to talk forever.'

'I've already seen your father. If you've finished for the time being, walk up the hill with me and tell me about it; I've nothing to do for the rest of the day.'

She looked down at her cotton dress. 'I'm not a bit tidy—my hair...'

'Looks perfectly all right, and who's to see, anyway?'

A bracing speech, but hardly flattering.

They walked in silence for some distance, but as they neared the summit of the hill she began, 'I don't know what to do. I'm so afraid that Colin will come up to the house and upset Father. Father knew that I liked Colin, I didn't make a secret of it; I even suggested that he might be made a partner—that was before—before...'

'You found him out. So that if he spoke to your father now, he might suppose that you were still in love with Colin.'

'Not in love,' she said quickly. 'Infatuated, I suppose, or at least only a little in love, but not any more. I'm suffering from outraged pride, and I'm scared that he'll do something to upset Mother and Father. How am I ever to convince him that I want nothing more to do with him?'

The doctor flung a large, comforting arm around her shoulders. 'There is a simple way of doing that. You and I, Beatrice, will become engaged.' She turned to face him, her mouth half open, her eyes wide, slow colour mounting into her cheeks.

'Before you utter a word, let me point out that I have not mentioned marriage, not even a proposal; but Colin wouldn't know that, would he? But if we let it be known that we are engaged, he will almost certainly realise that hanging around here in the hope of marrying you is a waste of his time; better by far that he should go in search of some other young woman with a comfortable background and good prospects.'

Beatrice's cheeks were their usual healthy pink, but she looked distinctly ruffled. 'It is very kind of you to offer,' she began haughtily, 'but I'm sure that's quite unnecessary. I'll think of something.'

The doctor wasn't in the least put out. 'You are a resourceful young woman, and I have no doubt that you will think of a great many ways of getting rid of him. When you've exhausted them all, my offer still stands!'

It was quite illogical of her to feel that he had let her down, especially when he started a cheerful conversation about Mabel, whom he had left at her father's house, enjoying a romp with Knotty. They had reached the top of the hill and stood side by side, looking at the wide spread of country before them.

'Is Germany as lovely as this?' asked Beatrice after a minute or two, searching for a safe topic.

'Parts of it, yes, but England is beautiful, and some of the best beauty spots are so hidden away that it takes a lifetime to discover them.'

He smiled at her as he spoke, so kindly that she said quickly, 'You're not annoyed because I don't want to be engaged to you?'

'Dear girl, of course not. I am rather too old for you in the first place, and in the second, we are not sufficiently good friends to cope with such a situation.'

'You're not in the least old, and you must know that we all regard you as a friend after what you have done for Father.'

'Too kind,' murmured the doctor. 'You forget that it is all in the day's work for me.' He glanced at his watch. 'Perhaps we should be strolling back? Your mother mentioned ham on the bone and potatoes in their jackets for supper.'

Soon, as they neared the house, she said quietly, 'Thank you for listening, Oliver. It helps a lot, doesn't it, to talk to someone…?'

'Oh, yes, and probably tomorrow you will find Colin gone and all your worries with him.'

But he was wrong there; buoyed up by the foolish idea that Colin might actually be gone because the doctor had suggested it, Beatrice went down to the village; there was Colin, strolling along, coming down the hill from the church, quickening his steps when he saw her. She was still some way away from the shop and there were no side roads, only grassy paths between some of the cottages. She walked on, and when they drew level wished him a cool good morning and made to pass him.

He turned around and walked beside her, saying nothing at all, which was oddly disquieting, so that she was glad when she reached the shop. He made no effort to go inside with her, and she sighed with relief as she closed the door on him. She was half-way through her shopping when Mr Drew said, 'What's he want, then? Hanging round outside… Why doesn't he come in instead of looking through the door like that?'

'I expect he's waiting for me.'

'Sweet on you, is he? Can't say I blame him.' And Mr Drew chuckled.

She spun out the order for as long as she could, but finally she had to leave the shop. Colin was strolling down the street some way from her and she crossed over and started on her way back home, to find him within seconds beside her again. There was no one about, so she stopped and faced him.

'Look, Colin, you're wasting your time. I have no intention of marrying you, and you would do better to find another job instead of hanging around here.'

He laughed. 'Come off it, darling. You were sweet on me and you can't deny it—led me on, you did, letting me think that your father would give me a partnership, or at least put up the money for us to settle down somewhere without money worries.'

'I did not lead you on.' Her voice rose indignantly, 'You're talking nonsense.'

He caught her by the arm and began walking down the street. 'We're going to have a talk, Beatrice, darling...'

She tried to pull away from him, but he was gripping her hard and just for a moment she felt scared; to make a scene wouldn't do at all... She closed her eyes for a moment, and when she opened them it was to see Oliver driving slowly up the street towards them. Her voice came out in a whisper and then a healthy shout, not that it had been necessary; she saw that he had seen them and was already pulling into the kerb, and a moment afterwards was standing before them, smiling a little.

'Oliver,' she was quite uncaring of the effect of her words, 'Oliver, do explain to Colin that we are engaged; I can't make him understand that I won't marry him.'

The doctor's smile didn't alter at all. 'My dear girl, until everyone reads of it in the *Telegraph*, no one knows.' He turned an almost benevolent face upon Colin. 'I dare say Beatrice had no chance to tell you, had she?'

He tucked a large hand under her arm, and she had never been so glad to feel its firm pressure. Colin looked from one to the other of them.

'Why didn't you tell me?' he demanded of Beatrice.

'You didn't give me the chance, but now you know, Colin, so please leave me alone.'

'I've been wasting my time,' he said furiously. 'Well, I wish you the best of luck, the pair of you.'

He turned on his heel and walked away, back up the street, and Beatrice watched him go in silence. Presently she said, 'I'm sorry—I panicked. And I had to stop him—I mean, right in the middle of the village, and you know how people look out of their windows—and he was holding me rather tightly—I didn't want to make a scene.'

The doctor listened patiently to this. 'You acted most sensibly,' he observed, at his most placid. 'And I have no doubt that we shall shortly see the last of young Wood.'

He bent a thoughtful gaze upon her worried face. 'There's really nothing that he can do, you know.'

'No. But what about—that is, I said that we were engaged.'

'Very wise. I'll see that a notice goes into the *Telegraph* tomorrow morning.'

'But we're not.'

'Ah, you know that and I know that, but no one else needs to know. Tell your family by all means, but let everyone else believe what they read. Once Wood is safely away, we can review the situation.'

'Yes, but...'

'Shall we get into the car? I was on my way to see you—we will go the long way round and discuss the matter in comfort.'

So she got into the car beside him, aware now that several interested faces were peering round cottage curtains.

'We seem to have created a good deal of interest,' remarked the doctor calmly. He tooled the car gently up the street, turned past the pub and took a narrow lane just beyond it. 'Now, what is worrying you?'

'Us—you. You said you would put a notice in the *Telegraph*, but if you're going to get married, won't she mind? The girl you're going to marry?'

'She is a most sensible young woman; I foresee no difficulties. Besides, I intend to marry her and no one else. No one else really matters.'

He spoke quietly, and Beatrice felt a pang of envy for the girl who could be so sure of him whatever he did. He must love her very much. 'She must be awfully nice.'

'She is everything I could wish for. Do you intend to tell your mother?'

'Well, yes, I think so, but not Father, because then I'd have to explain about Colin and he might get upset and angry.' She thought for a bit. 'But I'd better tell Ella.'

The doctor laughed. 'A good idea—she's an observant child.'

'Were you coming to see Father?'

'Partly, and partly to see how you were getting on with Wood; I rather thought he would be a nuisance. Now you will be able to settle down to your usual quiet life again.'

Perversely, Beatrice found no pleasure in the prospect. She was thankful that Colin would be gone, but a quiet life, stretching ahead for years and years, held no appeal. There was always James, but she suspected that he had transferred his affections to the rector's eldest daughter, a friend of hers and most suitable for him. Without a tinge of regret, she hoped that they would be very happy.

'Perhaps it might be a good idea if you were to go away for a week or two. No need to say where you are going to anyone but your family. Colin—if he hasn't already gone—might possibly get the idea that you were staying with me, which might speed his departure.'

'Oh, does he know where you live?'

'No, but he knows that I work mostly in London; even if he wanted to find you, he might not find it worthwhile.'

'Why should he persist? I thought he would go away now.'

'It is to be hoped that he will, but you must remember that you are the key to everything he wants: a partnership, the prospect of taking over the practice in the future, and a wife who is by no means penniless.'

'And I thought it was just me,' she said ruefully.

Her father was over at the clinic, helping Mr Sharpe with an unexpectedly busy morning surgery; her mother was sitting outside the kitchen door, shelling peas.

'Your father won't be long now. Go and make the coffee, will you, darling? Oliver, can you spare the time to have a cup with us? You've come to see your patient, I expect?'

He sat down on the grass beside her, and when Beatrice had gone to the house she added, 'He's so much better now Colin has gone; he didn't like him, you know, and he was so afraid that Beatrice would fall in love with him.' She glanced sideways at the doctor's impassive face. 'I think she was beginning to, but now he's gone...' She heaved a sigh of relief.

'He hasn't gone, Mrs Browning. He's in the village, and he's been pestering Beatrice every time she pokes that pretty nose of hers outside this house.'

Mrs Browning stopped shelling peas and stared at him, open-mouthed. 'Pestering her? She has never said a word.'

'She doesn't want to upset Mr Browning. It was quite by chance that I found out about it.'

'And?'

Beatrice came through the door with the tray, and he got up and took it from her. 'I think Beatrice may want to tell you herself.'

'But not her father?' Mrs Browning began to pour the coffee. 'He'll be another ten minutes or so, dear. Oliver has just told me that Colin has been bothering you—has he gone or do we send you away? Is it upsetting you?' She handed the doctor a mug of coffee and then a plate of biscuits. 'Of course, you don't have to say anything if you don't feel like it.'

'Well, Mother—' began Beatrice, and gave her an admirably brief account of Colin's activities. 'And then this morning I couldn't get rid of him and—and I saw Oliver and I shouted to him, and he came and I told Colin that we were engaged...' She heard her mother's sharp intake of breath. 'Yes, I know, I must have been a little mad, but I couldn't think of anything else, and Oliver very kindly told a lot of fibs about the notice being in the *Telegraph* tomorrow...'

She hadn't looked at Oliver once as she talked, but now she looked across at him. 'I am very grateful, I really am, and I hope you didn't think I was imposing on your good nature.'

'Think nothing of it.' His voice was nicely casual. 'I have hopes that your quick thinking may have the right effect. All the same, I think that you should go away for a week or so; it will save answering awkward questions in the village, and give Wood no opportunity of cross-questioning you. Another thing, perhaps it might be a good idea to mention our engagement to your father. There is no need to say anything about Wood, and we can be vague about the future. After a suitable interval, Beatrice, you can change your mind and we can all go back to our normal way of living.'

A sensible speech which left both Beatrice and her mother with feelings of regret, but for different reasons.

'And what about you, Oliver?' asked Mrs Browning worriedly. 'Won't it interfere with your life—your private life?'

'I don't believe so. I'm going on a lecture tour in a few days' time, so I shall see very few of my friends for several weeks, and I shall have a backlog of work to get through on my return, so I'm not likely to go out a great deal.'

'You make it sound very easy.'

He passed his mug for more coffee. 'My tour takes in Utrecht, Cologne, Copenhagen, Brussels and finally Edinburgh; it will take a fortnight, or perhaps a day or two more than that. In fact, I can see no reason why Beatrice shouldn't come with me. Lecturers usually take wives with them, and it is by no means unusual for fiancées to go along.' He had spoken in his usual calm fashion; now he looked at Beatrice and smiled. 'A good idea? No hurry to decide. I shall be at Salisbury for the next day or so. I'll give you a ring before I go back.'

He got to his feet as Mr Browning joined them, remarking

that he looked fit and well. 'I'll take a look if I may before I go, although I'm sure that I shall find everything satisfactory.'

Mr Browning sat down. 'You all look very pleased with yourselves,' he observed.

It was Beatrice who answered. 'Father, Oliver and I—we've got engaged. It was rather sudden and we haven't any plans at present; Oliver's busy.'

'My dear, what splendid news! Oliver, I am delighted. And here have I been worrying about young Wood. I quite thought that you were beginning to like him, Beatrice, and all the time it was Oliver. Well, well!' He beamed around him. 'Now I shall have to find someone to take your place.'

'Not yet, Father,' said Beatrice quickly. 'Oliver has an awful lot of work to get through.' And, when he looked doubtful, she added hastily, 'You know who is longing to step into my shoes? Ella—she might even train as a vet. She's been pestering me to let her work at the clinic during her holidays, and they begin next week.'

She succeeded in her efforts to divert his thoughts. 'You're quite right, Beatrice—she is a natural with animals. There's no reason why she shouldn't help out with exercising and feeding and learning something of the surgical work.' He put down his mug. 'I dare say you're busy, Oliver. Shall we go indoors? I never felt better in my life, especially now that I've heard your news. Beatrice will make a splendid wife, you know—a very level-headed girl and an excellent cook.'

He led the way indoors and Beatrice said softly, 'Oh, Mother, I don't think it will work—what have I started?'

Her mother gave her an untroubled look. 'Well, darling, it struck me that Oliver didn't seem all that surprised—I mean, one would have thought that he had thought of it himself.'

There was the faintest question in her remark.

'As a matter of fact,' said Beatrice carefully, 'he did—not then, but before Colin left he was being tiresome one morning—' Somehow she couldn't bring herself to tell her mother about Colin's telephone conversation which she had overheard. 'And Oliver happened to come along, and we had a talk afterwards and he suggested that it might be an idea, but I said no.'

'Things have a way of sorting themselves out,' observed Mrs Browning. She sounded quite pleased.

The two men came back presently, and after a few minutes' reassuring talk from the doctor he drove away with nothing more than a casual remark to Beatrice that he would see her in a day or two.

True to his word, the announcement of their engagement appeared in the *Telegraph* on the following day, and Beatrice spent the day answering phone calls from friends and people she knew in the village. There was a phone call from Great-Aunt Sybil too, with guarded approval of the match. 'A well-mannered young man,' she observed weightily, 'and Miss Moore, whom he recommended to me, has proved to be a treasure. He is one of the few members of the medical profession who has an inkling of my needs.'

A recommendation which Beatrice stored away to pass on to Oliver when next she saw him.

There was a letter from Colin the following morning, and she saw with misgiving that she was right in thinking he was still in the village. It was an impassioned missive, and if she hadn't had the clear memory of his phone conversation she might have been swayed by it. She read it carefully, tore it up and put the pieces tidily in the wastepaper basket. If she ignored it, he would surely go.

Only he didn't; he was still there three days later, sending her a letter each day, not attempting to see her, only begging her to break off her engagement and marry him instead. 'Your father won't object,' he had written, 'once he realises it is what you want; he can offer me a partnership and we can have Sharpe's house.' Only someone as selfish as he could suggest turning a man and his family out of house and job, thought Beatrice, and tore up yet another letter.

The doctor came on the evening of the fourth day, quiet and self-assured, and when she had poured out all her worries he remarked placidly, 'We can take care of that; you'll come on the tour with me. I'll have Miss Cross with me, so you won't lack for company while I'm lecturing. I'm leaving the day after tomorrow. Can you be ready by then? You have a passport? Good. Bring clothes for a couple of weeks, and something to wear at the rather boring dinner parties we shall attend.'

He smiled at her rather in the manner of a medical man who had just reassured his patient that she would get better, even if she didn't think so at that moment.

'Are you sure? I mean, won't your fiancée mind?'

He said evenly, 'The girl I am going to marry will have no objection.'

'Then she must be a saint,' said Beatrice roundly.

'Happily, no. Just flesh and blood, nicely put together.'

'Do you want me to come up to London?'

'No. I'll fetch you some time in the morning, and I shall drive very slowly down the village street so that everyone will be able to see us go.'

'You think of everything.'

'I do my best.' He sounded amused.

'But what about when we get back?'

'Let us cross our bridges when we get to them. The whole point of the exercise is to convince Wood that you are really unattainable. Let us deal with that first. What have you done with his letters?'

'Torn them up. At least, one came this morning, but I haven't read it yet.'

'Then do so while I take a look at your father. His surgery will be over by now?'

'Yes.' He had stopped the car short of the house, and she had been the only one to see him drive up. 'I'll go and make the coffee. I'll be in the kitchen.'

Her mother was there, stringing beans while Mrs Perry

cleaned the kitchen. She had been with the family for too long for anyone to have qualms about minding their 'p's and 'q's in front of her.

'Oliver's here,' said Beatrice. 'He's gone to see Father—he's staying for coffee. He wants me to go on his lecture tour with him and his secretary the day after tomorrow.'

'Now won't that be a treat?' remarked Mrs Perry. 'All over the place, no doubt, and plenty of fine folk to listen to him.'

'Well, yes, I suppose so. My passport's all right for another year—it's ten years, isn't it? And I had it for that trip after I took my A levels.'

'Clothes?' enquired her mother, getting to the heart of the matter. 'Will you go anywhere?' She meant, would Beatrice go anywhere special where she would need to dress up?

'Well, dinners and things. It's for about a fortnight.'

'Make the coffee, darling, will you? Ella's home, luckily. You and I will go to Bath this afternoon and do some shopping. What's that letter in your hand?'

Beatrice had forgotten Colin's letter. She opened it while the coffee brewed and read it slowly. It was even more urgent than the others—he couldn't understand why she hadn't answered his letters; surely she must see what a splendid future they could have together? Once again he pointed out that her father was bound to see them on their feet and make sure that she continued to live comfortably as she had always done.

'Well, really,' declared Beatrice indignantly, just as the doctor came into the kitchen; he removed the letter from her hand and read it.

He tore it into pieces when he had done so, and put them into the kitchen bin, and said placidly, 'Your father is remarkably fit—not to be worried, of course. Mr Sharpe seems to be just right for him—they get on well together.' He took the tray from Beatrice. 'In the garden?'

'I'll have mine here, young man,' declared Mrs Perry, and remembered a bit late to add, 'Doctor.'

Mrs Browning sliced the last bean. She was dying of curiosity to know what had been in the letter, but four daughters had taught her the value of a golden silence. This time, however, she was to have her reward.

With a glance at Beatrice, the doctor said casually, 'His letters don't vary, do they? The promise of a vague future, but no mention of how that will be achieved. A dish of herbs where love is is all very well, but nowadays one needs the money to buy the herbs.'

Mrs Browning chuckled. 'Poor boy; I still don't like him—but I'm a little sorry for him, too.'

Beatrice said nothing, but busied herself with the coffee, and the doctor said smoothly, 'From all accounts he is a good vet; he should be able to get a job wherever he wants to go.'

He accepted a mug of coffee and Beatrice gave him a grateful look; her mother was satisfied about the contents of the letter; he had somehow managed to dispel any suspicions she might have had about Colin, and at the same time implied that he would recover quickly enough from his professed love of Beatrice.

When her father joined them, the doctor asked in his mildest manner, 'You will be coming with me, Beatrice?' He glanced across at Mr Browning, who nodded happily. 'I've rushed you, rather, but I'm sure you will enjoy yourself. I don't have much time during the day, but Miss Cross is a pleasant companion. I'll be taking the car and we'll go from Dover and drive up from Calais. We shall be in Utrecht for two days.'

He glanced at Beatrice. 'Come back to my place for lunch, Beatrice, and I'll tell you exactly where we are going.'

She shook her head. 'I'd have liked to, but Mother and I are going to Bath—I must do some shopping...'

'Ah, of course, you will have nothing to wear.' His voice was bland. 'In that case, come to lunch, then we'll pick Mrs Browning up and I'll drive you both there and collect you whenever you say.' He added with a faint smile, 'I have some shopping to do, too.'

No one could find fault with this; Beatrice went indoors to change her dress and find Ella to beg her to take Knotty for his walk, then hurried outside again. They were still sitting over their coffee, but Oliver got up when he saw her, said his goodbyes and ushered her into the car in a businesslike manner, and drove off.

CHAPTER SIX

THE DOCTOR HAD little to say as he drove to his home, and Beatrice, her head for the moment full of worried thoughts about her clothes, hardly noticed his silence. She had nice clothes; her father paid her a salary for her help at the clinic and she was able to afford them, but she didn't go out a great deal and her stock of after-six dresses was small. 'And something to travel in,' she muttered, forgetting where she was for the moment.

'Oh, knitted cotton or jersey that will drip dry,' Oliver answered.

She turned to gape at him. 'Whatever do you know about drip-dry cotton?'

'You forget that I have sisters. You should wear honey colour with that hair, or that pale apricot pink. I'm partial to pink.'

She had to laugh, and he said, 'That's better. You don't laugh enough these days.'

He swept the car through the gates, and there was Jennings waiting at the open door with Mabel bouncing around, anxious to be made much of. Beatrice, going in to a chorus of cheerful barks and Jennings hovering, felt quite at home.

They ate their lunch with a map spread out on the table between them, while the doctor pointed out exactly where they would be going.

'And do you lecture in English?' she wanted to know.

'In Holland, yes, and in Copenhagen, but I manage to make myself understood in German and French, and of course a number of medical terms are universal.'

'And do you give the same lecture each time?'

'Well, basically, yes.'

'You must be very clever—cleverer than I thought...'

He said gravely, 'Thank you, Beatrice. You flatter me.'

'Oh, I didn't mean to do that,' she said forthrightly. 'I dare say there are a lot of things you can't do.'

His, 'Oh, dozens,' was so meek that she gave him a suspicious look which he countered with a bland smile.

They didn't linger over the meal, but got back into the car, this time with Mabel on the back seat, and drove back to her home. Mrs Browning, hatted and gloved, was waiting for them, declared herself perfectly willing to share the back seat with Mabel and was ushered into the car.

The journey took less than an hour, and was largely filled by Mrs Browning's voice murmuring over her shopping list.

'You'll need a new dress, dear; something pretty for the evening...'

Beatrice frowned; it sounded as though her mother was fishing for dinner invitations; if he offered her one she would refuse.

The doctor caught the frown out of the corner of his eye and smiled a little. 'Two, if I might suggest that. I did tell Beatrice that I am invited to attend at least one dinner in each place we visit, and I'm expected to bring my companion.'

'What about Miss Cross?' Beatrice asked.

'Oh, the secretaries have a gathering of their own; she has what she calls her little black number, and something called her brown crêpe.'

'You look awful in black,' commented Mrs Browning from the back seat.

Beatrice let out a very small sigh, and the doctor began to talk about the journey, so that Mrs Browning put away her list and listened. He could, on occasion, talk 'nothings' with great charm.

He dropped them off at the top of Milsom Street, promised to pick them up at the same place at half-past five, and drove away with Mabel sitting beside him.

Mrs Browning gave a satisfied sigh. 'Now, let me see—Brown's first, I think, darling. Your father told me that you had to have all that you needed. You buy what you want; I've my cheque-book with me.'

'Mother, I have plenty of money—I've not spent anything for weeks.'

'Yes, dear, but your father would like to give you a present—you've been so good and helpful.'

The two of them plunged into a delightful afternoon's shopping, emerging after an hour or so with a great many parcels and a much thinner cheque-book. Beatrice had found the knitted three-piece almost at once. What was more, it was in an apricot pink. 'Quite uncrushable,' declared the saleslady, 'and so suitable.' She didn't say what it was suitable for, but that hardly mattered; Beatrice was well satisfied. She had found two pretty dresses too—just in case she needed them, she pointed out to her mother. 'And since Father's paying...'

A patterned crêpe, very elegant with long, tight sleeves and a billowing skirt, and a blouse and skirt in satin, the blouse ivory, the skirt in a rich, dark red. To these were added a cotton dress with its matching cardigan, and a sun dress she thought she might never have the chance to wear, but which suited her so well that it seemed a pity not to buy it. They had tea at a nice teashop, and punctually at half-past five returned to the spot where Oliver was to meet them. He was already there, reading an evening paper, one arm round Mabel. No one, thought Beatrice, looking at him, would guess that he was an eminent physician at the very top of his profession. He looked far too much at ease. He looked up and, aware of them, got out of the car, ushered Mabel into the back, disposed of their parcels, tucked Mrs Browning smoothly in beside Mabel, whisked Beatrice into the front seat, climbed in beside her and drove off.

'I'm sorry we are a little late,' observed Beatrice.

'Five—ten minutes? I hadn't even glanced at my watch. Did you have a successful afternoon?'

'Oh, very, thank you. Did you?'

'I? Oh, yes. A consultation at Bath United.'

'Oh, do they call you in there as well?'

His firm mouth twitched with a hidden smile. 'I get called in all over the place.'

'Well, yes, I suppose you do.' They were silent while she tried to think of something to say, and couldn't. Her mother broke the long silence.

'You'll stay for supper, Oliver? Nothing much, just one of my pork pies with a salad and duchesse potatoes. Beatrice made a strawberry tart this morning—with cream, of course.'

'I'm going back to London this evening, Mrs Browning; I've a round to do in the morning and patients to see...'

'Well, you have to eat and it will be quite ready; I warned Ella. She's almost as good a cook as Beatrice.'

'In that case, I'll stay with the greatest of pleasure. You don't object to Mabel?'

'Good heavens, no! She can have her supper with Knotty. I dare say she'll be glad of a run around the garden. Will she go back with you this evening?'

'Oh, yes. She hates London, but she hates being away from me more.'

They talked about dogs for the rest of the journey.

Supper was a lively meal; no one mentioned Colin, the talk was all of Mr Browning's day at the clinic, the afternoon's shopping and the forthcoming trip.

Oliver could have known us all his life, thought Beatrice, watching him gently teasing Ella and carrying the dishes out to the kitchen. She thought it unlikely that the Jenningses allowed him to tidy away so much as a fork. He said all the right things to Mr and Mrs Browning, received a kiss from Ella with every sign of pleasure, waved casually to Beatrice, begged her to be ready when he came for her on the following day and drove away.

She went away to pack her bag, make sure that she had her passport and money while she listened to Ella's good advice about the right make-up and how to do her hair. 'You can't go around with a plait,' she pointed out. 'Do a french pleat or a chignon, and do use eye-shadow.' She sighed. 'I wish I had your eyelashes...'

To all of which Beatrice listened with only half an ear; she was thinking about Colin, although her thoughts were strangely clouded by a strong mental picture of the doctor. At least, she thought, by the time she got back home Colin would have gone and she would be able to stop thinking about him. She hated him for his duplicity, but at the same time it was hard to shake off the attraction she had felt for him.

'Don't look so sad,' said Ella. 'You're not old yet. You never know, you may meet a dashing Dutchman or a German professor.'

'I don't fancy either.' Beatrice began to loop her hair into a tidy chignon. 'Besides, I don't expect to meet any.'

'You're going to those dinner parties Oliver hates; find him a sexy blonde and hunt around for yourself.'

Beatrice let her hair fall round her shoulders. 'Ella, where do you get your ideas from? You're only fifteen...'

'Darling Beatrice, you're the one who's fifteen—being taken in by Colin like a teenager and not having an idea how to deal with him. You're a darling, but you've spent too many years with animals and not enough with men.'

To which remark Beatrice agreed, being an honest girl.

Wearing the new jersey outfit, she was ready when Oliver arrived.

His greeting was decidedly casual. 'Ah—you took my advice.' His eyes swept over her person; the casual look of a brother for a sister, she reflected peevishly. 'You're ready? We must go up to town and pick up Miss Cross. I told her to be at the flat—we can have lunch there and then drive down to Dover.'

They drove to town, making small talk in a desultory fashion, eating up the miles until the outskirts of London slowed them down. Beatrice had only the vaguest idea where the doctor lived; she supposed that it was somewhere close to his consulting-rooms in Harley Street—perhaps he lived in a flat at the same house.

He didn't. He drove up Park Lane, turned off into South Audley Street and, just short of Grosvenor Square, entered a quiet little tree-lined street with a terrace of Regency houses on either side. Almost at its end, he drew up.

'Oh, is this where you live?'

'When I'm in London, yes. Come along, we haven't a great deal of time.'

She was bustled across the narrow pavement to the front door, opened as they reached it by a tall, thin woman with a severe expression, made even more severe by the way her hair was drawn back into a tight bun and her lack of make-up.

'Hello, Rosie,' said the doctor cheerfully. 'I hope you've got a good lunch for us. Is Miss Cross here?'

'Good day to you, Doctor.' The faintest glimmer of a smile did its best. 'Lunch will be served in ten minutes, and Miss Cross arrived not five minutes ago.'

'Splendid. This is Miss Browning. Beatrice, Rosie runs my home for me and is indispensable.'

Beatrice shook hands and murmured and Rosie said graciously, 'If Miss Browning will come with me, I'll show her where she may tidy herself.'

Beatrice wasn't aware that she was untidy, but she went meekly enough in the wake of Rosie to the end of the narrow, elegant hall where there was a splendidly appointed cloakroom.

Presently, hoping that she would fulfil Rosie's expectations of tidiness, she went back into the hall.

The doctor poked his head out of a door as she did so. 'In here, Beatrice,' he said, and drew her into a charming room overlooking the street, furnished with deep armchairs and sofas and several very nice Regency tables bearing reading-lamps. Cosy in the winter, thought Beatrice, and advanced to meet Miss Cross.

She had imagined her to be a smart, youngish woman, exquisitely made-up, dressed with fashionable elegance and full of the social graces. Miss Cross was none of these things; she was dumpy and little and well into her forties, with a round face and twinkly eyes and a neat head of brown hair, going unashamedly grey. She was dressed neatly but unfashionably, and on the front of her dress hung her gold-rimmed spectacles. Beatrice liked her at once, and they beamed at each other as the doctor introduced them. 'Here's Beatrice, Ethel. Beatrice, Ethel has been with me for a long time now; she always knows where I have to go next and what I have to do—I'd be lost without her.'

'Such nonsense,' declared Ethel delightedly. 'How nice to meet you—may I call you Beatrice?'

'Oh, please—and may I call you Ethel?'

'Let us drink to that,' observed the doctor, handing round sherry.

They lunched in a smaller room at the back of the house, furnished in mahogany and with french windows opening on to a charming little garden. There was a bird-bath at the end of the centre path, and sitting on a bench near the window was a large tortoiseshell cat, watching two kittens playing on the small lawn.

'Rosie's pet,' observed Oliver, settling Beatrice in her chair. 'Her name's Popsie. She joined the household some months ago and took over the kitchen regions, and I suspect that the kittens have every intention of taking up residence with her. Rosie adores cats.'

'Does Mabel mind when she comes here?'

'Not in the least. But she doesn't like London, although she comes up and down with me.'

Rosie served lunch: lettuce soup, grilled sole and a salad, and a fresh fruit salad for afters. The coffee was delicious and served with tiny butter biscuits made, Oliver assured her, by Rosie to a secret recipe.

He was so well served, she reflected; Rosie here, obviously devoted to him despite her severity, and the Jenningses at his home in Dorset. But he deserved it, she conceded; his was a relentless life, despite the comfort of his living, and he wasn't a man who, having reached the top, would seek an easy life.

They didn't linger over the meal; Miss Cross was ushered into the back seat of the car, Beatrice got into the seat beside the doctor, and they began their journey.

They went over on the hovercraft and, since Ethel Cross and Oliver were both immersed in papers, Beatrice opened the paperback she had had the forethought to bring with her, and pretended to read. The doctor raised his eyes once to say, 'Sorry we're so unsociable, but it's an opportunity to get everything sorted out. My first lecture is tomorrow morning at nine o'clock, and we have to have some kind of plan for the day. Ethel will be with me, taking notes, but we'll meet you for lunch. I'll tell you where.'

On land, he drove steadily, stopping for tea just before they crossed the Dutch border. Miss Cross had dozed for most of the journey, and he and Beatrice had carried on a conversation which needed very little effort on either's part.

The doctor had taken the motorway through Antwerp and Breda, and entered Utrecht from the south. As they neared the city centre, Beatrice stared round her as he threaded his way through the evening traffic, pointing out the cathedral tower and the cathedral, the canals and the brief glimpse of the fish market. 'There's plenty to see,' he told her, 'and no difficulty with the language. I'm afraid Ethel and I will have to leave you to your own devices until the late afternoon, but we'll go out in the evening.'

She had expected that. 'I'll be quite all right,' she assured him. 'I like pottering.' And indeed, the city looked worth exploring, with its old houses and tree-lined canals. She wondered where they were to stay, and got her answer almost at once when he stopped before a hotel in the heart of the city. It looked grand in an old-fashioned way, and just for a moment she had qualms, to be reassured by Ethel's friendly voice.

'This is most comfortable. We stayed here a year ago when the doctor came over to test the medical students and deliver a lecture. And everyone speaks English.'

They had rooms on the first floor, Beatrice and Ethel beside each other and the doctor on the opposite side of the corridor. The rooms were extremely comfortable, with large bathrooms and balconies overlooking the street, and Ethel's had a table in the window on which she put her portable typewriter. 'We'll have breakfast together,' she told Beatrice cheerfully, 'and probably lunch, but I have dinner when it suits me; I like to get my notes written up each evening.'

Beatrice didn't like to ask about Oliver's arrangements; she supposed that he would meet colleagues in the evenings, so probably she would dine with Ethel. She went to her own room to unpack, mindful of the doctor's suggestion that they should all meet in the bar in an hour's time.

Bathed, her hair hanging down her back, she began to worry about what she should wear. She dragged on her dressing-gown and nipped out into the corridor. There was no one about, so she put the door latch up and started the few yards along the corridor to Ethel's door. She had her hand raised to knock when a small sound behind her sent her whizzing round. Oliver was standing at his open door, watching her.

'Oh, hello. I'm just going to ask Ethel what to wear…'

'You look very nice like that. I like the hair.' He watched with interest while she blushed. 'Wear whatever women wear to cocktail parties. I'm not a betting man, but I'm willing to wager a substantial sum on the certainty of Ethel's wearing her little black number.'

Beatrice edged her way back to her own door. 'Oh, well, thank you...'

He hadn't moved. He glanced at his watch now. 'You have fifteen minutes.'

She sat down at her dressing-table and did her rather flushed face and wound her hair into a smooth chignon, then got into the patterned crêpe, found slippers and evening bag, and with barely a minute to spare tapped on Ethel's door.

The doctor's money had been quite safe; Miss Cross was wearing the little black number, a sober dress with a discreet neckline and all the same elegant enough. She eyed Beatrice appreciatively.

'That's pretty,' she exclaimed. 'And of course, you have a lovely figure, if I may say so. I'd love to be able to wear a dress like that; it's a lovely fit.'

They went down together, talking clothes, and the doctor watched them coming down the staircase and across the foyer. He sighed gently and went to meet them.

Dinner was delightful, and the three of them were in the best of good spirits, but after Miss Cross had had one cup of coffee she declared that she would go to her room and get things ready for the morning.

'That first lecture, Doctor,' she wanted to know, 'you will be finished by eleven o'clock, I take it? Then you'll have coffee and see some cases at the St Antonius Ziekenhuis. Where will you lunch, and will you need me there?'

'No, Ethel, you're free until half-past one, when I'm due at the Whilhelmina Kinderziekenhuis. I'll want you there, but I don't expect to stay after five o'clock.' He stood up as she got to her feet. 'Don't worry about Beatrice, I'll see about her lunch, and don't forget there's a dinner in the evening.'

She beamed at them both. 'You'll enjoy that. I'll see you at breakfast.'

He sat down again and ordered more coffee. 'Now, let us get your day settled...'

'You don't have to bother about me. I shall be perfectly all right all day.'

She might just as well not have spoken. 'Will you come to the St Antonius Ziekenhuis at twelve-fifteen? Take a taxi. It's quite a short ride. We'll have lunch at the Hotel des Pays Bas in the bar there; the children's hospital is very central. You'll come to dinner at the university in the evening—half-past eight. The next day I have to lecture at the Academisch Ziekenhuis, that's very central; then there will be a noonday reception there—you'll come to that. We leave in the afternoon.'

She eyed him askance. He had it all nicely planned, and she wondered what he would say if she declined to join in his plans. On the other hand, he had been kind enough to help her out of the awkward situation with Colin. 'Very well, I'll do as you ask. Thank you for your kind invitations,' she added politely.

He gave a rumble of laughter. 'Am I walking roughshod over your plans? I'm sorry if I'm bustling you around. I only wish I had more time to show you round, but you have no need to get lost, I'll get a city plan for you from the desk and you can always ask, you're a sensible girl.'

She busied herself with the coffee-cups. She had taken pains with her appearance that evening, and all he could say was that she was sensible. A pity she hadn't bought a little black number like Ethel's.

'You're looking peevish,' said Oliver, putting his finger unerringly on the spot. 'I called you sensible, and I've not once said how charming you look this evening, and if I say it now it won't do at all, will it?'

She said thoughtfully, 'Well, I suppose that it would be better than nothing,' and he laughed again.

'Would you like to go somewhere and dance?'

She was too surprised to answer at once. 'Dance? Us? Isn't it rather late?'

'Very relaxing after a long drive. There's a place close by—we can walk there.' He smiled with such charm that she found herself smiling back at him. 'You'll need a shawl or something.'

She had a mohair stole with her; she went to her room and fetched it, and went back to the foyer where he was waiting for her. If they danced for an hour it would still be not quite midnight by the time she got to bed, and perhaps he needed to unwind. He didn't look as though he needed to unwind, she reflected as she went to meet him, and for a fleeting moment thought of Colin, who would have rushed to meet her as though she were the only girl in the world. She gave her head a little shake; she mustn't think of him any more. She had come away in order to forget him, and there was nothing wrong with the doctor's manners; they were, in fact, a good deal better than Colin's. Without haste he had reached her side, wrapped her stole around her shoulders and accompanied her to the door where he took her arm. 'Less than five minutes' walk,' he told her, 'and it's a lovely night.'

The club overlooked a canal; discreetly quiet and just full enough to make it pleasant and a little exciting. They had a table near the dance-floor and the doctor ordered champagne. In the becoming light of pink-shaded lamps Beatrice drank a glass and got up willingly enough to dance. She danced well, but then so did Oliver and the band was good. It was two hours later when she asked him the time and declared roundly that they should both be in bed. 'You've a lecture at nine o'clock,' she reminded him, 'and you've been driving all day. If you don't get some sleep, you'll forget what you have to say.'

'Oh, Ethel would never allow that; she hands me a sheaf of typed notes at the very last minute.' He spoke seriously, although she had the strong impression that he was laughing at her.

'So that you can read them—what a good idea.'

'Isn't it? I haven't done so so far, but I hold them in my hand or put them on the table before me so as not to hurt her feelings.'

They walked back to the hotel and said goodnight in the foyer. 'I enjoyed dancing,' said Beatrice. 'I do hope that you are not too tired.'

He smiled down at her, and for no reason at all she had the feeling that she had said something foolish. 'Never too tired to dance with you, Beatrice. Goodnight and sleep well.'

She contrived to peep over her shoulder as she reached the head of the staircase; he was still standing at its foot, watching her.

As she got ready for bed she told herself that he was a man of the world, well-versed in the art of flattering a woman. On the other hand, she mused, she had to admit he had been kind to her; and not just kind, he had offered practical help when she had needed it most, as well as a shoulder as solid as a rock upon which she had cried her eyes out. Her last thought as she drifted off into sleep was that he was a very nice man. Nice was a useful adjective—it covered a dozen others more specific, but she was too sleepy to think of them.

Breakfast was a businesslike meal with the doctor and Ethel arranging the day between them, although as they rose from the table he reiterated his plans for Beatrice, adding, 'Have you sufficient money with you?'

She had a small bundle of traveller's cheques in her bag. 'Oh, more than enough.'

They walked through the foyer together, and she stood with him while Ethel went to her room to get her coat and notebook. 'I hope you have a successful lecture. I hope you'll let me come and listen to one...'

He lifted his eyebrows. 'Why, thank you, Beatrice, and so you shall.' There was no time to say any more, for Ethel had joined them.

'There are some lovely shops,' she told Beatrice, and started for the door.

'Don't spend all your money,' begged the doctor, then bent and kissed Beatrice's surprised mouth, and had gone before she could do more than gasp.

She left the hotel half an hour later, and spent the morning window-shopping and buying one or two presents to take home; she sent a postcard too, had coffee at a chic little coffee-shop and went to gaze at the cathedral. She would have liked to have spent longer; she would have to go back a second time, there was so much to see, and she wanted to walk through the cloisters before it was time to get her taxi. There were quite a few people around, but the cloisters were peaceful all the same. She wandered around and found herself wishing that Oliver was with her, and although she thought of Colin, too, she had to admit that the doctor would be a far better companion in such surroundings. She sighed for no reason and went to look for a taxi.

It was exactly a quarter-past twelve as she paid off the taxi and went through the hospital entrance, uncertain what she should do if Oliver were not there. But he was, talking to two other older men and when he saw her he went to meet her, took her arm and introduced them to her. She shook hands and answered their polite questions, which were uttered in pedantic English, and when Oliver said they should be going they expressed the hope that they would see her that evening. The older of them twinkled nicely at her, and added, 'I do not see why our good friend here should have you all to himself!'

Oliver smiled and said nothing, and Beatrice murmured politely, registering a vow that, given the chance, she would take good care that he saw as little as possible of her at the dinner. She could of course plead a headache and cry off, but on second thoughts that would be a mean thing to do. In his own fashion, Oliver had helped her a lot, even though at times she had found herself thinking that it was more from a sense of duty than actual friendship.

She accompanied him to the car presently, talking pleasantly about her morning and making all the proper enquiries as to his lecture. They were seated at a small window table, studying the menu, when he observed blandly, 'What a little chatterbox you are, Beatrice—you don't have to entertain me with small talk unless you feel that you must.'

Which left her speechless.

They ate in silence for some time, amused on the part of the doctor, peeved on her part, until he said mildly, 'I couldn't think of anything to say.' A remark which she didn't pretend not to understand. She laughed then. 'Never tell me that you were at a loss for words.'

'Certainly not, but I'm not sure if they would have been the right ones! Would you like coffee?'

The hatchet, a very small one, was buried; they spent the rest of the meal talking about Utrecht, and presently parted company. 'But mind you're back at the hotel by half-past four,' he reminded her. 'We can all have tea together and Ethel can remind me of what I have to do next.'

Beatrice spent the afternoon in the cathedral again; there were a great many other places to visit, but she knew that once she poked her nose into a museum she would lose all count of time. Obedient to Oliver's instructions, she presented herself in the hotel lounge exactly on time, and found him and Ethel already there. Over tea and delicious little biscuits they discussed their day, and when Ethel left them in order to type up her notes they stayed where they were, not saying much, pleased with each other's company.

It would have to be the long red satin skirt and the white blouse, decided Beatrice as she changed for the evening. And they really looked very glamorous and worth every penny of her father's money. She did her face and hair with extra care, thrust her feet into black satin evening pumps, found her matching bag and went downstairs. It was a fine, warm evening, so that the question of a coat or stole didn't arise. They would have spoilt the magic of the blouse and skirt most dreadfully.

She swanned down the rather grand hotel staircase, pleased

with her appearance, and was rewarded by the look on Oliver's face when he saw her, although his rather casual, 'Oh, very nice,' was hardly flattering. The thought crossed her mind that probably she wasn't the type of girl he admired. This girl he was going to marry was very likely small and fair and blue-eyed and delightfully helpless. It was a pity, she reflected, accompanying him out to the car, that she was a big girl who, if ever she should faint, and that was most unlikely, would undoubtedly knock flat anyone she fell on to. She sat beside him, her self-confidence oozing through the soles of the pretty slippers she wore. And at the University, ushered relentlessly forward by her companion, she had a great desire to turn tail and run. There were many people milling round, the women all splendidly dressed. She felt Oliver's hand under her arm as she stood still, wishing very much that she wasn't there.

The doctor bent his head and whispered in her ear, 'You are easily the most beautiful woman here, Beatrice. Lift your chin and throw your shoulders back, and do me proud.'

She was so surprised that for the moment she didn't do anything at all, and when she looked up at him he was smiling, his face calm. She found herself smiling back, and all at once her peevishness melted away and she sailed along beside him to where the reception committee waited.

After that, the evening was a thundering success; she met any number of Oliver's colleagues and their wives, and managed very nicely on her own when he was compelled to leave her once or twice. She had him for a dinner partner though, with a stout, middle-aged man on her left, whose English was fluent, if heavily accented, and who paid her lavish compliments which she accepted with a pretty dignity and stored away to be recounted to Ella when she got home.

And after dinner people stood about talking, discussing future seminars and conferences while the women listened dutifully and managed to gossip among themselves at the same time. Beatrice, who was accepted, had she but known it, as Oliver's future wife, was led from group to group and made much of with frequent invitations to visit her new friends when she next came to Utrecht. To all of which she replied with a vagueness taken for shyness on her part.

It was late as they drove back to the hotel, and there were very few people in the foyer. They left the doorman to take the car to the garage, and wandered across the carpeted floor towards the staircase.

'Thank you for a lovely evening,' said Beatrice, suddenly shy.

The doctor took her hand and turned her round to face him. 'You enjoyed yourself? Good.' He sounded remote. 'A change of scene is the best cure for a damaged heart. It seems to be working well.'

She hadn't expected him to say anything like that. It was as if he were reminding her that she was there as one of his patients, being treated under his expert eye. She suddenly wanted to cry without knowing why, but she swallowed back the tears and said very politely, 'I'm sure you're right. Goodnight.' And she walked, with a very straight back, upstairs.

CHAPTER SEVEN

BEATRICE DIDN'T SLEEP WELL; she was healthily tired, but she wasn't happy. She supposed that she was missing Colin, although she had the greatest difficulty conjuring up his face, even though she was able to remember very clearly the flattering remarks he had made so often. They hadn't meant anything, though.

It was going to be a warm day, so she put on a cotton dress and went down to breakfast. The doctor and Ethel were already at their table, but he got up as she joined them, and she sat down, soothed by his good manners. His good morning was brisk.

'Don't forget there's a farewell reception at noon at the Academisch Ziekenhuis. We will come back here for lunch and leave for Cologne in the afternoon. Ethel, you'll be there, of course. Beatrice, walk in to the hospital and say you're my guest; Ethel will come for you if I can't manage it. It will last about an hour, and you'll have met quite a few of the people there already.'

He had barely glanced at her, but Ethel had noted her tired face and, being the soul of discretion, had said nothing. Beatrice, unaware that his quick look had taken in her unhappy face, thanked him politely and poured her coffee, buttered a croissant and took a bite. She was feeling better already; the doctor's bracing manner didn't allow time for melancholy, and listening to Ethel's cheerful voice she felt ashamed of her self-pity. They left the breakfast-table presently and went their various ways with last-minute instructions from the doctor as to the quickest way to reach the Academisch Ziekenhuis from the shopping centre.

The morning went pleasantly. She bought another present or two, had coffee and then began to stroll towards the hospital. She had gone to her room after breakfast and changed into the pink jersey outfit; the cotton dress hadn't seemed quite suitable for a reception, although the doctor hadn't said anything, and she had done her face after she had had her coffee. The doctor, watching her cross the hospital's forecourt from a first-floor window, thought she looked charming, and after a moment excused himself from the group of doctors around him and went down to the entrance to meet her.

He greeted her with his usual calm, enquired as to whether she had enjoyed her day and walked her to the imposing room where the reception was being held. There were a great many people there, and she recognised quite a few of them. Ethel was there too, and came to meet them.

'You found your way,' she observed. 'Have you had a nice look at the shops?'

'Lovely. I like Utrecht.'

'We must see what you think of Cologne,' remarked the doctor, and drew them both into a group of people Beatrice had already met. Waiters were sliding in and out of the groups with trays of drinks and dishes of canapés, and presently Ethel wandered off and Oliver escorted her around the room, making sure that she met as many people as possible. He seemed to know everyone there, and when in a quiet moment she remarked upon that he said, 'Well, I have been here several times during the last few years.'

'Have you been a consultant for a long time?'

He smiled slowly. 'Let me see, I'm thirty-seven. Six years or so.'

'You're clever, aren't you? I said that once before, but I can't help remembering that when you are like this...'

'Like what?' He sounded amused.

'Grey suit, silk tie and—and a bit remote.'

'Ah, I must remedy that, mustn't I? When we get home and I have time, we must climb the hill together again—I promise you that I won't be in the least bit remote.'

Beatrice went faintly pink. She felt a pleasant little thrill, unfortunately doused by the arrival of a powerful-looking man with a fierce moustache who wrung Oliver's hand and, on being introduced as the Burgermeester of Utrecht, clasped hers and addressed her as 'little lady'—which, while not in the least appropriate, did much for her self-esteem.

'Charming, charming. You will come again, both of you, of course!'

'Of course,' agreed the doctor blandly. 'We shall look forward to that.'

Alone again, Beatrice asked, 'Why did you say that? About us coming again?'

Two elderly gentlemen were bearing down upon them; Oliver turned to greet them. 'But we will come again,' he said over his shoulder, and then, 'This is the hospital director and a very important man...'

After that there was no more opportunity to talk together and presently they said their goodbyes, found Ethel and went out to the forecourt where the cars were parked.

They talked of their forthcoming visit to Cologne, the morning's reception and of the various people they had met while they ate their lunch. The restaurant was full, and the doctor paused to greet several people as they went to their table, his arm on hers, and invariably they all expressed the hope that they would see them again. 'We shall be over in London in the autumn,' said one serious-looking professor, lunching with his wife. 'You must both come and dine.'

Beatrice was tempted to point out to Oliver that the various acquaintances who had expressed a hope that they would meet again—and that included her—were mistaken, but she didn't want to say so in front of Ethel. She kept quiet, ate her lobster thermidor and a towering confection of ice-cream, chocolate and whipped cream, and joined in the small talk.

It was three o'clock when the doctor edged the Rolls out into the city's traffic. They drove south, over the Rhine, crossing into Germany at Emmerich and following the road through Xanten to Krefeld, a large industrial town, a blot on the scenery round about them. Presently they stopped in a village and had tea, and Beatrice studied the map.

'There are several roads,' remarked Beatrice, 'all going to Cologne.'

'Yes. We shall go back on another route so that you get a chance to see as much as possible of this part of Germany.'

'The Rhine must be lovely.'

'Oh, it is, but you need to get past Bonn. Last time we came I had a day to spare, and we drove along the Rhine, past the Lorelei Rock. Unfortunately there will be no time to go anywhere on this trip.'

'Did you—that is, was your fiancée with you?'

She was looking at the map and didn't see the look which passed between her companions. 'No, but Ethel was.'

'It was gorgeous,' enthused Ethel, and enlarged upon the beauties of the Rhine at some length, until they got up to go.

The doctor drove on, turning off the main road to go through Zons, a small medieval town about twenty miles from Cologne. It was a charming place, and he obligingly parked the car for a little while so that Beatrice could stroll through its streets with Ethel on one side and him on the other, pointing out the ancient buildings.

Cologne cathedral was visible before they had a clear view of the city, its twin towers soaring upwards, and once they reached its heart it seemed to overshadow the old houses with their gabled roofs. But there were a great many modern buildings too, and the streets were bustling with people and traffic. Beatrice didn't think, at first glance, that she was going to like it as much as she had liked Utrecht, although the sight of the great cathedral was awe-inspiring. The hotel, close to it, was awe-inspiring too, and very grand. She gave it a somewhat doubtful look as they stopped before its splendid entrance, and Oliver said, 'I agree with you—very five-star, isn't it? Not quite what I would have chosen, but of course everything is arranged beforehand. At least it is central, and I have no doubt very comfortable.'

Which it was. Their rooms were on the first floor again but at the back of the hotel, overlooking a quiet square. They were opulently furnished, and Beatrice and Ethel poked their noses into every corner of them. 'I only hope that my little black number will be up to standard,' said Ethel with a giggle.

It seemed they were to follow the same routine as they had in Utrecht, and presently they went down to the brilliantly lit bar and found Oliver waiting for them. 'The surroundings call for nothing less than champagne cocktails,' he observed, 'and I can only hope that you are both hungry, for the menu is sumptuous.'

The restaurant, when they reached it, was even more brilliantly lit than the bar. Beatrice took her seat at the window-table reserved for the doctor and studied the menu. It was indeed sumptuous. She chose cold watercress soup with cream, and then worked her way through the elaborate menu; far too much choice, she reflected, but perhaps the Hotel Excelsior Ernst had to live up to its five stars. Then she settled for grilled sole with a white wine sauce, straw potatoes and *petits pois à la flamande*. Ethel chose chicken, and the doctor, without looking at the menu, asked for fillet steak with *vigneronne*. The waiter looked quite upset as he removed the menus, their choice was obviously too modest, although the wine waiter treated the doctor's choice of a bottle of red burgundy for himself and a bottle of Chablis

Grand Cru for the ladies with the respect it deserved. Beatrice, tasting hers, declared it to be a very nice wine, unaware that it had cost more than twenty pounds a bottle.

She and Ethel chose the same sweet, a light peach tart which they pronounced to be perfection, but the doctor took his choice of the cheeseboard. Beatrice would have been content to have sat over coffee, but Oliver had some work for Ethel, so she declared herself tired and wishful of an early night and, armed with the guide to Cologne with which Oliver had thoughtfully provided her, left the restaurant with every sign of eagerness to get to her room. The three of them stood in the foyer for a moment, then Ethel went away to get some papers she needed and Beatrice made to follow her up the staircase. Oliver's large hand on her arm checked her.

'I shall have very little time to myself tomorrow,' he told her, 'but if you don't mind eating a snack lunch in a hurry, we'll have it together.' He frowned in thought. 'Now, where shall we meet? Somewhere you can find easily.' He smiled. 'The cathedral, of course. Inside the main door and the centre nave. Half-past twelve?'

'Oh, that would be nice. Are you sure that you can spare the time?'

He smiled again. 'Oh, indeed I can. Goodnight, Beatrice. I don't want to say it, but I must.' He picked up her hand and kissed it gently. 'Sleep well.'

Undressing slowly, Beatrice did her best to sort out her thoughts. They were a bit muddled; Oliver was beginning to loom rather large in them and, while she told herself that it was gratitude that she felt for him, she couldn't deny that he attracted her. 'I shan't sleep,' she declared to her reflection in the ornate looking-glass as she slapped cream on to her face.

She got into bed and slept within seconds.

Breakfast was a businesslike meal and brisk. Oliver was brisk too, while Ethel perused her notebook. They got up to go long before she was finished, and Oliver said, 'Don't forget to be in the cathedral, half-past twelve.'

He got up and was gone before she could say a word.

She spent the morning finding her way around the city. There was a street of shops close to the hotel, and she wandered down to it, looking at the windows and doing sums in her head, changing German marks into pounds and deciding that everything was rather expensive. All the same, she was tempted to buy a leather belt for Ella and a silk scarf for her mother. She still had an hour to spare by the time she reached the cathedral, so she found a small café and had coffee and tidied herself. Then she sat for a little while, looking around her at the vast place. It was magnificent, and presently she got up and walked around, clutching her guidebook and stopping every few yards to consult it. It took quite a long time. She was surprised when she looked at her watch to see that it was very nearly half-past twelve, and she hurried back to the central nave. She was at the wrong end, of course, so she hurried towards the great door, and half-way there was brought to a standstill by Oliver's hand.

'I would have waited for you, Beatrice,' he said, half laughing.

'Yes—well...' she was breathless with her haste and the pleasure of seeing him again '... I thought I was late, and you said you wouldn't have much time.'

'There's a coffee-shop in an arcade near here. I dare say we can get something there. I'll be finished by six o'clock; the three of us can meet in the bar at seven o'clock. Tomorrow evening there's a dinner at the town hall; you'll come, won't you? And the following day I shall be busy until the afternoon—there's a reception at three o'clock. I'll fetch you from the hotel. We'll leave for Copenhagen the next morning.'

While she was listening he was steering her out of the cathedral and through the crowds outside into a nearby arcade to the coffee-shop. It was almost full and very noisy, but he found a table against one wall and sat her down. 'Coffee—and what would you like to eat?'

She looked at the counter behind them, loaded with rich cakes and pastries and a variety of breads and rolls. She said, 'I'll get fat—all that cream... I'll have a *brioche* and butter. I'm not hungry.'

He gave the order. 'Nor I, although I believe that if I were to enter your mother's kitchen at this moment and smell bacon sizzling in its pan I'd be famished.'

Over their simple meal he told her about the journey to Copenhagen. 'Hanover, Hamburg, Lubeck and Copenhagen.'

'It's miles—why don't you fly?' she wanted to know.

'Driving gives me a respite between one lecture and another. You don't find it too tiring?'

'Me, heavens, no! I'm loving every moment.' She added, 'I liked Utrecht.'

'One of my favourite seminars! Did you do any shopping here?'

'A belt for Ella and a scarf for my mother. Everything's rather expensive.'

'I dare say you'll find something more to your taste in Copenhagen. Brussels isn't cheap, either.' He glanced at his watch. 'Have you something to do this afternoon?'

'I thought I'd just wander round. I suppose I couldn't come to your lecture?'

'Of course you can, though it will be in German. You can sit with Ethel, she'll be delighted.'

Beatrice got to her feet. 'Oh, thank you. You don't mind? Ethel has to take notes, doesn't she?'

'Oh, yes, but not all the time.'

They walked together through the crowded streets and down a narrow side street bordered on one side by the hospital where he was to lecture.

'There's a side door,' he told her, and ushered her through a narrow archway and into a covered passage which led to the main building. The passages seemed endless to her, and the faint hospital smells revived memories of her father's illness; she was relieved when he opened a swing door and she found herself standing with him at the side of a large assembly hall.

'Ethel's sitting near the front. There she is.' He led the way down the aisle and tapped his secretary on the shoulder.

She turned a beaming face to them. 'Beatrice—oh, how nice, have you come to hear the lecture?' She turned a suddenly severe face on the doctor. 'You are cutting it fine, doctor—barely ten minutes. Have you your notes?'

'In my pocket. Ethel, take Beatrice to tea when I've finished. I'll see you both back at the hotel.'

He disappeared and Beatrice sat down beside Ethel. 'Do you understand German as well as being able to speak it? I mean, the kind of German Oliver uses when he lectures?'

'Bless you, yes. My father was in the army, he was stationed here for years and I went to school here. It comes in handy. Do you want me to translate?'

Beatrice shook her head. 'Even in English I don't suppose I'd understand the half of it. I'd just like to listen.'

Ethel gave her a quick look. 'Yes. Well, he's got a lovely voice.'

Oliver looked frightfully different somehow when he came on to the platform. Remote and so assured, and at the same time self-effacing. She understood nothing of what he was saying, of course, but he spoke fluently and without haste, and several times the crowded hall burst into laughter. The lecture lasted a long time, and Beatrice allowed her thoughts to wander. Would the girl he was going to marry accompany him on these lecture tours? she wondered. And later on, when they had children, would they stay at home and she with them, or would there be a nanny, a nice, old-fashioned type, so that his wife could travel with him? Or perhaps he would give up lecturing... They wouldn't stay at the Hotel Excelsior Ernst, though; they would go to small, quite quiet places and spend as much time as possible together.

Ethel's hissed whisper, 'He's finished the lecture, now they ask questions,' brought her back to her surroundings, and she sat listening and watching with awe as Ethel scrawled shorthand on page after page of her notebook.

'Do you have to type all that?' she whispered.

Ethel nodded. 'I get paid an enormous salary,' she added.

'You must be worth every penny of it.'

Ethel nodded again, entirely without conceit.

Finally it was all over and they slipped out into the street, and Ethel led the way to a coffee-shop not far from the hotel.

'It had better be coffee. Shall we have one of those enormous cakes?'

They had a delightful hour, the two of them, discussing clothes and make-up and the tour so far. 'Very successful,' observed Ethel. 'But then, they always are.' But she didn't talk about Oliver, and Beatrice knew that even if she asked questions about him she would be very politely side-tracked. Ethel might earn a splendid salary, but that had nothing to do with her loyalty to the doctor. Discretion, thought Beatrice, was probably her middle name.

They didn't hurry back to the hotel, but stopped to examine the shop windows. In the foyer, Ethel said, 'You'll be all right on your own for an hour? I've these notes to type.'

'And I've kept you from them,' said Beatrice contritely. 'I'm sorry.'

'Don't be. It was fun. There's only one lecture tomorrow, so I shall have time to get my typing done. There's a lecture on the following morning, but I'm free in the afternoon and we don't leave till the day after that.'

Dinner that evening was a light-hearted affair. Getting ready for bed later, Beatrice reflected that Oliver was a delightful companion with a quiet sense of humour which was never unkind.

She went to sleep confident that the next day would be just as delightful as that day had been.

In this she was disappointed, for after breakfast Oliver went away and she saw nothing of him until the late afternoon; she filled her day with more sightseeing and window-shopping, and after a late cup of tea with him and Ethel she went away to dress for the evening. It would be the satin skirt and blouse again.

There were far more people at the dinner than there had been in Utrecht. She found herself between two youngish men who spoke impeccable English and were flatteringly attentive. Oliver sat across the table from her with a handsome, well-dressed woman on either side of him, and although he caught her eye and smiled at her once or twice he seemed to be quite content where he was. She felt a surge of peevishness, and responded rather more warmly than she had intended to the younger of the two men.

The dinner lasted a long time and there was a great deal of it. They rose from the table at last after a series of speeches—one from Oliver—and stood around in the adjoining room, talking. Oliver had joined her once more, and her dinner partner, still with her, asked politely, 'You are engaged to be married to the good doctor?'

'Heavens, no!' said Beatrice, and added coldly, 'Dr Latimer is a family friend.'

'Of course. A pity that you cannot stay longer in our beautiful city. I would have given myself the pleasure of showing you its various splendid buildings.'

Beatrice, well aware that Oliver's eyes were on her face, smiled with charm and allowed her eyelashes to sweep down on to her cheeks and up again. For some reason, she wanted to annoy him. 'That would have been delightful. If I should return, perhaps you will ask me again.'

He wished her goodbye and kissed her hand, and she smiled again very sweetly. She didn't like him very much, but since they were unlikely to see each other again that didn't matter. She enlarged on his charming manner as they went back to the hotel, until Oliver spoilt it all by remarking placidly, 'A nice enough fellow—married with four children and a very stout wife.'

Beatrice swept through the foyer ahead of him and stopped at the foot of the staircase. 'You could have said so hours ago,' she pointed out with a snap.

'My dear girl, who am I to put a damper on your pleasures?'

'Oh, pooh.' She tossed her head. 'Goodnight, Oliver.'

She debated whether to have a headache the next afternoon and not go with him to the reception, but in this she was forestalled by his unexpected appearance at the table where she and Ethel were having lunch.

'I'll come for you both,' he told them, 'and if you feel a headache coming on, Beatrice, take a couple of Panadol and lie down for an hour.'

He smiled at them both and wandered away again, and Ethel said, 'He never seems to get tired. Have you got a headache? You'd better go and rest, and I'll call you in good time.'

It was difficult to be annoyed with Oliver for more than a few minutes, for the simple reason that he ignored the fact that one was cross in the first place. She and Ethel were ready when he came for them and, truth to tell, she enjoyed the reception. Everyone there was very hearty and friendly, and the little cakes were delicious. Although Oliver left her from time to time, he was always at her elbow just when he was needed. The evening passed with the three of them enjoying another elaborate dinner while they discussed their stay in Cologne and their journey north on the following day.

'I've allowed two days to get to Copenhagen,' explained Oliver casually. 'We shall go as far as Salzhausen, just south of Hamburg, tomorrow and do the rest of the journey on the following day.'

He glanced at Ethel. 'Ethel fixed things up at the hotel there. It's in the country, the Luneburg Heath—and it's old and quiet.

A nice change for us all. I thought we might leave soon after breakfast in the morning and get there for a late lunch.'

'I've got the notes for Copenhagen,' Ethel reminded him. 'Would you like them now?'

'Why not, if you are not too tired.'

It seemed the right moment for Beatrice to declare herself tired and ready for bed. She got up when Ethel did, and the doctor got up too, strolling with her across the foyer, with Ethel hurrying ahead to get the papers he wanted. At the staircase he came to a halt.

'You stole quite a few hearts today,' he told her, smiling. He touched her cheek gently with one finger. 'You're a little pale; a few hours in the country will do you good. You're not unhappy?'

'No—no, I'm not. How could I be? I'm having such a lovely time. I'll never be able to thank you enough.'

He only smiled again. 'Goodnight, Beatrice.' He took her hand and held it for a few moments. 'Sleep well.'

He really was a nice person, she thought sleepily as she jumped into bed. Although she was never quite sure what he was really thinking.

It was raining as they left Cologne, but by the time they reached Hanover the sun was shining again and they stopped at a wayside café for coffee. They didn't linger over it, and by one o'clock they were crossing the heath to stop before the hotel. It was of red brick and thatched, and once inside they were transported into the sixteenth century. Not that it lacked a single modern luxury, skilfully tucked away behind the old and beautiful furniture and the ancient walls. Beatrice rotated slowly round the room she was to have; she was enthralled. This, she decided, was the real Germany, away from the bright lights and the chandeliers. They went presently for lunch: local fish, a splendid salad and a rich tart for afters, helped along by the wine the doctor chose. They had coffee in the lounge, and since Ethel declared that she wanted to work on her notes Oliver and Beatrice took themselves off for a walk.

It was a quiet countryside, and unspoilt. They walked for hours, talking when they felt like it, at ease with each other, and they went back for coffee and cakes and a leisurely hour sitting outside in the evening light.

It was nice to give the blouse and skirt and the printed dress a rest. Beatrice got into one of her pretty summer dresses, wound her hair into a chignon and wandered downstairs, where she found Oliver waiting for her.

'Ethel isn't quite ready,' she told him. 'She said ten minutes, if you don't mind.'

'We'll have a drink while we are waiting and have a look at the menu.'

Beatrice worried her way through the German. 'Why is this a *Romantik* hotel?' she asked.

'A chain of hotels throughout Europe, all living up to a certain standard. Candles on the tables, good food, comfortable rooms and so on, so that those with romantic intentions can indulge them.'

'Oh, but other people stay at them? I mean, people who aren't being romantic?'

'Naturally. You need only consider the three of us to prove it.' A remark uttered in such bland tones that she could think of nothing in reply.

The food was excellent. They dined at leisure, and Beatrice and Ethel went to their beds soon after. Tomorrow would be another long day.

They left after an excellent breakfast, circumventing Hamburg and crossing into Denmark, driving up the road to Kolding and then on to the island of Funen, crossing on the ferry to Korsor, across the island of Zeeland and finally reaching Copenhagen. They hadn't hurried, and it was late afternoon by the time the doctor stopped at a hotel overlooking the harbour. 'Myhavn 71,' he told her, 'another *Romantik* hotel, and a good deal quieter than the Royal or the D'Angleterre.'

It was charming none the less, and had a quiet air of luxury borne out by the rooms into which they were shown. Beatrice unpacked, showered and changed into another summer dress and went down to the foyer. Ethel and Oliver were already there, sitting at a table, and Ethel's notebook was open. She closed it now and the three of them talked in the pleasant, lazy way people do when they have been travelling all day, and presently they went in to dinner.

The menu was French, but by way of a speciality there was a vast centre table laid out with smorgasbord, and with their appetites nicely whetted they went on to lobster and then strawberries and finally coffee, strong and dark and unlimited.

Beatrice, watching the harbour beyond her bedroom window before she got into bed, felt contentment flooding her. Tomorrow she would be on her own until the early afternoon, but she had a map the ever-thoughtful doctor had got for her, and he had promised that he would take her to see the Little Mermaid before they both went to the evening reception at the University. 'Only an hour or so; we shall be back at the hotel by seven o'clock. We'll have dinner and we'll all go to the Tivoli Gardens,' he had told her. 'The dinner will be on the second day, but I shan't need Ethel in the morning, so the pair of you can go shopping or sightseeing.'

The next two days were every bit as delightful as she had known they would be. The shops were splendid and everyone spoke English. She had spent her first morning prowling around the department stores, and in the afternoon she had driven with Oliver along the road by the water to see the Little Mermaid—a wistful little figure, but disappointingly smaller than she had imagined she would be.

The reception had been a good deal livelier than the one at Cologne, and there hadn't been the language difficulty; she had loved every minute of it. And on the second day she and Ethel had poked around the shops, buying trinkets and small figurines of porcelain before going back to the hotel and having lunch, while they discussed their visit to the Tivoli Gardens the previous evening. It had been marvellous, they agreed, and the doctor had been more than generous, paying for them to take part in its attractions and waiting patiently while they tried their luck in the shooting galleries and gazed open-mouthed at the firework display.

The dinner had been rather solemn to begin with, but soon livened up. Beatrice, in the blouse and skirt once more, had been glad to find Oliver sitting beside her, while on her other side was a young Danish doctor who knew England well and moreover admired her quite openly.

She had been annoyed when the doctor had remarked upon that as they drove back to the hotel. 'Turn all heads, don't you?' he'd remarked cheerfully. 'I wonder who it will be in Brussels.' She had told him tartly that she neither knew nor cared, and he had chuckled to himself which had annoyed her still more. But on the whole they had got on very well indeed; she had come to miss him when he wasn't there.

The Rolls made light of the long drive to Brussels and they stopped on the German-Belgian border and had a leisurely lunch at a country restaurant, then took a stroll for half an hour before getting back into the car. Their hotel was in the centre of the city, an elegant building with the best shops close by, but, as the doctor pointed out, there were only two lectures to give in Brussels and both on the same day. 'So make the most of it,' he told Beatrice. 'There will be a luncheon at the hospital tomorrow and I would like you to come to that with me. I have another lecture in the afternoon, but we could go out in the evening if you would like that, while Ethel gets the last of the typing done.'

So she had spent the morning looking at the shops but buying very little; some chocolates for her sisters, a tie for her father and a pretty brooch for her mother, as well as biscuits for Mrs Perry and the Sharpe family. And by then it was time to pretty herself for the luncheon and go down to wait for Oliver.

She enjoyed herself, although she had felt a little doubtful of it. But it gave her an opportunity to air her French, which was really rather good, and the food was delicious. She spent the afternoon packing her things and went down to the foyer, refreshed by a tray of tea in her room and a leisurely bath. Ethel was already there with the doctor, and after dinner the three of them went out. Oliver seemed to know just where to go, but then she would have been surprised if he didn't; they had drinks at a fashionable café, walked a little, had coffee at another hotel and then strolled back.

'Well, there goes our last evening,' observed Oliver placidly. 'Back to the grindstone tomorrow. We shall leave soon after breakfast—we'll go over from Ostend.'

He bade them goodnight in the foyer, not giving Beatrice a chance to tell him how much she had enjoyed herself. Indeed, his manner was so remotely kind that she hesitated to do more than wish him goodnight. She went to bed feeling dissatisfied and vaguely unhappy. Somehow or other she would contrive to thank him properly before she reached home. She had much to thank him for, she reflected; she had only been away for two weeks, but already Colin seemed like a character in a book she had forgotten she had read.

CHAPTER EIGHT

IT WAS RAINING when they left Brussels, and it was still raining when they reached England and drove westwards. They stopped in Ightham at the Town House, a restaurant with a high reputation and an imaginative menu, and had lunch before Oliver joined the motorway and presently the A303, explaining that it would be easier and quicker if he were to take Beatrice home first and then drive back to London, first to Ethel's flat and then to his home.

'Will you stay in London?' Beatrice made her voice casual.

'For a week at least. There will be a backlog of patients, as well as urgent new cases. Ethel is to have a well-earned holiday—I only hope the temp they send will work half as hard. I'm lost without her.'

Ethel had heard him from the back seat. 'Well, if it's that Miss Duffield who came last year, she was most efficient...'

'She terrified me.' He glanced at Beatrice. 'Do you suppose your mother would give us tea? Then we shan't need to stop on our way home.'

'Of course she will. I sent her a card days ago, and told her to expect us any time after four o'clock.'

'Splendid.' After that, they didn't talk much, and Ethel dozed off. The doctor glanced in his mirror and said quietly, 'She must be worn out; she never misses a trick. She certainly deserves a week off.' He gave Beatrice a sideways glance. 'And you, Beatrice? What will you do now you're home again?'

'Help Father, and there's always heaps to do in the village—coffee mornings and the church bazaar and the children's summer outing, and if anyone's away or ill I help out with meals on wheels.'

'The mind boggles.'

Come to think of it, thought Beatrice, my mind boggles too. It never used to, I'm getting discontented... She said defiantly, 'Oh, I like doing those things.'

He murmured politely, 'Of course, you will get married. Is Kathy back from her honeymoon?'

And after that they talked about Kathy and Ella and Carol in general, and although Beatrice tried to lead the talk back to his own plans he gave nothing away, so that she was forced to fall back on dull topics like the weather and the likelihood of there being a good harvest.

He stopped before her home door soon after five o'clock, and it was flung open instantly to allow Mrs Browning, Ella and Carol with Knotty to surge out to greet them.

'Come in,' cried Mrs Browning, embracing Beatrice, shaking hands with Oliver and Ethel, and urging them indoors. 'Isn't this delightful? And I'm longing to hear all about the trip, but I suppose you won't have time to tell me. Tea's ready. Ethel—you don't mind if I call you Ethel?—Beatrice will take you upstairs. Oliver, go straight into the sitting-room. I'll fetch the tea-tray.'

He went with her to the kitchen and took the tray from her. 'Young Wood has gone?' he asked.

'Yes, a week ago. But there are several letters...' Mrs Browning looked at him with troubled eyes.

'Don't worry too much. I am almost sure that Beatrice has

got over him—he hadn't gone very deep, you know. Let her have the letters.'

'If you say so, Oliver.' Mrs Browning picked up a plate of scones and started back to the sitting-room.

'You don't mind if Ethel and I leave within the hour? She is tired and I am faced with an out-patients at nine o'clock in the morning.' He put the tray on a table. 'I'd like to take a quick look at Mr Browning before I go. He's well?'

'Yes. Mr Sharpe is just right as a partner, and they get on famously. He'll be glad to have Beatrice back, though Ella's been very good.'

'If Beatrice should marry, someone will have to take her place.'

'Yes, but there isn't anyone at the moment.'

Mrs Browning was arranging plates, and didn't see Oliver's face, only heard his quiet, 'Not at the moment, no.'

Ethel and Beatrice came in, and a minute later Ella and Mr Browning, and they sat round the open windows talking about their journey and eating Mrs Browning's scones and cakes. 'What a lovely tea,' said Ethel, and passed her cup for the third time.

The men went away presently, and Beatrice took Ethel for a quick look at the clinic. When they got back to the house, Oliver was waiting for them and goodbyes were said without delay.

'I still haven't had the chance...' began Beatrice, her well-rehearsed speech of thanks ready on her tongue, but never to be uttered, it seemed, for Oliver shook hands briefly, wished her a brisk goodbye and ushered Ethel into the front seat of the car. She watched him drive away. Now she would have to write a thank-you letter, for she had no idea when she would see him again. She stopped suddenly as they turned to go back indoors. She would have to see him again, she couldn't bear the thought of not doing so—just once more and then never again. He was going to be married to a nice girl who trusted him, and it was just a hideous quirk of fate that she had fallen in love with him.

Her mother, waiting for her to go indoors, said briskly, 'Are you coming in, darling?'

Beatrice found a nice normal voice to say, 'It's such a lovely evening now, I'm going to walk round the garden with Knotty.'

She walked aimlessly for some time, thinking about Oliver and trying to decide when she had fallen in love. She had always liked him from the moment they had met, and she had never thought of him as a stranger, but to pinpoint the moment when she knew that she loved him was impossible. It was because he had gone away so quickly and casually that the fact had been brought home to her now.

'And there is absolutely nothing to be done about it,' she added unhappily to Knotty. 'What a mess I have made of things, haven't I?'

She went back indoors presently and spent the rest of the evening giving her mother and father and Ella a detailed report on her travels.

'How very exciting,' remarked Mrs Browning, 'and to think that Oliver goes on these trips at least once a year. I'm not surprised he hasn't married; he can't have had much time to do so.'

'Well, he's going to soon.'

'Is he, dear? That will be nice.'

Her mother, thought Beatrice peevishly, could at times be quite infuriating.

It wasn't difficult to slip back into her usual working days again, and she welcomed the fact that they were busier than usual. It was only at the end of the day, in her own room, that she allowed herself to think about Oliver, wondering what he was doing and where he was. Somehow nothing else mattered; she had torn up Colin's letters without opening them, to her mother's secret satisfaction, and there was certainly no room in her mind for any thoughts of him. The week went past, and very nearly a second one, before something happened to disrupt her busy, unexciting days.

A letter came from Great-Aunt Sybil. Miss Moore was taking a week's holiday—for urgent family reasons—and, since Aunt Sybil could on no account be expected to manage without a companion, Beatrice was invited to spend a week in her place. 'Invited' wasn't perhaps the right word, the invitation was worded more in the form of a command but, as Mrs Browning said, the poor old thing was to be pitied.

'Why?' asked Beatrice, not best pleased at the summons.

'Well, dear, no one loves her, do they? We do our duty by her; your father manages her shares and things for her, and I go and see her once a month and you fill in gaps, but none of us likes doing it.'

'How right, Mother. But I'll go, if only to keep the peace. Nothing much can happen in a week.'

She went away to pack her bag, happily unaware that she was quite mistaken.

Great-Aunt Sybil gave her a grudging welcome. Miss Moore had already gone, leaving a neat list of things which had to be done for Beatrice. They were innumerable, and Beatrice, reading it, saw that the week ahead would be a difficult one, given that she wasn't Miss Moore in the first place, and furthermore would have to contend with her great-aunt's ill humour because Miss Moore wasn't there.

The first day went well enough; Beatrice, anxious to please, wound wool, fetched spectacles, read aloud and listened with an intelligent face and half an ear to Miss Browning's forceful opinions of the government. She had heard most of them before, and beyond a suitable, 'oh', or 'I see', she was free to think her own thoughts of Oliver.

But on the second day she blotted her copy-book badly by forgetting the pills that her great-aunt took for her indigestion; worse, forgetting where they were. 'Miss Moore,' pronounced Miss Browning in disagreeably loud tones, 'forgets nothing. If it were not for her, I should very likely be lying in my grave.'

'Oh, well,' said Beatrice cheerfully, 'it's only for a week, Aunt Sybil, and think how much you'll enjoy seeing her again.'

'You are still an impertinent young woman,' said Great-Aunt Sybil.

It was difficult not to be bored; the weather had changed as it so often did in an English summer, to drizzling rain and brief snatches of sun which lasted long enough for one to go out of doors and get caught in the next shower. Beatrice played card games with her aunt, read the papers from cover to cover, and thought about Oliver.

There was a thunderstorm on the fourth day of her visit; it rumbled all day and then, as night fell, reached a crescendo of noise, interlarded by flashes of blue lightning which Beatrice didn't like at all. None the less, Miss Browning elected to go to her bed at the usual hour, and Beatrice, left on her own since Mrs Shadwell had retired to her room too, decided that bed might be the best place. She pulled the curtains close, turned on all the lights and presently got into bed, where she dozed off over a book. When she woke an hour later the storm had died away; indeed, it was too quiet, with not a breath of wind and no sound of traffic.

She got up, switched off the lights, got back into bed and closed her eyes. She was asleep at once and didn't wake again until the rising sun woke her. It was six o'clock or thereabouts, and a lovely morning. To go to sleep again would be a waste of time. She got up, put on her dressing-gown, slipped into her slippers and went quietly downstairs, intent on making a cup of tea before Mrs Shadwell got down.

She was half-way down the stairs when she heard a faint sound. A drawer opening or being shut? A door closing? She paused, frowning. Mrs Shadwell never came down until just after seven o'clock, and her great-aunt remained in her room until she had breakfasted. It might be the milkman, but the sounds had come from the front of the house. Beatrice, not a nervous type, tied her dressing-gown girdle more tightly, tossed her mane of hair over her shoulders and trod softly down to the hall.

The front door was still locked and chained, but the drawing-room door was ajar. She pushed it open and peered round it. A man was standing in front of the handsome bow-fronted cabinet where Miss Browning's splendid collection of antique silver was housed. He had a case open beside him and was picking and choosing the best pieces.

Fright held Beatrice silent for a moment and then indignation took over. 'Put everything back at once,' she said in a voice which shook only very slightly. 'I'm going to call the police.'

Even as she uttered these brave words, she saw that the french window at the other side of the house behind him was open, and since the telephone was at the other end of the room he had a distinct advantage—which he took. Snatching up the case, shedding christening spoons, silver dishes, goblets and some really fine snuff boxes as he did so, he ran out. Beatrice went after him. Never mind the phone; she was a splendid runner and he was a heavily built man, lumbering across the garden which gave on to an alley-way at the back of the house. But half-way there, with her in hot pursuit, he turned, to run down the side of the house and jump the little iron railing and dash along the pavement. Beatrice, hard on his heels, wished in vain for the milkman, someone going to work—anyone. Characters in books always cried, 'Stop, thief!' but she had no breath for that; she was gaining, but once out of the square there were several narrow roads where he could get out of sight.

Oliver, on his way to spend a couple of quiet days at his home, saw the man first and then Beatrice, her hair flying, dressing-gown all anyhow, tearing along like a girl possessed. If he had been uncertain as to what was happening, the sight of a small Georgian coffee-pot at the side of the road would have helped him to understand the situation. But he didn't need silver coffee-pots; with a snort of laughter he overtook the man, got out of his car, knocked him down and then put a well-shod foot on him.

'Hello,' said Beatrice, and flung her hair out of the way and tugged her dressing-gown into decency. 'He was stealing the silver.'

The doctor smiled in his nice calm way. 'I thought that might be it. Get in the car, my dear, and phone the police, and stay there until they come.'

She turned to go. 'You always come,' she said, and his smile widened.

All he said was, 'Run along now.'

She sat obediently while the police came and put the man in their car and asked her a lot of questions. She answered them in her sensible way, and looked astonished when the police sergeant warned her in a fatherly fashion not to go running after thieves again.

'He could have turned nasty, miss,' he told her. She forebore from telling him that Great-Aunt Sybil could turn nasty too, especially if she had come downstairs and found her cabinets rifled. On the whole, she thought, she preferred the burglar.

She would be required to make a statement, said the pleasant police sergeant, but later in the day. He cast an eye over her appearance. 'You'll need to go home and have a nice cup of tea, miss,' he told her kindly. 'A bit of a shock it must have been.'

Oliver was leaning against the car's bonnet. 'I'll see her safely back, Sergeant. I'm a friend of the family and I know her aunt.'

So presently he got into the car and drove the short distance to Miss Browning's house, its quiet dignity disturbed by a police car parked on the street outside and a police officer standing at the door, while another one pottered up and down the square, retrieving teaspoons, snuff boxes and a badly dented teapot...

Inside there was a good deal of noise and confusion. Loud voices in the drawing-room seemed the signal for them to peer round the door, to see Aunt Sybil, clad in a magnificent dressing-gown, sitting very upright in a chair before the almost empty cabinet. Mrs Shadwell was standing behind her, wringing her hands, and the daily girl who came in to help stood just inside the door. She looked round at Beatrice and Oliver as they went in and exclaimed, 'Well, I never...' in a loud, excited voice, so that Great-Aunt Sybil and her housekeeper gave up contemplating the cabinet and turned round.

'Beatrice,' Miss Browning's voice trembled a little with shock, 'you are undressed, I am told that you have been in the square, I am deeply mortified.'

Beatrice, without realising it, clutched Oliver's hand. 'So sorry, Aunt Sybil, but I saw this man making off with the silver. I'm sure you'd have been a good deal more mortified if I'd let him go without trying to stop him.'

'You could have called the police instead of tearing round Wilton like a demented...'

The doctor stopped her, a cutting edge to his calm voice which would have silenced a howling mob. 'Miss Browning, you do not appear to understand the situation. Beatrice very bravely challenged the thief, and since the telephone was out of reach, did what any person with a spark of courage would have done: tried to stop him. I find your attitude utterly incomprehensible. You should be unendingly grateful to her.'

He flung a large arm round Beatrice's shoulders. 'I shall take her home as soon as she is dressed and has packed her bag.'

Great-Aunt Sybil went a delicate puce, made several attempts to speak and at last said, 'Young man, you are extremely rude...'

'I am not a young man, Miss Browning, though it is kind of you to say so, nor am I rude.' He took his arm from Beatrice and tapped her smartly on the shoulder. 'Upstairs with you. Is ten minutes long enough?'

As she went upstairs, she could hear her aunt's voice, its rich tones vibrant with feeling. 'I shall be alone...'

'You have these ladies—your housekeeper and her help in the house? You do not know what it is to be alone, Miss Browning. To sit in a small bedsitter with not enough to eat and nothing to keep you warm, and dependent on a neighbour's kindness if she remembers—that is being alone!'

Beatrice paused on the stairs to listen. Her aunt would shred him into little pieces. She was amazed to hear her voice pitched in a lower key and almost subdued. 'Young man, I do not like you particularly, but I think that you are a good man with the courage of your convictions. Should I be taken ill—as I probably shall after this terrible shock—I shall expect you to attend me.'

Beatrice didn't wait for more, she had already wasted two minutes of the ten she had been allowed.

She dashed water on to her face, raced into her clothes, brushed her hair in a perfunctory manner and rammed everything into her bag. There were several odds and ends lying around, and her forgotten dressing-gown lying in a heap by the bed. She snatched them up and stowed them into a plastic bag she had thrown into the wastepaper basket the night before, and went downstairs.

Her aunt was still sitting in her chair; she didn't appear to have moved, and Oliver was standing by the window, looking out, his hands in his pockets. He looked, she thought, completely at ease, and she loved him all the more for it.

'A plastic bag!' exclaimed Great-Aunt Sybil. 'Must you, Beatrice? In my day, no young lady carried such a thing—why have you no luggage?'

'Well, I have Aunt, but I didn't have much time and I haven't packed very well—these are just some bits and pieces left out.'

To her utter surprise, Miss Browning observed, 'I shall give you suitable luggage for your birthday, Beatrice. Your twenty-seventh birthday.'

No girl of twenty-six likes to be reminded that she is going to be twenty-seven. Beatrice swallowed bad temper and said perkily, 'I can't wait for it; I love birthdays.'

The doctor looked over his shoulder at her and allowed a small sound to escape his lips. 'A very proper attitude,' he said approvingly. 'Shall we go? Miss Browning, the police will require a statement from Beatrice, and she will have to return here to make it. I hope and expect that you will recover anything which was taken—thanks to Beatrice.'

'Well, and you too,' said Beatrice. 'I should never have caught him if you hadn't come along.'

'An open question.' He bade Miss Browning a polite good morning, nodded to Mrs Shadwell, who was still wringing her hands, smiled at the daily help and took Beatrice's bag while she said her goodbyes in turn.

'You'll have your nice Miss Moore back in another two days,' said Beatrice cheerfully.

In the car she asked, 'Isn't it rather early for you to be driving home?' She turned to look at him, and her loving heart was touched by the tiredness of his face. 'You've been up all night,' she said.

'Well, yes, for the greater part of it. But I have the weekend to myself, and Mrs Jennings will be waiting for me with a mammoth breakfast.'

He was driving steadily, looking ahead.

'Aunt Sybil will be all right? She did say that she simply had to have a companion. Supposing she falls ill?'

'Your Great-Aunt Sybil has a constitution of iron.' He added casually, 'You look untidy.'

Indignation swelled in her bosom. 'Of course I'm untidy. You gave me ten minutes to dress and pack, remember? And I cannot think why I did as you asked. I needed at least half an hour. I know of no other woman who would be such a fool...'

'Actually,' said the doctor at his most soothing, 'you look rather nice.'

The wind was taken out of her sails. She said contritely, 'I'm sorry, I didn't mean to snap and you're tired...'

'A couple of hours' sleep will soon put that right. I'll call for you after lunch; we can go for a drive, if you like, or go back and have tea in the garden, and lie about working up an appetite for one of Mrs Jennings' dinners.'

'I'd like that—just to sit in the garden. Aunt Sybil doesn't much care for sun and fresh air, and I've had to spend rather a lot of time indoors.'

'Two o'clock, then?'

There was a delicious smell of bacon frying as they went in to her home, and Mrs Browning was warming the teapot at the sink. She put it down rather sharply as they went in. 'Beatrice, darling, what's happened? How very untidy you are. You're not hurt? And you, Oliver, are you all right?'

'Perfectly. Beatrice surprised a burglar at her aunt's house and gave chase—I happened to be passing by—and as I was on my way home I gave her a lift.'

'Oh, I see,' said Mrs Browning, not seeing at all. 'You both need a cup of tea and then a good breakfast, then you can tell me all about it.'

'Tea would be splendid, but I can't stay for breakfast, Mrs Jennings would never forgive me—I told her I would be home between eight and nine o'clock.'

Beatrice hadn't spoken; now she said, 'Oliver came just when I didn't know what to do next. He always comes.'

The doctor smiled gently, and her mother gave her a thoughtful look. 'Yes, dear. Sit down and drink your tea, and then have a nice hot bath and I'll make the breakfast. Oliver, you're sure you can't stay?'

He shook his head. 'I wouldn't dare. The Jenningses are hand in glove with Rosie, my housekeeper in London; between them they order my life.'

'Won't your wife mind?' asked Beatrice suddenly, and went slowly pink because he would think that she was prying.

'Oh, they'll thoroughly enjoy having someone to look after. They are worth their weight in gold.' He put down his cup. 'Thank you for the tea, Mrs Browning. If I may, I'll just take a look at Mr Browning while I'm down here. He's due for a check-up in two weeks, isn't he?'

He crossed the room to where Beatrice was sitting, and bent

and kissed her cheek. 'I'll see you at two o'clock.' He turned to her mother. 'I've asked Beatrice over to keep me company for tea and dinner.'

Mrs Browning gave him a limpid look. 'Just what she needs after several days of her Great-Aunt.' She looked at Beatrice. 'Isn't it, dear?'

Beatrice nodded, thinking about the kiss. Of course, to him it had just been a casual salute which had meant nothing to him; unfortunately it had played havoc with her heart, which seemed to be choking her and making it impossible to speak. She watched him go, and when her mother came back from seeing him to his car she got up. 'I'll go and have a bath, Mother.'

'Yes, dear. Breakfast will be about twenty minutes, and your father will be back by then, so you can tell us all about it.'

So half an hour later, bathed and dressed in the pink outfit, her hair brushed and plaited, her face nicely made-up, Beatrice sat down to her breakfast. She was allowed to make inroads into bacon and eggs before her father said, 'Well, love, tell us what happened.'

So she told. 'In your dressing-gown,' commented her mother when she had finished. 'But at that hour of the morning there wouldn't be many people about.'

'No one, Mother. And I'd forgotten what I was wearing, I just wanted to catch the man.'

'Very brave of you, darling. I think I would have crept back to bed.'

'And then Oliver came along,' said Ella, who had sat quiet, for once.

'Yes, wasn't it lucky?'

'Not luck, fate—it was meant. You keep bumping into each other, don't you? Oh, not bumping, you know what I mean. Fate throws you together.'

'You've been reading the horoscopes again,' said Beatrice in what she hoped was a light voice.

'Mother says you are having tea and dinner with him. Does he fancy you?'

Mrs Browning drew in her breath sharply and cast a warning frown at her husband, who had his mouth open to speak. It was left for Beatrice to say something. 'He is getting married very shortly. She sounds a very nice girl, and when he talks about her you can hear that he's—he's very fond of her.'

Ella was irrepressible. 'Oh, well, someone else will turn up for you. There's a letter from Colin for you; it's on the hall table.'

Beatrice who felt like crying, laughed instead. 'Ella, you're incorrigible! Shall I put on an overall and come and give you a hand with the animals? What's in, anyway?'

Half an hour later, cleaning out the small room where the smaller animals went to recover after surgery, Ella said, 'You and Oliver ought to marry—you suit each other down to the ground. And what I want to know is why, if he's so smitten with her, doesn't this girl he's going to marry ever come down to his house here? He spends almost as much time in it as he does in his London house, doesn't he? Always racing up and down the A303 at all hours of the day and night. Do you suppose she's there and no one knows?'

'If she were, I would have met her by now.' Beatrice strove to keep her voice calm. 'Besides, they're not married yet.'

Ella gave her a pitying look, 'Really, love, you're dreadfully out of date—or do I mean old-fashioned? Two of the teachers at school live with boyfriends. They're even buying a house together...'

Beatrice gently moved a sick terrier belonging to the vicar to a clean cage. 'Well, they wouldn't need to buy a house, would they? He's got two already. And I should imagine that well-known specialists in the medical profession take great care of their reputations.'

Ella hadn't finished. 'But he took you all over Europe and pretended that you were engaged. Oh, I know all about that, I asked Mother...'

Beatrice began to fill the water bowls. 'Oh, I see. Oliver did that to help me, and his fiancée knew about it. He told me that she didn't mind—that she understood. You see, Ella, it was to stop Colin thinking that I might still marry him.'

'You don't want to any more?'

'No. It was infatuation, nothing more. I dare say you know more about that than I do,' she added drily.

'I expect I do. All the same, I wish that you and Oliver...' She caught Beatrice's eye. 'You like him, don't you?'

Beatrice didn't quite meet the eye. 'Yes, he has been kind to me, and I'm grateful.'

In the car later, driving to Oliver's home, Beatrice said, 'I don't think I'll come out with you again, if you don't mind.'

'I shall mind, unless you can give me a good reason.'

She fidgeted around in her seat. 'Well, it's a bit difficult to explain. I don't think it's fair to your fiancée. I can't believe that she doesn't mind—not about me going to Utrecht and all those other places with you and Ethel, because that was just to get away from Colin, but now—today—there's no reason...'

'Today is rather an exception, isn't it?' His voice was cool. 'You had an unpleasant experience this morning. You may not realise it, but it gave you a shock; the best cure for that is to do something to take your mind off it, hence my invitation to spend an afternoon snoozing in the sun and eating one of Mrs Jennings' splendid dinners. Look upon it as medical advice, Beatrice.'

She deplored his impersonal manner, while at the same time feeling relieved at his assumption that he had offered her a kind of therapy for shock. She said, 'Very well,' in a meek voice, and made a pointless remark about the weather.

It was a pleasantly warm afternoon; they lay on the well-cushioned loungers on the lawn behind the house, and presently Beatrice went to sleep, to wake to the gentle rattle of teacups. 'Too nice to go indoors just yet,' said Oliver. 'Be mother, will you? And tell me what plans you have for the future.'

She poured from a silver pot into wafer-thin and exquisite china cups. 'I haven't any,' she said baldly. 'Do you have sugar?'

'What—have you forgotten that already? Two lumps. Has Colin ceased to worry you?'

'Yes. I haven't thought about him for quite a while. I can't think how I ever imagined that I was in love with him.'

'One never can. But experience is valuable—it enables you to know the real thing when it comes along.'

She passed the sandwiches and didn't look at him. It was only too true in her case, and she would rather die than tell anyone, ever. She said in a wooden voice, 'I'm quite sure you're right.'

The long silence was broken by Mabel, wanting cake, and Oliver began a gentle chat about nothing much so that Beatrice was soothed into content. It wouldn't last, she knew that; sooner or later she would remember that he was going to get married to someone else, and even if he remained her friend, indeed a friend of the family, it wouldn't be the same. She bit into Mrs Jennings' walnut cake and hoped with all her heart that he would be happy.

They wandered round the garden presently, and then strolled along to see the horses and Kate the donkey. Since it was a fine evening, they took Mabel for a walk through the open country behind the house.

Beatrice was happy; she knew it wouldn't last, but just for the moment life was everything she could ask of it. She didn't have much to say, but there didn't seem to be the need to talk. They turned for home presently, and Mrs Jennings led her away to tidy herself before dinner.

Oliver was in his drawing-room when she joined him, and they sat by the open window, watching Mabel gallop around the lawn while they had their drinks. Presently they dined. Mrs Jennings had excelled herself: a terrine of leeks and prawns in a delicate sauce, red mullet with thyme, and raspberries and cream. Beatrice did justice to the lot.

They sat over their coffee, but at length she said, 'I think I should go home now.'

Yet she felt an instant sadness at his prompt, 'Of course, you must be tired.'

'Are you going back to London on Monday?' she asked as they drove back.

'Yes, I shan't be down again for some time. There's a good deal of work for me and I have some business of my own to settle. There are certain arrangements to make before one marries.'

She was glad that she didn't need to answer that, for they had arrived at her home, and although he went in with her it was to spend a short time with her father before bidding them all goodnight in his usual pleasant manner and driving away. She didn't think that she would see him again, not as a friend, anyway. Next time he would be pleasantly impersonal, intent on checking up on her father, probably relieved that she and her tiresome problems were no longer in need of any help.

CHAPTER NINE

IT WAS ONLY after he had been gone for an hour or more that Beatrice remembered that nothing had been said about their pseudo engagement. Since it had been announced in the paper, it would have to be revoked in the same manner. On the other hand, if Colin saw it, he might try and see her again. Perhaps Oliver intended to do nothing about it; it would be best to leave it to him.

She was grateful for the suggestion her mother made that she should go to bed rather early. 'A lot has happened today,' observed her parent, 'and you must be very tired. Your father has to go over to Telfont Evias in the morning. Perhaps you would drive him, dear? That Jersey herd there, they all have to have something done to them.'

Mrs Browning was delightfully vague about it, although her daughters suspected that she knew a great deal more about a vet's work than she appeared to.

'Yes, of course I'll go. If Father's going to be there a long time, shall I do any shopping for you in Tisbury?'

'Yes, dear. Mrs Perry wants several things, you could get them at the ironmonger's.' She glanced at her daughter's pale, sad face. 'Off to bed with you, love. Father will have to leave about eight o'clock if he's to be done by lunchtime. What a blessing Mr Sharpe is so very reliable.' She waited until Beatrice was going upstairs. 'You don't miss Colin, dear?'

'No, Mother, he doesn't mean anything any more.'

So it wasn't he who had put that unhappy look on Beatrice's face, reflected her mother, but Oliver. She frowned, for she had felt sure that he was more than interested in her. Of course, there was this girl he was going to marry. 'I'd like to see that girl with my own eyes,' muttered Mrs Browning. 'She's too good to be true, for one thing.'

The week went by, and a second followed it; Beatrice, once more back in her familiar routine, did her best not to think of Oliver and failed lamentably. She scanned the paper each morning, searching for his name among the marriage announcements, and she wrote a careful letter to Ethel, in which she took great pains not to mention the doctor, merely reiterating her enjoyment of their trip and hoping that Ethel had had a good holiday. She had a letter back in which, among other bits of news, Ethel mentioned that Oliver was working much too hard. She hadn't asked him why, it wasn't her place to do so, but she suspected the reason. This was followed by several exclamation marks which, to Beatrice's unsettled mind, implied that Ethel knew a good deal more than she intended to write.

She was in her room, making her bed, when she looked out of the window and saw the Rolls halting smoothly in front of the house. There was a back staircase, and without stopping to think very clearly Beatrice darted from her room, sneaked down to the back door and slid away into the line of trees and shrubs beyond the field, where the convalescent horses and cows were kept. Only when she paused for breath did she wonder why she had done it. The thought uppermost in her mind was that she couldn't bear to see him again, even though she longed to do so. She fetched up against an uprooted tree and sat down on its trunk. She wasn't far away from the house; she would hear when he drove away. Presently she heard her mother's voice calling her, and then Ella, free from school for the day, shouting for her. She took no notice, they would think that she had gone for a walk or biked down to the village, and in a little while Oliver would go away.

It was almost half an hour before she heard the gentle purr of the Rolls as he left. She sat for another five minutes, just to be on the safe side, and then started back. She went a little cautiously, intent on circumventing the house and appearing from the tumbledown shed at the back of the yard where her bike was kept. She reached the corner of the clinic and poked her head cautiously round the corner.

Her view was blotted out by the vast expanse of the doctor's waistcoat within inches of her nose.

'Now, I wonder why you ran away?' he asked, pleasantly casual. 'It struck me that you were probably hiding in that convenient little patch of trees. Why?'

She stared up at him. 'Oh, dear,' she said, 'I don't know why, really I don't.' And then, being a truthful girl by nature, 'Well, I do know, but I can't tell you.'

He smiled down at her. 'I hope that when you feel you can tell me, you will.'

'Never,' said Beatrice, and, at that moment at least, meant it. 'I should get back, I'm making beds…'

But he made no movement at all to stand aside, and short of turning tail and going back the way she had come, there was no way of getting past him. She took refuge in polite conversation. 'Have you come down for a few days' rest?' she asked politely.

'No, I must go straight back. Ethel has a row of patients lined up for me to see this afternoon.'

'Oh—then why…?' She stopped before she said something silly.

'Did I come?' he finished for her. 'To see you, but now I find that this is not the right moment, after all.'

'What about?'

He laughed down at her. 'Getting married, Beatrice.'

The pretty colour in her cheeks paled. 'Oh, yes, of course. I—I hope that you will ask us all to your wedding.'

'You may depend upon that. Does Colin still write to you?'

The question took her by surprise. 'Yes, but I don't read his letters.'

'He's still in England?'

'I don't know. I've never looked at the postmark.'

'You really have forgotten him, haven't you?'

She said quietly, 'Oh, yes.' She smiled up at him, learning his face by heart.

'Heartwhole and fancy free,' he announced softly. 'Do you wonder what is around the next corner?'

She shook her head, held out her hand and said in a pleasant, polite and wooden voice, 'Goodbye, Oliver. We'll see each other again, of course, but it won't be—won't be the same.'

He took her hand. 'No, it won't.' He laughed down at her surprised face. 'Off you go and make your beds.' He touched her cheek lightly with a finger, and she turned and ran past him, furious with herself for crying. Thank goodness he hadn't seen that!

She raced upstairs and went on with the beds, and by the time she had finished she looked almost the same as usual. Only Ella, in the kitchen making the coffee, took a look at her pink eyelids and opened her mouth to speak, and then shut it again at her mother's frowning look.

It was three days later, when her mother had gone on her duty visit to Great-Aunt Sybil, Mrs Perry had gone home and Ella was at school, that Beatrice found herself alone in the house. Her father had gone to an outlying farm and Mr Sharpe had gone to the calf sale in Tisbury. It was another summer day, and she had opened all the windows and left the door to the kitchen open while she pottered to and fro, pulling radishes and cutting lettuce ready for supper that evening. Knotty was lying across the step, half asleep, and she had turned the radio on. Presently, she decided she would make a cup of tea and spend an hour in the garden before seeing to the few animals in the clinic.

She had her back to the door when Knotty suddenly got up in a flurry, barking madly, and when she turned round Colin was standing just inside the kitchen.

He was smiling, but she didn't much care for that; she waited silently for him to speak, feeling nothing but indignation at the way he had walked into the house in such a fashion. It made her feel better to see that he was disconcerted by her calm response to his appearance, but he recovered himself quickly.

'Took you by surprise, didn't I? I told you in my letters that I'd be back—perhaps you didn't believe me.'

'I don't read your letters. Will you go away, Colin? I'm busy.'

He grinned. 'I know where everyone is,' he told her, 'and you're here on your own for at least another hour. Time enough for us to have a little talk.'

'We have nothing to talk about.' She was suddenly furious. 'Get out, Colin. Why do you keep pestering me?'

'Because I have a very shrewd suspicion that you're not going to marry that doctor of yours. It was a put-up job, wasn't it? Oh, I know all about it; you went to Europe with him, didn't you? I suppose you thought I'd be fool enough to go away. I don't give in so easily, Beatrice, my darling. He's not going to marry you, is he? For all I know he's already got a wife, so here you are, jilted. And don't deny it, there's not been a word about a wedding for weeks; I've had my ear to the ground in the village and I don't miss much. So now you should be glad that I still want to marry you. Of course, I shall expect a partnership—the practice is big enough to take a third man—a good salary in order to keep my wife in the comfort to which she has been accustomed and a decent house to live in.'

Beatrice said steadily, 'I think you're absurd. Perhaps I was infatuated with you for a few weeks, but now I really have no wish to see you again, so you can take no for a final answer and go away.' She added in a reproving voice, 'The weeks you have wasted, Colin!'

'Not wasted, my dear.' He had come into the kitchen and closed the door on a protesting Knotty. 'You can't deny any of the things I've said, can you?' He eyed her thoughtfully. 'I shouldn't be surprised to find that you're in love with this high and mighty doctor.'

He was astute. She had kept her face calm, but the look in her eyes gave her away, and he gave a triumphant chuckle. 'I thought so. All the more reason for you to reconsider marrying me. It would be one in the eye for him, wouldn't it? You must be feeling humiliated.' He clicked his fingers. 'Of course—he doesn't know! I shall enjoy telling him.'

'You're despicable, and he won't believe you.'

He had moved nearer and she had moved behind the kitchen table, facing him and taking comfort from its stoutness.

'Don't you believe it, darling. Can you imagine his tolerant amusement at your naïve idea? Just because he was good enough to help you out of a situation you didn't like, you have got besotted with him.'

'You are imagining a lot of nonsense,' Beatrice spoke with her usual calm, although her insides were shaking. She wasn't surprised when he said, 'I promise I won't tell, if you agree to marry me.'

She glanced at the old-fashioned clock behind him on the wall. In another half-hour or so her father would be back, and her mother too. She badly needed someone on her side, even Knotty, barking his head off again.

Knotty was barking at Ella, home earlier than usual from school and standing just out of sight, looking into the kitchen. Her first thought was to rush inside and help Beatrice bundle Colin out of the house, but prudence prevailed. Another man should deal with the situation. Mr Sharpe was just outside in the lane, talking to the vicar. She turned and ran round to the front of the house, just as the Rolls slid her handsome nose round the curve of the drive.

Ella didn't call out, she was too near the kitchen for that. She flew at the car, and the doctor slid to a halt, stopping with an inch or so to spare. 'Don't do that again, Ella, I very nearly died of fright.'

'Sorry, Oliver, do come! Thank heaven you're here. Colin's in the kitchen with Beatrice…'

He was a very big man and heavily built, but he reached the kitchen, opened the door and was inside while Ella was catching her breath. He hadn't appeared to hurry, yet there he was, leaning calmly against the doorjamb. Beatrice restrained an impulse to hurl herself into his arms, and wondered with a flash of temper at his almost casual attitude. True, he had come into the kitchen very fast. She gave him a rather tremulous smile, and thought thankfully that everything would be all right now.

Nobody spoke; the doctor gave the impression that he was half asleep anyway, and Colin was marshalling his wits, and Ella, who had slipped into the kitchen, held her tongue, which for her was unusual.

Presently Colin spoke. 'I'm staying in the village; it seemed a good chance to come and see Beatrice. I wanted to make quite sure that she was still open to persuasion to marry me. She might just as well—did you know, by the way, that the poor girl is head over heels in love with you?'

'Yes. I knew.' The doctor took a step, gripped Colin by the arm and marched him outside, closing the door quietly as he went and Ella let out a gasp.

'Oh, do you suppose he's going to kill him?'

Beatrice was shaking like a jelly, furiously angry and so humiliated that she would cheerfully have sunk through the floor if that had been possible.

'I hope they kill each other,' she said with a snap.

Several minutes elapsed before the doctor returned. 'Did you knock him out?' asked Ella eagerly.

'Er—no. But I don't think he will be coming here again.' He hadn't looked at Beatrice. 'Do you suppose your mother would invite me to tea if you went and asked her? We'll be along presently.'

Beatrice made for the door, but she had to go round the table and Ella was ahead of her; besides, Oliver put out a leisurely arm and caught her hand as she tried to pass him.

He shut the door into the back hall as Ella went out, and stood leaning against it. 'Colin won't bother you again,' he said gently. 'I give you my word on that. Forget him, Beatrice.' He patted her shoulder in an avuncular manner. 'How very fortunate that Ella came home early from school, but I hope someone will warn her not to run full tilt into cars. I missed her by a couple of inches.' He gave her a kindly, impersonal smile. 'Shall we have tea? All this excitement makes one thirsty.'

She went ahead of him. He wasn't going to say anything about Colin's spiteful disclosure, and she was most grateful for that; she got red again just thinking about it. More than ever now she must avoid him. As they went into the drawing-room, her unhappy mind was already exploring the possibility of going to stay with one or other of the more distant family.

Ella must have said something, but no one mentioned Colin as they had their tea. Oliver carried on an effortless conversation with her mother and father, completely at his ease, gave Ella a few useful hints about the biology paper she was preparing for her class, and without appearing to do so, drew Beatrice into the talk. He stayed some time then finally made his unhurried departure. From Beatrice's point of view, he couldn't go fast enough. She never wanted to see him again, although how she would be able to live without doing so was a moot point. She summoned up a stiff smile as he went, but she didn't go out to the car with the others. Instead she made some excuse about feeding Knotty. When they got back, she was so bracing in her manner that no one uttered a word about the afternoon's unfortunate event, and when she said in a bright voice that she fancied she would like a visit to an aged aunt of her mother's who lived with a great many cats in a cottage in Polperro, she met with an enthusiastic response.

'Why not, dear?' said her mother. 'There's that student coming from the veterinary college at Bristol; he can take over from you, and Aunt Polly will love to hear all the news.'

Which would have to be shouted, reflected Beatrice, for the old lady was deaf.

But any port in a storm… To get away as soon as possible was her one wish. She sat down that evening and wrote to Aunt Polly, and then waited anxiously for two days, during which no one mentioned either Colin or Oliver to her. And when the reply came, written in a spidery hand and violet ink, she showed it to her mother.

'Aunt Polly wants me to go as soon as possible. Tomorrow? The student comes the day after. I could wait another day…'

'No, love, you go.' Her mother was slicing beans and didn't look up. 'I'm sorry, darling. We all feel for you, you know, even if we haven't said anything.'

Beatrice put the letter tidily back in its envelope, taking time over it. 'Yes, Mother, and thank you all for not saying a word. I don't think I could bear that.'

'A week or so away, darling, and you'll feel able to cope again.'

'Yes, Mother, and please don't tell anyone where I am.'

Mrs Browning, rightly deducing that anyone was another way of saying Oliver, agreed.

Carol, with a few days off from her office, offered to drive her down, and they left on a wet day which, as they neared Cornwall, became shrouded in mist as well. Between Tavistock and Liskeard it formed a white wall which lasted until they neared the coast, and as they took the road from Looe to Polperro the mist lifted so that they had a glimpse of the little town below, snug between high cliffs, the cottages grouped around the small harbour. There were houses on the hillsides on either side, too, and any number of charming cottages tucked away on either side of the one narrow main road. Aunt Polly lived close to the harbour, up a tiny lane, with a steep flight of steps leading to her front door. Carol parked the car on the road and they went in together, already seen by their aunt, who flung open the door and, in the loud voice of the deaf, bade them welcome. Several cats came to welcome them too, and it took a few minutes for greetings to be exchanged before they all went indoors.

Aunt Polly was small and thin, with a ramrod-straight back and a fierce-looking expression. No one knew quite how old she was, and no one had dared to ask, but it was thought that she was eighty at least, although she didn't look much more than sixty. She had refused help on several occasions, and if the family ventured to do more than write occasionally and enquire as to her health she became remarkably testy.

She seemed glad to see Beatrice, partly because Beatrice had a fondness for small animals and partly because she didn't chatter, but she made no demur when, after a late lunch, Carol said she must go back home. Carol, she confided to Beatrice later, was a nice girl, pretty too, but far too smart and fashionable.

'She's very clever,' pointed out Beatrice, on her knees in the small sitting-room, brushing one of the cats. 'And everyone likes her.'

Aunt Polly snorted in a ladylike way. 'That's as may be. Why aren't you married? You must be all of seven and twenty.'

'I'm twenty-six, Aunt Polly.'

'Don't tell me you haven't had an offer?'

'Two serious ones.'

'And the others?'

'Not serious.'

'There's someone, I'll be bound, a pretty girl like you. He's married, I suppose?'

'No. Just engaged, and he's a friend, that's all.'

'A good basis for marriage, friendship. No good loving someone if you don't like them.' She removed a very large, fat tabby cat from her lap. 'We'll have tea. Go for a walk if you like before supper. I have it at eight o'clock. I like to go to bed early.'

The rain had stopped and the mist had lifted. The little town was quiet, the day tourists had left and most of the summer visitors had gone back home. Beatrice walked briskly round the harbour and climbed the cliff path on the other side. Tomorrow, she decided, she would walk to Talland Bay, unless Aunt Polly wanted her to do something else.

Aunt Polly suggested it over supper. 'I live in a nice little rut,' she explained. 'Don't think you have to entertain me. You can shop for me after breakfast and help me with the cats, and then go off and enjoy yourself until teatime.'

So Beatrice spent her days walking, taking sandwiches and sitting on the cliffs to eat them, watching the sea and occasionally getting wet from the sudden rain showers. There was colour in her cheeks again, and she was even able to laugh a little over Colin's visit. She did her best not to think about Oliver, but when she did she got red in the face with shame, even though there was no one to see her. All the same, with two days of her holiday left, she felt that she could face everyone again. Given time, everything faded, even love, she supposed.

On the day before Carol was coming to fetch her, she took a last walk over the cliffs and then a stroll through the narrow, cobbled streets. It was the kind of morning which gave a hint of the autumn to follow, with a cool breeze which blew her plait over her shoulder and left her a little chilly although the sun was bright, hidden from time to time by great billowing clouds crowding in from the west. She stopped to look at a collection of pottery in one of the small shops; there were shelves of Cornish piskies, handmade and all different. One each for her sisters and another for her mother. There was a nice little painting, too, which would do for her father.

'Hello,' said Oliver gently.

She spun round and he caught her arm to steady her. The

colour had left her face, now it came rushing back. 'How did you get here? Who told you?'

'I drove down and Mrs Perry told me...'

'But I asked Mother...'

'She said that she had promised not to tell—er—anyone. Mrs Perry happened to be there,' he added blandly.

'I'd rather not talk to you.' She was breathless, and any moment now she would burst into tears. 'I'm staying here with an aunt.'

'Yes, I know. A charming old lady. She's invited me to lunch.'

He took her arm and began to walk her away from the shops, back to Aunt Polly's house. 'A delightful place,' he observed chattily. 'Especially when the season is over. We must come again.'

'No,' said Beatrice, so loudly that several people looked at her.

The doctor came to a halt and turned her round to face him. 'You really are a goose,' he said, and smiled. Then, to the delighted interest of those passing by, he kissed her.

Beatrice closed her eyes and opened them again. He was still there, and she could feel his arms most reassuringly wrapped around her. 'You can't...' she began.

'Oh, but I can, and I will.' He kissed her again. 'The rest must wait.'

Beatrice sat through lunch in a bemused state, answering when spoken to, but taking no part in the conversation which Aunt Polly dominated with observations and tales about cats, and hers in particular.

'Beauty will have kittens in a few weeks.' She pointed to a grey Persian on the windowsill. 'She's pure bred, you know, thrown out when the people who owned her moved away.'

'Perhaps you will save one of the kittens for us,' suggested the doctor suavely.

Aunt Polly skewered his eyes with her own shrewd ones.

'Yes. Us?' She gave a chuckle. 'You shall have one for a wedding present.' She looked at Beatrice. 'You hear that, Beatrice?'

Beatrice muttered 'Yes, Aunt,' and didn't look up from the semolina shape she was pushing around her plate. She looked up pretty smartly when Oliver remarked that he would like to leave within the next hour. 'I'll wash up while you pack, Beatrice.'

'But I'm not...that is, Carol's coming for me tomorrow morning.'

'She was delighted when I suggested that I should take her place—there is some flower show or other that she wanted to go to.'

'So go and pack, child,' said Aunt Polly. 'I've enjoyed having you, but visitors do unsettle the cats, you know.'

So Beatrice packed and changed and got into the pink outfit, and presently went downstairs and found Oliver waiting for her in the hall. He took her bag from her and waited while she said goodbye and made her little thank-you speech, then he bent and kissed the old lady's cheek. 'You must come to the wedding,' he told her. 'I'll send a car for you.'

'The cats—they can't be left.'

'I'll find someone to mind them.' And Aunt Polly, by no means meek, nodded meekly.

The car was parked in a private car park half-way up the main street.

'No one is ever allowed to park here,' said Beatrice.

'I know.' He unlocked the car door and ushered her into the front seat, and went away to the man standing in a corner, presumably guarding his property. She could hear him laugh at something Oliver said, and watched money change hands.

She had been racking her brains for a suitable topic of conversation, something impersonal—the weather, the scenery, the state of the roads? A waste of time, for Oliver got into the car without a word, and beyond the remark that they would get back in time for tea he didn't speak. She found his silence disconcerting, and it lasted for the whole of the journey.

They were expected. Mrs Browning had tea ready and, since Carol was back from the show and Ella was there from school, there was no lack of conversation. And, if anyone noticed how quiet she was, no one said so.

Oliver got up to go after tea. 'You're staying down here?' asked Mrs Browning.

'Yes, possibly for a few days. It rather depends.'

He shook hands all round, but when he came to Beatrice he kissed her soundly without saying a word. When he had gone she stood in the hall for so long that her mother came back to look for her.

'Oh, Mother, I'm in such a muddle—he's not said a word...'

'He kissed you very thoroughly, love,' her mother pointed out.

Beatrice burst into tears. 'That's what I mean,' she cried.

She had thought that she would stay awake all night, but she slept at once and didn't wake until early morning. A lovely morning, too. It was going to be a splendid day. She got up and put on a skirt and top, and tied her hair back and slipped downstairs to let Knotty out and begin the climb up the hill. Perhaps she would be able to think clearly if she sat quietly and watched the sun rise in the pale sky.

She was almost at the top when she looked up. Oliver was there, watching her. She went on more slowly until she reached him, and he put out an arm and drew her close.

'Oliver, how did you know that I would come?'

'It's the best time of day. Do you remember, my darling, when we met? I fell in love with you then, and I believe you felt as I did, although you didn't know it then. You didn't know it for a long time, did you? I had to wait while you got Colin out of your system, so I allowed you to think that I was going to marry...'

'But why? There was no need.'

He kissed her slowly. 'I had to be sure, and I had to wait until you discovered that you loved me.'

'Oh, I do, I do. If you ask me, I'll marry you, Oliver.'

'I promised myself when we met that one day I would ask

you to marry me on this very spot, and now I'm fulfilling that promise. Will you marry me, my darling?'

'Yes, I will. Darling Oliver, I think I'm going to cry.'

Her dark eyes had filled with tears, and he wiped them away with a finger, then kissed her very gently, pulled her down on to the fallen tree-trunk, and put an arm round her.

'A day for making a wish,' said Beatrice dreamily. 'Only I've got all I ever wished for, haven't I?'

'If you haven't, my dearest love, I'll make sure that you do.'

She kissed him for that.

* * * * *

Grasp A Nettle

Tender-handed stroke a nettle
And it stings you for your pains;
Grasp it like a man of mettle
And it soft as silk remains.
—Aaron Hill

CHAPTER ONE

THE WINDING STONE staircase in the corner tower was gloomy excepting for the regular patches of sunlight from the narrow slit windows set at intervals in its thick stone walls, but the girl running up the worn steps thought nothing of the gloom; she was well accustomed to it. She paused now, half way up, to peer out of one of the windows, craning her neck to look along the back drive to Dimworth House. It was almost two o'clock and the first of the visitors were already driving slowly down the narrow, ill-made lane which ran for a mile or more on its way from the main road.

The girl turned her bright coppery head to look down at the wide gravel path bordered by lawns and herbaceous borders, to where, beyond the open gate at its far end, the field used as a car park was waiting, empty, for the cars to fill it. It promised to be a good day in terms of entrance fees; although Dimworth House was one of the smaller stately homes open to the public, it was doing quite nicely, although it meant hard work for the family, and indeed, for everyone connected with the estate. The girl left the window presently, ran up the last curve of the narrow staircase, and pushed open the arched door at its top. It led to a small circular lobby, panelled and empty of furniture. She crossed this, opened the door in the opposite wall and entered a short, carpeted corridor, the walls hung with paintings and with a number of doors in its inner wall. There was a rather fine staircase half way along it, leading to the floor below, and a long latticed window lighting the whole, although not very adequately. The girl hurried along with the air of one familiar with her surroundings and knocked on the end door, and on being bidden to enter, did so.

The apartment was large, low-ceilinged and panelled, furnished with a variety of antique furniture, presided over by an enormous fourposter bed, and was occupied by a very upright elderly lady, sitting at a writing table under the window. She looked up as the girl went in, said: 'Ah, Jenny,' in a commanding voice and laid down her pen.

The girl had a charming voice. 'I found Baxter, he was in the water garden. He'll do the tickets—he's putting on a tie and washing his hands, and Mrs Thorpe says she'll take over from me at four o'clock.' She glanced at the carriage clock on the desk. 'I'd better get down to the hall, the cars are starting to arrive, Aunt Bess.'

'Dear child!' declared her aunt. 'I can't imagine what we shall do when you go back to that hospital tomorrow.' She coughed. 'I'm afraid it hasn't been much of a holiday for you.'

Her niece smiled. 'I've loved it,' she assured her relation, 'it's been a nice change from theatre, you know. I'm sorry I can't stay here for the rest of the summer.' She had wandered to the window to look out, and the sunshine shone on her bright hair, tied back loosely, and her pretty face, with its hazel eyes, thickly fringed, little tiptilted nose and generous mouth. She was of average height, nicely rounded and gloriously tanned with a sprinkling of freckles across the bridge of her nose.

The Hon. Miss Elizabeth Creed, her mother's sister and a lady of forceful disposition, smiled as she watched her, for she was the only one, bar her great-nephew, for whom she had any affection. Jenny had never allowed her aunt's caustic tongue to worry her; and although she had been left an orphan at an early age, she had never once asked for money or help of any kind. True, she had a quite adequate income of her own from the trust set up for her by her parents, as well as her salary, but that was chickenfeed compared to the annual revenues enjoyed by her aunt and the very generous allowance given to her dead cousin's widow and small son, Oliver, who would one day inherit Dimworth and a handsome fortune with it. In the meantime, however, his mother chose to live in Scotland with her parents, and the house was run by his great-aunt until such time as he was considered old enough to do this for himself.

Jenny, who spent her holidays with Aunt Bess, thought it a great pity that the little boy didn't live at Dimworth, for it was a beautiful place and peaceful, and her cousin, who had died in an air crash a year or so after his marriage, had loved it dearly and would surely have wanted his son to have been brought up there, but Margaret, his widow, had never liked it over-much; she came to stay from time to time, but always made it clear to the rest of the family that she was glad to go again. She would be coming within a few days, bringing the little boy with her, and Jenny had every intention of spending all her days off at Dimworth while he was there, for the two of them were the greatest of friends, and Margaret, beautiful and languid and not particularly maternal, soon tired of his youthful high spirits.

Jenny, leaving her aunt to her writing, skipped down the staircase, crossed the landing below and opened a carved oak door on to a richly furnished sitting room overlooking the front of the house, and through which she threaded her way without loss of time, to go through a small, very old arched door cut into one of its walls. It led to another staircase, a very small one, down which she trod, to open an even smaller door at the bottom opening directly into the entrance hall of the house. There was a large table set in the centre of this vast area, laid out neatly with brochures, postcards, small souvenirs, pots of homemade jam and the like, and she made for the chair at its centre and took her seat just as the first of the visitors poked enquiring heads through the open doors.

The next two hours went fast. Jenny had been right, there were a good number of visitors, and when she had done her stint in the hall and Mrs Thorpe, the vicar's wife, very correctly dressed in her best summer two-piece and a good hat, had taken over from her, she went across to the old stables, converted into a tea-room, and found that it was nicely filled with family parties, tucking into their cream teas. Florrie, the indispensable housekeeper, and her niece Felicity were managing very well between them, so Jenny made her way back to the house, to enter it by a small door at the side, which led via a back hall into the last of the chain of rooms on view to the public—the dining room, sombre and panelled in oak, its refectory table and massive oak chairs protected by crimson ropes, and the silver goblets and plates on the great table protected by a burglar alarm which no one could see; they gleamed richly against the dark wood.

There were a dozen people there, standing about staring at the treasures around them, gazing without a great deal of interest at the dark oil paintings on the walls—family portraits, and not very colourful ones, although if any of them had studied them closely they would have noticed that most of them portrayed a variety of people with coppery hair, just like Jenny's.

The next room leading from the dining room was crowded, as it usually was; it was a small apartment, its walls lined with bookshelves, and arranged on a number of small tables was the collection of dolls which Aunt Bess had occupied herself in collecting over the years. This small room led in its turn to the blue drawing room, lofty and rather grand with its ornate ceiling and silk-hung walls, and furnished with gilded chairs and tables and a magnificent harpsichord. The little anteroom leading from it was far more to Jenny's taste; panelled in pinewood and rather crowded with Regency furniture, surprisingly comfortable to sit on. The family sometimes used the room in the summer, but once the evenings became chilly it was more prudent to stay in the private wing, for a small staircase led from the anteroom, up and down which the wind whistled, leaving anyone silly enough to sit there chilled to the bone.

Jenny didn't pause, but went up the staircase to cast an eye over the three bedrooms on view. No one had used them for very many years now. Their fourposters were magnificent, the heavy tables and mirrors and chests worth a fortune, but they held little comfort. There were quite a few people here too; she mingled with them, answering a few questions and cautioning people that the stone staircase leading down to the hall was worn in places and needed care before slipping away again, this time to go through yet another of the small doors which peppered the house, into the private wing. It was cosy here, with thick carpets underfoot, damask curtains at the mullioned windows, and a nicely balanced mixture of period furniture. Jenny's room was down a narrow passage, a roomy apartment with a small sitting room adjoining it and a bathroom on its other side. She had always occupied it, ever since, as a small child, she had spent her holidays at Dimworth.

She went straight to the wall closet now, gathered an armful of clothes and began to pack with speed and neatness. She intended leaving early the next morning, driving herself in the Morgan two-seater which Aunt Bess had given her for her twenty-first birthday; she had had it for four years now, and drove it superbly, making light of the journey to and from London, a journey she made at least twice a month. She would have liked to have spent all her days off at Dimworth, but she had a great many friends in and around the hospital—besides, Toby Blake, the elder son of Aunt Bess's nearest neighbour, might feel encouraged to propose to her yet again if she went down there too often. She frowned now, thinking about him; she supposed that sooner or later she would marry him, not because she was in love with him, but because they had known each other for such a long time and everyone expected them to. She was aware that this was no reason to accept him, but he did persist. 'Water wearing out a stone,' she commented to the room around her as she shut her case, took a cursory look in the mirror and went to find her aunt.

Tea was a meal which, on the days when the house was open to the public, was a moveable feast in the small sitting room on the ground floor. Anyone who had the time had a cup, and old Grimshaw, the butler, made it his business to tread to and fro with fresh tea as it was required. He was on the lookout now for Jenny and as she gained the lower hall, said in his fatherly fashion: 'I'll bring tea at once, Miss Jenny,' and disappeared through the baize door beside the stairs, kitchenwards.

Jenny called after him: 'Oh, good,' and added: 'I'm famished, Grimshaw,' as she opened the door and went in. Her aunt was sitting by the open window, her tea on the sofa table beside her chair.

'I must have an aspirin,' she declared in a voice so unlike her own that Jenny hurried over to her. 'I have the most terrible headache.'

'You've been working too hard, Aunt Bess. I'll get them... in your room?'

Her aunt nodded and she sped away to return at the same time as Grimshaw with the teapot. She poured her aunt another cup and shook out two tablets and offered them to her. 'Do you often get headaches?' she enquired, casting a professional eye over the elderly white strained face.

'I've never had a headache in my life before,' observed Miss Creed sharply, 'only these last few weeks...'

'And aspirins help?'

'Not really.' She was sitting back in her chair, her eyes closed.

'Then let's get Doctor Toms to see you.'

Miss Creed opened her eyes and sat up very straight. 'We will do no such thing, Janet. I'm never ill. You will oblige me by not referring to it again.'

'Well,' said Jenny reasonably, 'if you have any more headaches like this one, I shall certainly refer to it. Probably you need stronger glasses.'

Her aunt turned her head to look at her as she stood at the table, pouring herself her tea. 'H'm—perhaps that's it. You're a sensible girl, Jenny.'

Jenny smiled at her; her aunt always called her Janet when she was vexed, now she was Jenny again. They began to talk of other things and her aunt's indisposition wasn't mentioned again that day. Only the next morning when she went along to her aunt's room to wish her goodbye did that formidable lady declare: 'If ever I should be ill, Jenny, I should wish you to nurse me.' And Jenny, noting uneasily the pallor of the face on the pillows, said hearteningly: 'You're never ill, my dear, but if ever you are, yes, I'll look after you—you know that.' She bent to kiss the elderly cheek. 'You've been father and mother to me for almost all of my life, and very nice parents you've been, too.' She went to the door. 'I'll be back in ten days' time and I'll telephone late this evening unless anything crops up.'

London at the end of summer was crowded, hot, and smelled of petrol. Jenny wrinkled her nose as she drove across its heart and into the East End. When she had started her training as a nurse, her family, particularly Margaret, had been annoyed at her choice of hospital. With all the teaching hospitals to choose from, she had elected to apply to Queen's, large and old-fashioned and set squarely in the East End; not the type of place which, since she had insisted on taking up nursing, a Creed or a Wren should choose. But Jenny had had her own way, for despite her pretty face she was a determined girl with a quite nasty temper to go with her hair, and she had done her three years general training, followed it with a midwifery certificate and now held the post of Junior Theatre Sister. Her family still smiled tolerantly at the idea of her having a career, thinking no doubt of Toby Blake waiting in the wings, as it were; sure that very soon now she would realise that to be married to him would be pleasant and suitable and what was expected of her. But Jenny had other ideas, although she wasn't able to clarify them, even to herself. There would be someone in the world meant for her; she had been sure of that ever since she was a little girl, and although there was no sign of him yet, she was still quite certain that one day she would come face to face with him, and he would feel just as she did—and in the meantime she intended to make a success of her job.

Queen's looked grey and forbidding from the outside, and indeed, on the inside as well, but she no longer noticed the large draughty entrance hall, nor the long dark passages leading from it. She plunged into them after a cheerful exchange of greetings with the head porter, and presently went through a door, painted a dismal brown, across a courtyard overlooked by most of the hospital's wards, and into the Nurses' Home, an old-fashioned building which had been altered and up-dated whenever there had been any money to spare, so that it presented a hotchpotch of styles and building materials. But inside it was fairly up-to-date, with the warden's office just inside the door and a wide staircase beside the two lifts. Jenny wished the warden, Miss Mellow—who wasn't in the least mellow—a staid good morning, for it had barely struck noon, and started up the stairs, taking the handful of letters Miss Mellow had wordlessly handed her with her.

Three of them were from Toby; he was a great letter writer; his handwriting small and neat and unmistakable. Jenny sighed as she saw it and glanced at the others; from friends who had married and left hospital, inviting her severally for a weekend, to dinner, and to meet for coffee one day soon. She read them as she wandered upstairs, for she wasn't on duty until the following morning and she had plenty of time to unpack and get her uniform ready. But Toby's letters she didn't open, not until she had gained her room on the third floor, put her case down, kicked off her shoes and curled up on her bed.

There was nothing to say in any of them which she didn't

know already, and why he had to write on three successive days to point out the advantages of marrying him was a mystery—besides, she had seen him only four days ago, and when, as usual, he had asked her to marry him she had said quite definitely, with the frankness of an old friend, that it just wouldn't work. She put the letters down after a while and went along to the pantry to make a pot of tea. Clare Brook was there, putting on the kettle, having had a free morning from Women's Surgical, and she greeted Jenny with a cheerful 'Hullo,' and went on in mock dismay: 'You're on call tonight, ducky. Old Hickory (Miss Dock, the Theatre Superintendent) is off with toothache, Maureen's got days off and Celia being Celia and left in charge doesn't feel she should.' She raised her eyes to the ceiling. 'Our Celia is getting too big for her boots, just because Mr Wilson likes the way she hands him the instruments... So there you are, Jenny Wren, and for sure there'll be a massive RTA and you'll be up all night.'

Jenny spooned tea into the pot. 'Well, I've been away for two weeks,' she observed, 'so I suppose it's fair enough, though it's beastly to come back to.'

Clare eyed her with interest. 'Had a good time at that ancestral hall of yours? Seven-course dinners every evening, I suppose, and a dress for each one...' She spoke without rancour; everyone liked Jenny and nobody grudged her her exalted background. 'Not engaged to that Toby of yours yet?'

Jenny spooned sugar into their mugs and reached for the biscuit tin. 'No—it's silly of me, but I just know we wouldn't suit. Well, what I mean is...' she frowned, wishing to make herself clear: 'We've known each other simply years and years, and there's no...no...'

'Spice? I know what you mean—you're so used to each other you don't even quarrel.'

'He has a very even temper...'

'Huh—so there's nothing for you to sharpen your bad moods on, is there? You need someone with a temper as fine as yours, my dear, without an ounce of meekness in him, to give as good as he gets.'

'It doesn't sound very comfortable,' protested Jenny.

'Who wants to be comfortable? Chris and I fight quite a bit, you know, and we're only engaged. Heaven knows what it'll be like when we marry, but it'll never be dull.' Clare handed her mug over for more tea. 'Which reminds me, I saw the sweetest wedding dress the other day...'

The pair of them became absorbed in the interesting world of fashion.

Jenny had to get up during the night, not for the massive RTA which Clare had prophesied, but for a little boy who had fallen out of his bedroom window to the pavement below; it took hours to patch him up and his chance of survival was so slim as to be almost non-existent. Jenny, going back to bed at three o'clock in the morning, lay awake worrying about him for another hour, so that when she got down to breakfast at half past seven her pretty face was pale and tired, but the news that the child was still alive cheered her up and she ate her breakfast with a fair appetite, wishing, as she always did, that she was back at Dimworth, having her breakfast in the little sitting room overlooking the water garden, with Aunt Bess sitting opposite, reading indignant pieces from the newspaper and calling everybody, impartially, a fool.

There was a heavy list for the morning and Celia Drake, assuming the mantle Miss Dock had temporarily laid down, was at her most trying; if the morning's work was to run smoothly, then both of them would have to work, sharing the cases. But Celia, topheavy with importance, had elected to take the easiest of the list and leave the long-drawn-out ones to Jenny, which meant that Jenny wasn't going to get off duty punctually; the list would drag on until after dinner and there would be a wild scramble to get the afternoon list started on time, and although it wasn't a long one, Jenny guessed who would be scrubbing for it.

She eyed the cases she was expected to deal with and

frowned heavily, her lovely hazel eyes dark with temper, while her coppery hair seemed to glow. Celia had retired to the office, probably to sit at the desk and dream of the day when she would—perhaps—be Theatre Superintendent. Jenny poked her indignant head round the door and gave her a fuming look.

'Come on out and do your share, Celia,' she invited waspishly. 'You're not in Old Hickory's shoes yet, you know. We'll share this list, half and half, and if you don't like the idea, I'll drop everything and go off sick.'

Celia might hand the instruments with *éclat,* but her wits weren't all that quick. 'Go off sick?' she wanted to know. 'But you're not…'

Jenny nodded her bright head vigorously. 'Oh, but I am— sick of you. What's it to be?'

'Oh, all right,' declared Celia peevishly, and added nastily: 'I don't see why you should have it all your own way just because there's a baron in your family.'

'I've got his red hair,' Jenny pointed out, 'and his nasty temper.'

The day was long and hot and tiring; the cases ran over their times and small complications cropped up which no one could have foreseen; consequently by the end of the morning's list the surgeons were a little edgy, the housemen ravenous because they hadn't had a coffee break, and the nurses' dinnertime hopelessly late. Jenny saw the last case out of theatre, sent as many nurses as she could spare to their meal, drank a hasty cup of tea with the surgeons, and aided by the one nurse she had kept back, started on getting ready for the afternoon's list. Her staff nurse would be back in time to scrub for the first case, and the list was a straightforward one. She might even have time to eat a sandwich and have another cup of tea.

She did, while Staff took the cholestectomy, and as she made her hasty meal she wrote up the books and then put the rest of the paper work on one side before going into theatre to scrub for the rest of the list. They were finished by five o'clock, but there was still the desk work to get through. Celia, with a much shorter list, had already gone off duty, and Jenny sat in her office, writing swiftly in her rather wild handwriting, one ear cocked at the various familiar sounds coming from the theatre unit. She had two nurses on now, and a part-time staff nurse coming on duty at six o'clock. With luck, she would be finished by then.

It was too late to go out by the time she got off duty, and besides, she was tired; she took a bath and put on slacks and blouse and went to her supper, then sat around in the Sisters' sitting room, talking over the inevitable cups of tea. She was on the point of going to her bed when Miss Mellow arrived to request her presence in the telephone box in the hall. She spoke grudgingly, for she disliked what she called running messages, and she disliked Jenny too, partly because she was a pretty girl and partly because she came from that class of society which Miss Mellow always referred to as They. Jenny, who didn't like Miss Mellow either but had the good manners not to show it, thanked her nicely and went without haste to the callbox; it would be Toby—she sighed as she picked up the receiver. But it wasn't Toby, it was Doctor Toms. His voice, as mild as usual but carrying a note of urgency, surprised her. He wanted her at Dimworth. Miss Creed was ill and was asking for her.

'Now?' asked Jenny.

'Yes, my dear. Your aunt is very insistent that you should come.'

'Those headaches!' she exclaimed, remembering.

'Very severe—I want her to be seen by a specialist, but she says she'll do nothing until you're here.'

'Blackouts?' asked Jenny.

'Two today—probably she's had others and has told no one.'

Jenny glanced at her watch. 'I'll come at once, just as soon as I can fix things here. Will you ask someone to leave the side door open please—I ought to be with you by two o'clock.'

'Good girl! I shall be here, Jenny, with your aunt.'

She rang off and raced out of the home and across to the hospital. Night Super would be on duty by now, but heaven knew how far she had got with her first round. Jenny took five precious minutes tracking her down, and ran her to earth at last in the children's ward, where she held a hurried whispered conversation with her. Mrs Dent was a sensible, kindly woman, who listened without interruption before saying that of course Jenny must go at once and she would see that all the right people were informed in the morning. She even asked Jenny if she had enough money and if she would like a hot drink before she went. Jenny said yes, thank you and no, thank you with real gratitude and went back through the quiet hospital to her room, to fling clothes into a bag, explain her sudden departure to Celia, and go to the car park behind the hospital where she kept the Morgan.

She thanked heaven silently as she turned into the almost empty street that she had filled up on her way into London; there was enough petrol in the tank to get her to Dimworth. It was getting on for eleven o'clock by now, but once clear of London she made good time on the motorway; the clock tower bell chimed two as she stopped the car outside the private wing of the house. There was a light showing through the transom over the side door, and when she turned the handle, it opened silently under her hand. She stopped to bolt it before running up the stairs and along the corridor to her aunt's room. The door was slightly open and when she pushed it wide she saw Doctor Toms there, sitting in an arm-chair by the bed. He got up when she went in, but before he could speak Aunt Bess, her commanding voice a mere thread of hesitating sound, spoke.

'Jenny! You made good time. Don't let Doctor Toms frighten you. All this fuss about a headache...'

Jenny went to the bed and looked down at her aunt. She didn't like what she saw. Her aunt had looked off colour when she had left only two days earlier, but now she looked ill; her breathing was bad, her colour ghastly, and the pupils of her pale blue eyes were fixed and small. All the same, the lady of the house hadn't lost any of her fire. She spoke now in a snappy voice. 'Doctor Toms wants me to be seen by some puffed-up professor or other—he happens to be staying with him. I won't hear of it.'

'Why not, Aunt Bess?'

'He's a foreigner for a start,' Miss Creed's voice was slightly slurred. 'He's bound to be too big for his boots and make something out of nothing and then charge me a small fortune.'

Jenny had perched on the bed beside her aunt. Now she took one of the hands lying idle on the coverlet and held it between her own. 'Look,' she said persuasively, 'why not let this man take a look at you? If you don't like him you can say so and then you need not see him again—and as for the small fortune, you know quite well that you could pay a dozen professors and hardly notice it.' She lifted her aunt's hand up to her cheek for a moment. 'To please me?' she coaxed.

'Oh, very well,' agreed her aunt grumpily. 'You're just like your mother, she could charm water from a stone. But mind you, if I don't like him, I shall tell him so.' She stared at Jenny for a moment and added in a confused way: 'I don't feel very well, Jenny.'

'No, I know, my dear, but you will feel better, I promise you, and I'll stay with you. Now will you rest for a little while? I'm going to talk to Doctor Toms for a few minutes and then I'll come back and sit with you.'

Miss Creed nodded, seeing nothing unusual in the fact that someone should forgo their night's sleep in order to keep her company; she wasn't a selfish woman, but she had been used to having her own way and people to carry out her wishes without question for so long that the idea that it might be inconvenient for them to do so never crossed her mind.

Jenny waited until her aunt had closed her eyes and then followed the doctor out of the room, closing the door softly for her aunt had sharp ears.

'She's ill, isn't she?' she whispered, and when the doctor nodded. 'Can you get this professor quickly?'

Doctor Toms nodded again. 'By sheer good fortune he happens to be spending some days with me—we've been friends for some years and he has been lecturing at Bristol; he still has several lectures to give, so he won't be going back for a week or so.'

'Back where?'

'Holland. He's Dutch.'

Jenny frowned, her mind vaguely filled with windmills, canals and bottles of gin. 'Oh—Is he all right? Clever, I mean.'

'Brilliant,' said Doctor Toms. 'You know what I suspect your aunt has?'

'Subdural haematoma,' hazarded Jenny.

He looked surprised and then said: 'Of course you come across them pretty often. I'm not sure, of course, that's why I would like Professor van Draak te Solendijk to see her.'

Jenny's eyes opened very wide. 'Good grief, what a frightful name!'

The doctor smiled faintly. 'Everyone calls him van Draak.'

'Thank goodness for that. Aunt may not like him.'

Her companion smiled again. 'I fancy she will. Now I must get back home. I'll be here round about nine o'clock in the morning, but telephone if you're worried. What about your sleep?'

'I'll doze and get Florrie up between six and seven—that'll give me a chance to have a bath and breakfast.' She smiled at him. 'Thanks for letting me know, Doctor Toms. Poor Aunt Bess, we must get her better.'

Her aunt was dozing restlessly when she went back into the room. Jenny settled herself in a chair, kicking off her shoes and arranging the table lamp so that it didn't disturb the bed's occupant. She was hungry and longed for a cup of tea, but she would have to wait for it. She had no intention of disturbing Florrie or anyone else at that hour. They must have had a busy, worrying time of it—besides, she had told Aunt Bess that she would stay with her. She settled herself as comfortably as possible and prepared to sit out the rest of the night.

CHAPTER TWO

MISS CREED SEEMED a little better in the morning, but Jenny, making her ready for the day, wasn't too happy about her, but there were things she had to do. She left Aunt Bess in Florrie's capable hands and went away to unpack her things, have a bath and change her clothes. Doctor Toms arrived just as she was finished breakfast and took her back upstairs with him while he examined his patient again, made a few non-committal remarks which only served to make her snort indignantly and then took Jenny aside to explain worriedly that there was an urgent maternity case he had to go to, but that the professor would be over at the earliest possible moment on his return from Yeovil hospital where he had been delivering a series of lectures to postgraduates. He went away then, warning Jenny that it seemed very likely that her aunt would have to go to hospital herself.

Jenny set about making her aunt as comfortable as possible while she kept an ever watchful eye on her condition. There was no dramatic change, but certainly it was deteriorating steadily. Soon after one o'clock Florrie came to relieve her for her lunch, and stayed while Jenny did a brisk round of the old house, making sure that everything was ready for the visitors. The clock tower chimed twice as she went through the door in the entrance hall and up the circular stairs which led to the lobby on the next floor, and the private wing.

There was someone in the lobby and the small apartment seemed crowded by reason of the vast size of the man standing there, and he wasn't only large, but tall too, with iron-grey hair and bright blue eyes, and although he wasn't young he was nonetheless handsome. Jenny spared a second to register that fact before saying pleasantly:

'I think you must have missed your way; this leads to the private part of the house.'

She was affronted by his cool: 'I am well aware of that, young lady—perhaps you would tell whoever is looking after Miss Creed that I am here. Professor van Draak.'

'Te Solendijk,' added Jenny, who had a splendid memory for names. 'I'm looking after her, I'm her niece, Janet Wren, so perhaps you'll tell me anything I should know when you've seen her—treatment and so on,' she pointed out kindly, for he looked so surprised.

His thick eyebrows lifted. 'I hardly think I need to discuss these things with you, Miss...er...it is surely not your business.'

He had a deep voice, probably a delight to listen to when he was in a good mood, which he was not, Jenny decided. She turned her head to look out of the window at the small groups of people coming along the drive towards the entrance and spoke over her shoulder. 'Of course it's my business; Miss Creed is my aunt and I shall be nursing her. You have no reason to be so cross, you know.'

He stared down his arrogant nose at her. 'I am not cross, young lady. I do not allow my feelings to take control of me at any time.'

Her eyes widened. 'You poor soul,' she exclaimed warmly, 'it must be like walking about in a plastic bag!'

He didn't smile, although his eyes gleamed beneath their

heavy lids. 'You are foolish, Miss Wren, for in that case I should be dead.'

'That's what I meant.' She delivered this telling shot with a sweet smile and opened the door. 'If you would come with me, Professor…'

He stalked down the corridor beside her, making no attempt to speak, and Jenny, keeping up as best she could, was quite relieved when they reached her aunt's room. At the door, before she opened it, he said evenly: 'You do understand that Doctor Toms was unable to come with me—it is a little unusual…'

'Not to worry,' Jenny told him cheerfully, 'he's an old family friend, you know. Aunt Bess won't mind,' she paused, 'unless you do?'

'It is usual for the patients' own doctor to be present,' he pointed out in his almost faultless English. 'I am a foreigner—your aunt…'

'Oh, don't worry about that.' She spoke reassuringly. 'She doesn't like foreigners as a rule, but I expect she'll like you.'

She was about to open the door when his hand came down on hers, preventing her. 'Why do you say that?'

She smiled at him, wishing he didn't look so unfriendly. 'You look the part,' she told him, and when he took his hand away, opened the door.

Florrie, with a few urgent whispers to Jenny, went away, and Miss Creed said sharply from the bed: 'Jenny? Where have you been? And when is that foreigner coming?'

'He's here now,' said the Professor, his manner so changed that Jenny looked at him in surprise. He didn't look angry and withdrawn any more, but calm and assured, a rock for any patient to lean upon and pour out their symptoms. His voice was gentle too and although nothing could alter the masterful angle of his nose, his manner was such to win the confidence of the most cantankerous of patients. He had walked across the room, to stand by the bed in full view of his patient while Jenny introduced him, returning Miss Creed's fierce stare with a mild look which Jenny found hard to believe.

'You will forgive me,' said the Professor suavely, 'that I should come in this fashion without our mutual friend Doctor Toms. I believe he has explained the circumstances to Miss... er...' He paused and looked enquiringly at Jenny, who gave him a stony stare and didn't utter a sound; if he wanted to call her Miss Er for the rest of their acquaintance, then let him! She got her own back presently, though.

'Doctor Toms has told Professor van Draak—oh, dear what a very long name—te Solendijk all about you, Aunt Bess. Do you want me to stay?'

Two pairs of blue eyes were turned upon her, two mouths, firm to the point of stubbornness, snapped: 'Of course.' They should get on famously, the pair of them, thought Jenny, casting her own eyes meekly downwards.

The Professor took his time; he was not to be hurried by Miss Creed's voice, bossy still though weak and slurred, telling him what to do and what not to do. When at length he was finished, she snapped: 'Well, what's the matter with me? Or is it just a headache—though I daresay you'll make the most of it, whatever it is.'

The Professor ignored that, straightening himself slowly and eyeing her with calm. 'Yes, it is a headache, but that is only a symptom of its cause. I should like to operate on you, Miss Creed. Would you go into hospital?'

'No. To be mauled about and pay hundreds of pounds for something an aspirin will cure.'

He said impassively: 'I'm afraid aspirin won't cure this headache.' He gave her a long, considered look and she stared back at him defiantly, although it obviously needed an effort; Aunt Bess was pushing herself to her limit. He went on deliberately: 'If I don't operate, Miss Creed, you will die.'

'Plain speaking.'

'I don't think you will listen to anything else. I shouldn't myself.'

'You will tell me exactly what I have wrong with me and what my chances of living are.'

'Certainly. You wish Miss…?'

'Er,' murmured Jenny helpfully. 'I'm a nurse and I shall be looking after my aunt, Professor van Draak.'

'Ah, yes—just so. Then I will explain.'

Which he did very nicely; a minute haemorrhage in the brain, at present only causing severe headaches; difficulty with speech, with breathing, blackouts…'You will have had those, of course?' he asked offhand, and nodded when Aunt Bess said quite meekly that yes, she had had several. 'I shall find the site of the haemorrhage,' said the Professor, not boastfully but as a man who was quite sure that he would, 'repair it, and provided you do exactly as you are told, you will be as good as new within a very short space of time.'

Miss Creed considered his words. 'It sounds reasonable enough,' she said drowsily, 'but I'm too tired to decide today—come and see me tomorrow.'

He put his handsome head on one side, contemplating her. 'I should like to operate tonight,' he told her calmly.

The lined, elderly face on the pillow lost some of its firmness. 'Tonight?'

He nodded. 'The sooner the better. I can arrange through Doctor Toms to have the use of the theatre at Cowper's,' the local cottage hospital and not so very far away. 'You would have to remain there as a patient, but I promise you that the moment you are fit enough to move, you shall return here.'

'Jenny?' Miss Creed suddenly sounded very elderly indeed. 'What shall I do, Jenny?'

'Just what the Professor asks, Aunt Bess,' Jenny had been standing at the bedside, opposite the Professor, but she had taken no part in the conversation. Now she came a little nearer. 'Doctor Toms says that Professor van Draak is a brilliant man, and you know you will only have the best—besides,' she went on cunningly, 'you'll be as right as a trivet by the time Oliver comes to stay.' Which wasn't quite true, but she judged that a small fib was justified in the circumstances.

She watched her aunt thinking about it and nobody spoke until Miss Creed said: 'Get on with it, then.' Her voice was suddenly strong and autocratic. 'And be sure and make a good job of it.'

The Professor assured her levelly that he would do just that, adding: 'Might I have a few words with Miss...your niece? Perhaps someone could be fetched to sit with you for a short time.'

'Do what you like,' said Miss Creed rudely. 'I can see that you're a man who always wants his own way. Jenny, don't let him flatten you.'

As they walked back along the corridor, Jenny said: 'Aunt Bess doesn't feel well...' and was cut short by his patient: 'My dear young lady, no one with a subdural haemorrhage feels well, and if you are referring to her remark that you should not allow me to flatten you, I rather imagine that there would be little possibility of that.'

She stopped so suddenly that he, walking a little behind her and to one side, bumped into her and was forced to catch her by the shoulders to steady her. She brushed him away with a wave of one beautifully kept hand. 'I can't imagine why you are so rude, Professor. Do you dislike the English, or just women? Whichever it is, isn't going to help Aunt Bess very much.'

'My dear Miss...'

'Look,' she interrupted him impatiently, 'the name's Wren—quite easy and so much nicer than Er.'

He laughed then, and for the first time she realised with a little shock that when he laughed he looked quite different—years younger; someone she would like to know... She squashed the thought at once and prompted: 'You were saying?'

He had stopped laughing and was looking down his nose again, holding the door open for her at the head of the little staircase. 'Merely that I do not dislike the English, nor, for that matter, women. I hope your curiosity is satisfied?'

'Pooh!' exclaimed Jenny, and ran down the stairs very fast, but despite his size, he was at the bottom only inches behind her, to open the door and usher her politely into the entrance hall. 'Where can we talk?' he asked abruptly.

She led the way through the small groups of people wandering round, out of the door and turned down a little flagged path which led to the tiny church adjacent to the house. Through the churchyard gate, among the ancient tombstones, she said: 'Here.'

Rather to her surprise he remarked: 'A peaceful and quite beautiful spot,' and then leaned himself against the old grey walls of the church, crossed his elegantly shod feet, dug his hands into his jacket pockets and went on: 'Your aunt is very ill; the thing is to get to the haemorrhage before it does any further damage; any moment it could worsen, although somehow I don't think it will, but we mustn't take chances. If I can operate quickly she has a very good chance of recovery.' He glanced at the paper thin gold watch on his wrist. 'It is now three o'clock. I have already spoken to Cowper's; the theatre is available at six o'clock. Doctor Toms will be there, of course, and I have an excellent anaesthetist standing by as well as an extremely able assistant. Will you telephone for an ambulance and bring Miss Creed to the hospital at once? I presume that you will stay there until the operation is over.'

'Of course. I must see Mrs Thorpe—the vicar's wife, you know, and our housekeeper...' Jenny was half talking to herself and he looked amused. 'The ambulance first, of course, but don't I have to have your authority for that?'

'I talked to them a short time ago; they are more or less expecting a call for an urgent case, so there should be no difficulty.'

She eyed him curiously. 'You were so sure—you had everything arranged.'

'I like to be prepared—besides, I respect Doctor Toms' judgment, I merely confirmed what he strongly suspected.'

She said inanely: 'Yes, well... I suppose so. Have you a car here?'

He nodded in the direction of a magnificent Panther J72 drawn up on the gravel sweep outside the entrance and she opened her eyes wide. 'Is that yours? I thought...that is, I...'

'An unlikely car for a not-so-young Dutchman.' He smiled faintly.

'No—yes—I mean, she's a beauty.' She was suddenly a little breathless. 'And you're not even middle-aged!'

'Forty, as near as not—and you, Miss Wren?'

'Me? I'm twenty-five.' She hadn't meant to tell him that. 'Where shall I take Aunt Bess?'

'They will be expecting her. The usual routine before operation—nothing to eat or drink—but of course you know that.' They were walking towards his car as he spoke and after the briefest of goodbyes, Jenny went indoors to telephone and then see Florrie and Mrs Thorpe. There was no time to lose, but even in her haste she found herself wishing that she could have spared a moment to watch the Professor drive off his splendid car.

Florrie grasped the situation within minutes; Jenny knew that she would be able to leave everything in her capable hands. The same couldn't be said for Mrs Thorpe, who wasted precious minutes exclaiming: 'There, I only said to Mr Thorpe yesterday,' and 'Well, I never,' and 'It's to be hoped—' She would have gone on for some time in this tiresome manner if Jenny hadn't cut her politely short, begged her to organise the visitors on the following afternoon and arrange for Baxter to sell tickets again.

'Probably I shall be back by then, Mrs Thorpe, but I'll let you know. Mrs Trott'—Trott was the elderly lodgekeeper-cum-handyman—'said she would help out if it was necessary at any time, and I'm sure she will—it will only be for a day or two while I'm with my aunt.'

Mrs Thorpe looked important. 'Now, don't worry about anything, Jenny, I'll see to everything.' Her bosom swelled alarmingly. 'None of us would dream of letting Miss Creed down.'

Jenny thanked her nicely, glad that her aunt couldn't hear her doing it, for she had no opinion at all of the vicar's wife, although she used that lady's services quite unscrupulously whenever it suited her to do so, and hurried back to her aunt's room. Miss Creed hadn't been told that she would be leaving almost immediately; the ambulance Jenny had telephoned for would be arriving very shortly. She sent the devoted Florrie away, found an overnight bag, rammed in what she considered necessary for her aunt's comfort and approached the bed.

Aunt Bess had her eyes shut, but she spoke immediately in a slurred voice. 'Don't imagine that I don't know that you're arranging something behind my back, Jenny, because I'm perfectly aware of it.'

'Yes, Aunt Bess, I'm sure you are, but it's nothing you haven't been consulted about. The Professor wants you in hospital—he told you that just now—and I'm packing your bag to take with you. The ambulance will be here in a few minutes.'

'I'm perfectly able...' began Miss Creed.

'No, dear, you're not—not just at present. I'm coming with you and I shall stay for a bit. Everything's arranged, so there's no need for you to worry about a thing.'

'I'm not worried,' stated her aunt drowsily. 'You're sure that that enormous man knows what he's doing?'

'Yes, Aunt, I am.' Jenny, to her own surprise, discovered that she really was sure about that, which seemed a little silly considering that she had never seen him operate.

And hours later, when he came straight from theatre, still in his green smock and trousers, his grey hair hidden by his cap, to find her in Sister's office, waiting, she was just as sure.

He said without preamble: 'Your aunt will be all right. She's very fit for her age and should make a good recovery, although she will have to take reasonable care. Do you want the details?'

'Please.'

He gave them at some length and then said: 'Miss Creed should regain consciousness shortly. She will want to see you, will she not? You are prepared to stay?'

'Of course. They've very kindly arranged for the night.'

'Good. I'll be around for a while and I shall be in early in the morning. Doctor Toms had to go straight from theatre. He's quite satisfied.'

She looked at him rather shyly. 'Thank you, Professor van Draak, I'm very grateful,' and felt snubbed when he replied coldly: 'You have no need to be; it is my work.' He opened the door, preparatory to leaving. 'Someone will fetch you very shortly.'

He had gone, leaving her feeling that even if he didn't like her, and it seemed that he didn't, he might have been a little less terse. But he hadn't been terse with Aunt Bess, he had been kind and patient and moreover clever enough to see exactly how contrary she was, and deal with it in the only way she would accept. Jenny had seen her aunt make mincemeat of those who crossed her will too many times not to know that she was the last person to listen to cajoling or persuasion. She got to her feet and walked up and down the little room. Well, the man was a professor of surgery; presumably professors had that little extra something that set them above the rest. She stopped in front of a mirror and poked at her hair in an absent-minded fashion. All the same, he was arrogant and much too indifferent in his manner. She wondered if he were married and if so, if he were happy, although it was no business of hers. Only it had been providential that he happened to be staying with Doctor Toms, for Cowpers, excellent though it was was too small to have consultants attached to its staff and it would have meant her aunt travelling miles to Bristol or Poole or Southampton. As it was he had been allowed to make use of the small hospital's theatre. She had noticed that he was known to the staff there, too. Possibly he had stayed with Doctor Toms before and come to know the staff there—she would have to ask Doctor Toms.

A nurse came to fetch her then and she went along to the back of the hospital, where the three private rooms were. Miss Creed was in the first of these, surrounded by a variety of equipment, looking very shrunken and frail. She opened her eyes as Jenny went in, smiled a little and closed them again, but presently she said in a thread of a voice: 'All over?'

Jenny sat down by the bed. She had been keeping a tight check on her feelings, for Aunt Bess loathed emotion or tears. Now she could have wept with sheer relief, but she managed a steady: 'Yes, my dear, and very satisfactory, too,' aware as she said it that the Professor had come in silently and was standing behind her. He said something low-voiced to the nurse and went to the foot of the bed. Miss Creed opened her eyes again. 'Pleased with your handiwork?' she asked in a woolly voice.

'Yes, I am, Miss Creed, and you will be too in a very short time. Nurse is going to give you an injection and I should like you to go to sleep again.'

His patient submitted an arm. 'No choice,' she muttered, and then: 'Don't go, Jenny.'

'No, Aunt Bess, I'll be here when you wake.'

So she sat in the chair through the night's long hours, fortified by cups of strong tea the nurses brought her from time to time, trying to keep awake in case Aunt Bess should wake and want her. But her aunt slept on and towards morning Jenny let her heavy lids drop over her tired eyes and dozed herself, to be wakened gently by the Professor's hand on her shoulder, and his voice, very quiet in her ear. 'Your aunt's regaining consciousness.' And when she sat up, her copper head tousled and no make-up left on her face at all, he whispered, 'You're tired. You will go to bed when your aunt has spoken to you; I would send you away now, but of course she won't remember those few brief moments directly after the operation. You can return later on.' And when she would have protested: 'They will let you have a bed here for a few hours.'

It had been worth the long tedious wait. Aunt Bess opened her eyes and spoke in a normal voice. 'Good girl,' and then: 'Where's that man?'

'Here,' answered the Professor quietly. 'Everything is quite satisfactory, Miss Creed. I want you to sleep as much as you can. Jenny must go to bed now, she has been up all night.'

'We're fond of each other,' said Aunt Bess in a quite strong voice. 'I'd do the same for her. But send her to bed, by all means.' Her voice faded a little and then revived. 'You will anyway, whatever I say.'

'Yes. She shall come back when she has rested; you will feel more like talking then.'

Jenny found herself whisked away to an empty room in the pleasant nurses' home adjoining the hospital. She wasn't sure of the time, and she was too tired to care. She had a bath, drank the tea one of the nurses brought her, and fell into bed, asleep the moment her head touched the pillow.

She was wakened by one of the day Sisters. 'Your aunt is asking for you,' she was told. 'I'm sorry to wake you like this, but she's being a little difficult—you could come?'

Jenny shook the sleep from her head. 'Yes, of course. Is she worse?'

'No—just unable to settle and not very operative. Here's a dressing gown and slippers—you don't mind? We can go through the passage.'

Jenny wrapped herself in the voluminous garment, several sizes too big for her, and thrust her feet into equally large slippers and allowed herself to be led through the covered way to the hospital. 'What's the time?' she asked, half way there.

'Not quite midday. If you could persuade your aunt to have an injection... We'll bring you a light meal and you could go to sleep again. You must be worn out.'

'I'm fine,' declared Jenny sturdily, and stifled a yawn as she lifted dark, delicately arched brows at the sound of her aunt's voice, raised in wrath.

And indeed she was in an ill humour; flushed as well, sitting up against her pillows, her blue eyes brilliant under her bandaged head. 'There you are!' she cried imperiously. 'And where have you been, may I ask—leaving me to these silly girls? And where's that foreigner? I thought he was here to look after me? Heaven knows I shall be expected to pay him a king's ransom.'

Jenny perched beside the bed. 'I was having a nap, Aunt Bess—I sat with you during the night and I was a bit sleepy. And Professor van Draak was here for most of the night too, he must have been tired after operating. What's worrying you, Aunt?'

Miss Creed moved her head restlessly. 'I want to go home,' she stated. 'I'm sick and tired of these people, all shouting at me to have an injection; I do not want to sleep.'

Jenny sighed soundlessly. 'Look, dear, you've had an operation and of course you don't feel quite the thing, and until you have a nice long sleep you won't feel much better. We know you don't feel sleepy, but the injection will send you off in no time...'

'And what's he doing here?' interrupted Miss Creed, looking past Jenny's shoulder.

The Professor had loomed up beside Jenny. He said now in his calm way: 'I've come to give you your injection, Miss Creed—your niece has explained why you should have it.' He nodded to Jenny to hold her Aunt's arm firmly and slid the needle in without further ado.

'I'm not accustomed to being treated in this manner,' his patient began angrily. 'I like my own way...'

'And so do I,' agreed the Professor pleasantly. 'You will feel much more yourself when you wake up—tired and not inclined to do much, but much more comfortable in your head.'

'Bah...' began Aunt Bess, the lids falling over her tired eyes, 'I don't believe...'

Jenny heaved a sigh of relief. 'Poor dear, she must be feeling ghastly,' she said softly, and went on sitting where she was, overcome by tiredness once more. She yawned hugely, pushed up the sleeves of the ridiculous dressing gown and lifted her arms to sweep back her tide of hair, hanging all over the place. She would have gone to sleep then and there if the Professor hadn't said in a cold voice, 'Go back to your bed, Miss Wren. I see that you are still in need of sleep.' His tone was so very icy that she opened her eyes to take a look at him. His face looked icy too, the brows drawn together in a frown.

'Fallen down on the job, have I?' she asked pertly, tiredness forgotten for the moment in a wish to annoy him. He had been up most of the night too, but he didn't look as though he had; he was probably one of those iron-willed men who didn't allow himself to feel tired or happy or sad or anything else... She opened her mouth to tell him so, but yawned instead and fell asleep, sitting upright, swaying a little.

The Professor looked more annoyed than ever. 'Will you open the door, Nurse?' he asked the student left to sit with Miss Creed, and swept Jenny up into his arms as though she were a tiresome child and carried her back down the covered passage, to put her gently on her bed and pull the blanket over her. Jenny, dead to the world, rolled over. If she had been awake to hear his: 'Troublesome girl, to plague me so,' uttered in a cold voice, she would most certainly have answered him with spirit. As it was she gave a delicate snore.

CHAPTER THREE

JENNY DIDN'T WAKE until almost four o'clock and then lay for a few minutes gathering her still sleepy wits. She supposed she should get up; she had had another three hours' sleep and possibly, if her aunt was better, she would be able to go back to Dimworth later on in the evening.

But when she found her way to Aunt Bess's room presently, she found Sister there once more, and as she stood in the doorway, wondering if she should go in or not, she was lifted neatly out of the way by the Professor, who took no notice of her at all, but went straight to the bedside, where he bent over Miss Creed, murmuring to Sister with an infuriating softness, so that Jenny, very worried by now, couldn't hear a word. She was on the point of asking what was the matter when he spoke without turning his head. 'Come in, Miss Wren. I have something to say to you.'

She went to stand by him, looking first at his face and then at her aunt's, calm and unconscious. The look on her face caused him to say quickly: 'No need to get alarmed; your aunt has had a relapse. We're going to give her some more blood and change the electrolytes—I think that should put things right. She hasn't been as quiet as she should.'

'No danger?' asked Jenny anxiously.

'I think not.' He gave her a considered look and she said at once:

'May I stay here with her? I've had a good sleep, perhaps if I'm here when she comes round, I could persuade her to take things easy for a few days. She's rather strong-willed.'

He smiled faintly. 'Sister has had quite a difficult time of it this afternoon, I'm sure she will be glad of your help.' He glanced across the bed to where Sister stood. 'Perhaps Miss Wren could have a meal now and relieve you and nurse? I see no reason why she shouldn't sit up with her aunt, she has had a good rest.'

Jenny's charming bosom swelled with indignation. A good rest, indeed! Two periods of sleep of barely three hours on top of a night sitting up in a chair after driving down from London—the man wasn't only made of iron himself, he expected everyone else to be the same. She was willing to stay up for an endless succession of nights for Aunt Bess, she conceded illogically, but he assumed too much. She was in two minds to refuse a meal, just to show her independence, but she would probably be famished if she did. She said, outwardly meek, 'I'll be glad to do that, Sister, if you agree to it.'

So she was given her meal and installed in a chair by Aunt Bess's bed, primed with instructions and with the promise of relief for half an hour round about midnight. There wasn't much chance to sit down, though, what with half-hourly observations and keeping an eye on the drips. Adjusting them, Jenny thought that when her aunt wakened, she would want to know about those and probably do her best to remove them. Marking up her charts neatly, she sincerely hoped not.

The evening passed quietly. Aunt Bess showed no sign of rousing. The Professor arrived again about nine o'clock, this time with Doctor Toms, examined his patient, nodded distantly to Jenny and went again.

'And good riddance,' declared Jenny as the door shut quietly behind him, and then jumped visibly as it opened again. 'I heard that,' declared the Professor in his turn.

The hospital was quiet; the nights usually were, for casualties went to Yeovil and the patients, for the most part, slept for the greater part of the night. The night staff, small but efficient, managed very well, calling up the day nurses if anything dire occurred. About midnight Night Sister put her head round the door. 'Everything OK?' She smiled in acknowledgement of Jenny's nod and whispered: 'Someone will relieve you in a few minutes,' and went her soft-footed way, to be followed almost at once by a student nurse. Jenny ate a hurried meal and went back once more and the nurse, whispering that the patient hadn't stirred, crept away.

It was two o'clock in the morning, just as Jenny was changing a drip, that her aunt opened her eyes and said in a normal voice 'You should be in bed,' and then: 'I feel a great deal better.'

'Good,' said Jenny, 'and so you will if you stay very quiet, Aunt Bess. And I've been to bed, so don't bother about me.' She smiled down at her aunt, trying to be matter-of-fact and casual, because Aunt Bess hated tears or a display of emotion. 'How about a drink?'

She was giving it when the Professor came silently into the room, smiled at his patient and put out a hand for the charts.

He studied them carefully, grunted his approval and gave them back to Jenny without looking at her. 'You're better,' he told Aunt Bess, 'well enough for me to explain why you must lie quiet for a little longer.' And he explained very simply, in a quiet voice before adding: 'I should like you to go to sleep again now, but if you find that impossible will you lie still and relax, then there will be no need to give you another injection at present. Your niece will prop you up a little more, I think...'

'Don't you go to bed either?' asked Aunt Bess.

'Oh, certainly.' He smiled again and strolled to the door. 'I'll be in to see you again after breakfast.' His hand was on the door handle when he said: 'Miss Wren, will you hand me the charts? There are one or two things I should like to alter. Sister will return them presently.' He barely glanced at her and she supposed that she deserved it.

Aunt Bess went to sleep after that, remarking with some of her old tartness that Jenny and the Professor didn't seem to be on the best of terms, and Jenny, sitting in her chair once more, trying to keep awake for the last hours of the night, couldn't help but agree with her.

She was in bed and asleep very soon after the day staff came on duty, so that she missed Professor van Draak's visits in the morning, and in the afternoon he brought Sister with him, just as though Jenny were a visitor, and waited pointedly until she had gone out of the room before he examined her aunt. However, he joined her presently in the corridor, reassured her as to her aunt's condition, gave it as his opinion that she was now out of danger, and suggested that there was no need for Jenny to stay the night. 'I shall be passing Dimworth as I return to Doctor Toms,' he remarked without much warmth. 'I could give you a lift.'

It would have been nice to have refused him, but she hadn't much choice; there would be no one free at Dimworth to fetch her and she had no intention of telephoning Toby. She thanked him with a chilliness to equal his own and went back to sit with Aunt Bess.

Her aunt didn't seem to mind her going—indeed, she began to give a great number of messages, repeated several times in a muddled fashion, and added a list as long as her arm of tasks to be done at Dimworth, falling asleep in the middle of it. Jenny kissed the tired, still determined face and went out to where the Professor would be waiting for her. He got out and opened the car door for her and she had barely settled in her seat before he was driving away.

Jenny, having difficulty with her safety belt, said crossly: 'You don't like me at all, do you, Professor?' and was furious at his laugh.

It was a nasty laugh, full of mockery and the wrong kind of amusement, and his: 'My dear girl, you flatter yourself, and me too—I have no interest in you at all, although to be quite honest I must admit that I haven't much time for tart young women with red hair.'

'I expect you pride yourself on being plain-spoken,' said Jenny sweetly. 'I call it rude. Just by way of interest, what kind of girl do you like?'

He allowed the car to slow and shot a sidelong glance at her. 'Tall, calm, sweet-tempered—with good looks, of course; fair hair, blue eyes, a pleasant voice...'

'A cardboard creature,' cried Jenny, 'and even if you did find her, she'd be a dead bore as a wife.' A thought struck her. 'Have you found her? Perhaps you're married.'

'What an impertinent girl you are.' He spoke quite pleasantly. 'No, I am not married. When do you intend to visit your aunt again?'

A neat snub, if ever there was one. 'I'll drive over after breakfast. When do you return to Holland?'

'Wishful thinking?' he enquired. 'When your aunt is recovered.'

Jenny shifted in her seat, uncomfortably aware that she hadn't expressed nearly enough gratitude. 'Oh no...well, I'd like to thank you for what you've done for Aunt Bess. I know you saved her life and I'm deeply grateful—I hope it hasn't spoilt your holiday here.'

It was a nice little speech which he completely ruined. 'I get paid for it, you know,' he reminded her smoothly, 'and I haven't been on holiday.'

Jenny exploded with temper. 'You're impossible! We're right back where we started, aren't we? I've never met... You have no need to...' She drew a deep breath and swallowed the temper. 'What a lovely day it is,' she observed brightly.

The Professor's eyes gleamed momentarily and a muscle twitched at the corner of his firm mouth as he agreed suavely before launching into a businesslike discussion upon Miss Creed's illness. And at the house he refused her polite invitation to come in for a drink, and without pretending an excuse either.

She dismissed him from her thoughts the moment she was in the house, and indeed forgot about him entirely while she listened to Florrie's account of what had been happening during her absence—nothing much, it seemed. A good attendance on both days; they had run out of homemade jam; Mrs Thorpe had been far too bossy and annoyed Grimshaw...

Jenny lent a sympathetic ear, made a few tactful suggestions, praised Florrie, gave an expurgated account of her aunt's illness and went round the house. The rooms which were open to the public were exactly as they should be; she checked the burglar alarm and then went along to her aunt's room to collect a few more things she might require while she was in hospital, then went out of the side door, to take a short cut through the gardens and park to the vicarage. Mrs Thorpe might have been bossy, but she was kindhearted and well-meaning. Jenny found her at home, said all that was necessary, thanked her with charm and set off to the house once more. Supper and bed would be nice.

Aunt Bess was better in the morning. Jenny, herself rested after a good night's sleep, viewed her relative's still pale face with satisfaction. The relapse had been overcome: it was now just a question of the patient doing exactly as she was told to do. And for the next few days that was just what she did, much to Jenny's surprise, mildly accepting what she described to her niece as slops—served up daintily on a tray, but still slops—and allowing the nurses to get her out of and into her bed with the minimum of fuss. Jenny was completely mystified as to her aunt's change of manner until several days after the operation when she happened to be in the room when the Professor paid his visit.

'It's the sixth day tomorrow,' her aunt pointed out when he had finished examining her. 'I've won.'

He leaned against the foot of the bed, laughing down at her. 'Not until tomorrow morning—noon, I think we decided? And how about a further three days? You suggest the amount.'

Miss Creed chuckled. 'You come here tomorrow and pay up and I'll let you know then.'

Jenny waited until he had gone, smiling charmingly at his patient and giving her nothing but a brief nod. 'What was all that about?'

Aunt Bess grinned at her. 'We had a little bet.'

Jenny's eyes opened wide. 'A bet? Aunt Bess...'

'Fifty pounds that I couldn't hold out until tomorrow on the revolting food I'm forced to eat and twenty on the side that I wouldn't do exactly as I was told about getting up and all the other tiresome things I'm forced to do.'

Jenny let out a breath. 'You mean to say he betted...he couldn't, it's not professional...he's...'

'Huh,' Aunt Bess was positively smirking, 'what's to stop him?' She said gleefully: 'I shall make it a hundred tomorrow and buy you a pretty dress with the winnings.'

It would be exactly the same as if he marched her into a shop and chose a dress off the peg and gave it to her. 'No—it's sweet of you, Aunt Bess, but I've heaps of clothes. Why don't you put it towards that dear little chest we saw in that shop in Sherbourne a few weeks ago? You said you wanted it for Oliver...'

'So I did. Clever girl—that's what I'll do. Telephone the shop tomorrow, Jenny, and tell them to send it to Dimworth. When is Oliver coming? I've forgotten.'

'Next week. Margaret telephoned this morning early. She wanted to know if they should come because you hadn't been well—Oliver's a bit noisy, she thinks.'

'What a silly young woman she is; he'll be a tonic about the place. Besides, I shall be away for part of his stay. Professor van Draak says that I should have a change—a week or two away—we'll discuss that later. Now run along, child, and see about that chest.'

So Jenny ran along, saw to the chest, kept an eye on the day's visitors, did her share of the polishing and tidying up when they had gone, and went back to the hospital in the evening. Her aunt was asleep and doing very well, Sister told her. She would be fit to go home soon, provided she did as she was told to do. Professor van Draak would decide exactly when. Jenny nodded, dropped a kiss on the sleeping Miss Creed's cheek and went out to where the Morgan was parked.

It was overshadowed by the Panther de Ville, with the Professor at its wheel, looking disagreeable. 'I don't seem to have seen you for some time,' he commented as he got out to stand beside her.

'Nice for you,' observed Jenny flippantly. 'Aunt Bess is much better, isn't she?'

'Yes.'

She waited for him to say something else, but evidently he wasn't wasting his breath. 'You've been betting with her,' she said severely. 'I've never heard such nonsense.'

His smile made her wish that they liked each other. 'But it worked, did it not, Jenny Wren? Your aunt is a splendid woman but a shockingly bad patient—it was necessary to use guile.'

Jenny laughed—she hadn't done that for days. It bubbled up in a delicious trill, and the Professor stared at her as though he had only just seen her, his eyes hooded.

'When may she come home?' she asked.

'Another week, provided everything goes well. You will continue to look after her?'

'Yes.'

He nodded. 'I understand that her small nephew will be coming to stay at Dimworth. You do realise that there must be no untoward noise—no shouting—nothing to disturb her.'

'Oliver is six, but he's a very sensible little boy,' Jenny defended her nephew. 'If I explain why he has to be quiet, then he'll be quiet.'

'He has no mother?'

She thought of Margaret, who from one point of view wasn't a mother at all. 'Oh, yes, he has—she'll be coming with him.'

He stood back a little. 'Don't let me keep you. I'm sure you want to get back. Goodnight.' His voice was coolly polite.

She got into the Morgan without a word and drove away very neatly, not looking at him at all. Two can be rude, she reminded herself.

The Panther overtook her five minutes later, creeping up behind and then tearing past, giving her no more than a glimpse of an arrogant nose in a profile which ignored her. She said 'Phoo!' loudly to relieve her feelings and resisted a useless urge to overtake him in her turn.

And her temper wasn't improved at all when she found Toby waiting for her at Dimworth. He was full of helpful offers to do this and that, warnings as to her health if she didn't get enough sleep or eat enough and rounded off his remarks by reminding her that she hadn't answered any of his letters and had she thought any more about marrying him.

'No, I have not,' snapped Jenny. 'With Aunt Bess so ill and so much to do, I've had not time to think at all, and anyway, I don't want to marry you, Toby.' She added a polite 'Thank you.'

He was like a rubber ball, bouncing back whatever was said or done to him. 'Oh, well—I daresay you're tired. Is there anything I can do?'

The thought crossed her mind that the Professor wouldn't have asked; he would have known what wanted doing and done it without bothering to ask her, and then gone home and left her in peace. She said wearily: 'No, Toby—look, I've had a busy day and I'm tired.'

'You'd like me to go?' He got up out of the chair where he had been lounging. 'Suits me, old girl, I've got to be up early to go over and see that horse Mother wants me to buy.' He laughed. 'And I like my eight hours sleep, you know.'

She managed a friendly goodnight, although he had made her irritable. Such a nice young man, everyone said, and just the right husband for her, Margaret had observed on her last visit to Dimworth. Well, he might be nice, and young too, but he was too easy-going by far. Jenny went along to the kitchen, carved herself a hunk of bread and a slab of cheese and then, feeling better for her meal, went to bed.

She didn't see the Professor for two or three days. Somehow he had just been or was expected at any moment when she visited her aunt, and on two occasions he actually passed her driving back from the hospital, ignoring her on both occasions. They met eventually, face to face in the hospital's entrance and when he stood aside for her to pass she stopped in front of him. 'So there you are,' she exclaimed forthrightly. 'I was beginning to wonder if you'd gone back to Holland and forgotten to mention it to anyone.'

He allowed himself the faint glimmer of a smile. 'I overtook you just outside the village yesterday.'

She allowed her eyes to open widely and said innocently: 'Did you really? I had no idea... I should be obliged if you would let me know how my aunt is getting on. Sister passes on any news, of course, but that's not very satisfactory.'

The smile had gone, he looked down his nose at her and said austerely: 'It is unfortunate that we have missed each other just lately. I left sufficient information with Sister, or so I imagined. However, since we have met, I can tell you that Miss Creed should be well enough to return home in a day or two now. She will need a period of convalescence which presumably you will arrange and then a brief change of air—something different— a cruise would be ideal, for she would not need to exert herself in any way unless she felt like it. Someone would have to accompany her, of course. You?'

Jenny hesitated. It would mean giving up her job and her independence too, at any rate for the time being. 'Yes, of course I'll go with her if she wants me to. I'll have to go up to Queen's and see about leaving. I'm afraid they won't keep my job open.'

He wasn't very interested. 'You must do whatever you think fit,' he observed casually. 'Perhaps it would be a good idea if you arranged that while she is still in hospital.'

She agreed rather unhappily. 'Yes, I'm going to see her now. Thank you for sparing the time to see me.'

She slid past him and went along to her aunt's room, where she put on a bright face for the benefit of the invalid; entered with enthusiasm into plans for Oliver's visit, assured her aunt that it was of no consequence at all if she gave up her post at Queen's, and that nothing would be nicer than a cruise.

Only that night, in the quiet of her own room, she allowed herself the luxury of a good weep. She had expected her aunt to take it for granted that she would leave hospital and look after her—indeed, she had promised that she would, but she had expected that Toby would have understood a little how she felt about it. His: 'Oh, that's splendid news, old girl. We'll settle things when you get back from your trip, shall we? Once you're away from that place you'll realise how silly you've been hanging on so long. It isn't as if you need the money, and dash it all, everyone expects us to marry and I'm ready and willing, what more could a girl want?' had done nothing to dispel her gloom. What more did she want? she asked herself, sitting up in bed, hugging her knees. Just to be allowed to make her own life, prove that she could earn her own living, find herself a husband…someone, she told herself fiercely, who wouldn't call her old girl.

Getting Aunt Bess home wasn't as bad as Jenny had anticipated; indeed her aunt demonstrated a meekness quite unlike her usual forceful self. She was installed in a room on the ground floor so that she could, as she put it, keep an eye on things, and there had been a tremendous upheaval moving her bed and furniture from the room on the first floor. But once this was done, everyone had to admit that it was most convenient, for the new bedroom had a small sitting room leading from it and here Aunt Bess would be able to spend her days, ruling Dimworth from her chair.

She had been home three days when Oliver and his mother arrived, driving in the old-fashioned Daimler with Jamie, her father's gardener, at the wheel, for Margaret had never learnt to drive herself. She looked quite beautiful, Jenny thought, watching her get out of the car, her golden hair smooth, her expensive outfit in the exact blue of her eyes. She didn't wait for Oliver but started to walk towards Jenny, leaving him to scramble out on his own.

'How I hate the journey down!' she began, and kissed her perfunctorily on her cheek. 'But Father will insist that I have the car. Oliver gets so restless—I have quite a headache.'

Jenny murmured sympathy although she didn't feel particularly that way and turned to receive a boisterous greeting from her small relative, just as pleased to see him as he was to see her again. 'Come on in,' she invited. 'Margaret, you have your usual rooms; I've put Oliver next to me and Jamie's at the lodge. Aunt Bess is resting.' She looked inquiringly at Margaret. 'You did explain to Oliver?'

'About Aunt Bess? Oh, vaguely—he's only a little boy...'

Jenny sighed inwardly. 'Oliver, listen to me. You have to be as quiet as a mouse, because Aunt Bess hasn't been well. Presently, when you've had some lemonade, we'll go into the churchyard and I'll tell you exactly why.'

Margaret wrinkled her patrician nose. 'Oh, Jenny, must you? The churchyard, I mean.'

'It's a very pleasant place, and I must get him to understand about Aunt Bess, then he'll be good about it. Won't you, Oliver?'

They had reached the private wing by now and Jenny ushered the visitors into the sitting room where Felicity had already set the coffee tray. They were drinking it, while Oliver enjoyed his lemonade and a great many biscuits besides, when he said suddenly, 'I haven't seen Dobbs.' Dobbs was Miss Creed's chauffeur and Oliver's firm friend, and Jenny, glad of a respite from the trivial conversation she and Margaret were holding, said:

'He's in Canada, visiting his son. He'll be back in a day or two—we've all missed him dreadfully.'

'Don't ask so many questions, Oliver,' his mother begged. 'Jenny, I think I'll go to my room—is there someone to unpack for me?'

'Ethel...'

'Still here? She should have been pensioned off years ago.'

'Aunt Bess wouldn't do that, Margaret. She's been here longer than I can remember and she hasn't anywhere else to go. She does the mending and looks after Aunt Bess's clothes beautifully.'

Margaret brightened. 'Oh, does she? Good, she can look after my things.' She studied Jenny for a minute. 'Are you still working at that dreadful hospital?'

'I went up to London and resigned my job while Aunt Bess was still in hospital.' Jenny spoke quietly, still feeling unhappy about it. 'She'll need some help for a little while yet. I can always get another job.'

'I can't think why you don't marry Toby—he's so suitable...' Margaret looked her over. 'You're quite a pretty girl, you know, Jenny, and you dress very well. Don't you want to settle down?'

Jenny said no rather abruptly and asked about Margaret's health, a red herring which never failed to succeed, but Margaret had barely begun on her various little illnesses when Florrie opened the door and said in her nice cosy Somerset voice: 'The Professor's here, Miss Jenny—shall I ask him to come in here?'

Jenny frowned. He had said that he wouldn't be coming until the evening, but as usual he was doing as he pleased. 'Yes, do, Florrie—and perhaps you could send in some more coffee.'

She got to her feet as he came in and wished him a good morning and introduced Margaret. Margaret, she noted, had assumed her most beguiling air, reminding her of a Botticelli angel, and guaranteed to catch the eye of any man around. The Professor's eye was certainly caught; she gave him a few moments in which to feast his gaze before presenting Oliver.

She was a little surprised that the Professor behaved so nicely towards the little boy—indeed, his manner was that of a man entirely used to small boys, and when Oliver started to tell him about the pet rabbits he had left behind in Scotland, he listened with every sign of interest. It was Margaret who begged her son very prettily not to bore the visitor with his nonsense and then turned the conversation upon herself, while Jenny poured coffee and made what she always privately referred to as hostess murmurs. But presently when Margaret paused for breath, she asked him in businesslike tones if he had come to see her aunt, and if so, did he wish to do so at once, a remark which brought a decided twinkle to his eye.

'If it is convenient, yes. I have to go to Bristol this evening.' He looked at Margaret. 'It has been delightful meeting you,' he observed suavely, 'and I hope we may meet again before very long.'

And Jenny, watching, was aware of deep annoyance at this pretty speech; never once had he expressed a wish to see her again—on the contrary she had always had the distinct impression that he wished the reverse. It was wonderful what golden hair and blue eyes did to a man. She tossed her fiery mane over her shoulder and started for the door as he wished Oliver goodbye—in the nicest possible way, she was forced to admit.

Aunt Bess was awake and looking almost her usual self. 'You again!' she declared ungraciously. 'Heaven knows what your bill will be. I shall be forced to mortgage Dimworth...'

A remark which brought a crack of laughter from the Professor and a chuckle from Jenny. 'You share a sense of humour, at any rate,' observed Aunt Bess. 'Has Oliver arrived?'

'Yes, Aunt, he's downstairs having some lemonade.'

'Good—I'll see him when this fussing around is done with.'

She threw a look at the Professor, taking her pulse. 'What do you think of the boy? You've seen him, of course?'

'Yes. A splendid little chap—a worthy heir to Dimworth.'

His patient nodded, well pleased. 'I think so too. And his mother?'

'A very beautiful woman.' His usually cool voice held warmth.

'I'll grant you that—not a patch on Jenny here, though.'

Jenny watched his brows lift faintly and a mocking little smile curve the corners of his mouth, and went a bright pink. By dint of holding her tongue firmly between her teeth she managed to say nothing at all. His bland, 'Er—I hardly feel in a position to say anything to that,' merely added to her discomfort.

To cover it she said a trifle tartly: 'Do you want to examine Aunt Bess, or is this just a social call?'

'Both, I hope, but if you're busy...?' His voice was very bland.

She said with dignity that she wasn't and became strictly professional, addressing him—rather naughtily because she could see that it irritated him—as sir whenever she had the opportunity.

He came every day, although there was really no need now that his patient was doing so well, and it was more than coincidence that Margaret always seemed to be going in or coming out of the house when he arrived—and what more natural than that she should suggest a stroll in the gardens, or offer to show him the lily pond? Jenny, up to her eyes in visitors; getting ready for them and clearing up after them, still had time to notice that, and Aunt Bess, sitting in her great chair by the window and missing nothing, remarked with some asperity: 'Setting her cap at him, isn't she? Should have thought he would have had more sense.'

'It would be nice for Oliver,' said Jenny thoughtfully as she laboriously unpicked the knitting Miss Creed had mangled.

Her aunt gave her a long look she didn't see. 'Indeed it would; he needs a father. Eduard seems to like children.'

So it was Eduard now. Jenny speared a stitch with violence. 'A pity he hasn't married, then,' she observed lightly.

'Time enough, my dear, time enough. If you've finished with that knitting I wish you would go along and see how Grimshaw is managing with those pictures. I know he's good at those sort of jobs, but he's getting on a bit. And I'd like Oliver to come and sit with me for a bit.'

Jenny bent to kiss her aunt's cheek. 'OK—but I'll have to find him first; I bet he's up a tree.'

He was. She coaxed him down, warned him to be good and quiet and sent him on his way before going to find Grimshaw, who was managing very nicely. It was on her way back from this mission that she saw Margaret and the Professor. Margaret had a hand tucked confidently in his arm and was laughing up into his face as they strolled along the broad walk along the south face of the house. She had told Jenny the previous evening that she was enjoying her visit far more than she had ever done before. Watching her now, Jenny could see why.

CHAPTER FOUR

THE PROFESSOR, calling each day, yet managed to avoid meeting Jenny alone, and when they did see each other it was in Aunt Bess's company, listening to her giving dictatorial directions concerning her own welfare, the running of the house, and her forthcoming holiday. She had decided finally upon a cruise, the Professor having cunningly made sure that she did so by stating that possibly she would find it much too tiring. Madeira, she had settled for, and the Canaries—she hadn't been there for many years and she had a mind to see them again.

Jenny was to go with her, of course; Aunt Bess hadn't bothered to enquire about her niece's job at Queen's, she had taken it for granted that any sacrifice which Jenny made would be done willingly and for her benefit. And she had suddenly become quite overbearing about Toby. Whenever she and Jenny were alone, he was always the topic of conversation, it was as though Miss Creed took it for granted that Jenny wanted to marry him, despite her denials. It was rather like being in a net, thought Jenny despondently; she was aware that her friends at hospital had envied her; a lesser stately home to go to on her days off, money of her own, titled aunts and uncles, a nice young man waiting to marry her and transfer her to exactly the same kind of background...it was all so suitable, and yet she felt trapped. And now here was Aunt Bess positively pushing him at her!

To leave Aunt Bess to her own devices was unthinkable; she owed her a happy childhood and untold kindness; besides, she loved her irascible aunt. She would have to make the best of it, and once she was restored to health she would look for another job—and somehow she would have to convince Toby that she wasn't the wife for him. She had never given him any encouragement, but he still called each day, sometimes twice, always at the most inconvenient times, tagging along behind her while she arranged the flowers or polished the more valuable silver on display. Once or twice the Professor had seen them together, and for some reason that had annoyed her.

But she had fun too; Oliver was a delightful companion. They climbed trees, explored the wilder corners of the park while she taught him the names of the birds and small wild animals they encountered, fished for minnows in the stream which ran through the grounds, and fed the carp in the pond. And when she could spare the time, she took him round the house, pointing out its lovely furnishings and portraits, showing him the priest's hole and the cellars. The only place she wouldn't take him to was the top of the clock tower at the end of the south front.

'You'll have to wait,' she told him. 'There were a lot of starlings there this spring and it's full of old birds' nests. I must go up there and clear them away now the birds have gone.' And she had coaxed him to examine the glass case of family jewellery at the back of the hall instead.

It was a couple of days later when she found herself with an hour to spare before lunch. Armed with a broom and a sack, she took the unwieldy key from its hook behind the garden door and went to open the narrow arched door of the clock tower. There was no way in which to reach it from the house nowadays; the inside door had been walled up, and as the clock seldom needed attention, the outside door was enough. She climbed the narrow circular staircase quickly, not minding the musty smell and the dimness, and at the top produced a second key to open an even smaller door, and stepped into the square, stone-walled room which housed the clock. She had been right; the place was littered with old nests, feathers and all the debris of a large number of birds, and she set to work to clear it away. It took longer than she had expected and she had to hurry a little towards the end, dragging her full sack to the door and leaning it against the wall while she opened the door. It groaned and creaked as she went through and then shut behind her, and when she turned in a vain effort to keep it open in order to retrieve the sack, she dropped the key. She was bending to pick it up when the steps directly below her began to collapse slowly, tumbling down lazily, going out of sight round the angle of the winding stair. Jenny stood teetering on the top still, unable to believe her eyes, unable to go back—even if she had had the courage to move, for the key had tumbled with the steps—and certainly unable to go forward.

She took a long trembling breath and made herself think calmly while she clutched at the rough stones on either side of her. Panic she must not, that would be disaster, and shouting wouldn't help; there was the whole length of the south front between her and anyone likely to hear her voice. Perhaps when the ruin of steps below her had settled, she would be able to work her way down. She looked away from the still shifting rubble and tried to remember if she had told anyone where she was going, and concluded that she hadn't told a soul. Only at the back of her mind was the faint memory of having mentioned it to someone, but she couldn't remember who and even if she had it had probably not registered.

She was wrong. It had registered with Oliver, and when Miss Creed demanded that her niece should be fetched so that she might dance attendance upon her when the Professor called, and Jenny was nowhere to be found, and nor had anyone seen her in the house or grounds for quite some time, he joined the group of grown-ups discussing her probable whereabouts, but no one paid attention to him; they were too busy explaining her absence to the Professor, who had just arrived. He was inclined to think nothing of it. 'Probably gone for a walk,' he offered laconically. 'Perhaps Margaret could stand in...?'

But Aunt Bess wasn't going to have Margaret. 'Pooh,' she declared loudly, 'the girl's no use at all. If Jenny can't be found, then you can go home again, and don't dare to charge me a fee!'

The Professor hid a grin and then looked down at Oliver, tugging gently at his sleeve. 'I think I know where Jenny is,' he told him. 'She told me she would have to clean the clock tower room—it's full of old birds' nests—she told me so.'

The Professor eyed him thoughtfully. 'Did she know that I was coming this morning?'

'Course she did. She went to do her hair again after breakfast and when I asked her why she said: "Well, the old Prof's coming, isn't he? and I want to look severe."' Oliver paused. 'Why?'

A smile tugged at the corner of the Professor's mouth. 'We must ask her, mustn't we? I'll go and fetch her.'

'Shall I come with you?'

The big man smiled again. 'I think not, Oliver. Perhaps you would like to show me the carp later?'

He detached himself from the little group of people standing around and strolled off in the direction of the Clock Tower, along the south front, not hurrying in the least. The door was still open, he doubled himself up and went, still without haste, up the staircase.

Jenny heard the creak of the door and the unhurried steps and made herself look down from the spot on the wall where she had fastened her gaze because she was afraid of getting giddy. 'Don't come up,' she shouted in a not quite steady voice, 'the steps have crumbled.'

The footsteps didn't pause, and she shouted again urgently, 'For heaven's sake, listen!'

'I heard you very well the first time,' observed the Professor, rounding the last curve and stopping to contemplate the mass of masonry between them, 'but since I'm a humane man and unwilling to leave anyone, even you, in such a pickle, I considered it my duty to come and see what you were shouting about.'

Jenny choked back a strong desire to burst into tears. 'I'm glad you find it amusing,' she told him in an icy, shaking little voice. 'And now if you would be so good as to fetch someone—Florrie will know what to do…'

'Don't be silly,' he told her calmly, 'Florrie won't have the least idea what to do—besides, there's no need to fetch anyone—you only have to jump.'

'Jump?' uttered Jenny on a screech. 'It's ten feet—more. And where, pray, do I jump to?'

'Me.'

He was leaning back against the wall, poised in what she considered to be quite a dangerous manner on a pile of broken stones. He looked incapable of supporting himself, let alone her. 'No,' said Jenny.

'Afraid?'

'Well, of course I am—I'm scared stiff, if you must know. I'll stay here.'

'Which hardly solves our small problem. I'll count three and you'll jump.'

'I won't!'

'No pluck,' he observed to the opposite wall. 'Your illustrious ancestors would turn in their graves at your sad lack of courage.'

She said nastily: 'I don't suppose you've got any illustrious ancestors, but if you had, they must have disowned you years ago…ordering me about…'

He chuckled. 'My dear girl, come on. I'm getting cramp.'

'All the more reason why I should stay here.' Her hand slipped on the stones and she gasped with fright.

'You see? You only have to do that with both hands at the same time…' His voice held mockery. 'Jump, Jenny.'

'I shall knock you down.'

He let out a crack of laughter. 'You're what?—eight stone?—less, maybe. Well, I'm over fifteen.' He went on in a matter-of-fact manner: 'Your aunt was very annoyed. I daresay that by now she's allowed herself to get into a towering rage, and you know how bad that can be for her.' He smiled suddenly. 'Come on, Jenny, even if you can't stand the sight of me, you can trust me.'

Which, when she thought about it, was true enough. She closed her eyes, made a funny, helpless little sound, and jumped.

It was like hitting a tree trunk and just as solid. She had landed fair and square on to the professor's waistcoat and his arms held her tight against it. She could hear the hurried beat of his heart under her ear and mumbled: 'We'll never be able to move from here,' as another stair crumbled slowly away.

'Rubbish—you do as I tell you and we'll be at the bottom in a matter of seconds. Loosen your strangle-hold a little.'

She withdrew her arms from his neck so sharply that she almost overbalanced. 'I said loosen it,' the Professor pointed out mildly. 'And now do exactly as I say—you can argue about it afterwards.' She felt his arms slacken and gave a little gasp and heard his: 'No—now, remember those ancestors. I'm going to grip you by the elbows and swing you clear of the next two steps—I don't fancy they'll bear even your weight. I'll hold you until you've found your feet, then you must hang on to the wall until I join you.'

She clutched his waistcoat for a few seconds. 'All right, I'm ready.'

She felt herself swung down in a gentle arc. 'Grab the wall, left hand first—now the right. Good girl, I'm going to let go now. I'll be with you in a moment.'

And he was, balancing his weight beside her before trying the step below. 'Come on,' he encouraged her, and gave her a hand to hold. 'Get a foot on this one, but don't stay on it—get on to the next one if you can.'

It was quite easy after that, only they had to take care not to be on the same stair together, and once or twice the Professor had to stride over them as they slid away under his weight. As they reached the bottom they could hear the staircase breaking up very slowly behind them. The Professor shut the door and locked it and put the key in his pocket. 'Just in case Oliver decides to have a look,' he explained, 'and now stand still while I dust you down.'

She stood meekly while he brushed the dust off her linen dress, then took his handkerchief and wiped her face and lastly shook out her mane of hair. She should have been able to do these things for herself, but she was shaking so much that she was incapable of it. When he had at length finished, she said in a voice which still shook a little, 'Thank you—thank you very much. I was very tiresome, wasn't I? I should have known better. I'm an awful coward.'

He smiled very kindly at her. 'If you had been a coward, you would still be there on the top step. Do you feel you can face your aunt, or do you want a breather?'

'I'm all right now, thank you. Are you? I didn't hurt you when I jumped?'

He was brushing dust off his sleeve. 'No.' He sounded, even in that one brief word, as though he were laughing. 'Shall we go, then?'

It was Margaret who came to meet them as they went into the house. 'Jenny, where have you been? Aunt Bess is so cross. How could you go away like that, you knew Eduard was coming?'

Eduard indeed! 'I got hung up—so sorry.' Jenny moved away from the Professor and started to cross the hall to the cloakroom cunningly hidden in the panelled wall. 'I'll tidy myself—I won't be a minute.'

The Professor was already with her aunt when she reached the room. He must have told her what had happened because she said at once: 'Janet, you will be good enough to get someone to see about the tower staircase—it must be replaced or rebuilt. You're all right?' a little belatedly.

'Perfectly, thank you, Aunt Bess.'

'Humph—I hope you're grateful to Eduard.'

She didn't look at him. 'Yes, I am.'

'Fetch the brochure of that cruise I intend to go on.' Aunt Bess waved a beringed hand and turned to the Professor. 'It seems comfortable enough—I have arranged for us to have cabins on the sun deck. It will be quiet there, and any meals I wish to take there will be brought to me. I've made the ship's agent fully conversant with my state of health.'

'You have been busy.' The Professor's tone was dry.

'Well, Jenny has arranged it all, of course, she's good at that sort of thing. There is a doctor on board as well as a nurse—not that I shall need the latter. Jenny will look after me.'

'She has given up her post at Queen's?' he queried softly.

'Naturally.' Miss Creed shot him a suspicious look. 'I have never approved of her taking up nursing, especially at that hospital in the East End.'

'But if she had not trained as a nurse, you wouldn't have had her services now, Miss Creed.'

'That is beside the point,' said Aunt Bess grandly. 'She will be having a delightful holiday.'

'And afterwards?'

She stared at him and he looked back at her with a bland face.

'I'm sure I don't know—probably she'll marry. It's high time she did.'

Jenny had very little time to regret leaving Queen's. Aunt Bess, getting stronger every day, kept her busy with plans and arrangements for their cruise as well as overhauling her extensive wardrobe. And Jenny went to London and bought some new clothes for herself too—cool cottons and sundresses and several pretty evening dresses. She spent two days there, staying with one of her friends from Queen's, listening with nostalgia to the hospital gossip, and then driving back to Dimworth the next day, just in time to take her share of looking after the visitors to the house after she had given an account of her brief trip to Aunt Bess.

It was a lovely day and there were more people than usual. She was tired and hot by teatime, and the sight of Margaret, cool and serene, strolling in the rose garden with the Professor in tow did nothing to improve her mood. Margaret had a generous allowance from the estate and was free to regard it as her home should she wish to do so, but she made no effort to take her part in maintaining it. Indeed, when she came to stay, she expected that the whole place should be geared to her wishes, never mind how inconvenient it was, and even Aunt Bess's illness hadn't been allowed to spoil her gentle, selfish routine. As for little Oliver, he was left to his own devices, and if it hadn't been for Jenny, he would have had little enough fun.

Jenny, watching his mother sink gracefully on to a rustic seat, wondered how he would fare while she was away. Margaret had said that she would remain at Dimworth provided she wasn't expected to have anything to do with the visitors, which meant that Jenny had had to tour round the estate seeking helpers to fill in with the polishing of the furniture and silver, selling of postcards and the like, and carry on with all the small chores she attended to herself when she was at Dimworth. She took a last look at the pair, Margaret leaning back against the seat as though she were exhausted, and the Professor standing there, looking at her. 'Silly fool,' muttered Jenny, and sped away to make sure that the first batch of visitors hadn't strayed through any of the doors marked private.

She had crossed the hall and was deliberating as to whether she should go and find Mrs Thorpe or make sure that the collection of dolls was properly arranged, when the Professor, with the suddenness of someone who had popped up out of the ground at her feet, was beside her.

She looked at him with some interest. 'That was pretty smartish,' she observed. 'Did you run all the way? And how did you know...?'

'I saw you looking at us, and when you flounced off in that fashion I thought I'd better come after you and find out what had annoyed you this time.'

She had decided on the dolls and was already walking rapidly towards the tables where they were displayed. 'You always make me out to be bad tempered,' she snapped crossly, 'and I didn't flounce. And I'm not in the least annoyed.'

She twitched a wax doll's muslin skirt to exactness moved a baby doll carefully an inch to the left and stood back, her head on one side, refusing to look at him.

'Looking forward to your holiday?' His voice was friendly.

'Yes—no—I really haven't had the time to think about it—I have a lot to do.'

'While Margaret strolls in the rose garden.' He had spoken softly, but Jenny went a fiery red under his little smile.

She said stiffly: 'This is Oliver's home and Margaret is his mother, when she is here she naturally does exactly as she likes, and why shouldn't she?'

'Oh, quite. Only it seems to me that you don't always do exactly as you would like, Jenny.'

He sounded so kind and understanding that she found herself saying: 'Ah, yes, but you see it's a different kettle of fish with me. Aunt Bess has looked after me all my life, or most of it—and Dimworth has been my home. Margaret is quite entitled to tell me to leave, but she's too kind.' Too lazy to bother, too, she added silently.

'A charming person,' murmured the Professor. 'I'm sure she wouldn't do anything so unkind. Besides if you went away, someone else would have to be found to fill your place; dust and polish and run errands and keep an eye on the visitors and entertain Oliver while he is here.'

'I like doing it,' said Jenny sharply.

'You had a very promising career, so Doctor Toms was telling me.'

'That's none of your business.' She began to march back the way she had come. 'I have to find Mrs Thorpe.'

'In that cupboard place behind the hall where you keep the brochures. And it might be my business, Jenny.'

She stopped short to look at him. Was he serious about Margaret? Was he actually going to marry her? It would be nice for Oliver. She said quickly: 'Margaret is lovely and very sweet—she's been lonely since big Oliver died.'

She dived into the little room to confer with Mrs Thorpe without seeing the expression on the Professor's face.

She hardly spoke to him again before she and Aunt Bess left; true, he called to see her aunt and exchanged a few commonplace remarks to her concerning that lady's care while they were away, and although Jenny longed to ask him how long he planned to stay with Doctor Toms, she didn't do so.

Sitting beside Aunt Bess in the vintage Vauxhall Miss Creed refused to part with, being driven up to the docks at Tilbury to join their ship, she reflected that even after these weeks of seeing him almost every day, she still didn't know anything about him, only that he wasn't married and lived and worked in Holland. She wondered if Aunt Bess knew, but it was hardly the time to ask for her companion was resting with her eyes closed. Jenny looked at the elderly face with real affection; Aunt Bess was an old tartar, but a delightful one, with plenty of courage, determined at all costs that after her change of scene, she would return to Dimworth and take up the reins once more as though she had never had to relinquish them.

The ship was smallish and carried no more than three hundred passengers; moreover it was well appointed, with plenty of space. Their cabins on the sun-deck were all that could be desired, side by side well furnished and each with a bathroom. Jenny saw her aunt settled, summoned the stewardess to unpack for her, and retired to her own cabin, where she was presently visited by the purser with the news that they were to sit at the captain's table and that the ship's doctor would call upon them very shortly. They had only to ask for anything they required, he added. She thanked him warmly, unpacked, arranged her hair to her satisfaction, added a little more lipstick and went back to her aunt, who expressed satisfaction at the purser's message, gave it her opinion that her surroundings would do very well, and ordered tea.

The ship had set sail before they had finished and Jenny composed her aunt for a nap before going on deck to have a look round. In rather less than five minutes she was encircled by an eager little group of men, only too glad to explain just what the ship was doing and why. She treated them all with impartial kindness, refused a variety of invitations to have a drink, dance after dinner, explore the ship and try out the swimming pool in the morning with equal pleasantness, made her excuses charmingly and went off to the wireless room to send a message to Dimworth. She had promised Oliver that the moment they set sail she would let him know, and she remembered now how wistful he had looked when she had kissed him goodbye.

Something would have to be done about him; of course, if the Professor intended to marry Margaret, that would be splendid for Oliver, for he and the boy liked each other, but just supposing that didn't happen? The little boy had several years of loneliness before he would be sent to school; his grandparents in Scotland were delightful people, but hardly of an age to be his companions, and Margaret was of no use at all. He had one or two friends among the game-keepers' children who lived close by there, but although they might be good friends for him, their language sometimes left a lot to be desired and Oliver, like all small boys, had picked up the worst of it with all the ease in the world.

She sent her message and wandered back to her cabin; they were to have dinner there on their first evening, so that Aunt Bess might go to bed early after her long journey by car. It was still only nine o'clock by the time Jenny had helped her aunt to bed, saw to it that she had everything she might need for the night, and gone to her own cabin once more. She would have liked to have gone on deck, but she had already refused to join in the evening's activities. She undressed slowly, got into bed and opened her book, turning its pages without taking in a word for the niggling thought at the back of her mind that she hadn't said goodbye to the Professor quite distracted her. She flung the book down presently and turned out the light. After all, he could have taken the trouble to find her himself if he had wanted to couldn't he? Only he hadn't.

But she had no intention of allowing such a small—figuratively speaking, of course—thing as the Professor spoil the cruise. Subject to Aunt Bess vagaries, she joined in the deck games, danced every evening with a great variety of partners, sunbathed on deck in the increasing warmth, and tried her hand at the fruit machines. But not always; Aunt Bess took her place at the captain's table at lunch and dinner and had her own special corner in one of the bars before these meals, to which a select few were invited to join her, but she retired early and had her breakfast in bed, and moreover, liked Jenny to read to her while she rested in the afternoons, so that Jenny's time wasn't quite her own. Not that she complained, even to herself; they had come on the cruise for the benefit of her aunt's health, and that should come first.

All the same, she found herself looking forward to their arrival at Madeira. Aunt Bess had already decided that she wouldn't go ashore, but Jenny could if she wished; just for an hour or so in the morning before the ship sailed for Lanzarote.

They docked early in the morning and Jenny slipped on deck to get her first sight of Funchal, its white houses lining the water's edge and climbing into the mountains looming at its back. It looked lovely in the early morning light; she craned her neck in all directions to get a better view and went back to drink her tea and dress before going to see how Aunt Bess was. She had had a good night, she declared, but still had no desire to go ashore. 'On the way back,' she decided, 'but if you see anything you fancy, Jenny, buy it—the embroidery is exquisite, you know—something for Margaret and handkerchiefs for Mrs Thorpe, I suppose. Get what you like...' She pushed her tray aside. 'And get me a paper, child, will you? Now run along and have your breakfast and go ashore, but be certain to be back in good time.'

'You don't mind?' asked Jenny anxiously. 'You'll be all right? I've told the doctor...'

'Don't fuss!'

Jenny skipped away to eat an excellent breakfast, count her *escudos* and leave the ship. It had been a little difficult to avoid the offers of company she had received, for she hadn't felt sociable, but by dint of hanging about until almost everyone had gone ashore, she had succeeded, although she had been delayed at the last minute by a cablegram from Toby, asking her if she had changed her mind. Without stopping to think she had gone back to Aunt Bess and spoken her mind, scowling horribly as she tore it up and flung it into the wastepaper basket, and Aunt Bess had said sharply: 'You're being a silly girl, Janet. It would be an excellent marriage from every point of view.'

'Except mine,' snorted Jenny.

'Pooh!' her aunt had spoken strongly. 'You don't know what you want.'

Jenny wandered down the gangway after that, smiled at the first officer who was standing on the quay, and strolled through the noise and bustle around her, looking cool and very pretty in her blue cotton dress and wide straw hat. Perhaps she didn't know what she wanted, she mused, but at least she knew what she didn't want. She walked on, out of the dock and along the road towards the town. It was already warm and she had no definite plans of what she should do. A little shopping, she supposed, and a long, cool drink in a café.

CHAPTER FIVE

SHE HAD BEEN walking for perhaps five minutes when she saw the Professor strolling towards her, nattily dressed in light slacks and a cotton shirt. She almost fell over her own feet, stopping so suddenly at the sight of him, aware of a glow of pleasure flooding her person, which, considering that they didn't like each other, seemed strange.

His, 'Good morning, Jenny Wren,' was coolly friendly and showed no surprise.

'Well, I never!' she exclaimed. 'However did you get here?'

He forbore from telling her that he had flown his own plane over. 'Oh, there are ways and means,' he told her airily.

'Oh—on holiday?' she went on.

'Er—yes, one might call it that. Your aunt is on board?'

'Yes. Were you going to see her? I left her writing letters…'

'You have had your breakfast?'

'Ages ago.'

'Would it annoy you very much to come with me while I look her over?' He caught her by the arm and turned her round smartly and began to stroll back towards the quayside, without waiting for her reply. 'I remembered that your ship would be calling here this morning and it seemed a suitable opportunity...'

'You aren't worried about her?' asked Jenny quickly.

'If you mean do I anticipate any recurrence of the old trouble, I do not.' He went on to talk about nothing much until they reached the ship once more. As they went past the first officer, Jenny paused to explain: 'My aunt's doctor,' and when they were out of earshot:

'My dear girl,' observed her companion mildly. 'I'm a surgeon. You, a nurse, should know the difference.'

'Well, of course I do,' she was a little impatient. 'I didn't know you were so fussy about a little thing like that.'

The Professor made a small choking sound. 'There is a considerable difference—' he began, still mild to be cut short by her: 'Oh, don't be so stuffy!'

They had reached the sun-deck by now and she tapped on her aunt's door, looking at him over her shoulder as she spoke.

He swooped, there was no other word for it, and kissed her hard and with expertise. 'Stuffy?' he asked silkily, and hearing Miss Creed's voice bidding them enter, opened the door. Jenny stepped past him nicely pink in the cheeks, her chin up, her eyes very bright, so that Aunt Bess, looking up from her writing, exclaimed tartly: 'You look as though you've been quarrelling or kissing, Janet—which...' She paused as her eyes lighted on the Professor's vast frame in the doorway. 'Ah, it's you.' She didn't sound surprised. 'And are you on holiday too, Eduard?'

Despite her sharp voice she smiled at him and his mouth curved a little as he told her: 'A brief day or so. I realised that you would be calling here today and it seemed a good idea to look you up.'

'Huh—to examine me, I suppose, and send me a bill afterwards.'

'Er—examine you, yes, but since we are both on holiday I had intended to waive my fee.'

Miss Creed took him up smartly. 'You're more sensible than I thought. Certainly you may examine me. Now?'

'If it is convenient,' he murmured, 'and just a few questions…'

His patient threw down her book. 'Jenny, turn yourself into a nurse and see to me.' And to the Professor: 'Where is your stethoscope?'

'I hardly think I need it. Your pulse, a quick look at the scar, and as I said, a question or two.'

Miss Creed waved an imperious hand at Jenny. 'Then run along, child, I shan't need you. Be back for lunch.'

But Jenny stayed where she was. 'You don't need me, Professor van Draak?' she asked in a cool voice. His glance was quick and casual. 'Not at the moment, thank you.'

'Then be sure and return at the right time,' reiterated her aunt, and since there was nothing more to be said, she went.

But somehow the fun had gone out of the morning. She walked slowly away from the ship and along the road curving beside the water until she reached the town, where she pottered a little aimlessly round the shops, had a long, cool drink at a pavement café, quite unconscious of the stares her pretty face and bright hair induced, and then wandered on again. She was supposed to be buying things, but it was getting warm now and although she had an hour to kill, she felt disinclined to spend it in the shops.

The small side streets looked inviting and a little mysterious, leading away from the town's centre towards the mountains looming in the distance. Jenny turned into one of them and had taken barely a dozen paces when the Professor's large, firm hand gripped her shoulder, making her jump and turn sharply.

'Not up here, dear girl,' he begged her.

'Scaring me like that!' uttered Jenny peevishly. 'Creeping up behind me…'

'I didn't creep.' He sounded meek, although she was sure that he wasn't meek at all. 'I merely followed you to warn you that this part of the town isn't really for young tourists.'

'Who is it for?'

His eyes laughed down at her. 'Shall we say men only?'

She gave him a stony look. 'Well, there's no way of knowing.' She felt belligerent, caught unawares, and at a disadvantage.

His hand slid from her shoulder and caught her elbow instead and she found herself walking back the way she had come. 'I should have been perfectly all right,' she protested with slight pettishness.

He stopped to look down at her. 'With that face and hair?' He shook his head. 'Come and have a drink.'

'I've had one, thank you.'

'One should drink plenty in this heat. Doctor's advice.'

'But you're not a doctor—you're a surgeon, you said so.'

'Ah, yes—so I did. I'm a modest man; I tend to hide my light under a bushel. I do happen to be a doctor of medicine, but I never cared for the medical side and I tend to forget...'

'Well,' said Jenny, exasperated, 'you might have told me!'

'You didn't ask.' He had steered her through the streets to a pavement table outside one of the cafés and pulled out a chair. 'Now sit down and bury the hatchet while you cool your fiery feelings with a long drink. What would you like? Have you tried Sangria?'

'No—I had a soft drink.'

'Then you must sample it.' He sat down gingerly on the flimsy chair and gave their order, then went on chattily: 'So pleasant, these brief interludes.'

She let that pass. 'How did you find Aunt Bess? Better, I hope?' She wasn't going to give him the satisfaction of admitting that she found them pleasant too.

He waited until their drinks arrived. 'Remarkably fit—good reactions, and provided that she has told me the truth, she is making excellent progress. She will never be quite one hundred per cent again, you know that, but provided that she's moderately careful she should be able to resume a more or less normal life. Do you mind if I smoke?'

Jenny said that no she didn't and watched him fill his pipe. When it was nicely alight he asked: 'I take it there will be a good chance of you going back to your job?'

She shook her head. 'Not at Queen's and not for some time, I think. You see, Dimworth is quite a large place to manage. But the season will be over soon; if Aunt Bess feels quite fit by then, I'll see about getting another job.'

'You mind giving up your nursing?'

She sipped her drink and found it good. 'Well, yes—you see, while I'm in hospital I'm independent.'

'And when you're at Dimworth you have to conform?'

She had forgotten that she didn't like him, that he was arrogant and brusque and laughed at her. Just to voice her troubled thoughts was a relief, and he was easy to talk to. 'Yes.'

'And dwindle away into spinsterhood? I think not.'

'Well, no—actually Aunt Bess wants me to marry...'

'She has mentioned it—the young man Toby. Very suitable, I gather.'

'Yes, but I don't want to marry him.' She sounded pathetic without meaning to.

'This is a free world, Jenny—or at least parts of it are, and it's your life, isn't it? Throw him over, this so worthy young man.'

'Well, I've been throwing him over for years—but he's so—so nice—much too nice for me.'

'You wish to marry a man who is not nice?' There was laughter in his voice.

'Don't pick on words!' snapped Jenny. 'You know very well what I mean.' She sucked her drink through the two straws with childlike pleasure and went on. 'He's—he's...well, if you must know, he always lets me have my own way.'

Her companion puffed smoke gently, his eyes on the graceful rings he was making. 'Ah—and you are wise enough to know that wouldn't be a good thing for you.'

'I never...' began Jenny. 'He's a very nice man, I said so.' She added unkindly: 'He's young too.'

The Professor looked blandly across the little table at her. 'Another reason why you shouldn't marry him—although,' he went on judicially, 'perhaps you would suit each other very well after all. You could be bossy-boots for the rest of your life and he would become nicer and nicer—meek is I think your word for it. Your children would be simply ghastly.'

Jenny choked. 'Bossy-boots!' she exclaimed. 'Whatever next?' She swallowed the rest of her drink, anxious to be gone from this tiresome man. 'I am not—and my children will be simply super...'

'Given the right father,' conceded the Professor, and Jenny, choking again on the last few drops of her drink, caught her breath and had to be slapped sharply on the back, so that the tears stood in her eyes and she became quite purple in the face.

'You really shouldn't allow yourself to become so worked up,' advised the Professor kindly, 'nor should you gobble down your drinks in that fashion.'

Jenny, her breath back, let it out slowly. 'You are quite detestable,' she told him in an icy voice unfortunately spoilt by a hiccough. 'I am not worked up, only when you deliberately annoy me.'

'My dear Miss Wren—or may I call you Jenny?—I am the mildest of men...'

'Rubbish, and you've been calling me Jenny for goodness knows how long. You are a bad-tempered man, determined to annoy me!'

His look of astonishment was a masterpiece. 'Good gracious—I? Annoy you? Though I must confess to a bad temper. A man must have a few faults,' he added modestly. 'Have another Sangria?'

She said with dignity, 'Very well, I will, thank you.'

He beamed at her. 'Friends again?' He didn't wait for her to answer but embarked upon a gentle flow of small talk which required little or no answer. Indeed, he gave her very little chance of replying even if she had wanted to, and at length interrupted himself to say: 'It's almost lunch time, I'll take you back to the ship.'

They went by taxi, and Jenny was unaccountably annoyed at his very casual goodbye at the foot of the gangplank.

She lunched with little appetite and then, because Aunt Bess had changed her mind and wanted to go ashore after all, spent the next hour or so in a hired car which took them from Funchal along the coast road to Canico and Santa Cruz and Machico, before driving over the Portela Pass to Faial. Aunt Bess was getting tired by then, so they stopped for a cool drink and returned to the ship in plenty of time to settle her for a nap before dressing for dinner. She was already dozing as Jenny left her and went to her own cabin to review her wardrobe. There were several pretty dresses she hadn't worn yet, but she eyed them without much interest; any old thing would do, she decided for there was no one to notice what she wore. She didn't go too deeply into who the no one might be and perhaps in defiance of the half hidden thought, made up her mind to make the effort after all and wear a leaf green chiffon, a filmy creation which looked nothing at all on its hanger but did wonders for a girl once it was on, especially when she happened to have coppery hair.

Aunt Bess, refreshed after her nap, and with the stewardess to help her, had clothed herself with some splendour, zipped and buttoned into plum-coloured silk, a number of gold chains draped across her massive front. She lifted the old-fashioned gold-rimmed spectacles hanging from one of them as Jenny went in and studied her niece.

'Very nice,' she pronounced. 'We will have a drink.'

'Tonic water, Aunt,' said Jenny firmly, and led her elderly relative to the nearest lift.

The bar was quite full; Jenny knew most of the people there by now and she smiled and nodded to them as she accompanied her aunt to their usual corner, left empty by tacit consent. Only it wasn't empty. The Professor, in all the subdued elegance of white dinner jacket and black tie, was already there. He rose and came towards them and took Miss Creed's hand. 'This is delightful,' he observed, addressing her and smiling only briefly at Jenny. 'I've taken the liberty of ordering your usual drinks.'

He had settled Aunt Bess in her usual seat as he spoke, pulled out a chair for Jenny and sat down between them before she found her voice to say: 'Are you travelling on this ship too? I thought...'

His smile held a touch of mockery and his voice was cool. 'You forget, I'm on holiday too.'

She persisted: 'Yes, but this morning...'

'I don't remember it being mentioned,' he snubbed her gently, and turned to make small talk with Miss Creed while Jenny, in a quite nasty temper, studied his profile. Arrogant, she muttered silently, and rude he could at least pretend to be civil! She stared at the glass in her hand, gloomily contemplating several days of avoiding his company. His quiet observation, 'Yes, it is quite a small ship as ships go,' was so appropriate to her thoughts that she flushed and drank unwisely, almost all of her Pimm's Number One. It didn't help at all, either, when he leaned forward and took the glass from her hand and said in an avuncular manner: 'I did warn you not to gobble your drinks, Jenny.'

She shot him a fiery look, quite unable to answer for the moment, and in any case Aunt Bess had embarked on an account of their afternoon drive in her compelling voice, allowing for no one else to speak save when she paused for suitable comment.

The Professor was sitting at the captain's table too. What was worse, he faced Jenny across it, so that each time she looked up, it was to find his eyes upon her, a fact which caused her to carry on an animated conversation with the elderly man on her right—something to do with shipping, although she wasn't sure what—and presently she turned her attention to the famous journalist on her left, whose manner was a shade too charming for her taste. Until now she had kept him at arm's length, but now, with the Professor within a yard or so of her, his firm mouth curled into the tiniest of sneers, she allowed herself to be drawn into frivolous chat with the man. But before long she wished that she hadn't been so forthcoming, for he showed every sign of turning the inch she had given him into an ell. Moreover, she was only too well aware of the Professor's sardonic eye. She was doing her best to wriggle gracefully out of accepting an invitation to go on a sightseeing tour of Lanzarote in the journalist's hired car when the Professor came to her rescue.

'What a delightful prospect,' he murmured across the table, 'but aren't you forgetting that your aunt will need you while she has that treatment we have decided to try?'

Jenny was too grateful to express surprise at this piece of information—indeed, she admired the Professor for the convincing way he had spoken. Her 'Oh, dear—I'd quite forgotten, thank you for reminding me, Professor van Draak,' was a masterpiece of regret.

Aunt Bess wanted to go to her cabin directly after dinner, and Jenny went with her. It was still early and there would be dancing until the small hours, but Aunt Bess, after a leisurely half hour of undressing, had other ideas. 'You shall read to me, Jenny,' she decreed. 'You have a pretty voice and I find it soothing. The editorial in the *Guardian,* I think.'

So Jenny read. She read for a couple of hours and even then her aunt demanded that she should sit with her until she fell asleep, and by the time she had done that Jenny was too tired herself to join the captain and his party in one of the lounges, and certainly too tired to dance.

She didn't see anything of the Professor until lunch-time the next day, when he appeared at the table, wished his companions a good day and applied himself to the task of entertaining Miss Creed. It wasn't until that lady was being escorted to her cabin for her post-prandial nap that Jenny had the opportunity to ask: 'What treatment?'

The Professor, who had attached himself to them waved an airy hand. 'Purely mythical, Jenny, purely mythical. You were so completely bogged down, were you not? Only the unkindest of men would have left you in such a predicament.'

He opened Miss Creed's door so that both ladies might enter and Jenny edged past him without speaking. 'Ungrateful girl,' he murmured into the top of head, and shut the door silently behind them. It had barely closed when Aunt Bess exclaimed: 'My scarf—I left it in the restaurant.'

'Well, you don't need it at present,' said Jenny reasonably. 'I'll fetch it later.'

'I require it now. I refuse to take my nap until I have it.'

Jenny sighed, muttered under her breath and started back to the restaurant, to find her way barred by the Professor, lounging at the end of the corridor.

'You disposed of your aunt very quickly.'

She shot him a cross look. 'I haven't—she left her scarf in the restaurant, and she wants it this minute.'

'Do I detect a slight vexation? Where is your sunny disposition, Jenny Wren? Snappish, and no gratitude for your rescue, either.'

She made an effort to work her way round him. 'Well, I haven't had the time...'

'To express your deep obligation to me? But this will take very little time, my dear.'

He had kissed her soundly before she could dodge him and then disconcerted her utterly by standing aside without another word, to let her pass.

She lingered unnecessarily in the restaurant so that he would be gone by the time she went back, and was quite put out to find that that was exactly what he had done.

The ship had been delayed at Madeira, but now Lanzarote was clearly visible ahead of them. Jenny looked longingly at its mountains as she went back to her aunt's cabin, for she saw little chance of going ashore. They were due to sail again in the evening and although there was a coachload of passengers going on an afternoon tour, Aunt Bess had refused to consider staying quietly on board while Jenny joined them. She went into the cabin, handed over the scarf, picked up various articles Aunt Bess had dropped and prepared to go again, to be halted at the door by her aunt's voice. 'I understand the island is very interesting—Eduard has offered to drive you round this afternoon. I told him that you would be delighted.'

'Aunt Bess, I'm not a child—I can accept my own invitations, and the Professor hasn't said anything to me. In any case, I don't want to go, thank you—I'd much rather go with the coach.'

'Out of the question, Janet.'

'I've just told you I'm not a child!'

'You're behaving like one. I thought it very kind of Eduard. He pointed out that the coach will be hot and stuffy and probably break down. But if you won't go, you'd better go and tell him so now—he's on this deck, up in the bows.'

'Oh, Aunt Bess...!' Jenny shut the door quietly behind her, although she wanted very much to bang it. Aunt Bess meant it kindly, but why couldn't she stop interfering? Jenny went slowly out on to the deck, filled now with passengers watching the picturesque little town of Puerto de los Marmoles getting closer and closer. The Professor was standing with a number of other people, and she joined them silently, wondering how she was going to refuse his invitation without everyone around them hearing it too. There were two very pretty girls in the group, and either of them, from the way they were looking at him, would be only too delighted to take her place.

But it seemed that neither of them were to have that pleasure; he extricated himself from his companions with finesse, caught her by the arm and walked her briskly away.

'I have a car waiting,' he told her blandly. 'We should have two or three hours in which to see something of the island.'

'I don't want...' began Jenny, and then changed it to: 'Well, it's awfully kind of you, but Aunt Bess...'

He nipped this in the bud. 'She assured me that you wanted to go ashore and that she wanted a few hours' rest and quiet.

Ah, they're tying up now—you'll need a bonnet or something. I'll wait here.'

She saw that it was useless to protest, for he would either not hear or ride roughshod over any excuse she might be able to think up—and she couldn't think of any not without being rude.

In her cabin, searching for a pretty headscarf to go with her white cotton sun-dress, she toyed with the idea of staying there, only to discard it at once; to waste a glorious afternoon sitting alone when she could be exploring the island was just plain stupid. She arranged the scarf becomingly, put on a little more lipstick, and went back on deck.

The car was a small Citroën and rather battered, although it quickly proved its worth, for the Professor didn't linger in the town but made for the mountains towering to the north of the island. The road was a narrow one, but the surface was good, and he, who seemed to know his terrain, pointed out anything which he considered she might be interested in—dragon trees, the house built by Omar Sharif when he had filmed on the island some years previously, the once lived-in caves...

'It's like the moon,' declared Jenny, 'and there's no grass.'

'None at all—and you're right, it's so like the moon that the astronauts came here to train before their landing on the moon.'

She looked at him in surprise. 'However do you know all these things?' she wanted to know.

He looked suitably modest. 'Oh, I pick up this and that you know.'

They were climbing now, with mountains on either side of them and now and again a glimpse of the sea. It made a nice change of scenery when they reached Teguise, a sleepy town with an old Spanish style church in its square. But they didn't stop, climbing on towards the northern coast through the lava-strewn country, only slowing to look briefly at the village of Haria; white-walled, red-roofed houses and villas with colourful gardens and surrounded by palm trees and giant cactus.

'Well, that was nice,' observed Jenny, craning her neck to get a last glimpse of the pretty little place.

'There's something even nicer ahead of us.'

There was—right on the northern most coast and atop a steep mountain slope which Jenny privately thought the car wouldn't manage. The Professor parked in the clearing at the top and whisked her out to lead her through a door in the high lava wall surrounding them. It opened into a wide, white washed passage leading to a cave, converted to a restaurant, but he took no notice of the tables and chairs but led her to the enormous plate glass window at the end so that she could admire the view from it—a sheer drop to the sea below, and separated from the mainland by a small stretch of water, a fair-sized island, its only village facing them.

'No electricity, no gas, no telephone, no shops,' explained the Professor, 'just a fishing village—a quiet paradise, although I believe it's popular in the season. Nice if you want to be alone. Come and have a drink.'

Jenny elected to have tea—hot water, a tea-bag and no milk, but it was refreshing. Her companion settled for coffee and while he drank it, regaled her with odds and ends of information about their surroundings.

'You know an awful lot about it,' she said. 'Have you been here before?'

'Twice—no, three times. It makes a nice change from the Dutch climate.'

Here was a chance to find out something about his home there. 'Do you live in a very cold part of the country?'

'It can be cold in the winter. If you've finished we'll go,' he glanced at his watch. 'We'll take the coast road.'

She felt inward relief; she wasn't all that keen on mountains, and to be at sea level would suit her nicely. But it took a little while to get there; down the side of a mountain, along a narrow road full of hair-raising bends. It wouldn't have been so bad if the Professor had driven at a decorous pace, but it seemed to make no difference to him whether he was going up or down hill or on the flat; his pace was fast. They were within sight of the level road below them when he glanced at her briefly and said airily: 'Nervous? No need, I've been driving for years and I know this road. You look quite pale—where's your British phlegm, Jenny?'

'Thank you, it's still intact. I'm scared and I dare-say I'm as white as a sheet, but I have no intention of letting you have the satisfaction of frightening me. Pray go as fast as you like if that pleases your odious sense of humour.'

He laughed then and slowed down at once to a sedate pace. 'You don't like me at all, do you? Ever since we met and you tried to make me join the first batch of sightseers.'

She remembered how curt he had been. 'You were pompous.'

'Heaven forbid—but there, one is always prepared to think the worst of people one dislikes. This is the bend.'

They were out on the coast road now, with the sea not far away. It ran between sand and rock, with here and there a small village and isolated villas with carefully cultivated gardens. There was a camel, too, working in the sand with a diminutive donkey beside it, and the Professor obligingly stopped so that Jenny might look her fill. And soon after that they were back in the town, threading its narrow streets, picturesque and colourful, spoilt by glimpses of poverty almost out of sight. And then they were outside the town again, passing the heaps of salt on the flat fields near the water, speeding towards the ship. The Professor drew up neatly before the gangway, ushered her out and prepared to pay the man waiting while Jenny strolled over to the small stalls set up on the quayside, laden with souvenirs. She hadn't meant to buy anything, but the vendors looked so eager that she had purchased postcards, several rush mats and an embroidered traycloth before the Professor rejoined her, paid for them, bade her buy no more and walked her briskly on board.

'You're too softhearted,' he told her severely.

She stopped in the ship's vestibule, empty for the moment. 'Thank you for the trip,' she said coldly, 'and if you will let me know how much you paid for these things, I'll let you have the money.' She suddenly felt cross with him. 'And I'm not softhearted—why shouldn't one help someone poorer than oneself? A few pesetas to them may make all the difference between meat or no meat for their dinner.' She glared at him. 'The trouble is with you that you've got everything...'

He gave her a long thoughtful look and then without saying anything at all, turned on his heel and walked away from her.

There was nothing to do but to go to her aunt's cabin then, and that lady's crisp: 'You've been a long time, and in none too good a mood, I see?' did nothing to improve her temper. Luckily she didn't need to answer, for her aunt went on: 'Help me into my dress, child—we might go on deck for an hour before we change.'

Aunt Bess had her own corner with a chair always ready for her use; she reclined in it now, while Jenny gave a reluctant account of her afternoon, leaving out a great deal, so that presently her listener yawned, remarked that it sounded exceedingly dull and she would read for a while so that Jenny might do as she wished.

Thus dismissed, Jenny sauntered off to watch shuffleboard, hang over the side of the ship with several of her acquaintances and presently go with them to the bar by the swimming pool, where the younger passengers had formed the habit of gathering in the early evening. She stayed some time, sipping a long drink and pretending to herself that she wasn't keeping an eye open for the Professor. There was no sign of him. He had disappeared like a puff of smoke, which, considering his size, seemed unlikely. All the same, when she went to dress for the evening she did so with extra care, piling her copper hair into thick coils on top of her head and zipping herself into a rather lovely pink chiffon which she had been keeping for a special occasion, telling herself that she might just as well wear it as allow it to hang in the cupboard.

She had barely installed her aunt in her usual corner by the bar when the Professor joined them, a steward at his elbow with their drinks. He greeted Aunt Bess warmly and Jenny in an off-hand manner which made her grit her teeth, so that she said impulsively: 'Oh, hullo—I thought you'd jumped overboard.' She could have bitten her tongue out the moment she had uttered the words, for the look he gave her was amused and mocking too.

'You missed me?' he wanted to know blandly.

'No.' That didn't seem quite enough of an answer, so she added: 'I just happened to notice that you weren't around.' She picked up her glass and then put it down again; it would be just her luck to choke and have her back patronisingly patted.

'You don't like your drink?' he asked solicitously 'Let me get you something else.'

She snatched the glass up again, said: 'This is fine thanks,' and sipped cautiously, thankful when Aunt Bess took the conversation into her own hands, as she almost always did.

It was as they were on their way in to dinner that the Professor managed to separate her from her aunt for long enough to murmur: 'Such a pretty girl this evening, and so very cross. Seasick, perhaps?'

She spoke rather wildly. 'Of course I'm not—cross or seasick.'

'In that case I'm sure Miss Creed will spare you after dinner for a little gentle exercise—dancing.'

Jenny had her mouth open to say no, but Aunt Bess, whose ears were still much too sharp, said loudly: 'A splendid idea. I shall watch.'

He danced very well indeed, although his hold was as impersonal as a kindly-natured man's might be on an elderly aunt he wished to indulge. Jenny, ruffled in her feelings, was wickedly delighted when the slow foxtrot gave way to something more modern; he wouldn't know what to do…

But he did—better than most of the other men in the room. She twisted and twirled, but so did he, with the unselfconscious manner of someone who had done it a hundred times already and wasn't afraid of making a fool of himself. When they rejoined their party, Aunt Bess paused long enough in her conversation with the captain to remark: 'If I were half my age, I should enjoy all that gyrating.' She waved a hand in regal dismissal. 'Go away and do it again—I'm not ready for bed yet.'

Before she went to sleep that night, Jenny, reviewing her evening, decided that if the Professor should ask her to drive round Tenerife with him, she would accept. True, he annoyed her almost all the time, but he drove superbly. There would be Las Palmas too… She closed her eyes, thinking sleepily that the cruise was quite fun after all. They would reach Tenerife quite early in the morning; she must be sure and be up early.

CHAPTER SIX

JENNY AND AUNT BESS had breakfasted in the latter's cabin and the first coachload of sightseers were leaving the ship. There had been no sign of the Professor. Jenny had combed the ship without success, angry with herself for doing it, but somehow quite unable not to. Perhaps now that most of the passengers had gone ashore, he would seek them out.

She arranged the curl in front of her ear with exactitude and jumped visibly when there was a knock on the door and the Professor strolled in, wished them a good morning, made a few noncommittal remarks about the day's activities, asked his patient a few pertinent questions regarding her health and then looked at his watch, remarked that he must be gone, bade Miss Creed goodbye, whisked round on Jenny with surprising speed to kiss her hard and swiftly on her astonished mouth, and went his way.

Aunt Bess's voice broke the silence, to say surprisingly: 'Of course, he's nearly forty.'

Jenny shook the amazement out of her mind. 'That's not old,' she said before she could stop herself.

Her aunt gave her a thoughtful look. 'Heavens, no—did I say it was? And he of all men…'

Jenny was staring unseeingly out of the window, to the quay below. She didn't turn round. 'Oh? Why do you say that?'

'Very fit for his age—not an ounce of spare flesh on him. He could make rings round anyone half his age—has a good brain too. He won't look much different when he's seventy, which is more than I can say for some men I know.' She added sternly, 'Toby is not yet thirty and he has a decided bulge.'

Jenny giggled. 'Yes, he has, hasn't he?' And then with elaborate unconcern: 'I don't suppose we shall see Professor van Draak again.'

'As to that, child, you're quite out. He wishes to see me from time to time and suggested that I should go over to Holland, where I can have a check-up at the hospital where he's a consultant. It seems to me to be rather a nice idea—I haven't been to Holland for many years and there isn't anything much for me to do at Dimworth. Margaret is there and provided she exerts herself she should be able to manage. Eduard suggested that she might like to accompany me but I couldn't agree to that. You will come with me of course…'

Jenny wasn't sure what prompted her to say at once: 'Oh, I couldn't possibly, Aunt Bess,' although she was sure as she said it that there was nothing she would like better. For a man she didn't much like and who didn't much like her, the Professor loomed with an alarming clarity in her mind. The thought of not seeing him again had been niggling away at the back of her mind in a most unpleasant manner.

'Why not, Janet?'

'Well…' She sought for an excuse, and came up with: 'I did want to go back to nursing, you know. I thought I might go to Queen's and see if they would take me back…'

'If you're short of money…' suggested her aunt surprisingly.

Jenny couldn't remember Aunt Bess ever asking her that before. 'I've more than enough, thank you. Aunt Bess; it's not that—I just want to be independent.' As she uttered the words, the niggle exploded into amazing, solid fact; she had no wish to be independent, it was the last thing she wanted to be. She wanted above all things to be married to the Professor and be completely dependent upon him for the rest of her life. Probably they would quarrel, or rather she would quarrel and he would listen and smile in that annoying way of his, but that wouldn't matter in the least; she would love him however tiresome he was. Only he didn't love her. She frowned heavily. That was cold fact and she would have to think about it.

'Well, I expect another few days wouldn't matter,' she was surprised to hear that her voice sounded perfectly normal. 'How long do you intend staying in Holland?'

'Oh—ten days, perhaps. Eduard wants to do some tests.' Aunt Bess fiddled with a handful of the gold chains she so loved to wear. 'We might see something of the country while we're there; as long as I'm back at Dimworth before we close the house to visitors for the winter.' She dismissed the subject with a wave of the hand. 'And now go and see if we can hire a car, Jenny. I should like a drive—we are here until tomorrow, aren't we?'

Their drive was a rather different one from her trip with the Professor, but Jenny enjoyed it; it passed the morning hours and she had no time to think. Only in the afternoon, while Aunt Bess was resting, could she lie in the sun and think about Eduard van Draak. She would have cheerfully spent her evening doing the same thing, but there was cabaret and dancing and Aunt Bess, feeling festive, insisted that they should join the captain's party after dinner.

They went ashore at Las Palmas too, but although the scenery was delightful and shopping for presents to take home was a pleasant occupation, Jenny hardly noticed any of it. She joined in the cheerful groups of passengers, and laughed and danced when she was asked, but none of it mattered. She was impatient to get back now; the sooner they arrived at Dimworth, the sooner they would go to Holland.

The weather changed as the ship turned for home and Aunt Bess lay in her deckchair in a sheltered corner while Jenny, feeling lost, spent her time in the swimming pool or walked the decks. Now that the Professor was no longer there, the several young men on board were only too anxious to entertain her, but she treated them all with friendly impartiality and gave them no encouragement at all, and when they became too persistent, retired to Aunt Bess's side with the excuse that she must look after her elderly relative.

She danced in the evenings, of course, charming her partners with her sweet smile and ready replies to their talk, but all the while her head was full of the Professor. He had told her once, quite casually, that he had never wanted to marry; he had told her too that he had fallen in and out of love times without number, which was all very well. He had shown no sign of wanting to fall in love with her let alone take her to wife. Jenny smiled and murmured her way through the days, while she considered the best way to capture his serious attention—and that in the face of his interest in Margaret. He had wanted her to accompany Aunt Bess to Holland, hadn't he? and Aunt Bess had refused. Jenny, considering the matter, wondered what he would do next.

But once the ship had docked at Tilbury she had no leisure for her own thoughts. The business of getting Aunt Bess on to firm ground, as well as her considerable luggage, took all her time and attention, and as they went slowly through Customs and out on to the quay she saw to her vexation that it wasn't Aunt Bess's car waiting for them, but Toby in his Rover Metro.

He greeted them with a complacent smile and a: 'Thought I'd give you a surprise. I had some business to do in town anyway. Let's have the luggage, it can go in the boot. There's plenty of room in the back for you, Miss Creed.'

Jenny attempted to thwart this arrangement by declaring

that the front seat would be more comfortable for Aunt Bess, but he took no notice and Aunt Bess, strangely enough, raised no objection; indeed she said with some satisfaction: 'I shall do very well in the back, you two will have plenty to say to each other, anyway.' She looked a little cunning as she spoke, but Jenny didn't see that.

Later, thinking about the drive back, Jenny concluded that it had been Toby who had had a great deal to say, and he said it, repeating himself over and over again, giving her a dozen sound reasons why she should agree to marry him. If only he hadn't been so complacent about it, she remembered wearily, taking it for granted that marrying him was the best thing that could happen to any girl. He was a nice enough man, but so dull, and he hadn't contradicted her once when she had argued with him, and even when she told him firmly that she didn't love him, he hadn't believed her. If only it had been the Professor...but she couldn't imagine that gentleman behaving so tamely; he would probably have stopped the car and told her to get out and walk. She sighed and went in search of Oliver; she had promised to read to him before he went to bed.

He was curled up on a window seat with Florrie's cat beside him, doing nothing, which for him was unusual, and Jenny said at once: 'My, you're sitting there like a mouse—are you tired?'

He turned to look at her. 'I'm thinking. Do you think, Jenny?'

'On and off. What about—or is it a secret?'

'Mummy and Aunt Bess have had a row—I heard them because they were in the sitting room and I was on the stairs. Mummy's cross because Aunt Bess won't take her to Holland. She says...' he paused to get it right, 'she has a right to go because she's going to marry Eduard.' He turned blue eyes on to his listener. 'Who's he?'

Jenny answered faintly: 'Professor van Draak. You shouldn't listen to other people talking when they don't know you're there, Oliver.'

'Well, I did call to Mummy, but she didn't hear, they were

talking so loudly.' He climbed down off the window seat and held out a hand. 'Could we go into the gazebo while you read to me? I'm truly glad you're back, Jenny.'

She bent to kiss him. 'So am I, my lamb—I missed you.'

'But if you go to Holland you'll go away again,' He was faintly tearful.

'So I shall, but I'll be back very soon. Aunt Bess will only be there for a few days, you know. Besides you must stay here and look after Dimworth with Mummy.'

'Mummy doesn't like it here. She only stayed because Professor van Draak was here too.'

'Oh—did she?' She tried to sound casual. 'Well perhaps he'll come and see her.'

Oliver settled himself beside her in the gazebo, for they had walked as they talked. He said wistfully: 'I should like to go to Holland.' He gave her an engaging smile. 'With you, of course, Jenny.'

'And so you shall one day, when you're older and able to buy the tickets and look after me,' she assured him as she opened *Winnie the Pooh*. 'Shall I start reading?'

'Yes, please. Jenny, why haven't you got anyone to look after you? Would Professor van Draak do—if I were to mention it?'

He would do very nicely. Jenny sighed soundlessly. 'No, dear, I don't think so. Now, where were we?'

She settled back into the Dimworth way of life quickly enough. There was plenty to do, for the weather was still good and there were always plenty of visitors. She took her turn sitting at the table in the hall, selling brochures and postcards, helping with the teas, checking the stocks of tea and sugar and scones, polishing and dusting, keeping an eye on Baxter, who had been looking after the gardens for so long now that he tended to forget that they weren't his...

They had been back for the best part of a week when Aunt Bess told her that they would be going to Holland in three days' time. She offered this piece of news while they were all having tea, and Oliver burst into tears, while Margaret went white and said in a bitter voice: 'It won't make any difference—Eduard will come here.'

'What makes you think that he is in love with you?' asked Aunt Bess forthrightly. 'Has he actually said to?'

Margaret made a dramatic gesture. 'Not in front of the child,' she remonstrated.

'Pooh, he's bawling so hard he can't hear a word. And don't be dramatic, Margaret. Eduard has had ample opportunity to state his feelings. Personally I am of the opinion that you have imagined the whole thing.'

Margaret rose to her feet. 'I did not—how can you be so unkind? Just because men like me…and he doesn't like Jenny and she doesn't like him. They'll both hate it…'

Jenny had remained silent, but now she said in a colourless little voice: 'You forget that it's a professional visit, Margaret; nothing to do with who likes whom, and if you went, the Professor might be distracted from his work.'

Aunt Bess snorted fiercely, 'Rubbish!' and went on ruthlessly: 'Margaret, you will be good enough to remain here and look after Dimworth while we are away—it will do you good to bestir yourself. Go to Holland when we get back by all means—that is no concern of mine, although the mind boggles at the difficulties you will need to surmount. Do you really believe that Eduard will give up his work to come here and live as your consort—because that's what would be. However, that's your concern, as I've already said.' She glanced at Oliver, sitting beside Jenny blowing his small nose resolutely on the hanky she had offered him. 'We shall take Oliver with us. I enjoy his company.'

'But…' Margaret began furiously, then paused and Jenny knew exactly why. Aunt Bess had money, a great deal of it; she had indicated that when she died she would, provided nothing had occurred to annoy her in the meantime, leave most of it to Oliver. Dimworth was by no means a large estate, but it took a good deal of money to run it, and although there was enough for that purpose, her handsome fortune would be a splendid thing for Oliver when he took over his property, and in the meantime his mother would have charge of it. And Margaret liked money.

'Exactly,' nodded Aunt Bess, looking quite wicked and braced herself to receive the rapturous onslaught of her great-nephew.

They left Dimworth in some style. Miss Creed liked to travel in comfort; the Rover Sterling with Dobbs at the wheel would convey them to Holland, and they would stay a night on the way at the small, exclusive hotel in Mayfair where she had always stayed when visiting London before boarding the Hovercraft to take them across the channel. Oliver, sitting in front with Dobbs, was speechless with delight, and Jenny, beside her aunt on the back seat, felt exactly the same. Fortunately for her, Aunt Bess dozed for the greater part of the journey, so that she was able to give full rein to her thoughts. About the Professor, of course; she had at last discovered where he lived. North of den Haag, where he had beds in two hospitals, and not too far from Amsterdam, it seemed, for he held a teaching post at the medical school there. Aunt Bess had been annoyingly vague, though—somewhere close to the sea, she had hazarded, and when Jenny had asked where they were to stay she had been even more vague. 'Oh, Eduard has arranged all that,' Jenny was told.

Jenny frowned and hoped that she had brought the right clothes with her. The jersey dress and jacket would do very well for their necessary trips to the hospital and any sightseeing they might do, and she had packed slacks and tops in case there was a chance to take Oliver to the beach. She had added a couple of pretty evening dresses too; presumably they would be staying in an hotel and as Aunt Bess refused to alter her way of life, no matter where she was, Jenny guessed that it would be the kind of place where one dressed for dinner. She reflected rather unhappily that probably she would see almost nothing of the Professor, which was perhaps a good thing, for the more she saw of him the harder it would be to go on pretending that she didn't like him. On the other hand, she couldn't wait to see him again...

Safely across the Dutch frontier, Dobbs increased his pace. They would arrive in time for tea; Jenny calculated that while she looked about her at the flat, tranquil countryside. Aunt Bess was dozing again and Oliver, with the faithful Dobbs to answer his whispered questions was fully occupied. Fortunately Dobbs had been in Holland during the second world war and was ready with his answers. At least one member of the party was having a lovely time thought Jenny, smiling at the small coppery head in front of her. Oliver had been delighted at the prospect of spending hours in Dobbs' company while Jenny and Aunt Bess were at the hospital. For one thing he told him stories about the father he could barely remember, and for another he had an unending supply of toffees. She had no doubt that Oliver would be as well looked after as the Crown Jewels.

The country had become wooded and the road they were now on ran straight between trees. There were occasional glimpses of houses on either side, solid villas half hidden behind trees, and every so often a small neat village. It was hard to believe that den Haag and Amsterdam were neither of them far away. Dobbs was looking for signposts now, and presently he turned off into a country road with dense undergrowth on either side and Oliver turned round to Jenny, his face alight with excitement. 'Dobbs says we're there,' he whispered importantly, and pointed.

She looked obediently in the direction of his finger. She could see no hotel, only an open gateway leading to a drive bordered by a rose hedge, meticulously tended, but round the first corner she had her first glimpse of it; an austere, almost mediaeval place built of small red bricks, with narrow windows, a pepperpot tower at either end of its front and a very grand entrance. Old, thought, Jenny, and not in the least like an hotel—probably the owners had had to sell it in order to pay death duties. It would suit Aunt Bess exactly, though—the Professor had chosen well. She roused her aunt gently, set the toque she always wore—just like Aunt Bess's dear queen—straight on the elegantly dressed head, and prepared to alight.

Oliver was already standing on the gravel sweep, gazing up at the forbidding walls, his small mouth open, while Dobbs opened the car door ready to assist Miss Creed. It was left for Jenny to collect handbags, scarves and all the small paraphernalia with which Aunt Bess travelled, and then get out herself. She did so from the door furthest from the house, so that for the moment she couldn't see the entrance, hidden by the car's substantial bulk, but she heard the Professor's voice and stood still for a moment, catching her surprised breath. She had been looking forward to seeing him with her whole heart, but this was unexpected and she hadn't expected to feel quite like this when she did. It was like jumping off a high diving board, or finding oneself at the top of a mountain—her breath had been taken from her and her heart had shot up into her throat. She swallowed that organ back to where it belonged, steadied her breathing and walked round the back of the car.

He was standing with Aunt Bess, a hand on Oliver's small shoulder, giving some instructions to Dobbs about the luggage and when he saw Jenny he came to meet her. He showed no sign of pleasure at the sight of her—perhaps he had been expecting Margaret—but his greeting was pleasant if a little cool. 'You had a pleasant journey?' he wanted to know. 'I expect you would like a cup of tea before you do anything else. Shall we go in?'

The handsome door opened into a square hall of some size, with an enormous hooded fireplace to one side of it, flanked by massive armchairs. The table in the centre was massive too, with a great bowl of flowers on it. The walls held a great many paintings and a variety of weapons; Jenny eyed them as she looked round for the reception desk. There wasn't one, which seemed strange for an hotel—perhaps they didn't have them in

Holland. She asked: 'Our rooms are booked, aren't they? I can't see anyone to ask—it's very quiet...'

The Professor smiled with quite odious mockery. 'It had better be—I dislike noise in my home.'

'Your home...?' She goggled at him. 'I thought—that is, Aunt Bess said...'

He answered her blandly. 'A little forgetful, perhaps.'

Jenny gave him a puzzled look. 'Well, yes—perhaps she is. Did you know that Oliver would be with us?'

'Indeed I did.' He was staring at her rather hard. 'A pity that Margaret was unable to come.'

She looked away, studying a nearby portrait of some bygone van Draak te Solendijk; he might have been the Professor with a ruff and a neat little beard... She said soberly: 'I'm sorry about that, truly I am.' She frowned in thought. 'You know, once Aunt Bess is dealt with there's no reason why I shouldn't go back to Dimworth and she could come here...'

'My dear Jenny, I had no idea that you had such a kind heart—as far as I'm concerned, that is. I'm sure it does you credit.'

She glanced to where Aunt Bess and Oliver were absorbed in a vast painting of some sea battle or other. 'You have no need to be nasty,' she observed coldly, 'just because it's me here instead of Margaret. I didn't want to come,' she added with a complete lack of truth.

'I? Nasty? My dear girl, you are mistaken—I merely protect myself. Your poet Aaron Hill wrote something a long time ago—let me see—"Tender-handed stroke a nettle and it stings you for your pains; grasp it like a man of mettle and it soft as silk remains." Er—I daresay you can be as soft as silk, Jenny—you certainly sting.'

'What a perfectly beastly...' She was interrupted by Aunt Bess, her compelling voice uplifted.

'Some good paintings here,' she observed, 'comparable to those at Dimworth—probably better,' she conceded graciously.

The Professor was too well mannered to agree. He made a deprecating sound and led the lady towards the double doors to one side of the hall. They were opened from the inside by a short, stout man with a solemn face, whom the Professor addressed as Hans. He bowed with great dignity to the ladies and endeared himself greatly to Jenny by winking at Oliver, who winked back, delighted.

Tea was all that Aunt Bess could have wished for; thin cucumber sandwiches, a cake as light as air, little sugary biscuits, and tea poured from a silver tea-pot. And their surroundings matched the meal in elegance—a lovely room, long and narrow, furnished with what Jenny described to herself as Dimworth furniture. Only the curtains were a great deal more elaborate; thick brocaded velvet in a rich crimson, swathed and looped and fringed. She liked them, just as she liked the great chairs and dainty little tables and the enormous glass-fronted cabinet between the high, narrow windows.

'Is it open to the public?' asked Oliver.

The Professor handed cake to Aunt Bess. 'No, I'm afraid not. You see, Oliver, I should have to be at home a good deal if I were to do that, and I'm not—I'm at the hospital or my consulting rooms for a long time each day.'

Very nicely put, decided Jenny; probably the idea of helping out the revenue by charging so much a head to look round his home had never entered the Professor's head. Probably he was rich—well, he would have to be to live in such a house; large and difficult to heat, she suspected, and certainly needing a number of people to look after it. She longed to see more of it, and the wish was granted when he asked.

'Would you like to see your rooms? Miss Creed, I hope you will feel well enough to come to the hospital in den Haag tomorrow. There are several tests I should like to do—they won't take long, and it would be a good idea to get them over and done with.'

'Whatever you say, Eduard.' Aunt Bess sounded gracious and almost meek.

They went upstairs then, under the guidance of a small round woman, no longer young but very bustling in manner, with a cheerful face and pepper-and-salt hair severely dressed—Hans' wife, Hennie, the Professor had told them as she smiled a welcome, took Oliver by the hand and led them up the gracefully curved staircase to the floor above.

Their rooms were at the side of the house, close together, with Jenny's in the middle, separated from her aunt by a bathroom, and from Oliver by a communicating door. Hennie indicated that she would unpack for Miss Creed, and fussed her gently and not unwillingly into a chair, which left Jenny free to inspect her own room while Oliver ran backwards and forwards, inviting her urgently to look at this and that and the other thing in his own room. She smiled and nodded and said a little absently: 'Yes, in a moment, dear,' and went on with her tour of inspection. The room was furnished in a later period than the house had been built—Hepplewhite, with the bed, canopied with muslin, of satinwood, as was the dressing table and mirror upon it and the tallboy against one wall. The chairs were made for comfort, upholstered in pale pink striped silk, matching the curtains. The lamps were a rosy pink too and there were a variety of small silver and china ornaments which exactly suited the pale pastel portraits on the panelled walls. 'Very nice,' said Jenny out loud, and kicked off a shoe to feel the thickness of the moss green carpet.

Oliver returned hopefully to say: 'Isn't it super—do you think all the other rooms are like this one? It's a bit like Dimworth.'

'Yes, my lamb, though I think it's a good deal older than Dimworth.'

'Wait until I tell Mummy! Is he very rich?'

'And who is *he*?' asked Jenny reprovingly. 'If you mean Professor van Draak, I have no idea, but I should suppose he might be. It's no business of ours darling.' She was admiring a delicate porcelain figure she had picked up from a little work-table, and Oliver had gone to look out of the mullioned window.

'You don't sound as though you want to know Jenny. Mummy does—she said it mattered. Does it matter?'

She put the figure back carefully and gave him her full attention. 'Not one little bit, Oliver.'

And it didn't; she would settle most willingly for a completely penniless Professor, and if necessary live in one of those dreadful little modern houses like boxes, wearing last year's clothes and cooking cheap wholesome meals for him and the happy brood of children they would undoubtedly have. She was so lost in her daydream that she only just heard the little boy say in a small voice: 'Mummy wants to marry the Professor.'

Put into words, even a child's words, it sounded very final, but Jenny made a great effort. 'Well, dear, your mummy is a very pretty lady, you know, and although she loved your daddy very much, she feels lonely.'

'So do I. Professor van Draak wouldn't be happy...'

She went and knelt beside him and put her arms round his small shoulders. 'Why not, love?'

'Not at Dimworth—he's a surgeon.' His voice implied that she had asked a silly question, but Jenny was spared having to answer this awkward but wise remark by the loud barking of a dog, a distraction which sent Oliver to the window again, his worries forgotten. 'Oh, look—Jenny, it's two dogs and a cat, and the Professor's with them. May I go down?'

She went to look as she had been bidden. The grounds stretched away below them, turf with herbaceous borders leading to more open ground, well shrubbed and with trees in the distance as well as the gleam of water. The Professor was strolling across the grass, a great Dane treading beside him while a dog of extremely mixed parentage gavotted round them, while bringing up the rear was a very ordinary tabby cat.

'Very well, dear, but ask the Professor if you may go with him, don't just attach yourself to him.'

'He won't mind,' declared Oliver, making for the door. 'He likes boys, he said so, he's been a boy himself.'

Jenny turned her back on the window and unpacked before going to see how her aunt fared. 'I shall change for dinner,' declared that lady. 'You will go and tell Eduard so, Jenny, and come back in half an hour to help me with my hair before you dress.'

Jenny eyed her aunt doubtfully. 'Perhaps the Professor doesn't bother to change when he's home,' she offered, to be met with a positive: 'He has guests and will behave accordingly, Janet.'

She went slowly downstairs and out of the house door. The Professor, Oliver and the animals were already some distance away, making for the water—presumably a pond. Jenny reached them as they came to a halt at its edge to watch the ducks upon it, and they all turned round to look at her.

'Everything all right?' he wanted to know, and she had the feeling that he hadn't wanted her there. It made her say with a touch of haughtiness: 'Perfectly, thank you. Aunt Bess asked me to let you know that she intends dressing for dinner.'

He raised his eyebrows. 'How thoughtful of her—but hardly necessary.'

Jenny went pink. 'No—well, she didn't mean it like that. It's just that she's a little set in her ways.'

She waited uncertainly while he dug a hand into a pocket and handed Oliver a crust of bread. 'There you are, boy, and don't fall in.'

Oliver lifted adoring eyes to the big man's face. 'You do think of everything, don't you?' He started towards the reeds where the ducks were and then came back. 'Do I have to have my supper with you?'

His host smiled. 'No, I think not. Hennie will give you your supper when she gets back to the house and see you safely to bed. She's very kind.'

'Have you any more servants?' Oliver wanted to know, and Jenny said: 'Hush, my lamb, that's rude!'

But the Professor answered, just as though she hadn't said anything: 'Oh, yes, several, but Hennie is my old friend as well as my housekeeper and she will look after you especially well.'

Oliver nodded and wandered off happily, leaving Jenny to apologise for his lack of manners. 'But he's only six,' she explained.

Her companion had stooped to pick up the cat. 'I wasn't aware that I had complained about the boy,' he observed blandly. 'I expect you have things to do—I'll bring him back to the house presently.'

She wanted very much to burst into tears; he was rude and arrogant and quite unfeeling, and she hated him! No, hate was too good a word, she loathed him. She said in an icy voice: 'You don't have to take it out on me just because I'm here and Margaret isn't. I didn't ask to come, and now I wish I hadn't...'

She flounced off, using considerable self-control in not looking back, and having gained her room, spent a few minutes thinking up all the awful things she would like to happen to him. Considerably cheered by this exercise, she made her way to Aunt Bess's room, where she performed all the small tasks demanded of her and then went back to her own room once more, to dress herself carelessly in the first thing that came to hand, sweep her glowing hair into a severe knot, slap powder on to her pretty nose and put on the wrong lipstick. 'Who cares?' she asked her reflection ferociously, and went next door to see if Oliver was in bed.

He wasn't exactly in bed, but at least he was pottering happily around his room with Hennie in loving attendance. Jenny wrung a promise from him that he would be in bed in exactly ten minutes and went downstairs to join the others. She found them in the drawing room, chatting amiably, and because she was well brought up, she chatted too, seething beneath the bodice of her flowered silk dress. She ate her dinner too with every appearance of enjoyment, only her eyes flashed temper at her host when he addressed her, even though she schooled her tongue to utter platitudes by way of answer.

They sat a long while over their meal, round a mahogany table decked with silver and crystal and spotless white linen. The room was square and of a good size, and Jenny, peeping round her whenever she had the opportunity, loved its rich amber curtains and needlework carpet and the dark panelling of the walls. The Professor lived in comfort—not that he deserved it. She scowled at the idea and looked up to find his eyes upon her. His smile, knowing and mocking, made her scowl even fiercer.

It was when they had gone to the drawing room and had taken their coffee in a leisurely fashion, that the Professor had suggested to his patient that perhaps an early night might be of benefit to her, doing it in such a way that she was unaware that he had made the suggestion in the first place, only remarking that she considered it high time that they were all in bed as she rose to her feet. He got up too, walking unhurriedly to the door with her, crossing the hall, still talking casually before bidding her goodnight at the foot of the staircase. Jenny behind them, made to go upstairs too, but he caught her firmly as she passed him so that she was forced to stand still.

'I will settle the details about your visit to the hospital with Jenny, Miss Creed,' he suggested smoothly. 'I'm sure you won't wish to be bothered with them.'

'Very considerate,' agreed Aunt Bess, turning to look at them from halfway up the staircase. 'And don't keep Eduard up unnecessarily, Jenny; he has had a busy day. I'm sure.' She went on her stately way and turned once more to remark: 'A delicious dinner, Eduard. Goodnight.'

Her majestic back disappeared from sight and the Professor's hold slackened. 'We can't talk here, shall we go back to the drawing room?'

Jenny went with him, saying nothing at all. If he wanted to give her some instructions, let him do so, she couldn't stop him.

But when they were once more sitting facing each her he asked: 'What exactly did you mean about Margaret?'

'What I said. And if that's all you want to talk about, I think I will go to bed.'

'Carved from an ice block,' he mused, 'with your "Yes, Professor, no, Professor" as meek as you like, and your eyes killing me. Tell me, Jenny, do you really dislike me so much? Oh, I tease you deliberately just to see you get angry, but is that sufficient reason for you to treat me as though I had the plague?'

He crossed to her chair and pulled her to her feet, holding her hands fast in his, and turned her round so that the lamplight shone on to her face. 'Well—Do you dislike me?'

She must have been made to have supposed that she loathed him—hated him, even disliked him—how could that be possible when she loved him so much? He was the only man she would ever want to marry, she knew that for certain, and if he married Margaret her heart would break, but he mustn't be allowed to even guess at that. She said stonily: 'No, I don't like you, Professor van Draak,' because there was nothing else she could have said. And it couldn't matter to him in the least what she thought of him if he were in love with Margaret. Supposing she said 'I love you very much', what would he do? she wondered miserably. Despite his mocking smile and his nasty remarks he was a kind man, she was sure of that, and he would feel badly if she let him see that she had a *tendresse* for him.

He let her hands go and smiled a little. 'One of the nastiest stings the nettle has given me so far,' he declared lightly, 'but it's best to clear the air, isn't it?' He moved a little away and pulled the great dane's ears gently and went on pleasantly: 'Will you come with your aunt tomorrow? It may make things easier for her. There isn't a great deal to do—a sample of blood and I should like to do a scan…one or two tests…they should take two or three hours, no more. Hans will drive you there and bring you back, that will leave Dobbs free to stay with Oliver. I was going to suggest that you both came with me in the morning, but

I think now that it would be better if Hans takes you. I should like Miss Creed to rest when she comes back here; there will be several more tests and I don't want her to get tired. Three days should suffice, for I don't intend to overtax her strength.'

He smiled down at her, so kindly that Jenny only just prevented herself from putting out a hand to catch his sleeve and tell him what her true feelings were. But that would never do; she agreed politely, promised to have her aunt ready at the required hour and wished him goodnight. He didn't walk with her to the door and she didn't look back as she went out of the room.

CHAPTER SEVEN

Jenny found the next three days difficult even though they were interesting. The Professor treated her with the courtesy of a good host, but as he confined his conversations with her to her aunt's condition, suggestions as to times of appointments and similar dull topics; even if she had wanted to retract every word she had said on that first evening, it would have been impossible to get through the invisible but none the less solid barrier he had erected between them. After all, before, despite their disagreements, there had been a certain camaraderie between them, now there was nothing at all.

But if she was unhappy, Oliver was in the seventh heaven; with Dobbs as an ever-watchful companion, he had gone sightseeing; to the Maduradam at den Haag, to a number of castles in the vicinity and to the coast to see the sea and play on the sands. And when he wasn't at one or other of these places, he was pottering in a small rowboat on the pond, learning to use the oars under Hans' guidance, or eating the satisfying meals Hennie prepared for him. Life for him, at least, was bliss.

Aunt Bess seemed content enough too. True, her days were largely taken up with visits to the hospital and the rather wearisome hours there, and there were occasional visits to the Professor's consulting rooms too, but as these were organised with an eye to her comfort and convenience, she bore them with an equanimity which Jenny found nothing short of astonishing.

On their first visit to the hospital, driven there by Hans very shortly after breakfast, they had been met in the entrance hall by an elderly Sister whose English, although heavily accented, was more than adequate. She had whisked them away to the Surgical Floor and installed them in a waiting room, and Aunt Bess had barely had the time to complain at being kept waiting before a nurse came to usher them into the Professor's own sanctum.

It was much like any other consulting room. Jenny decided that if it hadn't been for some books on the shelves with ponderous-looking Dutch titles, it might have been in England, and indeed, when she looked more closely, there were a great many books with English titles, too, as well as French and German.

The Professor had risen from behind his desk to greet them and it was at once obvious that was no longer Eduard but Professor van Draak, about to examine his patient. Aunt Bess, ever one to speak her mind, had remarked upon this immediately with a: 'Ah—professional treatment, is it? I must remember not to call you Eduard. Jenny, take my jacket, I can't think why I brought it with me in the first place. Now, what am I to do first?'

The examination had progressed satisfactorily; from time to time Aunt Bess had demurred about something or other, but only because she felt bound to do so, and she was easily overborne by the Professor, suavely having his own way. Jenny, sitting silently close by, getting up and doing what she was required to do in her usual sensible fashion, couldn't help but admire the ease with which he managed his patient. At the same time she deplored the fact that he took absolutely no notice of herself. But that was her own fault.

Hans took them back to Kasteel te Solendijk afterwards, to a late lunch without the Professor, before Jenny settled her aunt for a nap. Having done which she felt free to do whatever she liked until teatime.

On that first afternoon she had toured the house with Hennie, and come to the conclusion that although it was vastly different from Dimworth, it was just as lovely, and certainly its contents were a good deal older, as was the house itself. She had remarked this at dinner that evening and the Professor had thanked her gravely without offering any further comment. This had the effect of making her feel peevish, so that she was glad when her aunt decided to go to bed very shortly after they had had their coffee and she was able to make her own excuses. Of course, if their host had even so much as hinted that he would enjoy her society for the evening, she would have changed her mind on the instant, but he did no such thing, only wished her a formal goodnight, which had the unhappy effect of rendering her sleepless.

The next day and the day after that were very much the same; Jenny, not sleeping well, presented a tired, pale face at breakfast, and it was perhaps as well that their host had already left in the morning before she and Oliver got downstairs, and if he did notice her quietness, he didn't remark upon it, although he was pleasant enough in a remote way and very considerate of her comfort as well as that of her aunt. And on the third morning, while she waited for Aunt Bess in the X-ray department, he sought her out to tell her that if she wished, one of the Sisters would take her round the hospital.

It was an enjoyable hour. Her guide had been a girl of her own age whose English, although limited, was enthusiastic. She was the Children's Ward Sister and they went there first, and Jenny, very impressed with the bright, cheerful place, peered and poked and asked endless questions before going to the Surgical Block; they spent so much time there that they had had to skimp the Medical side in order to see the Theatre Wing. Here Jenny was on home ground, and the two of them became immersed in a discussion on the best equipment for the recovery room and how it should be run, the number of nurses necessary to deal with it all, and they had their heads together over the newest thing in pumps for heart surgery when a student nurse came to tell them that the Professor was waiting for them.

They found him at the entrance, looking impatient, and Jenny made haste to apologise, still so full of her tour that she forgot to be distant with him. 'I got carried away,' she explained. 'There was such a lot to see in the Theatre Block.'

'I'm glad you found it interesting,' he told her repressively, and then turned to say something in a quite different tone of voice to her guide, who smiled and nodded and looked pleased with herself before shaking Jenny's hand and hurrying away.

'Your aunt refused to wait for you,' said the Professor crossly. 'You will have to come with me—I'll drop you off on my way.'

'Where to?' asked Jenny, and regretted her words when he replied, still cross:

'Since you are curious enough to ask—Amsterdam.'

He walked towards the door and a porter hurried after them to open it, and she was ushered out to the forecourt where the Panther de Ville was parked. They didn't speak at all until he drew up before his own front door, and when Jenny said politely: 'Thank you very much, Professor,' all she got was a curt: 'Well, don't expect me to say that it was a pleasure,' a remark which cast her into the depths for the remainder of that day.

There were to be no more tests for Aunt Bess, only a few days waiting for the results, so that she declared that she would enjoy a little peace and quiet in the gardens, recruiting her strength, and Jenny, egged on by Oliver, suggested that the pair of them might go to Amsterdam and have a look round. 'Oliver's dying to go, and so am I,' she declared. 'If Dobbs would drive us there, we could come back by train and telephone when we get to the station and he can pick us up there.'

The Professor wasn't there to cast a damper on her suggestion, and Aunt Bess could see no harm in it. Jenny was warned to take good care of Oliver, make sure that she had sufficient money with her and took care what they ate, and allowed to make her plans.

It seemed prudent to make them while the Professor was still absent, so that when the subject was broached at dinner that evening, there was really nothing much he could do about it, although she could see that he didn't approve. She sat, a delightful picture in the silvery crêpe dress she had put on with the mistaken idea that it made her look inconspicuous, her eyes on her plate, so that the lashes curled on her cheeks, trying not to look pleased because he was, for once, not to have his own way.

She could see no reason at all why she and Oliver shouldn't go to Amsterdam; Dobbs could drop them off in the heart of the city and from there they could take a canal boat and tour the waterways before having a good look at the shops. Left to herself she would have visited as many museums as she could have crowded into the time available, but one could hardly expect a lively six-year-old boy to do that—besides, he wanted to buy his mother a present. They would have lunch too, somewhere well-known; Jenny had a guide book and had ticked off the most likely restaurants.

She mentioned all this reluctantly to her host, but only because she was unable to do anything else in the face of his direct questions. His final grunt of disapproval made her all the more determined to go. It was ridiculous that he should consider her incapable of spending a day out without coming to grief.

And it was infuriating to watch his nasty little smile. She could imagine him saying 'I told you so' if by some remote chance their day should go awry. Spurred on by the smile, she remarked defiantly: 'It will be a day to remember,' and added for good measure: 'I don't suppose you enjoy that sort of thing any more.'

He had looked at her then with a sudden cold anger which caught the breath in her throat, aware that she had been rude and unkind too. She wanted to get up and run to him and beg his forgiveness and tell him that she hadn't meant a word of it.

Who was it who had said that one always wanted to hurt the one one loved? How very true! She had actually made a movement to rise when Aunt Bess, silent too long, began a rambling dissertation on the intricacies of family history, which allowed of neither of her listeners speaking until she had finished, and by then it was too late. All the same, Jenny tried again when they left the table, asking diffidently if he had a few minutes to spare her as she had something she wished to say to him, to be instantly snubbed with a chilly civility which froze her bones.

'Unfortunately I have several important telephone calls to make,' he told her with a smile which didn't reach his eyes. 'Tomorrow, perhaps?'

But of course he had left the house by the time she and Oliver got downstairs; moreover, Hans told her that the master of the house expected to be late home that evening and trusted that his guests would excuse him.

'So that's that,' sighed Jenny, and because it was Oliver's day, applied herself to the excitements lying head of them.

They left soon after breakfast, having bidden Aunt Bess goodbye and made sure that she had all she wanted before getting into the car with Dobbs at the wheel. Jenny, on the back seat by herself, studied her map of Amsterdam once more and then sat back to view the countryside. It was a fine day with a blue sky and a brisk wind and little chance of rain, which was a good thing for to please Oliver she had put on a pale blue jersey dress he particularly liked. If it rained it would be tiresome, but there would be shelter enough in the city and Hans had assured her that there were plenty of trains running when they wanted to return.

Dobbs didn't like leaving them when they reached the square in front of the main station; he spent quite five minutes trying to persuade them to get back into the car while he drove them on a personally conducted tour of the city, until Jenny said gently: 'Look, Dobbs, it isn't that we wouldn't like to come with you, it's just that we want to escape—just an hour or two...'

He understood her well enough and grinned in sympathy as he said goodbye, leaving them to join the queue for a canal boat.

The trip was exciting because they were in a foreign city and everything looked different, especially from the canals: the funny little gabled houses with their windows overlooking the water, the enormous mansions with their high windows and great doors, the narrow bridges and the people walking or cycling along the streets alongside them, even a street organ belting out some jolly tune which exactly suited their mood. As they stepped out of the boat, Oliver wheedled: 'Let's do it again, Jenny—please! I want to look at it all—it was so quick… look, there's another boat just going to leave!'

Jenny laughed at him. 'All right, my lamb, but I'll have to race to get the tickets. Wait here.'

There were quite a lot of people round the ticket booths even though the tourist season was almost over now. Foreigners like herself, she thought resignedly, waiting her turn. It was a minute or two before she had her new tickets and made her way back to where she had left Oliver. He wasn't there; she looked round carefully, for he couldn't be far away. But he was; she heard his shrill voice calling her name gleefully and turned round once more to see the boat gliding away at a great rate with him waving from a seat in the middle. He was perfectly happy, indeed she could see that he was laughing. She just had time to memorise the number of the boat before it disappeared under the first bridge; there was nothing to do for it but to remain where she was until it returned, almost an hour away.

She found a stone wall to sit on and fell to pondering what she should do. Must Oliver be punished by being taken straight back to the Professor's house? But probably he hadn't done it deliberately, only become impatient and gone on board in his eagerness not to miss a further treat.

And if he had done it deliberately, wasn't it the kind of thing all little boys did at some time or other? Margaret didn't allow him much freedom and he led a dull life… Jenny sensibly decided to wait and see what he had to say for himself when he got back, and waited patiently for the hour to pass while a dozen frightening possibilities chased themselves round and round inside her head.

The waiting time seemed long; when she saw the boat at last she made herself walk unhurriedly to the spot where it would berth, prepared to use more patience, for the boat was very full. But she knew real panic when the last passenger disembarked and there was no Oliver. There were already people boarding the craft for the next trip and she wormed her way through them, oblivious of the annoyed glances around her, and found the guide.

'A little boy,' she said breathlessly, 'six years with coppery-red-hair. He got on while I was getting the tickets. He hasn't come back.'

The guide was a tall girl with a cheerful face, 'I saw him,' she spoke in excellent English, 'he sat over there.' She pointed to a seat halfway along the gang way. 'He was talking to the people with him—I thought he belonged to them.' She paused. 'Not?' she wanted to know.

'Not,' said Jenny soberly. 'Did he get off, with them? I didn't know these boats stopped.'

The guide nodded. 'I am sure that he did. We are not supposed to stop, but sometimes if it is something very special, and these people were Dutch and had a reason—the lady felt sick.'

Jenny's mouth had gone dry, but she said steadily: 'Please will you tell me where that was? I must find him—he'll be lost...'

'Just past the Leidesstraat; we go under a bridge there and there is another canal crossing the Heerengracht at that point. There is a small landing stage there—we stopped for only a minute.'

'I don't even know where it is,' said Jenny wildly, and then, common sense coming to her aid: 'Thank you very much, you've been very kind—I'll get a taxi.'

The intending passengers were milling all round her now, annoyed at being delayed. It took her a few minutes to get off the boat, for as fast as she made for the exit, she was pushed back by a fresh wave of incoming people. Once on the quay she made herself stand still and think sensibly. Oliver had some money with him—not much, though, and although he was an adventurous little boy she didn't think that he would do anything foolish. He might even think of taking a taxi back to the boat stage. She went back to the ticket booth and found someone there who understood English. 'If a small boy with red hair comes here, will you please ask him to wait? That I'll be back very soon. I'm going to look for him.' She repeated the words for a second time, not quite sure that her listener understood, and finally turned away.

The Professor was so close behind her that she tumbled into him and had to catch his sleeve to avoid falling. Her spontaneous, 'Eduard—oh, thank heaven you're here!' was uttered before she remembered that they weren't on speaking terms any more, it seemed quite right and natural that he should be there when she wanted him, so she gave him a shaky smile, unaware that her face was quite white and that she looked scared out of her wits. 'I've lost Oliver—he got on the boat while I was getting the tickets...' The whole story tumbled out in a cascade of words, half of which didn't make sense.

The Professor removed her hands from his coat sleeve. 'So he has been gone for just over an hour.' His eyes, very cold and blue, stared down into hers. 'He could be anywhere. We will go to the landing stage you speak of and find out if anyone saw him leave the boat and which direction he took. If we draw a blank, we will go to the police.'

He walked her across the street to a taxi rank and told her to get into the cab. When he was seated beside her, he asked: 'How much money had he with him?'

'About twenty gulden—he was going to buy his mother a present.' Jenny spoke in a carefully controlled voice, her hands gripping each other tightly on her lap, while a procession of all the frightful things which could happen to a small lost boy wove its way through her brain.

At the landing stage she made herself stand quietly while the Professor made some enquiries and at the third attempt had success.

An old man, sitting on a stool, smoking and watching the world go by. He remembered Oliver quite clearly; the boy had stood for a few moments talking to a man and woman who had apparently been pointing out the way to him, for he had waved quite cheerfully to them and gone off down the *steeg* between the general stores and the tobacconists—and furthermore, in answer to the Professor's persistent questions, the boy had seemed perfectly happy—certainly not frightened. That was the extent of his memory. The Professor rewarded him suitably and rejoined Jenny.

She said at once: 'You've got news, haven't you? Is he all right? Where is he?' Her mouth, despite her best efforts, shook a little. 'I'm very sorry...'

'A little late in the day for that,' remarked her companion severely. 'Of all the silly things to do...however, that can wait. He went down this *steeg*, I imagine, on his way to the shops, for they can be reached from here, provided one knows the way I suggest that we walk down it now, searching every passage leading off it. You take that side, I will take this, and we will meet at the end. He may have fallen down or lost his way—the *steegs* all look alike—he may even be asleep in some corner, so look well. Can you whistle?'

Jenny understood him at once. 'Yes.'

'That is at least something to be thankful for,' he commented drily. 'One long and two short if you find him—and stay with him, for pity's sake.'

She had no idea of doing anything else, but she supposed she deserved his scorn and set off meekly beside him, to turn into the first narrow passage after a few yards. She went to its end—a blank wall, part of a factory, she supposed, and the tiny, derelict houses on either side showed no sign of life either. She retraced her footsteps and encountered the Professor returning from a similar search on his side, and parted from him almost immediately to turn into the next alley, with high walls on either side this time and ending in a shed neatly piled with bits and pieces of old cars. She searched every inch of it before going back, this time to see her companion's large back disappearing down a similar passage on his side. The next *steeg* wound itself between small houses at first and then blank walls again. Jenny had gone halfway down its length when she saw Oliver ahead of her, coming in her direction. He had a boy on either side of him, both coloured and in their early teens, each holding a hand. Jenny began to run, tearing over the cobbles at a great rate, calling his name in little gusty breaths while all the while she was wondering what he was doing there and who were the boys. Was he being kidnapped? He was calling to her now, but she didn't stop to listen—supposing the boys turned and ran off with him before she could reach them? She didn't see the banana skin on the ground; she skidded along the cobbles and fell, banging her head, aware at the last split second that she had knocked herself out.

When she opened her eyes, it was to encounter the Professor's blazing down at her, so that she closed them again at once, unwilling to face such fury. But she heard him say furiously: 'Why the hell didn't you whistle?' and before she could answer that: 'No don't talk. Oliver is here safe—these two boys were showing him the way back. His sense of adventure got the better of him, I fancy. You will stay exactly as you are while I get a taxi.'

Which remark naturally made her want to sit up immediately. 'I'm perfectly all right,' she said in a voice which wasn't quite steady.

'I know that,' he sounded annoyingly matter-of-fact about it, 'but you cut your head a little and knocked yourself out. You should pay more attention to where you are going.'

It was really the last straw—to be hauled over the coals like this when she had been doing her utmost...'Oh, stop pointing out my faults!' she cried furiously. 'That's all you do... I'm sick and tired...'

He said something she couldn't understand because it was in his own language and she didn't bother to open her eyes because her head ached. She felt his arm slide from her shoulders and instead Oliver's small hand wormed its way into hers. His voice, a little worried, whispered in her ear: 'Jenny, I didn't mean to frighten you, truly I didn't—I thought I'd look for a present for Mummy and then we would have more time for lunch. I was going to come back, but I got lost. Those boys were super—the Professor gave them some money. He's gone to get a taxi.'

She opened her eyes then and smiled at the small, earnest face peering down at her. 'Yes, my lamb.'

'You're not cross? He wasn't.'

She gave the Professor a good mark for that; he must understand children. 'No, I'm not cross—not a bit. Only you frightened me a little, Oliver—you see, you knew where you'd gone, but I didn't. Next time just let me know before you go, then I shan't worry. But it's really a much better idea to know your way around before you go off on your own—I'm sure the Professor would agree with that.'

She closed her eyes again and then opened them quickly because the taxi had arrived and she felt a fool, propped up against the wall, looking, she felt sure, like nothing on earth. And indeed, looking down at herself, she was a sight; the dress was a ruin for a start, for she had caught her heel in it as she fell, and the bodice was covered with small flecks of blood. Worse, her hair had come loose and was hanging round her shoulders in a very tatty fashion.

The Professor bent to lift her from the street and she protested fiercely—a waste of time and breath, for he didn't even bother to answer her, just settled her in the taxi, lifted Oliver into the seat by the driver, and then got in beside her.

'We can't go home,' she muttered.

'Not at once. You are going to have that head attended to and then we will have lunch—a meal will do you good. We can go home later.'

She would have argued about that, but her head was beginning to ache again. All the same, she asked: 'How did you know where we were?'

'Dobbs had already told me where you intended to go, and if you remember, you mentioned it yourself during dinner yesterday evening. And now stop talking and give that headache a chance.'

Jenny hadn't really bothered to think where she was being taken. It was only as the taxi drew up before a quite obvious hospital entrance that she exclaimed: 'Oh, there's no need for me to go here!'

'Be quiet,' said the Professor, and lifted her out, keeping an arm round her while he paid the driver. 'Go the other side of Jenny,' he told Oliver, 'and take her hand.'

For such a small cut she felt that a great deal of fuss was being made; perhaps because the Professor was known; he would be a consultant there, of course, which accounted for the immediate response to his wishes. She was provided with tea, sat comfortably in a chair and had her head examined carefully under his watchful eyes before the wound was cleaned, covered, and her hair combed and tied back neatly. She felt quite herself by now and was able to exchange a few words with the Sister and nurse who had helped her, given her an ATS injection and assured her that she had nothing to worry about before handing her back to the Professor with a tender care which he, however, didn't reflect. His casual: 'OK?' was presumably all that he felt it necessary to say before walking her out to the forecourt. True, his arm was under hers, but he would have done that for anyone who had just knocked themselves out...

The Panther de Ville was there; he must have fetched it from somewhere—the hospital itself perhaps? That made sense. What didn't make sense was the direction they took, for in a very few minutes they were driving down the Singel, the innermost semi-circular canal of the four principal ones which ringed the city, and Jenny wasn't so silly that she didn't know that travelling into the city's heart wouldn't get them on the road to den Haag. He had said something about a meal; perhaps he had a favourite restaurant. She felt hungry then, although she hoped that it wouldn't be too noisy, thoughts which led naturally enough to remembering the state of her dress. She couldn't possibly be seen in it—only a man, she thought crossly, would ignore such an important point.

Only the Professor hadn't ignored it; he turned into a narrow street lined with elegant houses and small shops and stopped outside one of them. He got out, saw Oliver safely on to the pavement and then opened the car door again. 'Feel up to buying a dress?' he asked casually. 'You can't go round in that thing.'

She stiffened; 'that thing' had cost her a pretty penny not so long ago, although she had to admit that now it wasn't fit to be seen. She allowed herself to be escorted into the shop—and a very elegant shop too—and wondered how he knew of it in the first place. The saleswoman knew him too; she smiled and chattered for a few moments and then broke into very fair English.

'I have just the dress for you, miss—not such a charming blue, but elegant.' She beamed widely. 'Miss has a charming figure.' A remark which drew no response from any of them as Jenny was led away to the fitting room.

The dress was pretty, duck egg blue jersey, with wide sleeves and an open neck and with a silk blouse of a paler shade to wear beneath it. It was a perfect fit too, but when Jenny asked its price the saleswoman seemed suddenly bereft of all knowledge of English so that Jenny was forced to ask the Professor's help. But before he answered her request, he took a long look, said: 'I like it, don't you, Oliver?' and then went on: 'I'll settle for it now, you can pay me later.'

Which he proceeded to do without waiting for her reply. She

thanked him as they got back into the car, but he only nodded carelessly and said: 'Now for lunch.'

She wondered where they were going next. He had reversed the car smartly and was back in the Singel, only to turn away from it again down a quiet, treelined street, bordered by tall, narrow houses, each with double steps leading to an imposing door. There was a canal running down the centre of the street and the willow trees beside it rustled gently in the wind. It was a charming backwater, left over from the Golden Age, and Jenny exclaimed: 'Oh, how delightfully peaceful!' and then looked enquiringly at the Professor when he stopped before one of the houses.

'My mother and father live here,' he observed as he got out of the car, helped her out and then gave Oliver a hand. 'They will be delighted to invite you for lunch.'

Jenny uttered a surprised 'Oh,' and then racked her brain for something else to say—something graceful and polite as befitted the occasion. She could think of nothing suitable, so contented herself with: 'Well, I am surprised.'

'Why?'

They were crossing the brick pavement with Oliver prancing along beside them. 'Well, I didn't suppose—that is, you never mentioned your family...'

'There are quite a few things I haven't mentioned.' He smiled his mocking smile and Jenny frowned and looked away. 'I had no idea that you were interested. Should I feel flattered?'

'I'm quite sure that you get all the flattery you could wish for,' she told him crossly as he banged the brass knocker on a door strong enough to withstand a siege.

An elderly woman, very tall and thin and dressed in black, admitted them. She greeted the Professor warmly, smiled at Jenny and Oliver and waved a hand towards one of the doors in the narrow panelled hall. Jenny found herself borne along, the Professor's large, cool hand under her elbow, Oliver hanging on to her other hand. She supposed it was the bang she had

had on her head which made the morning's happenings seem so unreal. It was like being in a dream where one had no power to do what one wished; the Professor had taken charge without so much as a by-your-leave—not that she would have been capable of doing much about anything. She felt sick just remembering her fright when she had discovered that Oliver had gone, and something of her feelings must have shown on her face, for her companion asked unexpectedly: 'Do you feel all right? Would you prefer to lie down?'

'No—thank you.' She gave him a grave look. 'Aren't you angry with me?'

His face was grave too. 'Yes, but probably not for the same reasons—and this is hardly the time or the place, is it?'

He opened the door and stood aside to let her pass him. The room was long and lofty and rather dim, with a big window at either end of it. Its dark panelled walls were hung with paintings and the polished wood floor was covered with fine silk carpets. The furniture was dark and solid and the chairs deep and comfortable. There were two people in the room; an elderly man, white-haired and as outsize as his son, and a small plump lady with a pretty face and dark hair only just beginning to turn grey. She appeared considerably younger than her husband and was dressed with great elegance; she came hurrying across the room to embrace her son and greet Jenny and Oliver with a charm devoid of curiosity. Jenny liked her; she liked the Professor's father too. He had blue twinkling eyes and a slow smile which put her at her ease at once as Mevrouw van Draak te Solendijk sat her down on an outsize sofa, sat down beside her, made room for Oliver to settle between them, and began a pleasant undemanding conversation.

The Professor hadn't said much when he had introduced them, but presently he interrupted the talk he was having with his father to ask: 'Shall I let Truus know that there will be three more for lunch, Mama?' And Jenny made haste to say: 'Oh, please—it's awfully kind of you, but we simply can't...'

The Professor ignored this and his mother smiled at her nicely while it was left to his father to say: 'Of course you must stay—we are delighted to meet you and Oliver, my dear, we have heard so much about you. And we don't go out a great deal; if you could bear with our elderly company?'

He was a poppet; perhaps his son would be like that in another three decades or so... Jenny blinked rapidly and assured him that they would love to stay.

Several hours later, driving back in the Panther, sitting in the back this time, while Oliver sat proudly beside the driver, Jenny mulled over her afternoon. It had been very pleasant; the Professor might be a bad-tempered, arrogant man, but not with everyone, it seemed. She had seen a different side of him and he had seemed ten years younger. They had lunched at a round table in a richly sombre dining room and Oliver had behaved beautifully. The food had been delicious, served by a cheerful, round-faced girl who called Oliver *schatje* and brought him a special ice-cream in place of the elaborate dessert served to his elders. He had shared Jenny's lemonade too, for the Professor had suggested mildly that after such a crack on the head, anything stronger might give her a headache again. She had agreed so meekly that he had given her a surprised look, this time quite without mockery.

Her thoughts occupied her nicely until they reached Kasteel te Solendijk, while she studied the back of the Professor's head and thought how handsome he was, even from that angle, but they received a severe jolt when she remembered that he was angry with her. He would save his rage until she had quite recovered from her tumble, of course, and then she would get the full force of it. Well, there was no point in dwelling upon it. She closed her eyes and when she opened them again they were almost there.

It was as they were going indoors that she asked him: 'Why doesn't your father live here? This is the family home, isn't it?'

He stopped to answer her. 'Oh, yes—although the house in

Amsterdam is a family home too. But it is more convenient for my parents to live there now that they are older—besides, this place is more suitable for a married man with a family.'

Her world spun around her. 'You're married—and a family...'

She didn't see the gleam in his eyes. He answered smoothly: 'Not yet.' He held the door open for her and when she was inside: 'I should go and lie down for an hour or two if I were you. I'll take Oliver with me in the car—I've a couple of calls to make.'

'Aunt Bess...'

'Leave her to me. Go upstairs like a sensible girl.'

Jenny did as she was told and fell asleep almost at once, to wake an hour or two later, immediately worrying away at the Professor's remark about getting married, so that her rest did her no good at all. She got up at last. A breath of air would clear her head and help her to be her usual sensible self before she dressed for the evening. She tidied herself quickly and went through the house, seeing nobody, although she could hear voices in the drawing room; she was intent on slipping into the garden through a side door. She had it half open when the Professor said from behind her: 'Ah, there you are...slipping away...'

Jenny was up in arms at once. 'I was not—I merely wanted to walk in the gardens. How dare you...'

He sounded amused. 'My dear girl, how you do take me up!' He took her hand off the door handle and closed the door, and she braced herself. He was going to take the lid off his temper and tell her off for being careless about Oliver. She made herself look at him and said snappily:

'All right, you're bursting to pick holes in me, aren't you, just because Oliver went off like that—well, you don't have to! I know that I shouldn't have let him go out of my sight for one single second, but I don't need you to tell me.'

'I wasn't going to.' His voice was mild.

'Oh, yes, you were!' Her cheeks were indignantly pink by now. 'You were fuming—and how was I supposed to whistle when I'd knocked myself on the head. You—you swore at me and you called me silly...' Her voice had risen a little and the desire to burst into tears was so great that she had to stop to gulp them down and found that she couldn't any more. 'I hate you!' she blazed and flew back across the hall and upstairs to her room. She stayed there, pleading a headache through the closed door to Aunt Bess, and refusing the tray sent up to her. What with hunger and weeping she passed a miserable night.

CHAPTER EIGHT

JENNY LOOKED AT her pale, puffy-eyed face with distaste in the morning. She was a fright, and no make-up could quite disguise her pink nose and red eyes. She did the best she could and was thankful to find that only Oliver was at breakfast. The Professor was leaving the house as she went down, but beyond giving her a quiet good morning as he shut his house door, he had nothing to say.

Aunt Bess had, though. Surveying her from her bed where she was enjoying breakfast, she observed. 'You've been bawling your eyes out, Janet, and I should like to know why. If you're still fussing about Oliver's little adventure yesterday, you may forget it—no one attaches the least blame to you.'

'Oh, yes they do,' cried Jenny. 'Professor van Draak was beastly—you have no idea! I wish I'd never come—I wish Margaret had come instead of me in the first place, then perhaps he'd be better tempered.'

Her aunt buttered toast with deliberation. 'You think that Eduard—and I do wish you would stop calling him Professor in that absurd fashion—is pining for her?'

She obviously wanted an answer. 'Well, Oliver said...and

I saw them together at Dimworth… I mean, Aunt Bess, it's rather hard on him that I'm here and not Margaret. He's not had much chance she's very pretty and someone will marry her sooner or later.'

'I should have thought that he had had a very good chance; he is rich, successful and good-looking—everything Margaret considers important in life. However, I do see what you mean.' Aunt Bess looked thoughtful and a little crafty. 'But there's no point in this discussion, is there, Jenny? And we shall be going home in a few days now. Eduard has asked me to stay for a further day or so and I've told him that we shall be delighted to do so. I should like the opportunity of seeing something of the country again and he would like me to meet his parents. A pity that his brother and sisters are away.'

'Brother and sisters?' repeated Jenny, just like a parrot. 'I didn't know that he had any—he doesn't look the kind of man to have any family at all. I was surprised to find that he had a mother and father…'

'Don't be absurd, Janet. There are three sisters and one brother, all younger than he,' said Aunt Bess briskly. 'The brother is at present in Ottawa—he is also a doctor, on some course or other. His three sisters are all married, two of them are living in Friesland, the youngest is travelling with her husband in France.'

'Well, I never!' muttered Jenny. Somehow the fact that the Professor was the eldest of quite a large family gave her a different idea of him; she had always thought of him as being withdrawn and solitary, and here he was in the bosom of a loving home circle. Her thoughts were interrupted by her aunt.

'I shall get up now and we will go for a drive. I feel very well, although I shall be glad to know the results of all those tests. Supposing we go to Scheveningen? We could have lunch there and Oliver can do his shopping.' She pushed the bedtable away from her. 'Now go along, my dear, and keep him amused until I'm ready.'

Jenny had been gone quite a few minutes before Miss Creed lifted the telephone receiver beside her bed and asked for an English number.

Scheveningen was fun, even though Jenny saw Eduard van Draak's face wherever she looked. If this was being in love, she thought morosely, then the quicker she found a cure for it, the better. They had lunch at the Corvette in the Kurhaus, a lively, noisy place which delighted Oliver and made conversation of a serious nature well-nigh impossible, which from Jenny's point of view was very satisfactory. And after lunch Aunt Bess stayed in the car while she and Oliver went to the shops to buy a present for his mother.

There were a great many things to choose from, but his choice fell on a gaudy table lamp in the shape of a Dutch girl in costume which, when the right button was pressed, played 'The Bluebells of Scotland'. It cost a good deal more money than he possessed and Jenny obliged with the difference, inwardly uneasy as to its reception by Margaret. But surely she would realise that Oliver found it a splendid gift and at least pretend to like it?

They bore the thing back to the car and unwrapped it to show Aunt Bess, who gazed at it with a wooden face before remarking warmly: 'Why, Oliver, what a lovely present—just what your mother would like to have. Did you choose it all by yourself?' She gave him an unexpected kiss. 'Clever boy! Now we will return to Kasteel te Solendijk and have our tea, I think.'

Jenny and Oliver were in the drawing room, trying out the lamp's raucous tune, when the Professor returned home. He flung the door wide with a thunderous face and a: 'What on earth...?' and Jenny could have hugged him for his swift: 'That's something quite out of the ordinary—is it for your mother, Oliver?'

The little boy looked at him anxiously. 'Do you like it?' he enquired. 'I chose it myself, and Jenny says Mummy will love it because I found it specially for her.'

'Jenny is quite right—presents chosen for someone you love are always doubly precious. Shall we have that tune again?'

He got down on his knees beside the child and listened to 'The Bluebells of Scotland' again, and when it was finished spoke to Jenny for the first time. 'Delightful, isn't it? Have you had a good day?' His voice was polite and formal.

'Yes, thank you. Aunt Bess enjoyed herself very much—I think it did her good. She's resting now.' Equally polite, she added: 'I hope you had a good day too.'

His blue eyes swept over her. 'Not particularly.' He got to his feet, towering over the pair of them. 'I have some work to do, I'm afraid, but I shall see you at dinner.' He bent to ruffle Oliver's hair. 'If you're in bed by seven o'clock, I'll come and say goodnight.'

The room seemed very quiet after he had gone. After a moment Oliver said: 'Isn't he super, Jenny?'

'Yes, my lamb.' It was lovely to be able to admit it to someone who would never know just how she felt. 'Now if you're to be in bed and tucked up we'd better wrap this up and go upstairs. You can say goodnight to Aunt Bess on the way.'

Jenny dressed with great care that evening, putting on the pink dress she had worn on the cruise; it was a little grand perhaps, but even she, a girl with no conceit of herself, was aware that she looked quite lovely in it. And she piled her hair, too, in shining rolls and coils which took a long time but was well worth it. At least her appearance boosted her *amour propre* and she went down the beautiful old staircase with her chin well up, touching the polished rail with her fingers as she went, humming a little under her breath. It was a pity that there was no one to see her beautifully groomed and gowned and without, seemingly, a care in the world. She executed a few dance steps as she went and then stopped abruptly, for there was someone to see her after all; the Professor leaning against an enormous pillow cupboard against a shadowy wall. He came forward to wait for her at the foot of the staircase.

'Don't stop on my account,' he begged her silkily, 'or was it on my account?'

Jenny came running down the last few steps and then, too vexed to look where she was going, tripped on the last step. He put out a hand and set her on her feet again with an amused chuckle which made her grind her teeth. 'I believe you lie in wait for me!' she accused him, and when he said: 'Of course I do,' stood looking up at him, her mouth open. 'Why?' she managed.

The arm that had saved her from falling was still round her shoulders. She felt it tighten and saw how right his eyes were. 'I think I shall take Aaron Hill's advice—"Grasp it like a man of mettle..."'

'I am not a nettle,' she protested.

He smiled so that her heart rocked in her chest. 'No, you're as soft as silk, Jenny...' He broke off to listen to the sudden commotion at the door and the argent banging of the knocker, but he didn't move to open it, nor did he loose her, but waited while Hans rod across the hall to answer the summons.

Margaret made a dramatic entry. Jenny, quite bewildered at her sudden appearance, yet had the time to wonder unkindly if she had rehearsed it on the way. Certainly it was very effective—effective enough to take the Professor's arm from her shoulders and send him to the door where Margaret had paused, trooping, to cry at exactly the right moment: 'Eduard, oh, Eduard—I've been in an agony of worry! My darling child kidnapped...' She struck another attitude and looked at Jenny. 'How could you!' she uttered. 'I thought better of you, Jenny— I thought you loved my Oliver, and to leave him alone in that manner—a defenceless little boy...'

Jenny took a couple of steps forward. 'Whatever are you

talking about, Margaret?' and then she made the mistake of adding: 'Who told you, anyway?'

'Ah, so you don't deny it!' Margaret turned to the Professor and caught his coat sleeve and gave it a tug. And he won't like that, thought Jenny, and wisely held her tongue.

'This is an unexpected pleasure, Margaret,' remarked the Professor, and gently removed her hand from his jacket. 'But I don't think I quite understand. Oliver is quite well and safe, you know—if he hadn't been I should have made it my business to let you know immediately.'

Margaret was one of the few girls Jenny knew whose eyes could, at will, be made to swim with tears without in the least detracting from her appearance. They swam now as she lifted them to Eduard's face.

'You didn't want me to know because you felt that you should shield Jenny—I can understand that because you're a man who helps lame dogs...'

A flicker of emotion passed over his face. Jenny wasn't near enough to be sure what it had been—mirth, anger...it didn't matter, anyway. She said in a matter-of-fact voice: 'Margaret, I'm not sure why you've come, but there was no need—Oliver got separated from me in Amsterdam, but he was perfectly all right and we found him again within a couple of hours, none the worse.' She looked at the Professor. 'That's true, isn't it?'

'Perfectly true. Margaret, who told you about it?'

'Aunt Bess. She telephoned me this morning—quite early. I got Toby to drive me to Gatwick and got on to the first plane I could. There's a taxi outside—you'll pay him?'

The Professor nodded to Hans, standing like a statue in the background, and he slid silently outside to come back presently with two suitcases.

The Professor glanced at them with an expressionless face. 'Take them up to the Blue Room, will you Hans, and ask Hennie to see if Oliver is still awake. If he is he will want to come down and see his mother.' He turned back to Margaret. 'Come into the drawing-room. I'm sure you could do with a drink while we explain exactly what happened. Miss Creed will be down presently.'

Margaret allowed herself to be led across the hall and as they passed her, the Professor said: 'You too, Jenny.'

Margaret sank into a chair with a grace Jenny frankly envied, and looked around her. 'How I've longed to see your home,' she murmured, and then: 'Could someone unpack for me? I must change for dinner, mustn't I, but I'll be very quick so that you need only put it back for a short time.'

The Professor was either very deeply in love or perhaps it was his beautiful manners, for he said at once: 'Of course we will put dinner back for you, but do see Oliver first, then you will feel completely reassured.'

He was standing with his back to the great fireplace and Jenny had taken a chair facing the door. It was flung open almost immediately and Oliver, in his dressing gown and slippers, rushed in, clutching his present.

'Mummy,' he cried, 'why are you here? You haven't come to take me back to Dimworth, have you? I'm having a simply super time!'

He allowed himself to be embraced at some length and then pushed his parcel on to his mother's knee. 'I've brought you a present, I chose it...'

Margaret looked at it without much interest. 'How lovely, darling. I'll open it later.'

'Now, please, Mummy,' he beseeched her.

He helped her to take off the layers of paper and the doll was revealed, and before Margaret could say anything, he pressed the button and then stood back listening to the tinny little tune, his small chest thrust out with pride. His mother pushed it away so sharply that it fell to the ground and the tune stopped abruptly. 'Darling, it's lovely, but what would I do with it, for heaven's sake?'

He had gone white, his eyes enormous, his small mouth buttoned tight against tears. 'You broke it,' he said. 'You don't like it…'

He turned away and hid his head in Jenny's skirts and she said in her soft, comforting voice: 'It was an accident, my lamb. Mummy's tired—she came hurrying all that long way to see you. Look, we'll pick it up and tomorrow we'll find someone to mend it—it'll be as good as new and you can give it to her again.'

His small lip quivered as he stared at her. 'Honour bright?'

'Honour bright.' She looked across at the Professor wishing that he would do something—anything but just stand there, looking as though he were watching a play, but now he spoke.

'I know just the man who will put it right, Oliver—shall I take it with me tomorrow and get him to see to it. It was only a little fall, you know.' He had bent to collect the lamp and was holding it in his hand. 'Look, the doll's all right, it's only the tune.' He smiled at the little boy, a gentle, kind smile which Jenny found very disturbing, and Oliver, reassured, said quite cheerfully:

'Oh, will you please find the man and let him put it right?' and when Jenny gave him a little push towards his silent mother, he went to her and kissed her cheek and said: 'I didn't know you were tired Mummy, truly I didn't,' and submitted to her embrace once more, and when the Professor suggested: 'What about bed, old chap?' he nodded and said goodnight. Only at the door he turned round to ask Jenny if she would go up presently and tuck him up.

She found him in bed five minutes later, tears pouring down his cheeks; it took her ten minutes to quieten him and another ten to get him to sleep. She went downstairs again, wishing that she could have gone to her room and stayed there for the rest of the evening and wondering why Aunt Bess had telephoned to Margaret. What could she have said to make her come tearing over to Holland as though Oliver were in grave danger? Unless she had used it as an excuse—after all, she had wanted to come in the first place, and anxiety or not, she had found time to pack two large suitcases before she left.

The Professor was still in the drawing room, a glass in his hand, looking perfectly calm and collected, and Aunt Bess was with him.

'Oliver was a little upset,' explained Jenny, accepting her glass and sitting down near her aunt. 'Aunt Bess, why did you tell Margaret?'

Miss Creed sought out a lorgnette from the various chains dangling down her front and levelled it at Jenny. 'Are you presuming to criticise me, Janet? I merely mentioned it in the course of conversation—she chose to put the wrong construction upon my remarks that is entirely her own fault. Eduard has explained everything very nicely, though; she quite understands that it was absolutely no fault of yours, and as I pointed out to her, if she had been in charge in the child, she would probably have had hysterics and been of no use whatsoever. That's a pretty dress do you not think so, Eduard?'

Jenny was aware that she was being studied at some length. 'Very charming,' murmured their host laconically—and only half an hour ago he had told her that she was as soft as silk... She took care not to look at him and made polite conversation until Margaret quite lovely in blue chiffon, came in, begging every one's pardon for being late and keeping them waiting and accepted a drink from the Professor with a smile which made Jenny seethe and ask: 'Is Oliver asleep?'

Margaret turned to look at her. 'Oliver? I don't know—I didn't look.' She smiled quite sweetly at Jenny; she had accused her of negligence and carelessness such a short time ago, but she had already forgotten about it, just as she would have dismissed as unimportant the little episode with the lamp. She tucked a hand into the Professor's arm and said prettily: 'I'm simply famished!'

The evening was hers, of course. Aunt Bess said very little, surprisingly enough, and although Jenny joined in the talk when someone addressed her, she made no attempt to focus any interest upon herself. The Professor didn't say much either, but he looked at Margaret a great deal and when she suggested that she would like to see something of Holland, offered to drive her to one or two places of interest. Madly in love, Jenny decided sadly. She had thought, for the briefest of moments, when they had been in the hall together… But now Margaret was here; he had been amusing himself with that silly talk about nettles.

Aunt Bess went to bed quite early after dinner, declaring that her outing had tired her more than she had supposed. 'And you might come with me, Jenny,' she requested. 'I'm getting slow.'

So Jenny had gone upstairs too, willingly enough, because to sit with the two of them for the rest of the evening was rather more than she could bear; better to go to her own room and wonder what they were saying to each other.

Surprisingly, the Professor was at breakfast in the morning, and when he suggested that she might like to accompany him and Margaret to Leiden she was tempted to agree, especially as he had included Oliver in the invitation, but Margaret, smiling sweetly, declared that if he went, she wouldn't be able to bear his chatter. 'The darling gives me such a headache,' she explained plaintively, 'and I haven't got over that nightmare journey.'

So Jenny said that she would stay home with Oliver. There was plenty to do, she declared enthusiastically, and as they would be leaving Holland soon now, it was a pity to miss the chance of going somewhere.

'Such as where?' asked her host gently, and when she didn't answer: 'The final results of the tests should be ready tomorrow,' he pointed out. 'I believe Miss Creed plans to return to

Dimworth as soon as possible once they are known. I thought a small farewell lunch, so that Oliver might join us.'

Margaret agreed enthusiastically, but he wasn't looking at her. He was watching Jenny, who, well aware of it, refused to look him in the eye but addressed a point over his left shoulder. 'I'm sure that will be very nice,' she said sedately. 'Oliver will love it. And now if you'll excuse us... Oliver, we'll go and find Aunt Bess and see if we may borrow Dobbs and the car.'

'There's a Mini eating its head off in the garage,' suggested her host, 'why not borrow it?' He was gathering up his letters and not looking at her. 'You might drive to Leiden and meet us for lunch.'

'How kind, but actually we've been wanting to go to Alkmaar—it's the cheese market today and Oliver is very keen to see it.' She turned a speaking eye upon the boy as she spoke, giving him a warning look which he understood at once, for it wasn't the first time... The Professor sat back in his chair, apparently blind to this byplay, receiving this mendacious statement with a bland expression which gave nothing away.

'Oh, well, in that case,' he said carelessly, 'take the Mini to Alkmaar. The market is great fun.' His tone implied that the fun was strictly for children and tourists.

'Where are you and Mummy going?' asked Oliver.

'Er—the Tropical Museum, the Pilgrim Fathers' House and possibly the Museum of Antiquities.'

'I think cheese sounds more fun.'

The Professor didn't answer this, only smiled.

Aunt Bess, invited to go to Alkmaar, declined. 'Tourists,' she sniffed, 'eating ices and gaping. Go and enjoy yourselves. I shall probably go into den Haag with Dobbs presently for some last-minute shopping. Janet, I shall decide today when we are to return.'

'Will Mummy come with us?' Oliver wanted to know.

Miss Creed gave him a searching look. 'And why do you ask, Oliver?'

'She said she was going to marry the Professor. If she does, where will I go?' He looked so forlorn that Jenny plucked him off his feet and hugged him close.

'With Mummy, of course—won't he, Aunt Bess?'

But before that lady could reply, he protested: 'But I don't want him for a daddy. He's my friend... Jenny, if he married you instead, I could come and stay with you here, couldn't I?'

Jenny frowned ferociously and went a bright pink, but her voice was quite matter-of-fact. 'Well, love, that wouldn't really do—if Mummy and the Professor want to get married, they'd hardly want to marry someone else, would they?'

'You've gone very red,' observed Oliver.

'That's because I'm out of breath hugging you. Say goodbye to Aunt Bess and we'll go and find that Mini.'

The Panther de Ville had gone by the time they reached the garage, but Dobbs was there, talking to Hans, and polishing the car.

'The little car's all ready, Miss Jenny,' he told her, 'and I was to tell you to be sure and be back by tea time.'

'Oh, indeed,' Jenny tossed her mane of hair over her shoulders. 'I can't think why. We shall stay until we've seen everything we intend to—and you can tell Professor van Draak so.'

'Well, I'm sure I don't know, Miss Jenny,' protested Dobbs in a fatherly way, 'but I do know that I'd rather not cross him—a very nice gentleman, but likes his own way, so to speak.' He nodded to himself. 'Quite right and proper too.'

'That's as may be,' said Jenny obscurely as she settled Oliver beside her and drove off.

There was a great deal to see in Alkmaar. They arrived before the cheese market opened, which gave them time to have their elevenses in a little café in the main street and then wander down its length, peering at the shop windows. And when they reached the Waaggebouw they joined the group of sight-seers, to watch the little figures moving round the clock tower as it struck the hour. It was only a firm promise to return and view this phenomenon as many times as possible that persuaded Oliver to leave and enter the cheese market.

Here the teams of white-clad porters in their gay boaters, carrying their enormous trays of cheeses, caught his fancy, so that they spent the rest of the morning there, sampling the cheese, buying highly coloured postcards and talking to any number of English and American tourists. Aunt Bess would have hated it, Jenny decided, prising Oliver away from a large family of children with the promise of lunch.

They went to the Schuyt restaurant on the Stationsplein and had a splendid meal; not perhaps well balanced, but very satisfying, especially for Oliver, who was of an age to enjoy *potat frites* with mustard pickles, followed by an enormous ice, rainbow-hued and smothered in whipped cream. They were strolling away from this repast, trying to decide whether to find the house with the cannon ball still in its wall—a relic of the Spanish Occupation—or go back for another sight of the figures prancing round the clock tower, when Jenny's suggestion that there was ample time to do both decided them to go in search of the cannon ball first, so they started off in its general direction.

But once over the bridge at the end of the main street they became quite lost. But it was a small town and they hadn't strayed far and there was plenty to look at as they wandered along. They found the house at last, paid their admission and started up the narrow little staircase. There were two or three rooms on each landing, all furnished in the style of a bygone age. Oliver, completely enraptured, peered and explored, begging Jenny to look at a dozen things at a time. 'Cheese, and now this!' he exclaimed ecstatically, and went on to the little landing to peer over the rail at the head of the stairs. 'Someone's coming up,' he informed her, and then gave a great shout. 'Professor van Draak—did you mean to come? How did you know we were here? Where's Mummy?'

'At Solendijk.' The Professor reached the tiny landing now and it was impossible for Jenny to pretend that he wasn't there.

She asked, not allowing her gaze to wander from the baby's cradle she was studying: 'Didn't she want to come?'

He was right beside her, because there was really nowhere else for him to go. 'Er—no.' And when she looked at him at last, he stared down his splendid nose at her and added: 'I have a patient here—I remembered that I had arranged to see her doctor. Margaret isn't interested in patients.' He added blandly: 'We had a delightful morning in Leiden.'

'And have you seen your patient's doctor?' asked Jenny, keeping to the point.

'Oh, yes—I did so before he started his afternoon surgery.'

'What a pity that you had to cut short your outing with Margaret.'

'I must agree, but then I had the happy idea of finding the pair of you so that we might finish our outings in company.'

'What about Margaret?' persisted Jenny doggedly.

'I think she had had sufficient of Leiden by lunch time—we had a meal in the town.' He smiled at her, his manner still bland. 'Such a charming and pretty woman.'

It was on the tip of her tongue to ask him why, if he found Margaret so fascinating, he hadn't rushed back to keep her company, but all she said was: 'Actually, she's beautiful.'

Oliver had been roaming round during their conversation. Now he declared that he had seen everything and was ready to go downstairs again. 'Perhaps we could have an ice?' he asked hopefully.

'We've only just had lunch,' Jenny said, so crossly that he looked quite startled and the Professor made haste to say: 'Shall we compromise with coffee and a glass of lemonade? there's a delightful coffee shop quite close by.'

Jenny made one more effort. 'Oughtn't you to go back?' she asked. 'I mean, haven't you any patients to see?'

He gave her an austere look. 'I am enjoying a rare free day—although enjoying isn't perhaps the right word.'

'Oh, I'm sorry.' She felt all at once mean and petty. 'I didn't mean to be horrid. Look, would you like to take Oliver with you, and I'll potter off on my own.'

His sudden smile warmed her to her very heart. 'Oh, Jenny, what a darling you are—why didn't we meet years ago?'

She stood speechless. He liked her after all, perhaps more than that—but he loved Margaret. Margaret had told her so, or at least, she corrected herself, she had said that she was going to marry him. Perhaps they had quarrelled and he had rushed off seeking consolation. She said in a sensible voice: 'Let's go and have some coffee and Oliver could choose what he wants to do next.' She smiled up at the blue eyes staring so hard at her. 'After all, it's his day.'

'I think it's my day too,' said the Professor thoughtfully.

They spent a riotous afternoon; there was a small *kermis*, a fair, tucked away behind the main street and the three of them tried each one of its attractions, and when they were tired of that, wandered round the booths, Jenny and Oliver licking large ice-cream cones while their companion contented himself with his pipe. But he did try his hand at the shooting gallery and won a hideous toy dog, its nylon fur a brilliant blue which Oliver found irresistible, and to equal things up, as he put it, he purchased a bead necklace for Jenny. She hung it round her neck and admired it at length, knowing that she would keep the gaudy thing for the rest of her life.

They were standing together watching Oliver whirling round on an old-fashioned roundabout, when he said abruptly: 'You were lying, weren't you?' Jenny gave him a wary look, aware that she had lied to him on several occasions. 'I asked you if you disliked me,' he went on, 'and you told me that you did. That wasn't—isn't—true, is it?'

Perhaps it was the carnival atmosphere around them, or just the intoxication of being with him, that made her answer recklessly. 'No, it wasn't true. I didn't—don't dislike you, though perhaps I did at first. I don't know any more…you are rather arrogant, you know, only I've got used to that now.'

His eyes were on her face. 'I'm not a young man—perhaps too old to marry.'

'Oh, nonsense!' she cried warmly. 'Of course you're not too old. Besides, Margaret is thirty—only ten years younger than you.'

'Margaret?' There was a wry amusement in his voice so that she hurried on:

'She seems much younger than that, but that's because she's so pretty, but she's really quite good at running a big household. Aunt Bess only does it because she prefers to live in Scotland with her parents besides, all her friends live there.'

'Giving me Dutch courage, Jenny?'

She didn't look at him because if she did she wasn't sure what she might say. 'I don't think you need it—only you've got this silly notion about being too old for a wife and children.'

'You think that I would make a good husband?' He sounded only a little interested.

'Oh, yes—and think how you could fill that lovely old house of yours with children. And there are the dogs, of course, and the cat—and you could have a donkey for the little ones and a pony for them to ride later…'

'Are we talking in dozens?' he wanted to know, and this time there was a laugh in his voice.

Jenny had a sudden vivid picture of Kasteel te Solendijk's old walls ringing to the shouts of little boys with bright blue eyes and haughty noses. There would be little girls too, of course—

perhaps with coppery hair? She said soberly: 'It's a house that needs children.'

'Well, there's Oliver for a start, though I hardly think that Margaret would marry on his account.'

'Well, I don't know about that—he needs a father, doesn't he, or an uncle or something. He'll inherit Dimworth when he's eighteen, but that's a long way to go.' She moved a little away from him. 'Here's Oliver now—I should think he must be tired out.'

Oliver declared that he wasn't tired at all, but he agreed willingly enough to the Professor's proposal that they should return home. 'But only if I may drive with you,' he declared.

The big man smiled down at him, 'Certainly you may,' and turned to Jenny. But she firmly refused his offer of a lift in his car and was indignant when he said mildly: 'Oh, dear—and I have already arranged for a garage to pick up the Mini and bring it down tomorrow.'

'Well, really!' she burst out. 'Of all the high-handed...'

'It is my car,' he reminded her silkily. 'Besides, I can't possibly drive and answer Oliver's inevitable questions at the same time.'

'He could have come with me.'

'He said he wanted to come with me. It is his day—you said so yourself.'

She choked back temper. 'Do you think I can't drive or something?'

'My dear girl, I would never have allowed you to drive the Mini if I had supposed that.'

She stood, muttering crossly until he said: 'I've enjoyed my afternoon—makebelieve, of course, but shall we not spoil it by quarrelling?'

She asked in a small voice: 'What do you mean—makebelieve?'

'Just that—doing something; being someone one wishes to be and cannot.' He added: 'At least for the moment.'

He sounded resigned and a little remote and her temper fled before a wave of love. 'It wasn't all makebelieve,' she assured him. 'I meant what I said—that I don't dislike you.'

She smiled up at him, her lovely eyes warm and soft. She hadn't meant to say that, but her truant tongue had had the last word. But she was quite unprepared when his arms caught her close, 'No, it wasn't makebelieve, Jenny,' and he didn't sound remote or resigned, 'and this isn't either.' He kissed her hard and lingeringly and then let her go without a word as Oliver, at last sated with the pleasures of the *kermis,* came trotting towards them.

CHAPTER NINE

THERE WAS NOTHING makebelieve about Margaret's face when they got back. She had too indolent a nature to be deeply angry about anything, but she had a decidedly pettish expression which quite marred her lovely features. She was sitting on the lawn as they drove up the drive and round the side to the garages with Oliver—for a great treat—sitting on the Professor's knee, steering the car. Jenny waved and called to her as they passed and received nothing but a cross look in return. In all fairness to Margaret, she had to admit that had she been in her shoes, she would have been more than just cross, although the expedition that afternoon had been innocent enough. She corrected herself—not quite innocent; there had been their conversation and the Professor had kissed her with a good deal of feeling, probably because he had wanted to kiss Margaret, who wasn't there.

When they reached the garage she got out with a murmured excuse and hurried into the house. Oliver had refused to go with her and she supposed that if the Professor wanted Margaret to himself, he would think up something to occupy the small boy. She went to her aunt's room first, but Miss Creed wasn't here, so she went slowly to her own room and sat down on the bed, wondering how best to keep out of the Professor's and Margaret's way until dinner time. A wasted exercise as it turned out, for standing by the window later on, idly looking out, she saw the Panther pass under her window. The Professor was driving and Margaret was beside him; both of them were dressed for the evening.

Jenny went downstairs to look for Aunt Bess then, and found her in the library, a lofty apartment smelling of leather and books and furnished with a number of deep armchairs, each with its own table and lamp. Aunt Bess was sitting at her ease, browsing through some old bound volumes of *Punch,* but she glanced up as Jenny went in.

'There you are,' she observed unnecessarily. 'Oliver is having his bath before his supper this evening—he's with Hennie. Eduard has taken Margaret to see some friends of his. Probably they won't be back until the small hours. That leaves you and me—we can discuss our journey home in peace.'

'Yes, Aunt Bess.' Jenny strove to make her voice interested and cheerful, with so little success that her companion said: 'Down in the dumps again! You'll be glad to get back to Dimworth, I dare say.'

Jenny said that she would, which was partly true. She wouldn't have to watch Margaret charming Eduard then; at the same time she wouldn't see him, full stop. She couldn't win either way.

'Has he come up to scratch?' asked Aunt Bess vulgarly.

'Who do you mean? Who with?'

'Margaret, of course.'

'I—I don't know, perhaps this evening...' Jenny's voice trailed off.

'Bah!' exclaimed Miss Creed in ringing tones. 'He won't, you know—not what he wants at all.' She looked sly and changed the subject abruptly. 'I'm going to Amsterdam in the morning to have lunch with Eduard's people, but I'll be back before tea—

the tests will be completed by then. I shall go home anyway.' She picked up *Punch* once more. 'Find a book,' she commanded.

So Jenny sat leafing through *Country Life* and several Dutch magazines which she couldn't make head or tail of until it was time to change for the evening. There was no sign of the Professor or of Margaret. She went upstairs to say goodnight to Oliver and then, after a fruitless suggestion that there was really no need for them to change their dress, to her room, to put on a rather sober dress which she had never liked. It was a silk flowered print in beige which did nothing for her at all, and she scraped back her hair in a style to match its dull cut before flouncing downstairs to the drawing room to find Aunt Bess, resplendent in purple and gold chains, waiting for her glass of sherry.

Dinner was delicious, but then all the meals in the Professor's house were; but she pecked at her food as though it were yesterday's porridge, saying 'Yes, Aunt' and 'No, Aunt' with a sad lack of interest in the topic under discussion. She emerged from a gloomy reverie to hear Aunt Bess observe:

'So that is settled—tomorrow evening on the night boat. Eduard must get us cabins. I shall telephone Toby in the morning and tell him to expect us, and you may telephone Florrie after dinner, Janet.'

Jenny said: 'Yes, Aunt Bess,' once again and played with her trifle. It was very short notice, but then Aunt Bess always did what she wanted when she wanted. Somehow or other there would be cabins put at her disposal and however inconvenient her unexpected arrival might be, Dimworth would be ready to receive her.

She telephoned Dimworth as soon as they had had their coffee, using the telephone in the small sitting room because Aunt Bess didn't wish to be disturbed in the drawing room, and listened to Florrie worriedly telling her that they would be ready for Miss Creed when she arrived. 'Though mind you, Miss

Jenny,' said Florrie's soft Somerset voice, 'there's the carpet in Miss Creed's room being shampooed and if it will be ready in time, I'm sure I don't know—and us run out of jam for the visitors and a nasty leak in the south wing.'

'Don't worry,' Jenny told her, 'Aunt Bess is going to be too tired to notice anything. I daresay she'll go straight to bed.'

'Who is going straight to bed?' asked the Professor from behind her and she turned round to see him stand aside in the doorway so that Margaret might come into the room too. He looked so pleased with himself that Jenny's hand shook a little on the receiver—and Margaret looked radiant. There was no other word to describe the look on her face—or perhaps a cat who had licked the cream pot empty...

She explained woodenly: 'Aunt Bess thinks she should go back to Dimworth. She's quite confident that the tests are OK, but even if they're not, she's going...she asked me to telephone our housekeeper.'

Margaret cast herself down on a deep crimson sofa, an excellent foil for her blonde beauty. 'Well, I shan't go,' she declared petulantly, 'just as everything is marvellous... You can take Oliver with you, Jenny—I'll come home later.' She turned to her host, still standing at the door. 'Eduard, you'll let me stay?'

His ready: 'Of course, my dear,' cut Jenny like a knife. She said, still very wooden: 'Yes, of course we'll take Oliver with us.' She forced herself to look at the Professor. 'I hope you don't think us rude and ungrateful, leaving so unexpectedly...'

'But your aunt had already told me,' he said cheerfully, 'provided of course that I get a good report from the hospital tomorrow, and the final decision to leave does rest with me... She is lunching with my parents tomorrow, isn't she? The Mini will be back in the morning. Would you and Oliver like to have it so that you can have a last fling together?'

Jenny never wanted to see the Mini again; she thanked him nicely but with some coolness, whereupon he asked her if she would prefer to borrow the Bristol 412 which he occasionally used in place of the Panther. 'It's a fast car,' he pointed out, 'if you found the Mini too slow, but very safe.'

She declined that too and was murmuring a few well-chosen words before getting herself out of the room, when he remarked casually: 'There is a donkey arriving in the morning, by the way—Oliver might like a ride on her. I'm buying a pony too, but he won't arrive until a week or so. You see I took your advice, Jenny.'

'How nice, I'm sure Oliver will love that.' She was aware that her voice was too high and turned with relief to the forgotten receiver in her hand; Florrie's voice was still rambling on, a little doubtfully now because she was getting no reply, so Jenny explained and rang off, anxious to be gone. But she was delayed once more, this time by Margaret.

'What time shall we go tomorrow?' she asked the Professor, and smiled at Jenny as she spoke. 'I'm so excited I feel exhausted; I simply must have a good night's rest.'

'One o'clock?' he suggested. 'I'll come and fetch you. No, that won't do, because I must see Miss Creed before she leaves. You will have to be fetched, but that will present no difficulties—I'll telephone presently. Margaret, are you going to tell Jenny?'

'No, certainly not! It's my lovely secret—well, it's your secret too, I suppose, and don't you dare to say a word.' She got up and stretched languidly. 'I'm off to bed—I must pack an overnight bag, I suppose.' She smiled again at Jenny: 'Wouldn't you like to know?' she murmured, and leaned up to kiss the Professor's cheek before sauntering to the door.

'I must go too,' said Jenny urgently. 'I promised I'd pack for Aunt Bess.'

It was a pity that he was standing in the doorway and showed no sign of moving. 'Not in the least curious, Jenny?'

'Well, of course I am,' she snapped, 'but don't think you can tease me into asking questions, because I'm not going to—besides, I can guess.'

'You might guess wrong.' He was smiling down at her, looking amused. 'You're very ill-tempered this evening. I thought that after this afternoon… That dress doesn't suit you, either.'

'It's a perfectly good dress,' she told him sharply, 'and this afternoon was makebelieve—you said so yourself.' She remembered how he had kissed her and went red, feeling the tide of colour wash over her face while he stared.

'Ah, so you remember, too,' he said softly. 'There's great deal I want to say to you, Jenny, but you're not in a very receptive mood, are you?' And he stood aside, wishing her goodnight in a voice which held a laugh, so that there was nothing for her to do but go upstairs, to pause outside Aunt Bess's door to gain composure. And once inside she was for once thankful that her aunt kept her busy helping her to bed and then packing for her under her sharp eyes. But presently Aunt Bess observed: 'That will do for the present. Go to bed, child, you look like skimmed milk—you need a good night's rest.'

Something Jenny didn't have.

By the time she and Oliver had breakfasted the donkey had arrived. A kindly Hans offered the information and they went without waste of time to the paddock behind the stables. It was a very small donkey and not in the best condition either, its mild eyes apprehensive as they made much of it, something which worried Jenny until Hans joined them with the carrots he had gone to fetch; to explain to her that the Professor had gone to a great deal of trouble contacting various societies until he had found one which had a donkey in need of a good home and at the same time were willing to transport the little beast without delay.

'But I thought it took weeks…'

Hans gave her a tolerant smile! 'It probably does, miss, but if Professor van Draak makes up his mind about something, he doesn't regard obstacles.'

'Oh—Well, yes. A week or two here and she'll be as fit as a fiddle, won't she? Is the pony coming from the same place?'

'No, miss. I understand he is a child's—what is the word?—mount no longer required by the owner. The Professor intends to buy a second donkey later on.' He paused to watch Oliver feeding carrots to the donkey. 'Perhaps Oliver would like a ride?'

So they all went for an amble round the paddock, until Hans gave it his opinion that the animal would probably be glad of a rest. Oliver slid off her back at once, saying loudly: 'I shall come here to stay very often, then I can ride...'

'Well, yes, my lamb, but you'll have to...' Jenny stopped. How very complicated life would be for Oliver if his mother married Eduard. He wouldn't need to be invited then, of course, because he would be living at Solendijk. But what about Dimworth? That was, after all, his true home and inheritance.

'Why don't you finish?' demanded Oliver.

'Oh, I've forgotten what I was going to say—it wasn't anything important.' She caught Hans' eyes upon her and had an uneasy feeling that he had known what she had been thinking and for some reason it amused him—almost as though he knew something she didn't.

'How about elevenses?' she asked, 'and Hans, it's such a mild day, do you suppose we could have a picnic lunch out here by the pool? I'll help carry it out.'

He beamed at her. 'Of course, Miss Wren, and there'll be no need for you to do anything.' His tone was mildly reproving at the suggestion.

They had eaten the last crumb of the delicious sandwiches which Hennie had made for them and drained the lemonade jug dry as the Panther swished up the drive and stopped before the front door. The Professor got out and went into the house, to come out again almost immediately and bend his steps in their direction. He had a glass of beer in one hand and a sandwich in the other and folded his length on to the lawn beside them with a cheerful: 'Hullo—have you enjoyed your morning?'

'Smashing!' declared Oliver. 'I went for a ride on your donkey and she liked it.'

'Good.' The Professor took a huge bite. 'And you, Jenny?'

'Very nice, thank you,' she told him demurely. 'Have you been busy?'

He polished off the rest of the sandwich. 'Yes. The test results are excellent. Miss Creed is in Amsterdam?'

Jenny nodded. 'Yes, but she'll be back before tea. Which reminds me that I still have a mass of packing to do and I'd better go and finish it.' She was kneeling beside him, tidying away the remains of their lunch on to a tray, aware that he was watching her. To break the silence she asked: 'Will Margaret be back before we leave?' She looked at him quickly and then away again. 'Should we say goodbye now?'

He glanced at the paper-thin gold watch on his wrist. 'Hasn't she gone yet? No, she won't be back until after you have left—probably not until tomorrow.' He drank the last of his beer. 'Oliver, you had better go and say goodbye to your mother now—she's to be fetched very shortly.'

The little boy ran off and Jenny got to her feet, anxious not to be alone with the Professor. 'I must go...' she began, but he chose to misunderstand her. 'Well, Miss Creed will certainly be safer with a companion on the journey.' He took the tray from her and put it down on the grass again, then tucked a hand under her arm. 'I have a fancy to stroll through the gardens,' he observed mildly. 'I'm sure you're very quick at packing and there can't be all that much.' He glanced down at her. 'I like that blue dress. Did you throw that flowered thing out of the window?'

She couldn't stop her chuckle. 'Of course not. I'll give it to someone when I get back, though; I don't much like it myself.'

She was being led away from the pool, towards the wide gravel path bordered by early autumn flowers very aware of his hand on her arm.

'Don't you want to say goodbye to Margaret?' she asked.

'My dear girl, I shall be seeing her again in a few hours. Tell me, what do you intend to do when you return to Dimworth?'

Was he going to meet Margaret, then? Where were they going together? And hadn't Margaret said that she had to pack an overnight bag? Jenny had no answer to the questions rotating round and round inside her head. She said a little absently: 'Well, I'll stay until the house is closed for the winter, then I—I suppose I'll look for another job. Perhaps Queen's would take me back...'

'So you have decided not to marry Toby?'

She tossed her bright head. 'I decided that years ago.'

'You have no other plans? There must be a number of young men dangling after you.'

He was very anxious to marry her off, she thought crossly, just because his future was all nicely settled and rosy. She didn't answer but asked instead, not really meaning to: 'When are you going to get married?'

'Oh, at the earliest possible moment,' he assured her suavely. 'I can't have a donkey and pony eating their heads off for nothing.'

She didn't know whether to laugh or cry. 'But it would be a year or two...'

'Ah, yes, but Oliver could keep them in practice, could he not?'

Jenny sighed, a sad little sound she wasn't aware of. 'Yes, of course.' Suddenly being with him wasn't to be borne a moment longer; he would walk here with Margaret and tell her about his day and talk about the children... She hoped that Margaret would listen intelligently and take an interest in the children, but perhaps he loved her so much that that wouldn't really matter.

'I must pack,' she said in a desperate little voice, and turned and ran back to the house.

Of course he had been right; she could have packed in ten minutes flat if she had needed to. She managed to spin it out until she heard the car which had come to fetch Margaret had driven away, very late, because Margaret hadn't been ready. She had told Jenny nothing when she had gone to say goodbye, only looked smug and pleased with herself and hinted at a marvellous surprise everyone was going to have very shortly. And when Jenny had tried to persuade her to tell her secret she had shrugged and said in her charming, indolent way: 'Oh, Jenny—not now can't you see I've got my hair to do? You'll know soon enough.'

Jenny wandered over to the window to stare at the lovely gardens spread below her. Well, she knew, didn't she—there was really no need to ask Margaret. She couldn't get away fast enough now, away from the lovely old house, its splendid grounds, the excitement of seeing Eduard every day...

She decided that it would be safe to go downstairs now, as the master of the house would be in his study, Oliver she had seen, his hand in Hans', crossing the lawn to take another look at the donkey. She would slip out of the side door behind the sitting room and go and look at the vines, so vastly superior to those at Dimworth.

She had reached the hall when the study door was flung open and the Professor stuck his head out, 'Packed?' he wanted to know carelessly. 'In which case, how about a stroll? We didn't finish the last one, did we? Miss Creed won't be back for another hour.'

Jenny restrained herself from bolting back the way she had come. 'No—no, thank you, I mean, I've still got things to do...'

'Such as?'

She stared at him helplessly, quite unable to think of any excuse at all. After a long moment he said smoothly: 'You don't want to, do you, Jenny?' His face had become bleak. 'And you must have a very good idea of what I'm going to say to you.'

She took a step backwards. 'Yes, of course—and I don't want...that is, I'd rather not...' Her voice trembled. 'Please, Eduard, not now.'

His brows rose. 'Not now? And supposing I should come to Dimworth, would I be allowed to tell you then?'

'I...yes.' By then she would be able to smile and congratulate him and wish him happy—Margaret too.

His smile was small and mocking. 'I shall remember that.' He had gone inside and shut the door before she could think of anything to say.

She didn't see him to speak to alone after that. Aunt Bess came back very satisfied with herself received the good news of her test results with an air of I-told-you-so, partook of tea and pronounced herself ready to leave. 'And you, Eduard, what will you do with yourself this evening? Margaret either would not or could not give me any coherent answers to my questions.'

'I have to go back to the hospital presently,' he told her pleasantly, 'and I shall be dining with Margaret.' He looked at Jenny as he spoke, but she pretended not to see.

They left a little later, after at least half an hour of loading luggage on to the car, installing Aunt Bess on to the back seat, finding Oliver, who had gone to say goodbye to the donkey, and finally taking a farewell of the Professor. He stood outside his front door, large and placid, saying all the right things. The last Jenny saw of him was his huge frame outlined against his lovely home, and she didn't see him very clearly for the tears in her eyes.

Their journey home held no hindrances. How the Professor had managed to get them cabins at such short notice was something Jenny didn't worry about; he was a man who would always get what he wanted. Margaret, for instance.

Back at Dimworth life settled into its old pattern once more; everyone was glad to see them back home and Aunt Bess, almost her former self, found fault with everyone, upset Mrs Thorpe, declared that it was a good thing that she was once more able to hold the reins because the household bills were shocking, and then toured the house, picking holes in everything and everyone. Just like old times, thought Jenny. No mention was made of Margaret and surprisingly she neither wrote nor telephoned for several days. When she did do so it was one morning when Jenny was dusting the doll collection. Aunt Bess took the call and presently swept along to where Jenny was carefully rearranging the exhibits.

'Well, she's done it!' declared Miss Creed in trumpet-like tones. 'Oliver is to have a new father.'

Jenny dropped her feather duster. 'Oh. I'm glad—when are they to be married?'

'As soon as it can be arranged. Presumably they have made some arrangement regarding Oliver—this is, after all, his home, or will be when he's a man.' Aunt Bess allowed herself a snort. 'Not that Margaret has made much effort to make it home for him. However, that must be gone into later, I suppose. He sounds a sensible type, and since they've known each other in their youth, he understands the situation.'

'Their youth?' asked Jenny, quite at sea.

'Well, yes, child. This Dirk van something or other was in Scotland for several years—he knew Margaret long before she met Oliver and married him. Now they have met again and have decided to marry. It seems a splendid arrangement.'

'Where did they meet? I mean, for the second time.' Jenny's voice was almost a whisper so that Aunt Bess begged her to speak up.

'He's a friend of Eduard, strangely enough. Eduard discovered that they knew each other and arranged to take Margaret to see Dirk what's-his-name. They practically fell into each other's arms.' She marched to the door. 'Don't forget the clock,' she said severely as she went out.

Jenny ignored the clock and the remainder of the dolls, too. So Eduard hadn't been in love with Margaret at all—so what had he wanted to tell her? She remembered how she had run away and begged him not to say any more. She picked up an exact replica of Queen Victoria and gave her a perfunctory dust. 'Fool fool,' she told herself loudly, 'he thinks you don't give a damn—I let him think that, and how on earth am I ever going to find out if it was me?' Her muddled thoughts gave way to several wild ideas, none of them feasible. She could of course go to Holland, but she would have to have a reason... 'And I'll find one!' she cried fiercely, flung down her duster and flew upstairs to her room, where she locked the door and cried her eyes red.

There were plenty of visitors that afternoon. Jenny watched them struggle through the gatehouse, up the broad path to the entrance and went to take her seat behind the big table, loaded with a fresh batch of jam, postcards and brochures. There was a school party, she noted, which meant that Florrie's niece would have to act as guide. The teacher in charge wasn't able to keep them an in order; ever since the time they had discovered a small boy sitting in a priceless William and Mary chair, eating a cheese sandwich, they had had to be careful.

The first few visitors appeared, making straight for the table, as they nearly always did, then armed with a brochure and a bag of sweets, they would wander off to look around them. There was, of course, a hard core of those who didn't know what they wanted, and for that matter, didn't know why they had come in the first place. Jenny pushed her hair off her forehead with a weary hand and opened the petty cash box as the first visitor picked up a handful of cards. One more week, she reflected, then the house would be closed and revert to its glorious winter peace, and she would be free to find a job—or go in search of Eduard. She handed change and wondered just what she would say to him.

An hour later she was still doing a fair trade, although the spate had spent itself and become a steady trickle. She handed a bag of fudge to a small, grubby boy with an engaging grin and gave him back his change with a warm smile and a souvenir pencil for free, and looked up at the next customer.

Eduard. She trembled a little at the sight of him and was furious with herself for it.

'I want to talk to you.' He didn't bother to lower his voice. 'Will you come out from behind that table, Jenny?'

'No.' It would have been little to have said more than that, but she had no breath.

'Then I shall come and sit beside you,' he said blandly, 'and we can talk here.'

'No, certainly not—of course we can't...' She gave him a quick glance and saw that he had meant what he had said. Two or three people were approaching, intent on buying postcards; she pressed the floor bell under her foot and hoped that whoever it was detailed to relieve her would come quickly, and watched the door, not looking at him. It was Mrs Thorpe who came bustling in, still wearing the best summer hat, her two-piece covered by a serviceable apron. 'Trouble, dear?' she wanted to know in her penetrating voice.

Jenny avoided answering that. 'I should be glad if you could take over for a little while, Mrs Thorpe—there's something I have to attend to.'

Mrs Thorpe's rather prominent eye had discovered the Professor. 'Why, doctor,' she cried archly and erroneously, 'how delightful to meet you again. No trouble, I hope?'

Jenny admired his suavity as he dealt with the question and

added: 'Don't let me keep you from your post, Mrs Thorpe.' His eyes took in the small queue which had formed behind him, but he didn't budge, only looked at Jenny. He wasn't going to move until she went with him and people were beginning to prick up interested ears. She got to her feet and walked round the table and started towards the small arched doorway marked private, and found him right beside her.

She stepped past him as he opened the door and then closed it behind him. The lobby was very small with the circular staircase spiralling up from its centre. Jenny, between staircase and Professor, had no room at all. All the same she asked in a dignified voice, addressing his top waistcoat button: 'What do you want?'

The Professor, probably with an eye to making more room, put his arms around her. 'You, my darling girl, you ridiculous, nettlesome creature, getting silly ideas into your head, taking everything for granted in your usual hoity-toity fashion. You said that if I came to see you here, you would listen to me, so I have come.'

'Well, I can't do anything else, can I?' she pointed out, glad that her voice was so nice and steady although she was very much afraid that in that confined space he would be able to hear her heart beating like a mad thing. And he must have done, for she was caught in a tight embrace and kissed in a purposeful fashion which left her in no doubt whatsoever as to his feelings.

'My dearest dear,' said the Professor lovingly to the top of her head, 'surely you knew that I loved you? Oh, not at once, I must admit, you're bossy and prickly to a fault and everlastingly managing to keep me on tenterhooks—and you're adorable… I'm a good deal older than you are, my love, bad-tempered and arrogant too. I shall have to learn to be a good husband, and I will. I promise you, for nothing I have is of any worth unless I have you.'

He bent to kiss her, gently this time. 'And why in heaven's

name you should concoct that fairy tale about Margaret and me…'

'I didn't! She told Oliver that she wanted to marry you, and you were always hanging round her…' She felt the Professor's enormous chest heave with silent amusement and went on indignantly: 'Well, you were—how was I to know? You see, you would have done very well for her—rich and living the kind of life she likes, and Oliver likes you…'

'He shall come and stay with us, my dearest. As I have already told you, someone must exercise those animals until our children are old enough to do it for themselves. But Dirk—Aunt Bess told you about him?—will see that Oliver has his fair share of living here. You haven't said that you will marry me, Jenny.'

Her voice was very quiet. 'I'm waiting to be asked.'

She felt his chest heave again and heard a rumble of laughter. 'Jenny soft as silk at last! Will you marry me?'

She stood on tiptoe to kiss him. 'I couldn't bear it if I didn't.' She was kissed at some length until she said: 'Eduard, just a minute—why didn't you tell me? I mean, at Solendijk—you see, it seemed as if you and Margaret…and yet in Alkmaar I almost… You did mean all those things you said in Alkmaar?'

'Oh, my dear heart, yes.'

Jenny heaved a sigh of pure happiness, and then: 'Eduard, your parents—do you suppose they'll mind? Will they like me?'

'They loved you. They couldn't understand why I hadn't snapped you up weeks ago.'

'Well, why didn't you?'

He smiled down at her, pulling her closer. 'I thought I'd told you; I'm too old and arrogant and…'

'Fiddlesticks,' said Jenny, 'you're exactly my idea of a perfect husband.' She kissed him to prove it. 'We'd better go and tell Aunt Bess. She will be surprised.'

They started up the staircase. 'No, she won't, my darling. I told her I was going to marry you.'

'Oh—did you? But I might not have wanted to.'

They had achieved the top of the narrow staircase by now. 'Then I should have persuaded you.'

'How?'

'Like this, my little love.' He bent his head to kiss her once more. Presently she said: 'Eduard—dear Eduard, there are a lot of questions…'

'Nothing that can't wait for an answer, my darling. This, on the other hand, can't wait either.'

And Jenny, kissed into silence, happily agreed.

* * * * *

Keep reading for an excerpt of
Unbridled Cowboy
by Maisey Yates.
Out now!

CHAPTER ONE

"THERE'S NO WAY around it. I'm going to need a wife."

Sawyer Garrett looked across the table at his brother, Wolf, and his sister, Elsie, and then down at the tiny pink bundle he was holding in his arms.

It wasn't like this was an entirely new idea.

It was just that he had been thinking the entire time that Missy might change her mind, which would put him in a different position. She hadn't, though. She had stuck to her guns. When she found out she was pregnant, she told him that she wanted nothing to do with having a baby. She wanted to go through with the pregnancy, but not with being a mother. Not even when he proposed marriage. Oh, they hadn't been in a relationship or anything like that. She was just a woman that he saw from time to time.

In fact, Sawyer Garrett could honestly say that he had a very low opinion of relationships and family.

Present company excluded, of course.

But when Missy had said she was pregnant, he'd known there was only one thing to do. His dad had been a flawed man. Deeply so. He'd acted like the kids were an afterthought and all he'd really done was let them live under his roof.

Sawyer wanted more for his child. Better. He'd determined

he would be there, not just providing housing and food, but actually being there.

If he could spare his child the feeling of being unwanted, he would.

And that was where this idea had been turning over in his head for a while.

The fact of the matter was, Garrett's Watch had a lousy track record when it came to marriage.

The thirteen-thousand-acre spread had been settled back in the late 1800s, with equal adjoining spreads settled by the Kings, the McClouds and the Sullivans, all of whom had now worked what was known in combination as Four Corners Ranch in the generations since.

And where the Garrett clan was concerned... There was nothing but a long history of abandonment and divorces. The one exception being Sawyer's grandparents. Oh, not his grandfather's first marriage. His biological grandmother had run off just like every other woman in their family tree. As if the ground itself was cursed.

But then the old man had happened upon an idea. He thought to write a letter to one of the newspapers back east asking for a woman who wanted to come out to Oregon and be a mother to his children. They'd had the only successful marriage in his direct line. And it was because it was based on mutual respect and understanding and not the emotional bullshit that had been a hallmark of his own childhood. He barely remembered his own mother. He remembered Wolf's and Elsie's, though. Two different women. Only around for a small number of years.

Just long enough to leave some scars.

Hell, he didn't know how he wound up in this position. He was a man who liked to play hard. He worked hard. It seemed fair enough. But he was careful. He *always* used a condom. And Missy had been no exception. He'd just been subject to that small percentage of failure. *Failure.*

He hated that. He hated that feeling. He hated that word. If there was one thing he could fault his father for it was the fact that the man hadn't taken charge. The fact that he just sat there in the shit when everything went to hell. That wasn't who Sawyer was. But Sawyer had to be responsible for his siblings far sooner than he should've had to be, thanks in part due to his father's passivity. If there was one thing Sawyer had learned, it was that you had to be responsible when responsibility was needed.

He wasn't a stranger to failing people in his life, but unlike his father, he'd learned. He'd never let anyone who needed him down, not again.

"Marriage," Wolf said. "Really."

"Unless you and Elsie want a full-time job as a nanny."

Elsie snorted, leaned back in her chair and put her boots up on the table—which she didn't normally do, but she was just trying to be as feral as possible in the moment. "Not likely," she said.

"Right. Well. So, do you think there's a better idea?"

"Reconsider being a single father?" Wolf said.

"I am," Sawyer said. "I'm aiming to find a wife."

Wolf shook his head. "I mean, reconsider having a baby at all."

A fierce protectiveness gripped Sawyer's chest. "It's a little late, don't you think?"

"Wasn't too late for Missy to walk away yesterday," Wolf said.

"Too late for me," Sawyer said.

It had been. From the moment he'd first heard her cry. The weight of... Of everything that he felt on his shoulders when this tiny little thing was placed into his arms. It was difficult to describe. Impossible. He wasn't good with feelings when they were simple. But this was complicated. A burden, but one he grabbed hold of willingly. One he felt simultaneously uniquely suited for and completely unequal to. He didn't know the first thing about babies. Yeah, he had done quite a bit to take care of Elsie and Wolf, and... He could see where he'd fallen short.

Elsie was just a hair shy of a bobcat in human form, and Wolf suited his name, and, well...big, a little bit dangerous, loyal to his pack, but that was about it.

"It's not too late," Elsie said. "In the strictest sense. You haven't even given her name."

No. It was true. He hadn't settled on anything yet. And he knew there was paperwork that he had to do.

"You want me to give her back?" He shook his head. "It's not like I have a receipt, Els."

"That's not what I meant," Elsie said. "It's just... It's a hard life here."

"And I aim to make it a little less hard."

"So, you're going to... What? Put an ad in the paper?"

"Granddad did," he said.

And it had changed their lives for the better. The history of Garrett's Watch might be rich with failed love stories, but it was a marriage of convenience that had brought real love to the ranch.

Their grandmother—their real grandmother (blood didn't matter here, staying mattered)—had loved them all with a ferocity their own mothers hadn't managed, let alone their father.

She had taught Sawyer to tie his shoes and ride a bike. She'd hugged him when he'd fallen and scraped his knees.

She taught him tenderness. And he was damned grateful for it now, because he had this tiny life in his care, and if it weren't for her, he would have never, ever known where to begin.

And thanks to his grandfather, he knew what else he might need.

However crazy his siblings thought it was.

"It's not 1950," Wolf pointed out.

Though, sometimes, on Four Corners you could be forgiven for not realizing that. For not realizing it wasn't 1880, even.

Time passed slowly, and by and large the landscape didn't change. Sure, the farm implements got a little bit shinier.

On a particularly good year, the savings account got a little bit fatter.

But the land itself remained. The large imposing mountains that surrounded the property that backed Garrett's Watch. The river that ran through the property, cutting across the field and the base of the mountain. The pine trees, green all through the year, growing taller with the passage of time.

They were lucky to have done well enough in the last few years that the large main house was completely updated, though it was ridiculously huge for Sawyer by himself. Wolf and Elsie had gone to their own cabins on the property, which were also sturdy and well kept.

In truth, this whole thing with the baby had been a wake-up call. Because whether or not he could look out the window and see it, time was passing. And when Missy had asked him what he wanted to do about the baby, the answer had seemed simple. It had seemed simple because... He had no excuse. He had plenty of money, and had the sort of life that meant he could include a kid in most anything. His dad had done him a favor by showing him what not to do. They were largely left to their own devices, but it was a great place to be left to your devices. And he'd had to ask himself... What was he hanging on to? A life of going out drinking whenever he wanted, sleeping with whoever he wanted.

He was at the age where it wasn't all that attractive, not anymore.

Thirty-four and with no sign of change on the horizon. In the end, he decided to aim for more. To take the change that was coming whether he was ready or not.

Turns out not very ready. But again, that was where his plan came in.

"I'm aware that is not 1950," he shot back at his brother. "I can...sign up for a... A website."

As if he knew how the hell to do that. They had a computer. Hell, he had a smartphone. They had a business to manage and it made sense. But the fact remained, he didn't have a lot of use for either.

Elsie cackled, slinging her boots off the table and flipping her dark braid over her shoulder. "A website? I don't think people swipe on their phones looking for marriage. I think they look for... Well, stuff you seem to be able to find without the help of the internet."

His sister wasn't wrong. He found sex just fine without the help of his phone. That was what Smokey's Tavern was for.

"The way I see it," Sawyer said, speaking as if Elsie hadn't spoken, which as far as he was concerned was the way it should be with younger siblings, "marriage can work, relationships can work, as long as you have the same set of goals as the other person. It's all these modern ideals... That's what doesn't work."

"Which modern ideals?" Elsie asked. "The kind that saw every woman in our bloodline leaving every man in our bloodline all the way back to when people were riding around in horse-drawn carriages?"

"Yes," he said. "That is what I mean. People thinking that they needed to marry for something other than...common need."

He was pretty sure his grandparents had loved each other in the end. But it reminded him of something other than romance. It reminded him of his connection to the land. You cared for that which cared for you. It sustained you. You worked it, and the dirt got under your nails. The air was in your lungs. It became part of you. Of all that you were.

That was something better than romance.

Romance, in his estimation, was screaming fights and other bullshit. Punishing each other—and your children—because you couldn't figure out how the hell to deal with yourselves.

He wanted no part in it.

"And what is it you have to offer a woman?" Wolf asked, grinning. "Why exactly would she agree to leave her life behind, to marry you and take care of your kid?"

"I've got this house," he said. "A fine working ranch, cute baby."

"A lot of bad habits, cheap beer and a bad temper," Elsie said, as if she were finishing his list.

"I didn't say I was perfect," he said.

"It's not going work," Wolf said. "You are not going to find some woman desperate enough that she's going to be willing to cross the country to marry you."

"And if you do," Elsie said, "I would be worried."

Wolf slapped his palm on the table. "Good point."

"Worried about what?" He frowned. "What do I have to worry about a woman for?"

"She could be a bunny boiler," Elsie said. "The crazy jealous type. Or just plain crazy."

"She's right," Wolf said.

"I'll figure it out," Sawyer said. "You act like I'm some kind of greenhorn. I know women. And I know what I need."

"Do you? Because it seems to me you got yourself saddled with a baby mama no different than your own mother," Wolf said.

And that bit down. Hard. Right on Sawyer's neck.

Leave it to Wolf to get right to the real issue. He felt guilty as hell. Because he'd done it, hadn't he? He brought a kid in this world under the exact same circumstances that he'd been brought into it.

Though he had to give it to Missy. She'd known that she didn't want to be involved. From the beginning.

His daughter... His *daughter*.

Damn.

That still hit him. Right between the eyes every time he thought it. He needed to give her a name so he didn't have to think of her in that way. He didn't have time to be going around feeling like he'd been punched in the heart every five seconds.

His daughter wouldn't have vague memories of her mother. She wouldn't have any of her at all. And if he got himself a wife fast enough, then she would only know one mother. One that shows her. One that chose to be here.

He wouldn't repeat the same mistakes as his father. Because Sawyer was a man who knew what he was about. Sawyer was a man who wouldn't sit on his ass and let his kids pay the price for his own bad mistakes. No. He wouldn't do it.

Sawyer Garrett was going to find himself a wife.

If a mail-order bride was good enough for his grandfather, it was good enough for him.

And he was going to get started right away.